1-2022

DATE DUE

PRINTED IN U.S.A.

Hayner PLD/Large Print
Overdues .10/day. Max fine cost of
item. Lost or damaged item: additional
$5 service charge.

Provenance

Center Point
Large Print

Also by Carla Laureano and available from
Center Point Large Print:

The Saturday Night Supper Club
Brunch at Bittersweet Café
The Solid Grounds Coffee Company

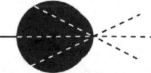

Provenance

CARLA LAUREANO

CENTER POINT LARGE PRINT
THORNDIKE, MAINE

For Steve Laube.
Thank you for helping make
all these books possible.
I couldn't have done it without you.

Chapter One

It was good to be home. Or at least it would be, if she had the faintest idea what *home* actually meant.

Kendall Green levered herself out of the back seat of her rideshare and heaved her roller case out after her, then gave a quick wave to the driver before starting up the steep asphalt driveway. In the month since she'd left Pasadena, the season had switched from summer to autumn—at least as much autumn as one ever saw in Southern California—the turning leaves of the valley oak a striking counterpart to the palms that surrounded the property. Her suitcase bumped over the uneven surface in time with the click of her high-heeled boots until she pulled up short in front of a wrought iron gate bearing a laser-cut metal sign with the words *Chronicle Design*.

Kendall smiled to herself and pressed the button on the intercom. "Sophie . . . it's me."

Instantly a buzz came through the speaker, and the gate unlatched with a metallic click. Kendall pushed through with a creak and clanged the gate shut behind her, then inhaled deeply as she stepped onto the Saltillo tiles that paved the front courtyard of the property. If she were going to claim a home, this was where it would be. Never mind that the stately Spanish-style property was only a rental and served as both office and living space. It was where her antiques lived, which meant it was where she belonged. At least for now. The rent went up every year in November; one more hike and they would be out on the street.

Or Kendall would. Sophie actually had family as backup, as little as she liked to ask them for help.

As soon as Kendall stepped through the arch-topped front door, a pretty brunette appeared in the hallway, a cordless office phone pressed to her ear. She held up a finger as she finished the call, then shot a bright smile in Kendall's direction. "Thank goodness! You're back early!"

Kendall laughed and hugged her friend and assistant, Sophie Daniels. The string of wooden beads Sophie wore as part of her usual boho ensemble pressed painfully into Kendall's sternum, but she didn't pull away. She wouldn't say she'd exactly missed Southern California while she was gone, but she'd missed her friend, overpowering rose perfume and all. "Only a day early," Kendall said, finally letting go and pushing the front door shut behind her. She froze while a horrifying thought occurred to her. "There's not a mouse stuck in the bathtub again, is there?"

Sophie shuddered. "No. Thank goodness. If that had happened again, the house would probably be burned to the ground." She grabbed Kendall's roller case and dragged it into the room right off the hallway. "Come sit down. I want to hear all about Europe."

Kendall followed her into the space they used as an office, noting that it looked just like she'd left it—desks piled high with paperwork and fabric samples, stacks of catalogs crowding the conference table. Sophie's goal to clean up their office obviously hadn't materialized. She shoved aside a box of cement tile samples to make room for Kendall to sit and plopped down across from her.

"Well, despite all the auctions, London was pretty much a bust," Kendall said. "I did pick up a modernist painting for the Vergara project at Christie's and some serving pieces at London Silver Vaults for Rebecca Moon, but—"

Sophie rolled her eyes. "I don't want to hear about what you bought. I want to hear about who you *met*."

That was Sophie, always the optimist. When Kendall traveled for business, she was lucky to see anything beyond the auction house and antique markets, let alone any of the city's more . . . attractive . . . sights. But that didn't stop Sophie from urging Kendall to live a little. Secretly she probably hoped Kendall would fall in love with a European prince or be swept away by a whirlwind romance with some sexy Scotsman.

Never mind the fact that Kendall's seven-year friendship with Sophie was the longest relationship she'd had with any human, ever.

"You know me better than that. What happened while I was gone? Other than a tornado hitting my desk."

"We got a new client . . ."

"And you didn't lead with that? Tell!"

Sophie's face broke into a smile and she jumped up to grab her tablet off her desk. "Wait until you see this place. It's a Thornton Ladd mid-century modern in Long Beach. La Marina Estates. It had a terrible 'update' in the 1980s, but the Thomases want to take it back to its original details." She pulled up her gallery and started swiping through the photos of the house, taken from every angle. No matter what else Sophie might be, she was definitely thorough.

"Wow. Diagonal walnut floors. You don't see those often." Kendall swiped back and expanded the photo to see detailing of the home's cement fireplace, which had been covered with a horrible faux brick. "At least it's just a veneer. That shouldn't be too difficult to remove, though it will have to be skim-coated when it's done." Excitement began to build in her. Her style ran more toward European antiques and elaborate finishes, anything with the weight of tradition behind it—French provincial, Spanish, Tudor—but it could be fun to work on something so streamlined and modern, especially since their clients were beginning to demand more eclectic spaces with a mix of origins and styles. "When do we get started?"

Sophie didn't answer immediately, and Kendall raised her eyes to her friend's face. "What?"

"It's just that . . . they asked for me specifically. Not you."

"Oh." Kendall licked her lips and shoved down the pang of hurt. "Of course. I just . . . No, that's great."

"Are you sure? The style is right in my wheelhouse, and after you let me take the lead on the Najarian project—"

"No, absolutely. It makes total sense. You'll do a great job. It's high time you start doing some projects without me, and if we're working independently, that gives us more income."

"That's what I was thinking." Sophie exhaled in relief; then her expression shadowed. "I was going to wait until you were settled in to tell you . . ."

Kendall froze. "You're not quitting and going out on your own, are you?"

"No! Of course not." Sophie laughed, then sobered quickly. "We got the notice from the landlord."

If she'd been feeling hurt before, now all Kendall felt was panic. "How bad is it?"

"Not great. Eight thousand."

"A month?"

"Well, it's not per year, that's for sure."

Kendall closed her eyes and tried to calm the sudden frantic thump of her heart. Eight thousand dollars a month didn't sound like so much compared to renting commercial space, but since they lived there, only part of that amount could be written off on their business taxes. The rest came out of their salaries, which were fairly paltry considering how much money they always had tied up in inventory and receivables.

"It's a good thing you're taking on your own clients then," Kendall said finally, straightening her spine. "With two of us working independently, we can make it work. And in that case, it's probably time that we list you on the website as a designer." She forced a smile. "Let me drop my things in my room and change, and you can show me what you're thinking."

Sophie returned the smile, and Kendall pushed herself to standing, her steps more subdued now as she pulled the roller case down the bumpy clay-tiled floor to her bedroom. The Spanish-style house had dual masters—large rooms each with their own en suite—so she and Sophie didn't have to share a bathroom, though it wouldn't have bothered Kendall if they did. She felt lucky enough to be living in a multimillion-dollar house in one of the nicest parts of Pasadena, a luxury she hadn't dared imagine as a kid. Until now, their work relationship had always been divided along certain lines: Kendall had the designer skills and the experience; Sophie picked up the slack on administrative duties and acted as a design assistant. It was only within the last few months that Kendall had let her take the lead on projects, and that was simply because Kendall's schedule had become untenable. She hadn't expected to come back from one of her sourcing trips to find that her assistant had been taking on clients of her own.

"Don't be silly," she whispered to herself, pushing down a sudden bubble of what felt suspiciously like jealousy. Kendall might be young for this business at only twenty-nine, but she'd made a name for herself with both her impeccable taste and her ability to find unique furnishings with interesting—and fully documented—stories. Everyone from movie stars to TV producers to socialites wanted to own a cabinet that was passed down from Catherine of Aragon's great-great-great-granddaughter or a Hans Wegner Danish modern prototype that never made it into production. It was her reputation for doing whatever it took to source the pieces and uncover their provenance that made her something of a wunderkind in the Southern California design

13

world . . . and most likely the reason they got the Thornton Ladd house in the first place.

But it was Sophie's design portfolio that closed the deal, and don't you dare take that away from her. Kendall was going to have to push down her urge to oversee the project and let Sophie have her day in the sun. And she would be there to swoop in if anything went wrong.

Kendall pushed open the door to her bedroom and let out an exhale, then dragged her bag over to the closet. While the rest of the house was filled with antique furniture and richly colored textiles, her room was minimal, almost spare in its decor. Its only furnishings were a simple iron bed covered in a fluffy white duvet, a bench with a woven seat at its foot, a single painting on the wall, and a large, threadbare Persian rug that covered the wood floor almost to the edges of the room. Beautiful, simple, and calm. A place for focus and relaxation. Her sanctuary, one that no one, not even Sophie, entered.

Except she didn't own it, and it could go away at any time. Would go away soon, if the rent hikes continued.

Kendall toed off her boots and placed them carefully on the shoe rack in her closet, then pulled out a pair of woven flats made from recycled plastic. The leather jacket got hung up beside her blazers, swapped out for a cozy knit cardigan. Her long blonde hair, which had started out in soft waves but gotten smushed from the ten long hours on the plane, went up into a messy bun on top of her head. Now she was ready to work.

But when she walked back out into their office space, Sophie was hurriedly packing things into a canvas messenger bag.

"What's going on?"

Sophie looked up guiltily. "I'm sorry. I just got a call from Renee Thomas. She's at the tile showroom and she's found something she loves. She wants me to go over there right away."

"Oh." Kendall blinked. "Of course. Go. We'll talk when you get back. I need to catch up on my mail anyway."

Sophie grinned. "I'll pick up something to eat and a bottle of wine on the way back."

Kendall forced a laugh. "Make sure it's a good bottle of wine then. Have fun. Go rescue your client from herself."

"Right?" Sophie rolled her eyes, but the excitement in her face said there was nothing she'd rather be doing. "Back later."

Kendall nodded and slid into her office chair, turning her back to Sophie like she'd already forgotten she was leaving. She didn't blame her—clients did things like this all the time. They said they trusted you to pick out their finishes and oversee construction, but they still spent all their free time poring over catalogs and wandering through design showrooms. Sometimes they had impeccable taste and made your job easier; more often, you found yourself diplomatically explaining that glass mosaic tiles went out of style years ago and didn't suit a Craftsman bungalow in the first place.

The front door closing behind Sophie just highlighted the sudden quiet in the room, so Kendall went over to the bookshelf and flipped on the Bluetooth speaker connected to her phone, then settled back at her desk in front of her overflowing in-box. Half of it was junk mail; the other half were bills, which she'd have to reconcile with her job sheets and send on to Sophie for payment. And then her fingers touched a thin business-size envelope, its linen texture standing out from all the cheap paper that surrounded it.

"Jasper Lake, Colorado?" Kendall murmured, looking at the return address in the upper-left corner. She'd been born and raised in Colorado, but she didn't have any family there. Didn't have any family, period. And she'd certainly never heard of any place called Jasper Lake. This better not be an "invitation" to a unique money-making opportunity. Kendall slid the blade of her silver letter opener under the flap and withdrew a single sheet of paper. Bold black letters at the top announced *Notice to heirs* followed by smaller print: *In the matter of the estate of Mrs. Constance Green.*

To the heirs and devisees of the above estate: This is formal notice that Mrs. Constance Green, the decedent, died on September 8, 2016, and you have or may have an interest in Mrs. Constance Green's estate. Mr. Matthew Avery, whose address is 21 Main Street, Jasper Lake, Colorado, has been appointed as the administrator of the estate. All documents, pleading, and information relating to the estate are on file in the Clear Creek County Courthouse under case number R000049872. The last day to file claims against the estate is October 21, 2021. The assets of the estate of Mrs. Constance Green will be disbursed 30 days following the date of this notice. Executed by the administrator of the estate of Mrs. Constance Green . . .

Kendall lowered the paper to the desk when she could no longer read the print. Her hands were shaking too hard to hold the letter still.

Constance Green.

She'd never heard the name before, but they shared the same last name, and someone was informing her she'd inherited part of this woman's estate. Surely that meant they were related somehow.

In the twenty-four years since she'd been abandoned at a day care center in a Denver suburb, she'd always imagined something like this happening. But now that it was here, she had absolutely no idea what to do about it, other than call the lawyer whose name and number were printed on the letterhead.

And maybe, just maybe, she would finally know what had happened to her mother.

Kendall hesitated for a moment before she picked up her cell phone and dialed the number.

The phone rang, and she half expected a secretary to answer, but instead a gruff voice came through the line. "Matthew Avery."

Kendall cleared her throat, the words suddenly sticking somewhere in her esophagus. "Mr. Avery. My name is Kendall Green. I just got a letter—"

"Kendall Green!" The lawyer's voice boomed out, now more enthusiastic than gruff. "You certainly know how to cut it close."

She blinked. "I'm sorry?"

"The cutoff date. October 21. It's less than two weeks away."

"Yes, I know, but I just received the letter. I've been traveling for the past month, and I just got home today."

"Right, but it's been almost five years since she passed, and this is a rather critical situation for Jasper Lake."

Kendall pressed her fingertips to her temples, trying to work through the stream-of-consciousness information coming from the lawyer. "For the town? I was under the impression this had something to do with a relative's estate."

The line went silent. She pulled the phone away from her ear to check if they were still connected, then pressed it back. "Hello?"

"Sorry. I . . ." Matthew Avery sounded discomfited. "Did no one contact you when Connie died?"

A laugh bubbled out of her, and she was aware it was tinged with hysteria. "Mr. Avery, I was abandoned at five years old and raised in foster care. I wasn't aware I had any family left. I don't even know their names."

The lawyer sighed heavily on the other end of the line. "Well. I certainly didn't expect to be the first to tell you this. You probably know your mother's name was Caroline, and I'm afraid I can't tell you much more than that. The estate in question, however, belonged to Constance. Your grandmother."

A grandmother. She had a grandmother. Of course she had a grandmother, but one who actually knew of her existence? If she knew that Kendall was out there somewhere, why hadn't she gotten in touch with her? And why had it taken someone five years to let her know she had died? Kendall hadn't even met the woman, so she was shocked by the sudden pang of loss.

Avery was talking again, and she realized she'd

missed a big chunk of the conversation when he said, ". . . come take a look at it yourself and decide what you want to do with it."

"I'm sorry, what?"

"I know it's a lot to take in, Ms. Green. But it is a sizable amount of property, and as you're the sole heir, it is going to revert to the county in less than two weeks if you don't file a formal claim against the estate. You can do it remotely, but I think it would be easier if you did it in person."

Avery went on, but Kendall had stopped listening. A sizable amount of property. Colorado was getting expensive, wasn't it? That meant even in a small town, it had to be worth something. She had no time for sentiment with a massive rent hike staring her in the face.

"Of course," she said, her voice resolute for the first time during this phone call. "I'll be there as soon as I can."

Chapter Two

When Kendall turned off the highway at the sign marked *Jasper Lake*, she was disappointed to feel absolutely no spark of recognition. Which was silly. She hadn't been born here, as far as she knew, and even if she had been, she wouldn't remember it, so there was no reason she should feel any connection to this place, roots or otherwise.

No, the only thing she felt right now was lingering nausea from the bumpy descent into Denver International Airport, followed by the twisty ascent into Colorado's high country in her rented Ford Explorer.

Or more likely, the nausea came from the knowledge that, in five minutes, she would find herself face-to-face with a piece of her past she'd never known existed.

The asphalt transitioned to hard-packed dirt, or maybe it was actually asphalt that had so much mud deposited on top, you could no longer see the black. Dirty snowdrifts, their surface pitted and gnarled by the sun's rays, piled up on either side from where the plow had left them, the occasional pocket of fresh white standing out in a crevice. She slowed her speed when the road jostled her to her teeth, noting the log cabin–style buildings on either side of her. One advertised snowmobile rentals and white-water rafting boats; another, tackle and ice-fishing gear. A quick look at the car's thermometer put the outside temperature at a balmy forty-two degrees at two o'clock in the afternoon.

There could be no doubt she wasn't in Southern California anymore.

She glanced up at the navigation screen on her cell phone and made a turn onto the town's main street, then caught her breath. Wood and brick buildings clustered together along a wooden boardwalk, their cheerily painted signs identifying them as cafés, ice cream shops, fudge factories. Every block or so, a break at the intersecting street gave a glimpse of blinding blue beyond—the eponymous Jasper Lake, its rippled surface reflecting the sun like diamonds. Even knowing that it was probably only a month away from freezing, the water lover in her yearned to dip her toes in.

But she wasn't here on vacation. She was here to settle the matter of an unknown grandmother's estate, and none too soon . . . It had taken her nearly a week to get things in order enough to fly to Colorado—and to find an affordable flight— leaving less than a week for her to file her claim before it reverted to the county. For reasons she still didn't understand, it sounded like Jasper

Lake had a vested interest in not letting that happen.

The dot on the navigation screen told her that Matthew Avery's office should be coming up on her left, and she swung quickly into one of the angled parking spaces that lined Main Street, right in front of a blue-painted, clapboard-sided building marked with *Matthew Avery, Attorney-at-Law*. She grabbed her purse off the passenger seat, her down jacket from the back, and jumped out of the car.

And instantly regretted it. The second the cold air hit her bare skin, it sent her into a full-body shiver. Kendall fumbled her arms into the parka and zipped it up as quickly as possible, shocked by the frigid bite of the wind. How could it possibly be so cold when the sun was shining down so brightly?

"You just have to deal with it for a few days," she muttered to herself as she stepped onto the wooden boardwalk and made her way toward the attorney's office, her boots making dull thuds with every step. Then she froze—figuratively, this time. A hand-lettered sign taped to the inside of the window stated, *Gone elk hunting*.

"What?" she burst out. She twisted around, hoping to see someone—even Avery himself—to tell her this was a joke, but the boardwalk was pretty much empty.

That was just great. She had flown all this

way—had let him know when she was arriving even!—and he was out hunting? Oh, excuse her, *elk* hunting. Because that made all the difference in explaining why he was not in his office working like a normal attorney. She pulled out her cell phone, punching numbers with angry determination, and waited as it rang.

Inside the building, an old-fashioned office phone jangled.

Seriously? He hadn't even forwarded his office phone to his cell? She'd thought she was in the Colorado mountains, not the year 1972.

Well, in a town this small, surely everyone knew everyone. There had to be someone who had his cell phone number. She did another spin to orient herself, not that it helped much when she had no idea where anything was, and decided on the direction that led to the lake. It had more buildings than the section she'd already passed, so surely there had to be a city hall or a chamber of commerce somewhere?

There was both, she found after a single block, and they were combined into a huge building in the same log-cabin, rustic style that dominated the rest of the quaint Main Street. A dark-haired man wearing jeans, a hoodie, and a shearling-lined leather jacket was standing on a ladder just outside the front door, hanging a vinyl banner.

"Excuse me?" she called up to him.

He drove a nail through the grommet on one

end of the banner before he turned his face toward her. She was hit immediately by the force of a pair of bright-blue eyes.

Well, hel-*lo*. Maybe this trip to Jasper Creek was looking up.

She'd thought she was immune to pretty faces by now, but her thoughts were coming just a fraction too slow for her liking. "Hey . . . I don't suppose you know how to reach that attorney down there, Matthew Avery? We were supposed to meet today, but he's not in."

Something akin to recognition lit on the man's handsome face, and he backed down the ladder. "You must be Kendall Green. Matthew told me to keep an eye out for you."

"Oh." Kendall was momentarily taken aback by the idea that maybe the lawyer hadn't just disappeared without a trace. "He did?"

The man started to stick out a hand before he realized he was still holding the hammer, then swapped it to the other hand and tried again. "Gabriel Brandt. You can call me Gabe. Just about everyone does."

Gabriel Brandt. Kendall sized him up surreptitiously. Somewhere in his early thirties, she figured, with dark hair that was longish on top and mussed from the stiff breeze that whipped down the boardwalk. He was also a couple of inches taller than her, which meant he was pretty tall, considering she was five-eleven in these boots. His jeans had a spot of paint on the thigh, and the work boots were well-used and scuffed. Town handyman, maybe? City hall maintenance?

She realized he was still waiting for her response, so she gave a half-hearted nod. "So . . . I guess you found me. Or I found you. What now?"

"Well, he left some paperwork for you to sign inside. We can start there." Gabe Brandt moved the ladder away from the wood-and-glass door and then pulled it open for her to precede him.

Warmth from a heater on full blast hit her as soon as she stepped inside, and she shrugged out of her coat, though she kept the scarf looped around her neck. Just the few minutes outside had put a chill in her bones that would take all night to get rid of. There was a reason she'd settled in California despite her Colorado upbringing. The weather had never quite suited her, and she'd absorbed the summer heat like she could store it up for the rest of the year.

Gabe brushed by her. "Right this way." Despite the rustic exterior, the inside was all wood and glass—high-end, like she would have designed a ski resort or mountain retreat. Various vinyl decals on the doors they passed identified the different offices contained in this one building: chamber of commerce, code enforcement, city council chambers. Finally he stopped before one that said *Mayor of Jasper Lake* and pushed carelessly through the door.

There was no one in the outer office, where a secretary was evidently meant to sit—maybe she was out elk hunting too?—but he didn't seem thrown by the absence, just pushed through another open doorway to a small, nicely decorated office.

Kendall hung back. "I can wait until someone comes back, you know. I'm not in that much of a hurry."

"Oh, Linda had to go pick up her daughter from school. Stomach flu. Besides, she doesn't know anything about this." He began moving stacks of paperwork around the desk, riffling through piles and shoving them aside.

"Should you be doing that?" Kendall asked.

He looked up and a slow smile spread over his face. "Considering it's my desk? I think it's okay."

Understanding hit Kendall like an avalanche, and her cheeks immediately heated. *"You're* the mayor."

"According to 642 citizens of Jasper Lake, yes."

"But the sign said 750."

"What can I say? A hundred or so of the others had their doubts." He shrugged, his smile still lingering. "You really didn't know? Matthew didn't tell you?"

Now that she knew this guy was the mayor, she had no compunction about flopping herself into one of the armchairs in front of the desk. "Matthew has told me next to nothing. Just that my time is running out and I have to file something with the county. I don't even know how he found me, and if I was so easy to find, why he didn't do it five years ago."

Gabe's expression turned sympathetic. But instead of sitting behind the desk, he propped himself on the edge of it. "We owe you an apology for that. It turns out that the executor of your grandmother's will was sick. He claimed he'd done everything necessary to find you, and then he died. And quite frankly, it fell through the cracks. Only when it was brought to my attention—when I took office—that the unclaimed property was going back to the county did I realize the executor's firm hadn't passed the files on to his successor, Matthew Avery, and it hadn't been properly dealt with. I hired a firm that specializes in finding missing heirs, and a lot of research later, you turned up. I just can't explain why they wouldn't have found you five years ago."

"Actually, I can," Kendall said. "I started my own business four years ago. Until then, I would have been pretty much off the grid. I didn't even have a checking account."

"Ah. Well, that makes sense. They mostly search public records in order to narrow down the most likely candidates for a given name."

"What no one has explained to me is the sense of urgency. What's the big deal if the property went back to the county anyway? I mean, thank you for bringing it to my attention . . . but why are you so invested in doing the right thing? You could have just let it revert."

"This isn't your run-of-the-mill housing track. This property is . . . special."

Kendall stared at him. "Special? Special how?"

He stayed silent for a long moment, studying her. "I think maybe it's better if you see for yourself."

Chapter Three

Gabriel Brandt locked the door to his office and gestured for Kendall to follow him down the hallway and back out onto the street. Even after Matthew told him that the long-lost heir was coming to Jasper Lake to make a claim on Connie's estate, Gabe hadn't quite believed it. The six weeks between when they'd located her and when she'd finally responded to the letter had felt interminable, like a slowly ticking time bomb they were powerless to defuse. And in many ways, that's exactly what the unclaimed property had become.

"Your grandmother's home is on the other side of the lake," he explained. "If you don't mind, we can take my car."

"That's fine," Kendall said easily. "And please don't call her that. I never knew her as my grandmother. As far as I'm concerned, she's a complete stranger who happened to give me a winning lottery ticket."

Gabe's eyebrows rose at the cold assessment. He hadn't exactly grown up in Jasper Lake, but he'd spent his teen years here, and there wasn't a resident who hadn't known and loved Connie Green. She had been something of the town's grande dame, with her elegant white hair and infectious laugh. The chair of every celebration committee, a member of the historical society—at least until the town flooded and destroyed most of their records—and the Sunday school director at Jasper Lake Presbyterian Church. In fact, if you grew up Protestant in this town, most of your early biblical education came courtesy of Constance Green.

But then, Kendall and her mother had been estranged from Connie, for reasons that Gabe didn't understand. His own grandmother might have, as she had been a close friend of Connie's, but she'd passed away not long after Kendall's grandmother. His grandfather had little to say on the subject, either because he didn't know or because he didn't feel it was his business. The end result was the same.

Gabe stopped in front of his vehicle—a Ram with big tires that had his friends joking that he was compensating for something. But the winch on the front wasn't purely decorative, given his place on the Clear Creek 4x4 Rescue, a volunteer group that bailed out stranded travelers who got on the wrong side of the thirty-plus-inch monthly snowfall in the winter. Kendall didn't seem to bat an eyelash when he unlocked the door and opened her side for her, just gripped the grab handle and hoisted herself into the passenger seat.

Gabe circled to the other side and climbed in,

then started the truck and backed it out of its parking spot. He glanced at Kendall, suddenly at a loss for words. She wasn't what he had expected. When the investigator had forwarded her information to him, he'd had little more than a tiny thumbnail on her design business's website to go off of: she'd looked stylish and very California-casual. Well, that still held. The slim-cut North Face jacket and fur-cuffed boots were the type of thing flatlanders thought they should wear when they came to the mountains. Functional, but it made her stand out as a visitor as surely as if she had been wearing a neon sign.

No, that was exactly as he'd thought. He just hadn't expected her to be so . . . attractive.

Pretty, yes. Pretty was a dime a dozen and had as little effect on Gabe as a coming snow forecast. But sharp intelligence glinted in Kendall's green-gray eyes, and both her sly smile and husky voice hinted at depths of humor he suspected but hadn't seen yet. Not to mention the way she placidly endured the jostling of the dirt road as he left the town's main drag and circled around the lake. California chic, maybe. But her spurt of cynicism left no doubt that whatever else she was, Kendall Green was tough.

Now, that . . . that he didn't see often.

When Kendall didn't speak, Gabe cleared his throat and reached for a topic of conversation. "What do you know about the town?"

She glanced at him, a smile playing at her lips. "Only what Wikipedia told me. Elevation 9,200 feet. Annual snowfall, 180 inches. Chances of getting charged by a moose, high."

"Did it actually say that?"

"Not in so many words. I extrapolated."

Gabe grinned. So he'd been right about the sense of humor. "Let me fill you in. You do, in fact, have a *moderate* chance of being charged by a moose, but only if you get too close during rut or you run up on a cow with calves. However, that's not nearly our most interesting feature. Jasper Lake was founded in the late 1880s, the exact date unknown, by miners looking for the holy trinity of ore: gold, silver, and lead. In fact, there's a nearby town called Trinity for that very reason, because it's the only region in Colorado that has all three in high concentrations near to each other. Jasper Lake is thought to have been named for the semiprecious mineral that's found in abundance around here." He broke off, realizing he was in danger of sounding like the town's website. Well, he was the mayor. People expected him to be knowledgeable about its history.

"Interesting. Any old buildings up here? I remember going to a ghost town with my class when I was a kid, but I can't remember where it was. You don't pay attention to local geography when you're a child."

"That's right; you grew up in Denver. I forgot." Gabe broke off. "I'm sorry. It's weird that I know so much about you and we just met. I read the report when they found you in California."

Kendall shrugged. "It's not like I keep it a secret. It's just not anything I like to talk about."

Noted. Somehow he'd pegged her as the chatty type, but so far she seemed satisfied to listen to him talk. "Anyway, you asked about old buildings. Yes, there are still some prospectors' cabins up in the hills, and there's a smattering of turn-of-the-century brick buildings from when it turned into a proper town and not just a mining camp. But the most interesting ones are the ones we're about to go see."

Kendall perked up. "Connie's property was old?"

"You could say that." He glanced at her intrigued expression. Of course being a designer who specialized in antiques, she would be intrigued by old houses. That was exactly what he was banking on.

Jasper Lake itself was shaped like a jagged kidney, no more than a mile long at its furthest point and approximately half a mile wide, but its frequent inlets and coves and natural bays meant that the meandering lakeside road took nearly twice as long to traverse as it would if it were a straight shot. Kendall was looking out the window at the scenery with interest, however,

34

just as he'd planned. He could have gone out to the highway, across the county road, and back to the other side of the lake in half the time, but he was banking on the town's natural beauty striking a chord in her. The decisions she made in the next few days would affect them all.

"During the summer, there's boat and kayak rentals near town. On this side of the lake, we have both a sailing club and a rowing club. We host regattas every summer that draw people from all over Colorado."

"And during the winter?"

"Ice fishing. We've just started hitting our first hard freezes of the year, but given another month or two, the lake's surface will be solid enough to walk on."

"Too bad I won't be here to see it," she said, and she actually did sound like she thought it was too bad. "Even though I've never been much of a cold weather person."

"You never skied?"

She shot him a look, and he inwardly cringed. Of course she hadn't. The words *ward of the state* had been prominent in the heir finder's report. He imagined not many foster parents took a kid skiing.

The conversation fell stagnant for several moments until Kendall spoke again. "So you're young. I'm guessing, what? Thirty? Thirty-one?"

"Thirty-two," he said.

"Right. So how does a thirty-two-year-old guy become mayor of a town that, so far, looks to be largely populated by the over-fifty set?"

She had done her homework. "Probably because said over-fifty set is worried about the future of their town if we don't start attracting younger families. Eventually the older generation will die and there will be no one left to take their place."

"Which makes sense," she said. "But why you exactly?"

There went the full force of her attention on him, her gaze fixed on his profile while he drove. He felt the sudden urge to reprise his mayoral campaign for her and then just as swiftly gave himself a mental kick in the rear for being stupid. "Short version or long version?"

"Depends. You know how far away we are. I'm a captive audience."

They were coming to the turnoff to the Gable Pines neighborhood, so he settled on the short version. "Undergrad in sociology, master's in urban planning. Six years of experience with a nonprofit in Detroit that created workable plans for revitalizing depressed neighborhoods. And I happened to spend my teens here, living with my grandparents. Also, I ran unopposed."

Kendall barked out a laugh, obviously not expecting that. "So what about the—" she did a quick mental calculation—"108 people who didn't vote for you?"

"Abstainers. Some only live here during the summer and so weren't present." And some had long memories and couldn't forget the troubled thirteen-year-old he'd been when he arrived, angry at the world and determined to make everyone as miserable as he was. When he remembered the mouthy—and destructive—punk he'd been back then, what he wanted most was a time machine so he could go back and slap himself upside the head. Fortunately, the rest of the town considered him a success story of their way of life, an example of what outdoor activity and attention and a takes-a-village mentality could do for difficult children. There might have been an element of truth in that, but Gabe knew it was due more to his grandparents' patience and unflagging faith that God had more planned for him than his initial delinquent direction.

Gabe slowed as he made a sharp turn down a dirt road, which transitioned back to pitted asphalt half a mile down. Kendall was busy oohing and aahing over the gorgeous view of the lake out the driver's side window, something that required her to partly lean over the console toward him. He wasn't complaining. It also meant that she was looking in the utter wrong direction when he finally pulled to a stop. "This is it."

Kendall whipped her head around, and her jaw dropped. "This is it?"

She grabbed the door handle and levered it open

before he could respond, jumping to the gravel shoulder with a crunch. The wind immediately whipped the stray tendrils from her blonde bun, and she quickly zipped up her jacket against the cold. "I don't know what to say. When we were talking about old houses, I didn't expect this."

"No one does. To our knowledge, there are no other Victorians like these in the county. Maybe even in the state." Gabe came around to stand beside her, feeling something suspiciously like pride as he gazed at the neighborhood.

Or at least it was intended to be a neighborhood. Whereas the rest of the homes on this side of the lake were spaced haphazardly along the shoreline, here five structures perched close together, proud and straight as if they were part of the gracious neighborhoods of Chicago or San Francisco, all sweeping porches, gabled fronts, and bright colors. Some of them were better kept than others; a sagging front porch on one and a shutter swinging on a single hinge on another spoke to the fact they'd been left vacant for some time now.

Kendall stared for another long moment, the expression on her face somewhere between fascination and awe. "Which one is mine, then?"

For once, Gabe wasn't even mad at the way Matthew had bumbled his duties, because it meant he got to see her shocked expression when he told her:

"All of them."

Chapter Four

"All of them?" Kendall snapped her gaze toward Gabe and her voice came out as a squeak. It was enough of a surprise to find out that the home she'd inherited wasn't the rustic cabin or characterless lake house she'd been expecting, but to know that she'd actually inherited *five* houses? Her mouth opened and closed several times before she could make sense of that statement.

"And quite a bit of the land around it, in fact. Connie was fairly well-off, and as the town population began to dwindle, these houses went vacant. She began buying them up from the owners as they moved out. She thought renovating them and using them as short-term vacation rentals might help with tourism in the town."

"And did it?"

"She never got that far. She fell ill, and before she could follow through with the plans, she died." Gabe studied Kendall's face, his expression sympathetic. He seemed to be concerned about her emotional state; he still didn't understand that to Kendall, Constance Green was a complete stranger.

A stranger who, despite leaving Kendall everything she owned, hadn't cared enough to track her down in the twenty-four years since her mother had abandoned her.

"Can I look inside one of them?" she asked finally.

Gabe nodded. "Sure. Let's take a look at the middle one. This was your—this was Connie's place, so it will be the most intact."

Kendall hugged her arms to her body against another gust of wind and followed him across the street. The third house was indeed the most well-kept of the five, its wood siding painted in a seafoam green, its brickwork recently repointed. "These aren't Victorians, by the way," she said, standing aside at the front door while he pulled a ring of keys out of his pocket.

"They aren't? What are they?"

"Gothic revival. Carpenter Gothic, to be exact. There's probably a number of these up here, though I doubt many were this elaborate." She looked over the porch, sure of her assessment. The pointed-arch window, the board-and-batten siding, even the gingerbread trim. It was all characteristic of the style, even if the sprawling wraparound porches were indeed far more Victorian. "Probably some architect putting his own twist on the style. I would have guessed 1870s, but this porch is more American Queen Anne, so I'm going with 1880 or 1890."

Gabe threw her a curious glance. "I thought your specialty was antiques, not architecture."

"They go hand in hand, especially in restoration work. You have no idea how many unholy mismatches of eras I run into. It takes a bit of detective work to uncover the original details. Which, fortunately, *is* my specialty." Excitement spread through her, similar to when she was about to view a client space for the first time. "Can I go in?"

"Of course." Gabe twisted the key in the lock, which sprang free with a well-oiled click, and stepped back for her to pass.

Kendall pushed the door open slowly. A single step landed her in a small, closed-off foyer spread with an oriental rug. She caught her breath. It was . . .

Not what she expected from the outside. In fact, for all her surety about the Carpenter Gothic exterior, she wasn't even sure how to categorize the interior. She took a tentative step forward and pushed open the second door that led into a front hallway. Gleaming wood floors—because surely they had gleamed; she could tell that even under their current dull coating of dust—stretched in all directions, punctuated by a variety of Persian rugs in tones of red and blue. Quartersawn oak paneling covered the walls three-quarters of the way up, above which was plaster painted the palest shade of cream. Ahead and to the right lay a staircase with an ornately profiled wooden banister; to each side, rooms that appeared to be a library and a parlor respectively. She stood there, taking in the wooden beams and molding. The overall effect was Craftsman, but in place of simple Arts and Crafts corbels, these displayed miniature carved renderings of columbine flowers.

Gabe came up behind her, jingling keys in his hand. "Pretty impressive, isn't it?"

"Very." Kendall moved off to the library, which was papered in a William Morris print—she couldn't tell if it was original or reproduction on the first look—and glanced around the room, her excitement building. For all the distinct historical flavor, Connie Green hadn't been a slave to architectural style. If she wasn't mistaken, that was an original Eames lounge chair in the corner, its saddle-colored leather blending into the room just as well as the simple Danish modern cabinet. If she knew only one thing about the person who had left her this home, it was that she had impeccable taste.

And for the first time, this began to seem like more than just a trip into her mysterious past or a financial stopgap. It was beginning to feel like the solution to Kendall's problems.

She kept a running tally as she moved from room to room, admiring not just the house's architecture but also its exquisite antique furniture. Dozens of Persian rugs, some in perfect condition, some threadbare . . . all worth a fortune to her Los Angeles clients. Furniture spanning eras from classical to mission, Danish modern to American mid-century, even a couple of pieces that looked like British Victorian antiques. Belatedly, she thought to pull out her cell phone and begin snapping pictures, annotating them quickly with her sketch app, while Gabe trailed silently behind her.

Finally, when they'd made a full circuit of the house, he stopped in the foyer again. "I have to ask. What are the photos for?"

"So I can remember the details later. I need to look up the values and determine which ones I'm going to ship back."

He blinked at her. "Ship back?"

"For my clients. She had some beautiful pieces. I can think of at least four projects that they would be perfect for. I'll need to go back and look more closely later, of course. There's no point in paying to move things that are just reproductions."

Gabe stared at her, something akin to horror on his face. She frowned. "What else did you think I was going to do with it?"

He shook himself. "I don't know. I guess I thought . . ."

"I'm certainly not going to *move* here." Kendall laughed. "What would I do in Jasper Lake? And with five houses, to boot?"

"There's always the Airbnb option."

"Well, sure, if I lived here. But my life is in Pasadena. My clients are all over Southern California. And no offense, but I don't really see myself living in a town like this."

"None taken." From his tone of voice, she thought it was probably a lie. "So that means you're going to sell the houses."

"I haven't really gotten that far," Kendall said, though that was exactly what she was beginning to think. She itched to get someplace with Wi-Fi, pull out her laptop, and find out what homes of this quality and era were selling for in the county. Probably a fraction of what they'd be back home, but then she could see these appealing to the well-heeled ski-slopes set, anxious to claim a bit of their own mountain paradise.

"There's something you should know before you decide, given your appreciation for architecture. Do you have someplace to be?"

"Other than going through the other four houses, which I can do on my own time, no."

"Then let's go back to the office. I want to show you something."

Gabe remained quiet on the drive back, while Kendall scrolled through the photos on her phone. Her delight in the home had been genuine; she was truly knowledgeable about both the architecture and the furniture, but he couldn't help feeling like all she was seeing were dollar signs. Maybe it had been a vain hope that she would somehow feel a sense of connection to the house in which her grandmother had raised her mother. After all, she'd never known her family. But he'd thought maybe she'd feel a spark of . . . something.

That hope wasn't strictly confined to the houses. He was hyperaware of Kendall sitting next to him in his truck: the fall of blonde tendrils across her cheek, the faint waft of a heady jasmine perfume, the husky laugh that emerged when she exclaimed over some unexpected detail of the furniture she was reviewing. Her enthusiasm was contagious, and it only served to stoke the attraction that had been building from the moment he saw her on the boardwalk.

An attraction that seemed to be completely one-sided. In fact, she had not budged from her professional mode the entire time they'd been together. Not to say she was cold—her enthusiasm said otherwise—but it was the kind of enthusiasm that a rare book dealer might express over finding an early manuscript of Shakespeare. Right now, her fingers flew over the screen of her cell phone in a string of text messages. He glanced over and saw the square images that said she was sending photos to someone. A partner? A client?

"I'm sorry," she said suddenly. "I'm being

completely rude. It's just that my assist—design partner took on this mid-century renovation back home, and I think the lounge and the cabinet in the library would be absolutely perfect for it. I want to get her the photos immediately so she can work them into the design before it's too late."

"It's no problem," he said evenly, though to him it felt as if she were a circling vulture. She couldn't possibly know that he'd sat in that very chair, listening to music on his headphones while his grandmother visited with Connie. That was back in the days when he was being such a delinquent that he was required to stay by Oma's side every waking minute. He'd hated it at the time, but in some ways, the Green house held as many memories as his grandparents' home did.

Clearly he wasn't going to get through to her with sentiment. He'd have to appeal to her love of architecture and her professional sensibilities. When they finally pulled up in front of the town hall again, he hopped out and circled to open her door, but she beat him to it.

"Okay," she said. "What do you want to show me?"

He led her back to his office, pausing for a brief introduction to his secretary, Linda, and then pushed into his own space, gesturing for her to take a seat. From the credenza behind the desk, he pulled out a roll of architectural plans and spread them before her.

"You know that beautiful little tract of homes? If you sell them, this is what the property becomes."

Kendall leaned forward to study the plans, her expression morphing from confusion to horror. "They're going to tear them down? For this?"

"For this." A monstrosity of a high-end lodge, all mountain-rustic kitsch and designer bedding. Gone would be the stands of pines and aspens, the sloping fall toward the lake. In its place, a massive fake-log building with hundreds of rooms, two swimming pools, and a dock where people could rent paddleboats and Jet Skis. "The developer wants to turn this into a summer destination, not just for the flatlanders, but to draw in all the people who live in the surrounding ski communities."

"And the town is actually considering letting him?" Kendall's voice came out strangled, and he felt a surge of optimism.

"Unfortunately, the town isn't doing all that well. We lost most of our tourism and our residents after a flood isolated us a few years ago. We got hit less severely than some of the surrounding communities, mostly because we have another way out. But in order for us to continue to provide essential services, like road repairs and the fire department, we need to increase our income. Until now, the developer hasn't been able to move forward because your houses are sitting smack in the middle of his proposed development, but . . ."

"But if I sell, he's going to be the one to buy them, and they'll be razed to the ground." The horror in Kendall's voice was palpable. "Can't I talk to the city council, tell them about how unique the buildings are? Surely they wouldn't allow—"

"Money talks. And honestly, considering I got elected on my promise to revitalize the town, I'm not sure there's much I can do about it if they decide to go this direction. It may not be the vision that I wanted for Jasper Lake, but there's no doubt it would help the tax base."

Kendall sighed heavily and fell back against the chair. "You have no idea what you're asking me to do."

"I think I do."

"No, you don't." She met his eye, and for the first time since she'd arrived, he caught a glimmer of vulnerability. "My partner and I are struggling to stay in our space. It's not just our office; it's our home as well. The landlord keeps raising our rent, but we use the house as a showroom and proof of concept . . . and we can't afford commercial space anywhere else. If I sold the houses here, I could buy my house from the landlord."

Gabe sank into the chair beside her. "I understand. I really do. But, Kendall . . . there are alternatives. You could lease the houses. You could follow through on Connie's idea to put them up as vacation rentals. I'm working on another plan for the town that wouldn't require us to raze the buildings or sell out to a developer and turn this into Summer Mountain World or whatever theme park nonsense he has in mind."

Kendall gave him a small, pitying smile. "The market value on my house is $1.7 million."

And Gabe's last spark of hope died. Selling the homes individually could probably garner at least that much; selling them to someone who desperately wanted the property so he could rake in buckets of money meant she could name her own price. There was no question she could get $1.7 million for the land. And if he were in her place, there might be no way he could pass it up either.

"Before you do anything, you need to file a claim on the estate at the courthouse. And by my calculations, you only have two days left to do it." He forced a smile. "Let's get that taken care of first. And then . . . will you at least take a few days to think on it? Let me try to change your mind?"

She studied him and then gave a sharp nod. "It will take me at least that long to catalog the furnishings. And I know you don't want to hear this, but if I end up selling and they're going to tear the houses down anyway, I will probably take out some of the architectural elements to reuse elsewhere. That's better than them being scrapped, isn't it?"

It was a bit like saying that organ donation mitigated the death of a loved one, but he nodded anyway. "If you'll give me a few days, I'll stand by any decision you make. Let's get this paperwork going. I also meant to ask you, do you have a place to stay?"

"I thought I'd find a motel. Or worse come to worse, I could drive back to Georgetown or Golden for the night."

"No, don't do that. I have something better. And I know someone who has been looking forward to seeing you."

Chapter Five

Kendall followed Gabe's truck in her rented SUV, traversing a few short blocks down Main Street and then turning toward the lake. Even another stunning glimpse of water couldn't quell the uneasiness in her middle. She'd come to Jasper Lake thinking that this would be a quick and easy process: file a claim against Constance Green's estate, hire a trucking company to transport anything of value back to California, put the house on the market with a local Realtor. Her hopes had lifted when she'd seen that it was not one but five houses and a sizable plot of land as well. It was the relatively quick influx of cash they needed, the first good thing she'd ever gotten from anyone claiming to be related to her. And yet now that she knew the likely buyer would bulldoze these gorgeous examples of American historic architecture and put up some insulting, kitschy behemoth in their place . . . the process didn't feel nearly so quick or so easy.

Well, why shouldn't it be? She had absolutely no obligation to this town. She'd never set foot in it before today, hadn't even heard of it before the letter from the lawyer arrived. And while

Gabe might have been banking on sentimentality to keep her from disposing of the property as quickly as possible, he couldn't know that she'd abandoned any curiosity about her past a long time ago. Obviously Constance had known about her existence and never tried to find her. Done nothing to save her from the string of foster homes and group homes she'd gone through before she'd finally landed at something more permanent. Done nothing to save her from the long years of hoping her mom might suddenly come back, followed by the constant pain of having her hopes shattered.

Kendall shook her head sharply. No. She didn't owe Connie Green or this town anything. She'd made a new life in California. That was her priority.

Gabe pulled up to the curb alongside a traditional blue Victorian that had small American and Colorado state flags waving from a flagpole on a front porch. Even this late in the year, the grass was green, and cheerful pots of autumn mums stood on either side of the cement steps. A sign out front proclaimed *Brandt Bed-and-Breakfast* with a cute interlaced triple-B logo up top.

She climbed out of her SUV and retrieved her duffel bag, and when she stepped onto the sidewalk, Gabe was waiting for her. He flung his arms wide. "This is it. Best bed-and-breakfast in Clear Creek County."

"Is it the only bed-and-breakfast in Clear Creek County?" she threw back with a smile, unable to remain sullen in the face of his enthusiasm. No matter his ulterior motives, his cheerful demeanor was infectious.

"No. But it is owned by my family, so I might be slightly biased." He pretended to think. "Nope. Still the best. Come on in."

Gabe took her bag from her hand and gestured for her to follow him up the front walkway. He let himself in without knocking, then called, "Opa?"

An older man appeared in the back hallway, dressed in a pair of pressed trousers and a knit vest over an oxford shirt. He walked slowly toward them, a slight frown on his creased face. "Gabriel? What are you doing here in the middle of the day?" His voice held the faint trace of a German accent.

"I've brought you a guest, Opa."

The man faltered for a moment and fumbled for the glasses hooked in his collar. He studied her in surprise, the sharp blue of his eyes startling in his wizened face. "You must be Kendall Green. I would know you anywhere. You're the spitting image of your mother, Carrie."

Kendall glanced at Gabe, discomfited. She'd been envisioning a homey grandmother or aunt, someone who would sit her down with a cup of tea or a cookie, not a stern-looking German who, despite his slight shuffling gait, carried himself with a thread of steel.

He was still waiting for her response, though, so she nodded. "I am Kendall. You must be Gabe's grandfather."

He didn't offer his hand, just gave her a nod that struck her as both old-fashioned and chivalrous. "Werner Brandt. Pleased to meet you." He swept a hand toward the stairs. "Please. Follow me."

Kendall hesitated, but Gabe didn't seem to notice her uncertainty. "Opa, are we putting her in the Lake Room?"

"Of course we're putting her in the Lake Room," Mr. Brandt—she couldn't think of him otherwise—responded with a touch of reproach. "It's a waste of a good view otherwise, and it gets the morning sunlight. Plus, she can see you coming and decide if she wants you bothering her."

Kendall smothered a smile and just caught the roll of Gabe's eyes when she cast a look back at him. Despite her initial misgivings, she couldn't help but like the brusque old man. There was a twinkle in his blue eyes—already so much like Gabe's—that made her think his sternness was just an act or a habit. She followed him up the well-worn wood stairs, covered with an oriental runner, unable to help trailing her fingers over the original wood paneling, now painted white. This home had all the history and charm that she loved, even if it was more worn-in and less distinctive than Connie's. Mr. Brandt made a turn down the upstairs hallway and stopped in front of the first door, a bedroom that seemed to face the front of the house. He pushed the door open for Kendall.

"Oh, wow." A carved four-poster bed in keeping with the age of the home dominated the room, its mattress spread with a cozy handmade quilt, and upholstered armchairs flanked an antique table in front of the bay window. A quick peek into the en suite bath displayed a traditional scheme of black and white with gleaming white fixtures. Most girls didn't get chills over original hexagonal floor tiles, but she'd spent her entire career trying to infuse this kind of period charm into new builds. She wandered over to the window, which provided a glorious bird's-eye view of the lake beyond.

"I take it this suits you?" Mr. Brandt asked formally, but the twinkle was back.

"It's perfect, thank you." She smiled at the innkeeper. "How much is it a night? Just so I'm prepared . . ."

"Bah." Mr. Brandt waved a hand impatiently and turned away. "No Green is going to pay to stay under my roof."

The glow Kendall had felt moments before disappeared, and his charity chafed like sand in her swimsuit. "No," she said firmly. "I insist."

Mr. Brandt seemed not to hear or, more likely, chose to ignore her. "Come down when you're ready. There are scones and coffee in the kitchen."

Gabe shot her a helpless smile and shrugged, then brushed past her to drop her duffel on the bed. "I'll wait for you downstairs."

"Thanks," she murmured, waiting for him to close the door behind him before she sank into one of the chairs with a sigh.

The surroundings were so beautiful, she could almost let herself believe she was here on a mountain getaway and Gabe was a friendly local determined to show her a good time. He was personable and intelligent—not to mention easy on the eyes. But she could never forget he was also Jasper Lake's mayor, and his sole purpose in bringing her here was to enlist her in his vision of the town's future. That made this whole trip an exercise in propaganda. As wonderful as the town might turn out to be, she couldn't forget about her bigger responsibilities and visions back home.

She glanced at her watch and then dialed Sophie on her cell phone. The line rang twice before Sophie picked up and started talking without saying hello.

"Is it horrible? Is it amazing? Tell me all about it."

Kendall leaned back in the chair and laughed, just hearing her friend's voice draining the tension from her. "It's not horrible. It's actually beautiful. You wouldn't believe this lake. And the trees have almost completely turned, but there's still all this red and orange and yellow. I wish you'd come with me."

"I wish I had too. What about this house?"

"Well . . . it's more like *houses*." Kendall explained the situation to Sophie, how she had come to inherit five houses and some property. "The only catch is, the town's mayor is trying to convince me to keep them, or at least not sell to a developer who wants to level them. He's building this huge summer resort on the far side of the lake."

"That sounds ghastly," Sophie said, but clearly her mind wasn't on the conversation. Kendall heard clicking in the background.

"Are you typing? What are you doing?"

"I'm just looking something up." She gasped. "Oh, my word, Kendall, do you have any idea how much those houses could be worth? Even in the middle of nowhere, they're at least a quarter of a million each. I thought we were talking shacks or something, but . . . $1.25 million? That's what I call an inheritance."

"Yeah, and they're even better than you can imagine. It's actually pretty depressing to think of them being torn down. If I end up selling, I'll want to take the stained-glass windows and some of the woodwork."

"What do you mean *if* you end up selling? You're seriously going to leave over a million dollars wasting away in the mountains? You don't even like the cold. You don't like skiing and you hate snow!"

"I know. And you're right." Kendall twisted around to catch a glimpse of the lake from her window. If she squinted, she could make out the tiny street with its five Carpenter Gothics through the shimmer of the setting sun on the water. "I just need to be strong. I haven't even filed my claim with the court yet, so that's the first step. And after that, I guess I need to consult a Realtor. But first, I want to inventory the houses."

"And how long do you think that will take?"

Kendall hesitated. "That was the other thing I wanted to talk to you about. I think it's probably going to be a week or two. Everything was wrapped up on my design projects before I went to Europe; I just have a few commissions from past clients to fill, and they know it will take me a while to find the right pieces. Can you handle things there without me for that long?"

"Of course I can. Take as much time as you need. Get all those delicious antiques crated and shipped back to me posthaste, and you can deal with the real estate stuff when they're empty. But *sell the houses.*"

"Noted." Kendall smiled, bolstered by her friend's assertive tone. She knew what she had

58

to do; she just had to be reminded what was at stake. "I have to go now. Fresh-baked scones downstairs."

"*Do not be seduced by the baked goods,*" Sophie intoned. "Also, I'm a little mad you can still eat gluten. Call me later."

"Done." Kendall clicked off the line and squared her shoulders. Baked goods indeed awaited her downstairs. And no matter how charming or persistent the Brandts were, she would stay strong.

Chapter Six

Gabe followed his grandfather down the stairs and around the staircase landing to the kitchen, where the fragrance of butter and wheat and the floral scent of citrus water perfumed the moist air. This was Werner Brandt's domain, and his past as a professional baker was evidenced by the no-nonsense approach he had taken with its decor: rather than the elaborate Victorian style his grandmother had favored, the kitchen was all functional tile, flat-paneled cabinets, and stainless steel. Back when the town had been thriving and the B and B was regularly booked, the cooking and baking for guests had kept him busy enough; now Opa baked for several of the town's cafés and restaurants. He said he did it to keep busy in his retirement years, but Gabe suspected it also covered expenses that the guesthouse and his Social Security checks didn't.

Gabe reached for one of the dozen round scones perched on a cooling rack, and Opa fixed him with his signature glare. "Don't touch them. They're still hot and they'll fall apart the minute you pick them up."

As soon as he looked away, Gabe snatched one

off the rack. It immediately crumbled into pieces, and he shoved half of them into his mouth. His grandfather shook his head in mock disgust. "Didn't I tell you?"

"Totally worth it," he mumbled around a mouthful of crumbs. "Orange and almond?"

Opa relented slightly at his words, his expression softening. Gabe blinked to restore his sudden blurry vision. Opa might have done the official baking for the B and B, but it was Oma from whom Gabe had sat across the island, watching her fix dinner. Guessing the spices in her food had turned into a game that even his most sullen teenage self hadn't been able to resist. Oma and this kitchen had been his touchstone when he needed it most. Even five years later, it was hard to believe she was gone.

Apparently Opa was thinking the same thing, because he placed a glass of chocolate milk in front of Gabe and slid another scone in his direction.

"I miss her," Gabe said softly. "I can't help feeling she would have taken one look at Kendall and known exactly what to say to convince her not to sell."

"She did know how to read people, your grandmother." Opa dragged a stool around the side of the island and perched on the edge. "The first time she and I met, she took one look at me and said I was going to take her out to dinner."

"Oma? She always said she'd played hard to get."

Something close to a guffaw escaped Opa's lips. "Your grandmother? Hard to keep, maybe. Hard to get, no. She knew what she wanted, and once she went after it, no one could stand in her way. I'm just lucky one of those things was me." He sent Gabe a look. "I sense a bit of that in your Kendall. It ran in the family. Stubborn as an ox, Connie Green. Her daughter, too."

"Trust me, she's not *my* Kendall. And she wants nothing to do with her Green history, stubborn or otherwise. They're strangers to her."

"Then maybe that's your task. Make them not strangers. Help her understand her connections to this town. Or at least that's what Greta would say." Opa looked at him significantly and reached for the damp rag to wipe down the countertop.

Gabe sighed. That was easier said than done. If the stubborn Green blood ran through her veins, she wasn't likely to change her mind once it was made up. He changed the subject. "Does she really look just like her mother?"

"Spitting image. A little older, of course. Caroline was barely eighteen the last time we saw her. Your grandmother always wished . . ." He shook his head. "But wishing doesn't bring anyone back, does it?"

Gabe had the feeling they weren't just talking about Caroline Green now. Opa's gaze had gone distant, and Gabe hesitated to interrupt what he expected was a deep dive into memory. After forty years of marriage, he had a lot of material to choose from.

Kendall chose that moment to poke her head into the kitchen. "Can I come in?"

"Of course, of course." Opa waved her to a seat. "Have a scone. I'll get you a cup of coffee."

Kendall pulled up the stool next to Gabe and shot a look at his glass. "That doesn't look like coffee."

"What can I say? I still like my chocolate milk. Just don't tell the voters. Half of them asked me if I was shaving yet when I put myself up for the office of mayor."

Kendall chuckled. "To be fair, you do have a young face."

Just what every guy wanted to hear from an attractive woman. "Not that young, I hope. It's been at least two years since anyone asked me if I wanted a kids' menu."

He saw Kendall repressing a smile behind the mug of coffee his grandfather set in front of her and counted that as a point in his favor. "So what are your plans for the rest of the day?" Gabe asked. "We can go back to my office and fill out the forms for the court, but you won't be able to file until tomorrow. I'm happy to drive you to the courthouse in Georgetown. It's about thirty miles."

"You don't have to do that. I'm sure you have things to do."

"Not really. All the planning for the fall festival is complete, and anything else my staff needs, they can reach me on my cell." He leaned over and lowered his face. "I'll tell you a secret. Mayor doesn't really do that much. The city council has to make all the decisions. I just execute them."

"You execute the members of your city council?" Kendall cracked, her eyes sparkling.

Gabe grinned. "Only if they make the wrong decisions. I tell you what. You finish your coffee—or better yet, take it in a to-go mug—and I'll show you around town. But you might want to put on another layer or two. The temperature is going to drop quickly as soon as the sun goes down."

Opa obviously understood what he had in mind, because he smoothly produced a stainless steel travel mug from one of the cupboards. "That's an excellent idea. Take her over to the Pine View Cantina for dinner when you're done. Their dessert menu is excellent."

Gabe laughed, even though Kendall looked confused as to what was so funny. "Humble as always, I see." He hopped off the stool and then circled the island to give his grandfather a quick hug. "I'll have her home at a decent hour; don't worry."

Opa ignored him and instead turned his attention to Kendall. "Here. Take another scone to go. I'll give you a little paper bag for it."

Gabe smiled to himself as Opa transferred Kendall's coffee to the mug, pressed a bag into her hand, and shooed them out of the kitchen. His grandfather was right: he had to make her feel a personal connection to the town. Operation Win Over Kendall Green had officially begun.

Chapter Seven

Kendall took her coffee and her to-go bag up the stairs to her room, where she riffled through the small collection of clothing she'd brought with her. When she'd boarded with just a carry-on duffel, it wasn't because of any specific decision to pack light. It was just that everything she owned was oriented to the sunny Southern California weather, not this winter wonderland with its rapidly falling temperatures. Still, she had packed a couple of sweaters, so she took a cable-knit pullover from the bag, slipped it on over her T-shirt, and then wrapped a long knit scarf around her neck. At the last minute, she pulled a beanie from the side pocket and let down her bun so it would fit on her head, taking a moment to arrange her waves over her shoulders. When she came downstairs a few minutes later, Gabe was waiting in the foyer. He took one look at her and started to laugh.

"What?" she protested. "You said to dress warm."

"I said to dress warm, but I didn't think you'd go Shackleton expedition on me." He shook his head, the grin staying plastered to his face. "Left coaster."

Kendall arched an eyebrow. "I grew up in Colorado, thank you very much."

"But your blood has thinned from all those matcha lattes." Gabe winked at her and offered his arm. "Come on, Miss California. Let me show you around a proper mountain town."

Kendall ignored his arm with a smirk of her own and opened the front door. "You know, for a mayor of a town, you're not very kind."

"Oh, I'm very kind. I'm just not very nice. There's a difference."

"Is there?"

"Of course. I'm kind, so I'm going to tell you that you've still got the price tag sticking out the neck of your jacket." He gave it a quick yank, snapping off the plastic tag, and then tucked it into her pocket. "If I were nice, I wouldn't say anything so you wouldn't be embarrassed."

Kendall reached for the neck of her jacket, feeling her cheeks warm. She'd hoped that she could pass this off as something already hanging in the closet, not a purchase that took four hours and $200 at REI before she left. The salesman had convinced her that you could do no less than 600 fill power down if you were going to Colorado, but before she'd gotten halfway down the street from the Brandt Bed-and-Breakfast—*Triple B,* she thought with a laugh to herself—she had to unzip the front.

Gabe smirked again.

"Okay, Mr. Mayor. You're supposed to be giving me a tour. Let's hear it."

"Let the record show that you asked for it."

She'd been joking, but he really did know everything about the town. As they walked down the quiet residential street, its asphalt potholed and covered with a fine brown layer—remnants of the magnesium chloride used as a deicer on the interstate—he told her more about Jasper Lake's history: how this neighborhood with the Victorian homes had been built by mine and business owners who settled in Jasper Lake permanently; how the smaller clapboard homes on the other side had once been used as boardinghouses before they were converted to single-family homes in the 1920s. When they finally reached the boardwalk area again, Kendall asked, "And how about this?"

"This is pure 1980s tourist bait," he responded with a grin. "We're only a couple of hours from Denver, so we get lots of day-trippers up here from April to September. Or at least we used to. By October, it's starting to slow down because the risk of a freak snowstorm or highway closure starts getting too high. Denverites—"

"Are barely better than left coasters when it comes to driving in snow," Kendall finished.

Gabe laughed. "Exactly. But I'm too *kind* to say that out loud."

She was well aware of the high country–flatlander animosity, especially considering so many of the latter types swarmed to the ski towns in their expensive SUVs like they owned the place. But she took no offense at the words. Despite having grown up in Denver, she felt no more connection to it than she did to Jasper Lake. She'd learned long ago that the way to be happy was to look to the future, not to the past. At least when it came to her own past. Ironically, she'd built a career on investigating other people's pasts.

They walked slowly down the wood-planked walkway, Gabe keeping a respectable space between them, his hands shoved in his pockets while she looked into shopwindows. Most of the shops were predictable tourist traps: candy and fudge factories, gift shops with alpaca sweaters and gold-dipped leaf jewelry and Christmas ornaments, even a T-shirt shop that was filled with variations on the ubiquitous Colorado flag. The town's quaint, charming air would probably annoy her were she back home, because it would be so obviously put-on. But there was something appealingly earnest about this place, something so authentically small-town—from the hand-churned ice cream parlor painted in shades of pink and white, to the tiny closet of a real estate office with its current listings printed on plain white computer paper and taped to the inside of the window—that she couldn't fault it. Suddenly, walking into that tiny Realtor's space to list her houses felt downright callous.

"What's this?" Her steps slowed in front of a small lot wedged between a sandwich shop and the next block of businesses, fenced off with a low-slung sweep of chain link. A run-down concrete building, its windows covered with curling brown kraft paper, stood forlorn and abandoned before wide swaths of green Astroturf. "It's a miniature golf course?"

"It *was* a miniature golf course," Gabe corrected. "And an arcade. Take a look." He pulled aside a roll of chain link that had been left unanchored at the edge of the plot and held it back so Kendall could step through. He took her elbow as she picked her way through debris that littered what looked like it was once a "green," half its metal obstacles missing, the plastic hole filled with decaying leaves. When they reached the building, Gabe wiped the window with his sleeve so he could peer through a gap in the paper covering.

She'd expected to see open, empty space, but the arcade was packed with games—pinball machines, Skee-Ball, animatronic fortune-tellers, and strongman games. In the back, there was even a toddler-size carousel, the horses and its mirrored canopy covered in a layer of dust.

"That's just . . . sad," she murmured. "Why did it close?"

"Not enough tourists. Hardly any kids in town." He cast her a look. "Only 5 percent of the population is under sixteen."

She did the math. "There's only thirty-something kids in the whole town?"

Gabe nodded. "And most of them are teens. They'll move away for college and never come back."

"You don't know that," Kendall said. "It's so beautiful here."

"Beautiful or not, there are no non-service jobs in town, and few people want a fifty-mile commute. Not to mention the lack of social opportunities." He fixed his gaze on her significantly, then inclined his head back toward the street. She followed him across the minefield of abandoned Putt-Putt fairways and through the gap in the chain-link fence. Back on the boardwalk, after the temporary reprieve from the wind, she felt chilled and pulled her cap down over her ears. But she wasn't cold just because of the wind. The picture Gabe painted was indeed stark. She could understand why they'd elected him in the hopes that he and his youthful enthusiasm could revitalize the town. But from what she could tell, it would take more than one man and his determination to fix Jasper Lake.

Maybe the resort wasn't such a terrible idea after all.

"I know what you're trying to do here," she

said finally. "And I'm not unsympathetic. This place has history. And charm. I think anyone could agree they'd rather see it restored to its former glory than turned into a Breckenridge clone. But . . . it doesn't change the reality of my situation. Or yours. It's just . . . wishful thinking."

Gabe nodded slowly. "Maybe I'm hoping that an alternate solution will present itself."

An alternate solution worth over a million dollars? She doubted it. But she kept her mouth shut and nodded, instead peeking into more store windows as they passed. For such a small town, they had a lot of businesses. Or maybe they were all oriented around the boardwalk instead of scattered across blocks like most small towns.

"Here we are," she said, relieved to have a change of subject as they approached a corner restaurant with the rustic sign pronouncing it *Pine View Cantina*. Gabe opened the door for her before she could, ushering her into a cramped lobby marked by a barrel of peanuts next to a hostess stand with a hand-lettered sign.

A middle-aged woman in a plaid shirt and a short black apron spotted them from near the bar area and bustled over. "Mayor Gabe! Nice to see you. Table for two?"

"Thanks, Julie, yes."

"Right this way then." Julie shot an appraising glance at Kendall and led them to a small booth in the back near the window. As soon as they seated themselves, she handed them menus in cloudy plastic sleeves and plunked a galvanized steel bucket of peanuts on the table. But rather than taking their drink orders, she lingered, looking between them. "I don't think I've seen you around town before. New here?"

"Just visiting," Kendall said, at the same time Gabe said, "This is Kendall Green."

Julie's eyes widened. "Kendall Green? Wow. I guess I should have known. You look just like your mother. Carrie and I went to school together, you know. She was a year ahead of me, cheerleader and everything. I always looked up to her so much until—" She broke off, embarrassed. "Anyway. It's nice to have you back in town. Moving into the old Green place on Lakeshore?"

"Haven't decided," Kendall said. It was easier than the real answer that lingered on her tongue: *Not a chance, lady.* "Can I get a Coke?"

That seemed to snap Julie back to the present. "Of course. You want your usual, Gabe?"

"Yes, please. Thanks, Julie."

She looked between them again, as if she couldn't quite make out what was going on. "Go ahead and look over the menus, and I'll be back in a minute to take your order."

Kendall watched Julie go, unsettled. Did everyone in this town know her name and her history? Because if they did, they knew a heck of a lot more than she did. She looked at Gabe, not sure if she really wanted to ask, but she couldn't help herself. "What did she mean by 'until'? What happened that Julie suddenly didn't look up to her?" She had a sinking suspicion that she knew.

Gabe cleared his throat, but he looked her straight in the eye. "She got pregnant her senior year of high school."

"With me," Kendall said, her voice choking.

"Yes. She was forced to leave school. It's my understanding that she had to get her GED instead."

Kendall arched her brow, irritated on behalf of a woman she'd always both longed for and hated. "That's terribly 1950s of them."

"It *was* thirty years ago. They thought that being seen condoning unwed pregnancy would encourage other girls to . . ."

". . . have sex?" Kendall snorted. "I've got news for them. No one plans to get pregnant in high school, but it doesn't stop anyone from doing what they want. What else? How do they all know my name?"

Gabe hesitated again. "Are you sure you want to hear all this?"

"Now that I know the entire town knows more about me than I do, absolutely." Until now, it hadn't really dawned on her that she had a history. If the houses were in Los Angeles or Denver, she would probably be dealing with a lawyer and a real estate agent, both strangers. Her past would have been erased, lost to everyone except the people involved, just how Kendall wanted it. It had taken her three years to tell Sophie about her abandonment and upbringing in foster care. But here . . . just introducing herself brought up her entire bio in the town's collective memory.

"Okay then." Gabe spread his fingers out on the table, palms flat against the sticky resin finish. "I don't know the whole story, and while my grandfather might know pieces of it, he wasn't close to Connie like Oma was. As I understand it, Caroline gave birth to her baby—you—and for a while, it looked like she was going to stick around town. But she got in a big argument with Connie and either left or was kicked out of the house. There was apparently plenty of speculation on that at the time."

Kendall kept her expression impassive, unable to interpret the myriad feelings jolting around inside of her. "Same end result. What happened then?"

Gabe spread his hands wide. "That's all we know. Caroline left when you were less than a year old, and no one ever saw the two of you again. There were rumors of course. Some people thought she moved to Los Angeles to try to be a movie star. I hear she was beautiful." He smiled slightly, a hint of humor in his eyes. "Given that everyone says you look just like her, I'd have to agree."

"That was a backhanded compliment," Kendall said, but she still smiled, feeling a tiny flush of pleasure. Then something else occurred to her. "What about my . . . Carrie's boyfriend?" She couldn't bring herself to use the word *father,* figured she could already guess the situation. But somehow, up until this point, she'd never really thought about the man who had made his contribution to her existence.

"That I can't tell you. At least I've never heard anyone talk about it. Towns have a long memory, but they do move on."

Julie came back before Kendall could answer, which was good, because there was no adequate response to what she'd just been told. It sounded like her mother left town with her when she was only a baby. Had it taken four more years for Caroline to decide raising a child alone was just too hard? If she didn't want Kendall, why hadn't she just left her with her grandmother?

Unless that's why Connie had kicked Caroline out of the house. Because she didn't want to deal with a baby. That put a far uglier cast on the situation. Kendall's stomach gave a little flip, and she took a reflexive drink of her Coke to settle her queasiness.

"Are you ready to order?"

"Oh." Kendall looked at her menu, which she hadn't even opened. "I'm sorry. I haven't decided yet."

"May I?" Gabe asked.

Kendall nodded mutely.

"We'll take the Pine View Feast." Gabe collected her menu with his own and handed them back to Julie, a friendly look on his face, but a definite dismissal in his tone.

"I'll put that right in," Julie said with a smile and then walked back to the kitchen. Kendall didn't miss the glance she threw back over her shoulder, though.

"It's killing her not to know what we're saying, isn't it?" Kendall asked.

"Can you blame her? Wouldn't you be curious if a classmate's long-lost kid showed up in town again?"

"Not really. But I wasn't very close to any classmates."

"Why? Did you move around a lot?" Gabe halted. "Sorry. Maybe that was an insensitive question. I thought because—"

"Because I was a foster kid, I got shuffled around? Yeah, I did, when I was younger. But I landed with one family and stayed with them until I graduated high school."

"That's good, I guess," Gabe said slowly. "Are you still in touch with them?"

Kendall unwrapped a straw and plunked it in her glass. "Why would I be?"

He shook his head in answer. "Anyway. I thought maybe we could go to my office early tomorrow, have you fill out the paperwork, and then we can go to the courthouse in Georgetown to file it."

"You don't have to do that. I've got a rental. I can drive myself."

"It's no trouble. I'm familiar with the roads and the courthouse. It will just make things easier."

It would make sure that she actually did it, he meant. Like she would forget or blow it off given what was at stake here. Still, he seemed like he was genuinely trying to help, and she could potentially use his assistance while she was here—not to mention the fact that she was staying at his grandfather's B and B—so she nodded. "Thanks. That's fine with me."

"Okay, good."

Before the topic could go back to her inheritance or her past, she folded her hands in front of her and fixed her gaze on him. "So. Tell me what you do when you're not busy mayoring."

"Mayoring?" He grinned. "A little bit of this and that. You know."

"You'll have to be more specific. Is it embarrassing or something? Are you secretly the only male member of the Jasper Lake Water Ballet troupe? A foot model for flip-flops? Or maybe your thing is more like microscopic taxidermy."

He threw his head back and laughed. "Microscopic taxidermy? Is that even a thing?"

"I don't know. You tell me."

"No, I'm afraid it's nothing so interesting as microscopic taxidermy. I like music. I like books."

Kendall sat back against her seat. "Now that *is* interesting. A man who reads. What do you read exactly?"

"Oh, a bit of everything. Bestsellers. Thrillers. Spy novels." He lowered his voice. "Even the odd romance."

"Oooh, Mayor Gabe likes bodice rippers?"

"Shh, lower your voice. I have a reputation to uphold." But he really didn't look that embarrassed or that serious about the statement, so she had no idea whether he meant the romance thing or he was just yanking her chain.

"Okay, then. What's the last book you read?"

He thought. *"Art and Architecture in Colorado, 1850–1950."*

"No. Seriously?"

"Seriously. It was interesting. Always looking for things to help the town, you know."

She sighed. So they were back to this topic. She was about to tell him that work-related reading didn't count when Julie returned with a giant platter heaped with food and carefully set it down in the center of the table. Kendall's eyes widened.

"Thanks, Julie. Can we get a couple extra sides of barbecue sauce?"

"Coming right up."

Kendall stared at the food. It was barbecue of every conceivable type: brisket, ribs, chicken, pulled pork, what looked like several different types of sausage. Gabe pointed to each of them. "Wild boar, elk, and buffalo."

"No kidding?"

"No kidding. Locally made. It's pretty incredible. I bet you've never had any of the three."

"You are absolutely right on that count."

Julie dropped off the sauce with instructions to call her if they needed anything, and then Kendall started heaping meat on her plate. As if the meat weren't enough, there were also sides of beans, coleslaw, and fresh-made corn bread, the kind that was baked in a skillet and then cut out in wedges. She took her first bite and gave a sigh of happiness. "This is amazing."

"It is pretty good," Gabe admitted, transferring food to his own plate. "Julie's parents own the place, but they're getting up in years, so she runs it. They smoke all their own meats in the back lot. Everything comes from local farms. So you can't get much more Colorado than this."

"I am not complaining. I just got back from Europe, and I missed good old-fashioned American barbecue."

"They don't have it there?"

"Not unless you go to an American chain, and then it's rarely as good." Kendall slathered her corn bread with butter and took a bite. Maybe it was the fresh air, but she couldn't remember the last time she'd tasted anything quite so delicious.

When they'd decimated more than half of the platter and Gabe asked for a to-go box, Kendall studied him carefully. It had to be the full stomach, but she was suddenly feeling warmer toward him. "Tell me about these alternatives."

"The what?"

"You said that you were hoping I'd stick around and explore the alternatives. So what are the alternatives? Besides the one we've already discussed, renting out the houses."

Gabe fell back against the plastic back of the booth. "Honestly? I have no idea. I feel like I've exhausted every option."

"You could just push hard for them to turn down the zoning request by the developer."

"It's not that easy."

"Why? What's the point in being mayor if you can't throw your weight around a little?"

"It's a small town, Kendall. Everyone has alliances. Half of the council would go along with the developer because their families have known each other for generations. Half of them are afraid to see our way of life destroyed, and they'd rather sacrifice the character of the town than see it disappear altogether."

"And you?"

It was as if the question stumped Gabe, because

after casting around for an answer, he finally said, "It doesn't matter what I think. It only matters what I can convince the council of."

"Of course it matters what you think. If you don't have the passion of your convictions to fall back on, how are you ever going to convince the council to see things your way?"

"You don't understand."

"What don't I understand?" Kendall folded her hands on top of the table and leaned over them. "You're so worried about the future of the town, you'd let them cave and do something you're adamantly against. That's a terrible reason to do anything. If you believe there's another way, convince them of that. I have no doubt you can be very convincing."

Something glinted in Gabe's eyes that she couldn't quite define. It could have been amusement or doubt . . . or hope? "You know me that well after a single day, do you?"

"I know enough." And she did. As long as she silenced the niggling part of her brain reminding her that sometimes you couldn't will people to change their minds, that sometimes no matter how hard you wished for something, you still came up short. But Gabe didn't need that right now. He needed a pep talk that would give him the strength to go find a solution to his problem, one that did not involve demolishing historic homes or Kendall losing her Pasadena property.

"Now, if I recall, someone said something about dessert?"

By the time they left the Pine View Cantina, Kendall was so stuffed she could barely move. As good as the barbecue had been—and it had been exceptional—his grandfather's pastries were even better. She'd finished her slice of cake *and* still managed to steal a couple bites of Gabe's brownie à la mode. The fact that he hadn't protested made her like him even more.

When they stepped out onto the sidewalk, full night had fallen, and the temperature with it. Kendall's breath puffed out in front of her, and she zipped her coat up and arranged her scarf so it didn't let any trickle of air in down her neck. Even with the sparse lights of the town around them, the sky overhead was spread with a dizzying array of stars. She stopped on the sidewalk and tipped her head back, her mouth open. "I've never seen so many stars. I'm always in the city. There's too much light."

"That's one thing we have an abundance of." Gabe stopped beside her and tilted his head back as well. "Stars, I mean. Not light."

She threw him a smile and started walking again. "You love this place, don't you?"

"I do. I mean, it's beautiful, but there aren't that many small towns left, not the kind where everyone knows and cares about everyone else. Of course, when I came here, I thought it was the worst place in the world." He cast her a wry glance. "Thirteen and taken away from all my bad influences? Yeah. I made my grandparents absolutely crazy for a while."

"You? Bad influences? That seems hard to believe."

"Let's just say I went through a rebellious stage. I was angry and looking for ways to get back at the world. Fell in with some kids who were dealing drugs, and before long, they'd roped me into being their lookout. And then their delivery boy. When my mom found out, naturally she freaked."

"Naturally."

"So she sent me up here. Nothing to do. In fact, my grandmother homeschooled me for the rest of the year, just so she could keep an eye on me."

"I bet that went over big," Kendall said. When she was nine, she'd been fostered with a home-school family, but she'd been so disruptive, they'd sent her back before three months were up. She still refused to take the blame for that one. She'd just been yanked out of a two-year placement where she'd had friends, had some semblance of normalcy, in order to sit at a kitchen table with five-year-old triplets all day. To say that she rebelled would have been an under-statement.

Gabe gave a soft laugh at her assessment. "About as well as you're imagining. But Oma

84

was patient to a fault. Even when she had to get tough with me. And that pretty much went for everyone else in the town, including your grandmother."

"I'm glad someone got to spend time with my grandmother."

Gabe slowed. "Kendall, I don't know what happened and how you ended up . . . where you did, but your mother loved you. Connie used to say that and Oma used to say that. Whatever the reason, I'm sure your mom thought you were better off without her."

"A child is never better off without her parents, no matter how bad they are." Kendall shook her head as if she could shake off the dark thoughts. "It doesn't matter now anyway. I'm grown. And I've done a pretty good job of taking care of myself."

Gabe didn't reply, but whether it was because he disagreed with her assessment or he didn't know what to say, she couldn't tell. They walked in silence the rest of the way to the bed-and-breakfast, where Gabe escorted her into the foyer. "Your car should be okay on Main Street overnight, but I can drive it over for you if you want me to."

"That's okay. I'll get it in the morning. Are we meeting at your office?"

"No, here. I wouldn't miss whatever Opa is making for your breakfast. When he gets that glint in his eye, it means he's got big plans."

Kendall laughed. "In that case, I wouldn't miss it either. Thanks for dinner, Gabe. And thanks for driving me tomorrow."

"No problem. I'll see you later." He gave her a smile and a little wave, then let himself out the front door. Reflexively, Kendall flipped the dead bolt behind him. Then she climbed the stairs to her room, which she had forgotten to lock before she left. Not that it mattered or that she'd brought much of value with her.

She toed off her boots with a sigh of relief and unwound her scarf, then plopped into one of the armchairs in front of the window. It had been a good day, all things considered. She'd found out she'd inherited a virtual town block and she'd spent a day with a pleasant, good-looking guy.

Which was why it made absolutely no sense that she started to cry and couldn't stop, even after she climbed into bed and turned off the lights.

Chapter Eight

Gabe climbed into his truck and sat with the key in the ignition and the headlights off. The day had undoubtedly been more trying for Kendall than him, but he still felt exhausted.

Kendall confounded him. He would have thought she'd be floored by the revelations about herself and her past, but she brushed them off like they meant absolutely nothing to her. She challenged his passion and his vision for the town. She joked around with him like they were best friends and yet closed off the minute they touched on anything too personal. Maybe that was her defense mechanism, and it would make sense given her upbringing: *Don't get too close, because you'll eventually have to leave.* Normally he would think that was a sad, disconnected way to live, but right now he wondered if she was onto something. Because tonight he could sorely use a defense mechanism of his own.

She held the town's future in her hands, and that alone should make him keep his distance, not want to learn more. But besides being beautiful, Kendall was funny and corny, free with her laughter and her opinions. She had no problem putting away a massive amount of barbecue and dessert in front of him, which he found inexplicably sexy—he couldn't stand when he took a woman out and she only ate a salad, as if he were weighing and judging her food intake.

All of that added up to a person he would like to get to know better.

The reality was, he would never get to know Kendall Green as well as he'd like, because nothing he said would sway her from selling those properties. Whatever life she left back in California meant far more to her than an unknown past in the Colorado mountains. Which posed two problems: he needed to kill his interest in Kendall while it was still but a whisper, and he needed to come up with an alternative plan for Jasper Lake—which seemed easy enough except for the fact he'd been trying to do that very thing since he was elected. Somehow he thought he'd have no more luck with the former than the latter.

He sighed and twisted the key in the ignition. The truck roared to life, and he pulled slowly onto the deserted street. Two short minutes later, he pulled onto the gravel driveway of his small house and killed the engine. Unlike the B and B's historic facade with its gingerbread and multiple stories, his house was a low-slung log-cabin type, its long profile and dark colors meant to blend into the forest from which this neighborhood had been carved. He tripped climbing the front steps and wished he'd thought to leave the porch light on. Then again, when he'd left the house this morning, he hadn't thought he'd be returning home after a full day of showing around the town's prodigal daughter.

He smiled at that thought as he put the key in the lock. Kendall would probably have a few choice words about that description, not the least of which being that in the Bible story, the prodigal son had actually *wanted* to come home.

As soon as the door scraped open, the scratch of nails on the hardwood floors and the jingle of metal started in the back of the house. Gabe barely got the door closed before a hundred-plus pounds of Irish mastiff slid to a stop against his legs.

"Oof. Why do I think this is the most you've done all day, Fitz?" He reached down to scratch the dog's shaggy, floppy ears and was rewarded with a lolling-tongue expression of ecstasy from the massive beast. Fitz bumped up against him and Gabe fell to a knee. "Okay, okay. A belly rub it is."

Gabe laughed as he scratched his dog and then pushed himself to his feet. It was like sharing the house with a good-tempered elephant. When he rescued Fitz from the county shelter, he hadn't known he was adopting an enormous lapdog who would take over both his sofa and his bed.

"Okay, buddy, let's go eat."

Fitz rolled back to his feet, gave himself a shake, and trotted off to the kitchen, about as much speed and enthusiasm as the dog showed for anything. Gabe tossed his keys on the dining room table as he passed and then squeezed through the kitchen door in the little space the dog had left for him.

"Sorry I'm so late tonight," he said as if Fitz had any idea what he was talking about. He scooped dry food from a large, snap-top bin in the corner of his outdated kitchen and deposited it into the stainless steel bowl sitting in an elevated frame. The dog was so big, if he put it on the floor, Fitz practically had to lie down to eat it. "I met a girl today."

Fitz cocked his head as if he were really considering his words. Then Gabe realized he was still holding the second scoop of food. He dumped it into the bowl and the dog dug in hungrily.

"She's very pretty. I didn't ask her if she liked dogs, but I bet she'd like you, because who doesn't like you?" It wasn't far from the truth—his friend Luke had called Fitz a chick magnet for good reason. He was sociable, well-behaved, and handsome—"everything you aren't." In fact, anytime he'd walked him through town this week, he'd had to stop for Fitz to be petted every block. Maybe he should text Luke to meet him a little earlier tomorrow, so he could give the dog some exercise before he had to meet Kendall at the office.

He fished his phone from his pocket and pulled up his running text conversation with his best friend. Meet at Main Street Mocha at 6 instead of 7 tomorrow? Bringing Fitz.

A couple of minutes later, the reply came through. Does this have anything to do with a certain woman you were seen with in Pine View Cantina tonight?

Gabe sighed. He should have known that word would travel so quickly, especially given Luke's connections to just about everybody. I'll fill you in tomorrow. It's not nearly as exciting as it sounds.

Is it ever?

Gabe chuckled and tossed his phone on the counter. As much as he'd like to climb into bed and get a decent night's sleep, Kendall's challenge still rang in his ears. He had to come up with an alternate plan. This should be easy for him. He had a degree in urban planning and five years of experience in redeveloping depressed neighborhoods, for pete's sake. It wasn't like he'd never done this before. It had just never been this personal.

He dumped coffee beans into the grinder on the chipped tile countertop and then transferred the fresh grounds into the basket of his coffee maker. Five minutes later, he had a giant mug of coffee, a spot on the couch with his laptop, and sixty pounds of dog—Fitz's front end—draped over his legs on the ottoman.

"You know, you're making it really hard to move," he said.

Fitz dropped his head on his paws and lifted an eyebrow.

"Okay, lazybones. Stay there."

Three hours later, he couldn't blame his lack of progress on the weight of dog on his legs any more than he could blame Kendall for what was going to happen to the houses after she sold them. He wiped a hand wearily over his face and lifted a silent, helpless prayer.

He'd been so sure he'd been brought here for a reason. An urban planner laid off and forced to come back home, just as the town he loved was facing changes that could destroy their way of life forever? It had so clearly felt like God's hand, His will, that Gabe had never stopped to consider if he could actually deliver on his promises. At the time, it had felt like faith. Now he was afraid it was only hubris. And it wasn't just he who would bear the fallout from his overconfidence, but the town he loved, the people who had put their trust in him.

It was only a matter of time before Jasper Lake found out the truth: their mayor, the big city planner, the hometown boy made good, was a complete and total fraud.

Chapter Nine

"So. Tell me about this woman."

Gabe dropped to one knee on the dew-covered turf and wrestled the slobbery ball out of Fitz's mouth, then lobbed it across the park before he dared answer. "You mean Connie Green's granddaughter?"

Gabe's best friend, Luke Anderson, raised an eyebrow at him over his paper cup of coffee. "Of course I mean Connie Green's granddaughter. Unless you had two dates last night and the Jasper Lake grapevine failed me completely. Which it wouldn't."

There was a reason for that, considering that on top of his web design business, Luke was also head of the Jasper Lake Chamber of Commerce and the one most often responsible for manning the visitor center in the community building. He checked in with businesses on a regular basis, which meant that he was the first one to pick up any town gossip.

Still, that was fast, even for him.

"It wasn't a date. I'm taking her to the courthouse in Georgetown this morning to file her claim against her grandmother's estate."

"With what, less than two days on the clock?"

"Something like that." Gabe cast him a look, knowing full well where he was going with this. "It's just a stay of execution, though. She wants nothing to do with the town. Needs the money."

Luke shrugged. "Then you're just going to have to change her mind."

"You sound like my grandfather." It was an easy enough thing to say, just like it was easy enough for Kendall to say he had to come up with an alternative to the resort development. The reality was much more difficult. "Hey, she's single . . . maybe you could change her mind."

Luke almost choked on his coffee. "You're pimping me out?"

"You know that's not what I meant. But you'd have a better chance at convincing her than I would." Luke was pretty much regarded as the town's most eligible bachelor—he'd heard some of the teenage girls referring to him as "a Hemsworth." He guessed that was the standard these days, and if he squinted and pretended Luke was a stranger, he supposed he could pass for a Norse god. Kind of.

"Whatever. You're single too. Amanda Lee is still dropping hints with me, by the way."

Fitz finally made it back to Gabe, having taken his sweet time at fetching, and dropped the slobbery ball at his feet. Gabe picked it up gingerly and snapped the leash back onto the dog's collar. "I'm not interested in Amanda Lee."

By silent agreement, they made their way over to the rustic wooden bench and sat down, Fitz shoving his way between them to be petted by whomever would oblige. Luke reached down and scratched his head automatically. "So what are you interested in?"

"At the moment? Inspiration." Gabe fell back against the bench. "I spent three hours last night browsing the internet, hoping for some sort of idea that would convince the council we do not need the summer resort. And I've got no more than I did when I got elected. Attracting visitors during the summer with festivals and events? They've tried it. Two years in a row, the rowing regatta got canceled because of high winds, and the outdoor art festival ended up damaging thousands of dollars of canvases because of a freak hailstorm. To say that the members are jaded would be putting it mildly."

Luke cleared his throat. "I know you don't want to hear this, but would it really be the worst thing if they actually did demolish those houses and put in a resort? I mean, yes, they're beautiful and they've been there as long as the town, but if it's between them and us . . ."

Gabe shook his head resolutely. "It's not just that. When you build a resort, especially a luxury one, it does bring in taxes and improve tourism. But it also encourages investors to buy up land cheap, build massive houses, and drive up real estate prices. Which is great for those people who want to sell their homes and move. But it raises property taxes and the cost of living for our elderly citizens who are barely surviving as it is. It ends up saving the town but hurting the people. If we're going to let that happen, we might as well all move to Vail."

"And that is why you are the person who needs to stop this." Luke poked Gabe in the shoulder emphatically. "Because you understand the impact on the community. You're a city planner. Why not build out a model of what the town will look like? Be honest . . . show them the shiny. And then demonstrate how it will hit everyone in their wallets. Most of the council members have been in the high country their entire lives, their families for generations. You hear how they gripe about the flatlanders in their Land Rovers gentrifying our small towns and making it unaffordable for anyone to actually live where they own businesses. It's one thing to tell them. It's another thing to *show* them."

Gabe stared at him. It was so simple he felt like an idiot for not thinking of it before. "You're right. You're a genius."

"That's what I keep trying to tell you."

"Are you willing to put your money where your genius is? I've got less than a month to put this together before the next council meeting. I've already stalled the vote once."

Luke gave him an emphatic nod. "Whatever you need."

For the first time in months, Gabe's spirits lifted. Right now, the town only saw the good side of development. But once they understood the long-term negative impact on their community, perhaps they would see the value in a more conservative approach. It didn't solve the problem of *what* to do, but it could at least get them to change the zoning, which would block the county from issuing permits for the resort, buying him time.

"Imagine seeing you here." A female voice caught their attention and Gabe twisted around to see Kendall picking her way across the grass, hands hidden in her pockets. She was dressed even more casually today in a pair of leggings, ankle boots, and a quilted vest over a fuzzy sweater, an ensemble that did nothing to disguise a slim figure and soft curves.

"Now I see why Amanda Lee doesn't have a chance," Luke murmured, pushing to his feet.

"Shut up," Gabe gritted out from the corner of his mouth before he smiled and rose as well. "Morning, Kendall. You found me out. Playing hooky in the park."

She grinned and glanced at the dog. "And who is this handsome guy?"

"That would be Luke, but don't say that to his face, because his ego is big enough as it is."

Luke elbowed him hard in the ribs.

Kendall laughed and dropped to the ground before Fitz, who looked to be in ecstasy while she scratched his ears and neck. "You're such a big boy. I bet you're a good boy, aren't you? What's your name?"

Luke sent Gabe a look and Gabe shot it right back, laced with a threat. "Fitz," he said finally. "He's an Irish mastiff. Seemed like it fit."

Kendall straightened, but Fitz decided that he was going to lean against his new best friend and almost knocked her off her feet before she could brace herself. "I think I might have named him Secretariat."

"Trust me, the thought did occur to me, but he's too lazy to be named after a racehorse. He thinks he's a lapdog."

"Aww, you're just a sweetheart, aren't you?" There went the baby voice again, followed by another affectionate pat. Fitz was officially in love. She focused her attention on Luke finally and held out a hand. "I take it you really are Luke? I'm Kendall."

"Yes. It's nice to meet you, Kendall. I was actually just going."

"Oh, don't leave on my account. I got up early and wanted coffee, but I didn't want to disturb Mr. Brandt. I'm supposed to be back at the B and B for breakfast in a little bit."

"No, really, I have to get some work done before I open the visitor center." Luke smiled.

"Have fun, you two." He gave a wave and turned on his heel, his smirk just a shade too knowing. There was no way Gabe was ever going to convince his friend that he had no interest in Kendall now, especially when Luke had seen his eyes just about pop out of his head like a cartoon. The only thing that could have made it more obvious was an "ooga" horn for sound effect.

"He seems nice," Kendall said, watching Luke walk away, her brow slightly furrowed. Apparently their nonverbal communication had not escaped her.

"*Nice* isn't the word I'd use, but we've known each other forever, so he knows where all the bodies are buried." Gabe smiled to make it clear he was joking. "Opa's place treating you okay? How'd you sleep?"

"Like a log. I think that's the most comfortable mattress I've ever slept on. I'm not going to want to leave."

Score one for his grandmother's decorating. Gabe glanced at his watch. "You said something about coffee?"

"Please." The word came out in a relieved whoosh, and she disentangled herself from Fitz so she could fall into step beside Gabe. "It's not as cold today."

"It's every bit as cold. You're just adjusting to the weather."

"Maybe," she said, though she didn't sound

convinced. "As soon as we're done with breakfast, we'll head over to Georgetown?"

"Absolutely. While we're there, we really should do some sightseeing. There's a cool old steam train and a mine tour."

Kendall shot him a look. "Seriously?"

"Yeah. Why not? It's something that is pretty much required for all fourth graders—"

"—which means that I did it in fourth grade. Went to school in Denver, remember?" She shook her head like she found him amusing. "No offense, but I really need to get over to the houses and start working. As good as Sophie is, my clients will start to notice if I'm not around."

It *had* been a rather lame way to try to interest her in the area, and Gabe kept forgetting that she'd grown up in Denver, considering everything about her screamed California girl. Maybe this was a lost cause.

Nope, he could not think that way. The easiest way to prevent the building of the resort was to prevent the sale of the property, and to do that, he needed her on his side. She needed to feel connected to this place, which made their next stop ideal.

Gabe nudged Kendall to indicate they should cross the street and led her straight to an old brick building emblazoned with a graffiti-style mural that proclaimed *Main Street Mocha*. He looped Fitz's leash around the bike rack, where the dog plopped down with a resigned sigh, then held the door open for her. The harsh sound of the grinder and the hiss of a steam wand met them as soon as they stepped through the door.

He inhaled the scent of coffee appreciatively. Secretly—or maybe not so secretly, considering that every candid photo of him at town events involved him holding a paper cup—Main Street Mocha was his favorite spot in town. It was all black steel and raw wood with mottled rust-and-gray acid-stained concrete, kind of industrial-rustic chic. A burnt wood placard with a passport stamp design and the words *Solid Grounds Coffee Company* sat just behind the bar, a tribute to the Denver roastery from which Delia sourced her beans. She was adamant about only using fresh, local, and sustainable, so the shop was littered with photos and logos from the Colorado businesses she considered partners.

Gabe watched Kendall's face as she surveyed the place, wondering if it would meet her evidently high design standards. Her expression gave nothing away, but there was a slight lift of her eyebrows when she leaned over and murmured, "I love the floor treatment. People have no idea how hard it is to get this effect on concrete."

They were next, so Gabe stepped up and smiled at the middle-aged woman behind the counter. "Morning, Delia."

"Morning, Gabe." Delia Crawford was the only

101

one who didn't call him Mayor Gabe. Of course, she was also the only one in town who looked like a roller derby queen with her forties-inspired clothes, victory rolls, and armfuls of tattoos. "Twice in an hour? That's a record even for you."

"Actually, my new friend Kendall here needs her caffeine fix."

"That's what we're here for." Delia shot Kendall a welcoming smile. "What can I get you, hon?"

"Large pumpkin pie latte?"

"Coming right up."

Kendall reached for her wallet, but Gabe bumped her arm with his elbow and handed a couple of bills to Delia before she could. "Make that to go, if you would. Opa is expecting us back for breakfast."

"Tell him I said hi. And also tell him that the almond scones were a runaway success. I'm going to make a double order next time."

"He'll be happy to hear it." Gabe stepped away to make room for the next customer, and Kendall followed him to the end of the counter where her drink would come up.

She continued to survey the coffee shop approvingly. "This place is amazing. If I go missing, check here first."

Gabe's phone rang in his pocket and he pulled it out, hoping it was just Opa checking in. But no, it was the office. If he was getting a call this early, it wasn't good. "Will you excuse me a minute?"

"Sure."

Gabe stepped back out the door onto the patio and pressed the phone to his ear. "Hello?"

Linda's familiar voice came through the line. "Hey, Gabe. I just got a call from Sheriff Martinez. He needs to move your meeting tomorrow to the week after next. Is that okay?"

He exhaled. It was nothing critical, just the annual review of the town's contract with the county sheriff's office. "That's fine. Thursday is best if he can make it."

"Okay, thanks. Are you still planning on being in late?"

"Yeah, probably about noon." He turned to glance through the window, but Kendall wasn't alone . . . and the man she was standing with made him clench his hand so hard around the phone he thought he'd crack the screen. "On second thought, I may not be in at all today. But you can reach me on my cell."

"Okay, just let me know."

Gabe clicked off the line and shoved his phone in his pocket, then marched back into the coffee shop, ready to do battle.

When Gabe stepped out to take his phone call, Kendall was left standing conspicuously at the end of the bar. For all the trendy decor, most of the people in this place were older, dressed in utilitarian jeans, fleeces, and cowboy or work boots. A place like this should be packed with telecommuters on cell phones and laptops, little kids getting a hot chocolate before school, businesspeople in their suits and dress shoes trying to get a little jump on alertness on their way in to work. The breadth of Gabe's challenge hit home now that she observed it with her own eyes. The town wasn't dying because of lack of tourism; the town was dying because the average age of the population was well over fifty. Families drove industry and growth; they needed businesses and schools and services.

The realization was oddly troubling, especially since she'd already determined that she had no obligation to this place.

"Excuse me." A tall, broad man in a Patagonia down jacket leaned past her to grab a napkin from the dispenser on the end of the bar and then paused, studying her carefully. "You're Kendall Green."

She frowned. Midfifties, fit, and wearing an obviously expensive pair of boots, he didn't look remotely familiar to her. "I am. Have we met?"

"No." White teeth flashed as he held out his hand. "I'm Phil Burton."

She struggled to place the name until she remembered the logo emblazoned on the plans that Gabe had shown her yesterday afternoon: *Burton Property Group*. Her instincts immediately went on high alert, but she put on a pleasant smile. "Oh yes. You're the developer who wants to build over on the south side of the lake."

He looked surprised. "Exactly. I see you've done your homework. That will make my job a lot easier."

"Oh?"

"I won't ambush you with business this early in the morning, but I'd like to set up a meeting at your earliest convenience. I imagine you're not going to stick around here that long."

There was something about his smug delivery, his conspiratorial tone, that raised her hackles. Like they were on the same side of something, when she'd never seen him before. She decided to play dumb. "Oh? Why is that?"

"Well, you're clearly not from around here." He looked her over as if that should explain everything. "And with the exception of this fine establishment, there's not much for someone like you to do here."

"Pumpkin pie latte!" Delia called, a little louder than necessary. The coffee shop owner's gaze flickered between them.

Kendall took her time retrieving her drink, then took even longer with her first sip. She was momentarily distracted by the taste of good espresso, bolstered by a not-too-sweet hit of spices. "Someone like me?"

Phil smiled. "A California designer with a taste for European antiques? I imagine this place is a little rustic for you. Listen, I know you're probably impatient to get back home. I'll make you a fair offer for the houses, take them off your hands, and you can get back to your life."

And that was what did it. Not the implication that he knew everything about her, but the idea that she hadn't done her homework and he was going to do her a favor by giving her a "fair offer." He figured he could get the property for a bargain, eliminate the last barrier to his development, and she would thank him for it.

If there was one thing she despised, it was being underestimated by a man like Phil Burton. "Have you even looked at the houses?"

He shrugged. "I don't need to. Folk construction. There's hundreds of them up here, some more interesting, better preserved, and better located."

"I take that as a no?"

"Take it that it doesn't matter. I don't need the land. I own everything around it. You think it's going to be worth anything when it's surrounded on three sides by my hotel and the lake views are of my docks? You're smart enough to see the truth." He produced a business card from his pocket. "Call me. I'm ready to move quickly. We can get this wrapped up and send you back to your life with a minimum of fuss."

"Mmm." Kendall took the card, giving him a terse nod. He gave a smarmy smile and then turned on his heel just as Gabe came back through the door. She didn't miss the silent exchange between the two men, Burton's expression triumphant, Gabe's thunderous.

"What did he want?" Gabe asked when he neared her. "Or do I even need to ask?"

"Oh, you can ask. He took one look at me, figured I was someone he could fool by down-playing the architecture and the land's importance to him, and pressed me to 'wrap it up quickly' so he could 'get me back to my life.' If I'd been a little shorter, I think he might have actually patted me on the head." Kendall lifted her cup to her lips, then immediately lowered it. She didn't want to ruin her enjoyment of this excellent latte with the bad taste Burton's condescension had left in her mouth.

"Are you going to call him?" Gabe asked.

She turned the business card over in her hand, feeling the weight of the stock he'd chosen, watching the shine of gold foil. When she looked up at Gabe, she'd be willing to bet that her eyes glinted with something feral. "Not if I can help it."

"So you're on board?"

Kendall watched the space where Burton had just been. "Nothing has changed, Gabe. I still need the money and I still need to sell. Just not to him." She finally turned to him, hoping that he understood exactly what she was saying. "We need to come up with a plan. And fast."

Chapter Ten

Had Gabe known that all it would take to get Kendall on his side was a meeting with Philip Burton, he would have arranged for him to be the first person she ran into. He had thought that perhaps he was the only one who felt like threatening violence just because Burton was in his personal space, assumed it was because of his strong feelings toward the town, but Kendall had no such ties and she was still fuming.

"I hate men who think women have no head for business," she mumbled between sips of her pumpkin pie latte on their way back to the B and B. "As if I was just standing around waiting for someone to tell me what I should do with my property."

The fact that she was calling it *her* property instead of *Connie's* was an improvement; finally she was a little bit invested in the houses, even if it was only because she felt like Burton was trying to cheat her. Gabe wouldn't complain if it finally put them on the same side of the argument.

"He's definitely got a 'punch me' kind of face," Gabe said lightly, and Kendall shot him a grin.

"Oh, if only I had thought that fast."

Gabe nudged her with his elbow. "Probably

best that you didn't. Burton is the type to press charges and then offer to have them dropped in return for stealing away your land."

"Probably," she said with a hint of malice, her eyes narrowing. And that's when Gabe decided he really liked this woman. Funny that all it took was a shared enemy and the threat of violence to bring them together. Despite her tone, the mood was comfortable now, conspiratorial, and from the way she settled her stride beside him, he thought she felt it too. "So tell me about Delia. She seems like an unusual type for this town."

"You mean under sixty?" Gabe grinned.

"Well, that. And the tattoos and the makeup and the hair and the vintage clothes . . . you know, the whole look. Transplant, right?"

"Replant, like me. Went away to college, got married, moved back after a divorce. Opened the shop and the rest is history."

Kendall nodded. "Now we just need another three hundred exactly like her, huh?"

"I would venture to say it would be difficult to find *one* other person exactly like her, but yeah, I get your point. We definitely need to attract working people and not just retirees to survive. Most of the younger folks moved out a long time ago and didn't come back."

"So that's got to be goal number one: attract the younger set to town." Kendall took another sip of her latte, brow furrowing. "What's required to attract young professionals or new graduates? Affordable housing, right? Which you already have."

"Compared to the Front Range, yes. But mostly it's jobs, and everything here is either service-oriented or seasonal retail. What good is afford-able housing if you're making zero dollars?"

"Hmm. Well, that's not something you can exactly wave your magic wand and make happen, is it?"

"You see my challenge."

"I do." She cocked her head. "What about Luke?"

Instantly, caution cut through him. Scratch that. Jealousy. "What about Luke?"

"He's young. What does he do?"

"He's a web designer. He works remotely. He has clients all over the country."

Kendall walked on, thinking for a minute. "I assume that means you have good high-speed internet in town, then?"

"We're in the mountains, not on the moon." Though considering how sketchy cell service could be at times, the question wasn't completely out of left field.

"So what if you tried to market it as a haven for telecommuters? 'Work virtually in the most beautiful town in Colorado . . .' You know, we millennials are really into work-life balance."

"Are we?" He shot her an amused glance.

"So I'm told. The balance of my life is work, so I'm not really sure that I'm a good example. But seriously . . . why couldn't you?"

He considered it for a moment. As an urban planner, he typically thought of things in terms of physical infrastructure, especially coming from Detroit: manufacturing and the like. But there were entire industries that operated virtually. Why couldn't they try it? It required little of the town itself other than the amenities needed to support a community, and while those might be thinner than they were in Clear Creek's larger towns, Jasper Lake was still livable.

"I think the big challenge then is housing. It's affordable, yes, but it's not like there's an over-supply of it."

"Yes, but surely you know a developer—who is not Phil Burton—who would be interested in putting in condos and some commercial space." Kendall's face lit up. "You know, hip and modern little cubicles with phone and high-speed internet that people could rent on a monthly basis. Bigger offices and conference rooms for small companies or meetings. They're all the rage in Los Angeles, especially the ones that are dog-friendly."

Gabe looked down at Fitz and automatically gave the pup's furry head a scratch. He could think of dozens of things that would need to be done before that could ever be a reality, many of which would take years . . . but he didn't have to actually accomplish it. All he had to do was show how his vision was preferable to Burton's. Enough for them to block the permits, shut down the resort plans, and save Kendall's homes. Then with the city council invested in the plan, they could take slow and steady steps toward a sensible implementation. It wasn't as sexy as having a resort pop up in a year, but there was very little about urban planning that qualified as sexy.

"You know, you do have five rather large houses in a choice location . . . ," he said slowly.

"Rent them, you mean? We've been there. I need a lot more money than rentals could bring in."

"Maybe not rent them. Maybe more like . . . subdivide and sell them individually as condos." He shook his head. "I'm just spitballing."

"Trust me, I've seen what you have to do to houses like that in order to subdivide them, and it's not pretty. I would hate to destroy the layout and the period details in order to make a multi-family unit. People spend hundreds of thousands of dollars to convert them back."

"Right. But we can't launch a massive marketing campaign to draw new citizens here without affordable housing. That creates the same problems as the resort development."

"I don't suppose there's any chance you could

convince Burton to change course? I mean, if you could change the zoning and block his permits, it's not like he'd be able to follow through with his plan. What's he going to do with his land then?"

"Hold on to it just to spite us?" Gabe guessed. "I haven't found him to be overly cooperative."

"That may change once he's no longer holding all the cards."

Gabe shot Kendall a sidelong glance. "Don't forget . . . you're still holding five of them."

She made a face, her gaze fixed on the horizon. "How could I forget?"

He felt a pang of guilt. She'd had a lot thrown at her in the past couple of days. Finding out a bit of her mother's story from Julie, having the entire future of the town hinging on her decision. And everywhere she went, there was someone to remind her of that. He suddenly wanted nothing more than to tell her not to worry, to do what she needed to do, and he would figure out the rest. A chivalrous impulse, maybe, but also a disastrous one. He was still Jasper Lake's mayor, and his first and most important priority was doing what was best for the town. Even if it meant putting Kendall Green through the wringer.

They finally arrived at the B and B, and Gabe opened the front door for her, then circled around to the backyard, where he let Fitz loose. The huge hound went galloping off, thrilled to be free, though that energy wore off quickly enough, and he made a beeline for the patio furniture. It was a good thing Opa was secretly fond of the beast or Fitz wouldn't get off so easily.

Gabe went through the back door into the kitchen, where Kendall was again sitting at the island, chatting with his grandfather. From the smell, he knew that Opa was cooking up some of Ellie Hernandez's famous pork sausage, raised and made only a few miles away on the Hernandez ranch. Not only was the meat amazing, but Ellie's special sausage blend was second to none. Even Opa admitted that he couldn't come close, and for a German, that was saying something.

Kendall was finishing up her latte while Opa told her about the flood that had stunted Jasper Lake's growth and destroyed so many of the neighbors. "Took almost two years for them to rebuild the bridge on the other side of Silverlark, and by then it was too late. Of course, you could come around the back side of the highway to reach us, but Silverlark was almost completely isolated unless you were comfortable with rutted dirt roads."

"Wow," Kendall said. "What did everyone do for supplies?"

"You don't live up here unless you're prepared to be snowed in for months, so the situation wasn't immediately dire. Eventually they graded the back way in for deliveries, but it still wasn't accessible to tourists."

Kendall finally noticed Gabe standing there. "Oh, hey. Your grandfather was just telling me about the flood and how long it took for them to get the emergency funds to rebuild."

"Yeah, and by then, the damage had already been done."

Opa set two plates down on the counter, one in front of each of them, piled high with fried eggs, thick country bacon, Ellie's sausage, and toast cut into triangles. Gabe didn't tell her that the English-American–style breakfast was reserved strictly for guests. He'd grown up with brötchen and marmalade alongside slices of salami and cheese for breakfast, but few guests saw pumpernickel as breakfast food.

Kendall dug in, trying the bacon first, and gave a groan of appreciation. "This is amazing."

Gabe smiled. "You should try the sausage."

"I will." She gave him a look that glinted with humor. "I'm glad I wore my stretchy pants today."

Gabe covered his mouth so he could laugh without choking on his food. Stylish she might be, but prissy she was not.

"So, Mr. Brandt, what do you know about Phil Burton?"

Now the cough did turn into a choke. Kendall patted him on the back, and Opa slid him a glass of water. When it was clear that he wasn't going to die, Kendall prompted, "Do you know Burton?"

Opa's expression hardened. "I know him. Why?"

"I was just talking to Gabe about whether or not he would be willing to change direction if the city council shoots down his resort. I met the man this morning, but I can't say I have any sense of what kind of person he is."

She was soft-pedaling that for sure, because she'd made no secret about the kind of person she thought Burton was.

Opa's expression tightened. "Philip Burton always does what's in Philip Burton's best interest."

Kendall didn't seem to catch the tension in the words, because she just nodded thoughtfully. "So maybe Gabe needs to convince Burton that this change of direction was his idea."

Gabe snorted. "That's likely to happen."

"You never know. If you tell him the town is more concerned with affordable multifamily housing, and that's the one thing the resort doesn't address, you don't think he'll smell an opportunity? Men like him are territorial. If you bring in another developer or even hint at it, you might force his hand. He won't want a stranger taking his business in his backyard."

"You know, that's not a bad idea." For someone

who looked so sweet and innocent, she had a remarkably devious mind. Score another point for Kendall Green.

"Thank you." She turned back to her food with satisfaction, but Opa's gaze remained fixed on Gabe.

"What?" he said finally, then cleared his throat when his grandfather scowled. "Sorry. You wanted to say something?"

Opa resumed wiping down the counters. Gabe had never pointed it out, but it was his tell when he was about to deliver news that his grandson wasn't going to like. "I know someone you could call on that front. And I know he would be more than happy to help out."

Now Gabe didn't even care if he was rude. He stared at his meal and stabbed the egg so hard that yolk bled across the plate. "That isn't going to happen."

"Gabe—"

He shook his head, and Opa dropped the subject, leaving Kendall to study him curiously. Thankfully, she didn't ask what the unspoken conversation was about, though he suspected of all the people he'd met, she would most understand his feelings on the subject.

The atmosphere in the bed-and-breakfast's kitchen got uncomfortable fast, thanks to Gabe's pronouncement, and Kendall scrambled to fill the silence with something, anything. She asked about the source of the meat on her plate, what Mr. Brandt enjoyed most about running a B and B, how long he'd lived in this house. Turned out that while he was one of the older residents of Jasper Lake, he was a relative new-comer to the town, having moved here with his wife only thirty years ago.

"Greta, God rest her soul, always wanted to live in a big city. New York, San Francisco. Said it reminded her of Berlin, where her family was from. We did that for a while, and then she said it was my turn. So I picked here. In some ways, it reminds me of Bavaria, where *I* grew up."

"Did either of you ever consider going back to Germany?"

"No." His eyes took on a faraway look, the downward corners of his mouth hinting at unpleasant memories. "Greta's family left Germany before the war. Mine was not so lucky, though luckier than some. By the hand of God alone, our Jewish roots were not discovered. Still . . ." He shook his head. "I know Greta felt isolated from her homeland, but she did not see what I saw: the destruction, the privation after the war. I could never go back."

Kendall listened in rapt attention. Maybe it was because she knew nothing of her own past, but she found other people's stories fascinating. She was about to ask more questions when Gabe took

118

their empty plates and moved them to the sink. "We need to get going, Opa. Kendall needs to file her paperwork at the courthouse this morning."

A surge of disappointment rose in Kendall, but she nodded. "We do, unfortunately. Thank you for the breakfast. It was delicious."

Mr. Brandt waved away her thanks. "It's nothing. Here, take some scones with you."

"It's only a half-hour drive, Opa. You've filled us up until dinnertime!"

"Still." He was already packing up leftover scones in a paper bag and digging out paper cups for the remnants of coffee in the large pot. Kendall expected Gabe to protest, but he didn't say a word, just took the food and hugged his grandfather goodbye.

He handed Kendall one of the cups when they stepped out onto the back porch. She half expected Fitz to bound toward them, but the dog merely raised his head from his perch on the patio furniture and looked at them hopefully. "Do you mind making a stop by my house first to drop this beast off?"

"Does he not like car rides?"

"Oh no, he loves them. Unfortunately, twisty roads don't like *him*."

Kendall made a face. "In that case, no, I don't mind dropping him at home. Is it far?"

"Not at all. If you haven't noticed, there's not much in this town that's far from anything else."

He whistled and Fitz slid off the sofa and trotted over, letting Gabe clip the leash to his collar without resistance. Once through the gate, the three of them fell into step on the sidewalk, Fitz happy to walk calmly beside them but for the occasional stop to sniff an interesting plant or post.

"Why are the Lakeshore houses so far away from the rest of town?" Kendall asked. "Seems like it would have been difficult to get water and power and sewer out there."

"There were no utilities here at the time they were built," Gabe said. "In fact, they were the only ones in town that actually had running water. You can still see the old gravity-fed water tanks up the hill behind them."

"Fascinating," Kendall said. "But still, why build them so far away?"

"That's a good question. No one has any idea since the builder is unknown. One would think that we'd have records of it somewhere, but most of the town historical society's records were lost in the flood, and I guess no one really felt the need to look it up before then. I would think it was a rich man who didn't want to mingle with the rabble—remember, this was a mining town."

It was a reasonable guess. Whether it had been a mine owner building his own home and ones for his children or an early industrialist with visions of an elegant community in the mountains, her

120

houses were certainly grander than anything else in Jasper Lake from that time period.

Their walk transitioned from a sidewalk to a paved road to a dirt one, deep ruts grooved into the surface. Here the houses were placed scatter-shot, the road winding around them rather than the other way around. Gabe stopped in front of a small log cabin surrounded by a picket fence. "This is it."

Her eyebrows rose. This tiny, modest structure was the home of the town's mayor? It looked more like a hunting cabin, even if it was clearly newer than the homes around it.

Gabe caught her expression. "Not so impressed, huh? Let me put the dog inside and grab my car keys, and we can go." He opened the gate and stood aside to let her through. She picked her way across the gravel path to the door, which was set into the side of the house without a porch or a landing to protect it. Gabe seemed surprised that she was following him inside, but he opened the door for her and followed her in.

"It's not much," he said apologetically. "Give me just a minute . . ."

He was right. It wasn't much, but it was still better than she'd expected from the outside. The whole house seemed to be done in hand-scraped hardwood floors, their surface scarred by shoes and dog claws. His living room had some real furniture—a rather worn but handsome leather chesterfield sofa and what appeared to be a hand-knotted Persian rug. She probably wouldn't have chosen the imitation Tiffany lamp on the rustic side table, but it was far better than the horrendous glass-and-brass constructions she'd found in a lot of bachelor pads. All in all . . . not bad for a single man who wasn't a designer. Gabe Brandt actually had a bit of taste.

Smiling to herself, she moved to the corner of the room where a compact electronic drum set stood. She picked up one of the wooden sticks and gave a mesh head a thump. It bounced back with hardly a sound. "You play?"

"Do I play?" he repeated and then poked his head out of what she assumed was the kitchen. "Oh, the drums. A little. Just for fun."

Kendall cocked her head and studied him. She guessed she could see that. He did kind of have a drummer vibe, at least more than any other type of musician. "Everyone needs a hobby, huh?"

He disappeared again, his voice echoing a little from the other room. "Something like that. Speaking of which, what's yours?"

"I—" She stopped. "I don't have one, I guess." Once, it had been design, but now that she did it for a living, nothing had slipped in to replace it. She moved toward the kitchen and then stopped. "Oh, my."

It was a time-capsule kitchen from the eighties, with chipped ceramic-tile countertops and a backsplash that alternated dark-green glazed Mexican tiles with hand-painted white tiles—each featuring a different mountain animal. The cabinets were typical builder's grade, which the homeowner had attempted to make look rustic by putting on bronze pulls shaped like twigs. It was . . .

"Horrible, isn't it?" Gabriel caught her expression and surveyed the kitchen with a bemused expression. "I mean, it could always be worse, but . . ."

"Not much worse," Kendall finished for him. "I'm going to give you the benefit of the doubt and say these weren't your design choices."

He chuckled. "Hardly. The place is a rental. One of the only ones around here with a fenced yard, in fact. Some of the furniture is mine, and some of it was here. That gaudy lamp out in the living room, for example."

"Sofa and rug?"

"Mine." He studied her amusedly. "You're judging me by my furniture choices, aren't you?"

"I absolutely am. But I'm happy to say you passed. The rug especially is beautiful."

"One of the only things I packed up and brought with me from Michigan. I rented a pretty little Craftsman, but I wasn't there long enough to really put down roots. Or buy real furniture." He put down the water bowl in what looked like a hastily handmade stand and then straightened.

"If I thought I was going to stay here long term, I'd have you decorate the place."

She flashed him a coy smile. "You probably can't afford me."

"Probably not." He gave Fitz one last pat and nodded toward the living room. "Ready to go?"

She followed him out, but she waited until they were both buckled into his truck before she asked the questions on her mind. "How long have you been back in Jasper Lake anyway? And why do you say you're not going to stay here long term?"

He put the truck in reverse and backed out of his driveway onto the street, glancing at her before he shifted into drive. "I've been here over a year. It was never meant to be permanent."

"But you're the town mayor."

"For the time being. I'm just . . . trying to get Jasper Lake on the right track before I go."

"I don't understand. Why put all the work into the town if it's not even your town?"

"I didn't say it wasn't my town. I just said that I never meant moving back to be permanent."

Either he was being purposely evasive or she didn't get Gabe Brandt at all. "I don't understand."

He glanced at her again. "This will always be my town. It saved me. But let's face it, it's not like there's a lot of work for an urban planner in this tiny mountain town."

"I don't know—it sounds like you've got your

work cut out for you here, especially if you can block the development and move in a different direction."

"Yeah, but what then? I'm thirty-two. So I spend five years here getting zoning straightened out and some sort of city plan on the books . . . and then I'm thirty-seven moving to another new city?"

He had a point. It felt like once you hit your late thirties, your direction in life was set, and good luck trying to deviate from it. It was part of the reason why she didn't want to make any big changes now. Her business was established. She and Sophie had an arrangement that worked for them, a beautiful home that acted as their showroom and design lab, and plenty of clients who knew exactly where to find them. Were they to uproot their business and move to someplace more affordable, like West Covina or Rosemead, not only would they suffer from the lack of proximity to their clientele, but it would look like they weren't doing well . . . and by extension, like they were incompetent designers.

Unfortunately, *fake it till you make it* applied to most careers.

"In any case, it seems very altruistic of you."

"Actually, it's pretty selfish." He threw her a rueful glance. "All my life, I knew that if things went wrong, I would have someplace to come back to. It was a safety net of sorts. And I was right. Jasper Lake was here when I needed it, just as it had always been, and I want to make sure it stays that way."

And that right there was the difference between Gabe and Kendall. He had a safety net, someplace to go back to. She had . . . the present. Only what she had made for herself, what she had scraped together with hard work and gumption. He might not want the town to change, but she had no such luxury. She had to do what was necessary to survive.

Still, she wasn't entirely unsympathetic. Had she grown up in a single place with any kind of meaning to her, she might feel the same way. For his sake, she hoped that they'd be able to make their interests align. Because as much as she was starting to like him, if she had to choose between his life in Jasper Lake and her life in Pasadena, it would be an easy decision. If there was one thing that being a foster kid taught you, it was to rely on yourself.

Gabe seemed unaware of the thought that now hung between them, but to her it was as impenetrable as a brick wall. She couldn't help but think that his confidence in her—or his hopes at least—was misplaced. It was unkind to let him believe otherwise.

Fortunately, the drive to Georgetown was short, and they were soon parked in front of the county courthouse. Kendall grabbed her handbag and steeled herself for the maze of bureaucracy she was about to encounter.

"Do you want me to come in with you?" Gabe asked.

"No, I'll be okay. As long as you're fine with waiting. I don't know how long it's going to take."

Her expectation: at least two hours. Reality? Less than ten minutes.

She had to ask for directions to which window to file at, then waited for one person in front of her to be finished. She handed over the paperwork; the clerk stamped it received and then gave her a receipt for her filing. "That's it?" she asked.

"That's it."

Kendall walked back out and climbed into the truck in a daze. Somehow it should be harder to make a claim on an estate that was worth over a million dollars. Not just dropping off a form and paying a nominal fee. "That was easy."

"I figured it would be. It's not Denver."

"I can see that." She glanced at him. "What now?"

"We can eat our scones and walk around town a bit, if you like. Or we can head back to Jasper Lake. Completely up to you."

The memory of the work awaiting her snapped her focus back to her objective. "Back to Jasper Lake, I think. I want to get started on my inventory today."

He nodded and put the truck in reverse without a hitch. "Back home it is. I probably ought to spend a little time in my office this afternoon anyway."

Judging from his easy acquiescence, he wasn't disappointed with her choice. But for some inexplicable reason, she thought she might be.

Chapter Eleven

Gabe dropped Kendall back in front of the B and B, where her rental vehicle was parked, which she climbed right into without going inside the house. Gabe waited in his idling truck, feeling like he should have seen her to her car, but it wasn't like this had been a date. Even the thought that he should be acting like it was a date showed how very long it had been since he'd had one.

Kendall gave a cheerful wave once she was settled inside the vehicle, a clear dismissal, so he flipped a U-turn and continued back into town. With the temperature finally rising above forty degrees, there were more people out and about, though in a town this small, they were mostly people heading into their stores for the day. During the winter, many shops didn't open until ten, and half the time they didn't open at all. The fact that so many were still keeping regular business hours in the middle of October showed a surprising degree of optimism. Optimism that he desperately needed to catch. What he and Kendall had brainstormed this morning was no panacea for what ailed the town, but it did at least offer them a fighting chance.

Gabe poked his head into the town clerk's office and waved to Elizabeth, the older lady who had been the town's administrative backbone for longer than he'd been alive, then proceeded to his own office, where Linda was already seated at her desk, her fingers flying over the keyboard. Between the name and her professional demeanor on the phone, most people were surprised to find she was actually younger than he was. Or they would be surprised if everyone hadn't known Linda her whole life.

She glanced up when he walked in and pulled one of her earbuds out of her ear. "Good morning, Gabe."

"Morning. How's your daughter? Recovered from her flu, I hope?"

"Oh, you mean the math flu?" She arched an eyebrow. "The kind that comes on suddenly when you haven't studied for a test?"

"Ouch." Gabriel winced. Linda's ten-year-old daughter, Cecily, was adorable and charming and had never met a situation she couldn't talk her way out of. Apparently she'd graduated to faking illnesses at school, which did not exactly endear her to her mother when the elementary school was twenty-five minutes away. "How much trouble is she in?"

"Let's just say that my yard will be completely leaf-free by this evening."

He looked at her quizzically. "You don't have a yard. You live in a condo."

Now a hint of mirth sparked in her eyes. "Exactly. The condo association should send me a Christmas card for doing their landscaping work for them."

Gabe grinned and high-fived her as he passed into his office. There was no mistaking the spine of steel in his assistant, something he suspected came from becoming a single mother at the age of eighteen. She'd had to fight and scrabble to make a life for herself and Cecily, and he was impressed by how well she had done it. Of course, that made him think of Caroline Green and her disappearance from Jasper Lake at that same age. To hear his grandmother talk, Caroline and Linda had been cut from the same cloth. What could have happened to make her abandon Kendall only four years later?

He shook his head, trying to wipe Kendall from his mind. He wished he could write off his fascination with her as infatuation, but while there was undoubtedly a spark of attraction there, his feelings were far more troubled than that. She too had that tough outer shell, that determination to make it on her own no matter the cost, a kind of grit that only came from a difficult, independent childhood. When he thought about what it must have been like, his heart ached for her . . . and he didn't consider himself a heart-aching sort of person. So why did he feel so invested after a mere day and a half?

Because he knew what it felt like to be abandoned, even if it wasn't in such a literal sense. And unlike him, she hadn't had anyone to fall back on.

Enough of that. He couldn't spend all his time worrying about Kendall when she would land on her feet more surely than any cat. The town, on the other hand, needed him. He sat down at his desk, plugged his own set of earbuds into his phone, and turned on his eighties metal playlist. Linda had once pulled them out to hear what he was listening to while he worked, and the horror on her face still made him laugh. He couldn't explain why the loud, aggressive music helped focus his thoughts. Maybe it was because it took all his attention to keep his mind *on* his work and the music out of his head. He pulled out the blank, gridded notepad he used to mind-map his projects and set his favorite gel ink pen to the paper.

Within minutes, he had a messy scrawl of ideas around the central thought *Resort Development,* all the things that would have to be taken into account should they approve the permits: traffic flow and road improvements, watershed impact reports, real estate price appreciation, property tax increase, cost of living . . . Some of the markers were negative, while some were positive.

Then there were the intangibles: quality of life, traffic, outside investors who bought real estate but didn't actually live in the town, impact on the public school system, and so on. He was aware that what he was doing was wildly speculative and his perspective might be slanted, but if he was going to convince the city council, he would have to give a realistic view of what their town might look like in another ten to fifteen years should they go forward with the development. Growth didn't have to be bad if it was done in a sensible way. He just wasn't convinced this was it.

Now there was little he could do without creating a 3D model. He pulled up his modeling software on his laptop and—after a quick check of the coordinates—input the GPS locators to load satellite images of the town. The software wasn't without its glitches—it occasionally picked out things like large traffic circles as buildings—but within hours, he had begun to build a respectable model to work from.

"Are you staying late?" Linda poked her head into his office, her bag slung over her shoulder.

He glanced up in surprise and checked his watch. Five thirty already. The afternoon had flown by while he was engrossed in the grown-up version of The Sims. "Not much longer. Don't wait for me."

"Thanks, Gabe. Don't stay too late. You work too hard."

He waved her off, as much a demurral as a dismissal, feeling like she had him completely wrong. He'd done very little for the town; this was the first concrete step he'd made toward his campaign promises. And even now, he was dealing in guesses, wishful thinking, and speculation. If only he had a crystal ball to guide his plans.

Or you know, you could try praying. The wry thought was half out of his own mind and half from his grandmother's mouth. Without a doubt, she had been a pray-first type of Christian, whereas it was easy for Gabe to let his analytical nature take over, especially when it came to work.

"Okay, Lord," he said out loud, leaning back in his chair. "What do You think about all this? Am I even headed in the right direction?"

After he stared at the ceiling for a minute or two, hoping for some sort of answering nudge, he concluded that it was time to knock off for the day and try again tomorrow. Maybe he'd wake up with a conviction one way or another. Or maybe he had to plow forward and hope it was made clear to him as he went along. This whole time, he'd been thinking he'd been sent to Jasper Lake to fix this, so he just had to believe that the solution would be made clear to him.

Or maybe he'd just gotten laid off and had to come crawling home, and he'd invented the whole right-time-right-place story to make himself feel better.

No, he couldn't believe that. The town needed him. And he wouldn't fail them.

It was cold. That was Kendall's first thought as she let herself into the easternmost home with the keys. Of course the power and propane had been turned off for some time now, but somehow she hadn't noticed how frigid her grandmother's house was when she'd gone in yesterday. Today, it was hard to ignore her shivers and chattering teeth.

She clutched her arms to her body, wishing she'd worn the coat and not just a down vest. She'd have to make this quick and then head back to the hardware store just outside of town to pick up a space heater. Or Gabe would come out here only to find her a blue Popsicle, frozen with her hand around her cell phone.

The thought of Gabe gave her an oddly unsettled feeling. She kept having to remind herself that she'd met him yesterday, that they had opposing priorities, that she really shouldn't trust him so easily. But his friendly and straightforward attitude was downright disarming. She couldn't help but like the guy, especially when she saw him with his grandfather and his huge, silly dog.

There were also those arresting blue eyes, the lean physique, and chiseled features just a touch too masculine to be called beautiful, not that she'd given it much thought.

"Stop being stupid," Kendall said to herself and marched through the parlor into the bare kitchen, her phone at the ready.

It didn't turn out to be needed, though. The house had some of the same impressive architectural features as Connie's, minus the period wallpaper, but absolutely no furniture. The old owners had taken everything with them but a battered breakfront that was good for little more than firewood. Kendall snapped a few photos of the home's two fireplaces, which she would definitely salvage from demolition if necessary, locked up the house again, and headed straight for the warmth of her rental SUV.

Forty-five minutes later, she was back in the same place, this time carrying a small propane space heater and an extra bottle of fuel she'd purchased at the hardware store. She flipped through the keys in her hand, taking four tries to find the one for the second house. Tomorrow she would bring a bottle of nail polish and mark them so she didn't have to go through this song and dance every time she wanted to open a door.

She didn't even end up firing up the heater, though, because the second house was the same situation as the first. No furniture, period details, nice fireplaces. This one at least had some interesting built-in corner cabinetry in the dining room, which she thought might be removable if she were careful. But the most striking details, like the carved columbines on the molding's corbels, were again absent. Did that mean Connie's house was the original build, the house of the "big boss," and the others were just copies for family members or high-ranking employees?

Kendall went through the two west-side houses with just as much speed, only documenting what she thought she might like to salvage, and then returned to Connie Green's home, where she stood on the street and stared, her chest tight. If she were honest with herself, she'd been wasting time with the others because she didn't want to face what might be inside.

If Connie Green had known she was alive, what might she find about herself in there? What might she find about her mother?

Kendall pulled out her phone and video-called Sophie, but her friend didn't answer. She tried texting instead. What are you doing? Are you available?

A message quickly came back: with client ttyl.

Kendall shoved her phone in her pocket and sighed. She couldn't even count on her friend to stall her entry into the house. Okay. No more dillydallying.

She let herself through the front door and paused in the vestibule. She had to be disciplined about this. No standing here, wondering if her mother had thrown her backpack on this bench in the entry, if Kendall had crawled across this Persian rug as a baby. This was about the furnishings and the architectural details only.

Kendall decided to start in the library, though her throat already felt tight. It was easy enough to tell herself to stay impassive, but years of looking at pieces with not only an analytical eye but a creative one couldn't be turned off at will. It was what made her good at her work, what allowed her to uncover the stories of the most obscure pieces—that willingness to imagine what the furniture had seen, the kind of people who had used it, how it had made its way from its place of origin to its current location. When she looked at these pieces, all she saw was a history that she should have been a part of but wasn't.

The sob caught her by surprise, choking her throat and tightening her chest. She fled the library, through the hallway and out the front door, where she collapsed onto the first step, her head in her hands.

"I can't do this," she murmured, trying to still the sudden storm inside. The indifference she had managed to maintain for years felt broken open in the face of her past, what should have been her home. If she even really knew what that meant. She glanced at her phone, but there was no other response from Sophie. She was doing what she should—putting clients first—but Kendall still felt inexplicably cut loose.

The rumble of a diesel engine drew her head up, and she swiped at her eyes when she recognized Gabe's truck. Slowly she got to her feet while he parked alongside the curb and got out of the truck.

"What are you doing here?"

"Just thought I'd check in." He spun his keys around his index finger as he approached. Then his expression changed. "What's wrong? Are you all right?"

"I'm fine. Just taking a break."

He glanced back at the house before focusing on her again. "It's harder than you thought."

She started to deny it, but something about the understanding in his eyes made her change her mind. "It is."

"What do you say we call it a day, then, and try again tomorrow?" He nodded back across the lake toward town. "We still have several restaurants you haven't tried. Or if you want to experience what my life is truly like up here, I have a rather impressive collection of breakfast cereals."

His mock-serious expression brought a laugh bubbling from her mouth. "Are you trying to warn me that cooking is not part of your charm?"

"Cooking is *definitely* not part of my charm. To be honest, I mostly get by on looks." He winked at her, eliciting another laugh, and gestured to the house. "Come on. Lock up and we'll go."

Kendall only hesitated a moment before she turned back to the house. After a quick check to make sure that the heater was off, she returned to the stoop and locked the front door behind her. The tightness in her chest remained, but at least there was a lightness layered atop it that hadn't been there before.

"What are the choices for dinner then? Besides cereal, I mean."

"Sandwiches, burgers, or Italian. All of them are good."

Kendall came down the steps toward him. "You know what? You choose. I trust you."

"Do you now?" Another glimmer in his eyes made her feel suddenly unsteady. "In that case, I have an idea."

Chapter Twelve

Gabe led the way back to town, where they dropped off Kendall's vehicle in front of the B and B, and then he drove her back to Main Street to pick up their dinner: sandwiches, huge dill pickles, and bags of salt-and-vinegar potato chips from the deli. Gabe half expected her to balk at his dinner choice, but true to her word, she calmly ordered her pastrami on rye and an unsweetened tea. Minutes later, they were heading back to his truck with their brown paper bag dinners in hand.

"You're not afraid of heights, are you?" Gabe asked as he put the truck in gear and headed out of town to the highway.

She cast a suspicious look at him. "No . . . at least I don't think so."

"Good." He grinned. "And I'm not telling you where we're going."

He realized he was asking for a lot of trust, considering they barely knew each other, but after finding her crying on the steps of her grandmother's house, he figured she needed an escape from town. He drove back around the lake the way they'd come, but instead of turning toward Lakeshore Drive, he continued onto a dirt road that wound upward into the hills. They jostled over a rut, and Kendall reached up to steady herself with the grab handle.

"Sorry. The later in the season it gets, the worse the roads get. We only have the resources to grade it once a year if we're lucky."

"I guess that's a good reason to have four-wheel drive, isn't it?"

"Something like that." He smiled and continued up the hill, then pulled off onto what was little more than a path. When he finally stopped, they were perched on top of a rocky promontory, the mountain sloping steeply down to the lake. The town was spread out before them in miniature like the buildings on a model railroad, simultaneously realistic and whimsical because of their tiny scale. It reminded him of the model he had been building in his CAD application today, reminded him of the things that couldn't be communicated in a rendering.

Kendall opened the door and stood on the running board so she could take in the view. "Wow."

"My thoughts exactly." Gabe hopped out of the truck and withdrew a heavy wool blanket from the back seat. Then he grabbed their dinners and circled around to the front of the truck, where he climbed up on the hood. "You joining me?"

Kendall's eyes widened, and then her face

softened into a delighted smile. "Okay." It took her a couple of tries to get onto the bumper, so he held out his hand and hauled her up next to him. She shifted uncomfortably. "I don't want to dent your hood."

"Trust me, you're not heavy enough to dent my hood. Besides, can't you see all the hail damage?" He indicated the golf ball–size dents that peppered the hood and the top of the truck.

Kendall cringed. "I bet that hurt."

He shrugged. "I bought it this way. Made it more affordable, and I knew if I was going to be spending any time up here, I would need something rugged. Last March we got fifty inches of snow." He peeked into one of the paper bags and handed it to her.

Instead of digging into her food, she scooted back against the windshield and stretched her legs out in front of her. The waning, pink-tinged sunset added a warm glow to her blonde hair, the color in her cheeks. She took in the view silently as the horizon melded into a collection of sherbet shades, the sky above it starting to drift into a hazy violet-blue. "This is beautiful."

"One of my favorite spots."

She cast him an amused look, but there was something guarded beneath it. "I bet you bring all the girls here."

"When I was a teenager? Of course. It was

known as Make-Out Point when I was in high school." He grinned at her. "But I haven't been up here since I was seventeen."

She reached for her iced tea and took a sip while she considered his words. "I take it you don't have a wife or a girlfriend." She held up a hand. "I'm not fishing; I just figured you wouldn't bring me here if you did."

"No, I don't have a wife. Or a girlfriend." There had been someone back in Michigan, his coworker. He thought he and Madeline had potential, but that evaporated when he was let go from his job. Maybe she was afraid that the layoffs would rub off on her, or maybe she just hadn't been that interested in him. Or maybe it was the fact that they'd seen each other on and off for over a year and they'd never slept together. He thought that made him a Christian and a gentleman, but he was finding that some women took it as an insult. They hadn't been as in sync as he'd initially thought.

Gabe shifted the focus back to Kendall. "How about you?"

"No, I don't have a wife or girlfriend."

For a second, he wasn't sure what to think, but then she cracked a smile. "No boyfriend or husband either."

"Cute."

"I couldn't help it. You were very nonspecific."

Gabe leaned back against the windshield beside

her and reached into his bag for his sandwich. "I find that hard to believe."

"Why is that?"

"Because you're beautiful and accomplished, and you probably have men asking for your number wherever you go."

She lifted a shoulder, which he took as grudging acknowledgment. "If they can't be bothered to have a conversation with me first, I can't be bothered to give them a call."

He could understand that. He'd had a few of those interactions in Jasper Lake, though he'd chalked them up to the dearth of young single men in town. Which, he supposed, proved her point.

"Their loss," he said finally.

Kendall fell silent and removed her own sandwich from the bag, then took a big bite. She chewed thoughtfully for a minute and lowered her food to her lap. "I don't think I can do this."

He glanced at her. "Eat the sandwich or sit here with me?"

A ghost of a smile. "Go through Connie's house."

He'd been wondering if she would say any-thing about that. It was part of the reason he'd brought her up here. Somehow, sitting on the top of the world made it easier to face your problems. "Why do you say that?"

"It's like having amnesia. I know that this

145

place is somehow connected to me, but I have no recollection of any of it. It doesn't mean anything, even though I know it should. It feels like . . ."

". . . an alternate reality?"

She cocked her head and studied him. "Sort of. You sound like you know how that feels."

Gabe took a deep breath. He hadn't intended on talking about himself, but now he felt compelled. "You know that whole rebellious phase I went through when I was twelve and thirteen?"

She nodded.

"Well, that was because I found out the man I thought was a family friend, the guy I called Uncle Bob, was really my father."

Her eyebrows arched upward and her mouth rounded into an O.

"My father was always out of the picture, so my mom raised me by herself. It wasn't easy. She was living off a secretary's salary, which was enough to get by on but not enough to have any extra, you know?"

"How did you find out the truth?" Kendall asked softly.

"I got pneumonia one winter and ended up in the hospital. They wanted my family health history, and she told them she didn't know about my father. But then when she thought I was asleep, she made a phone call. The next time she left the room, I hit Redial. It was 'Uncle Bob's'

office." He made quotes with his fingers around the name. "I demanded to know what was going on, and she broke down and told me."

"Wow. Who was he, then, that they kept his true identity from you?"

Gabe grimaced, a ghost of the disappointment and dismay he'd felt still present all these years later. "He was her boss. And he was married at the time. With two daughters."

"Oh." She took in the revelation. "I would be angry too."

"I was furious. Even more so because he knew we were struggling and never paid her more. He ate up my gratitude when he brought me new soccer equipment for school or a bike for Christmas. I thought he was this great guy doing things out of the kindness of his own heart, when really he was a deadbeat who refused to take care of his own kid because he already had a family."

"I take it you two haven't reconciled?"

If she guessed that from his tone, he wasn't hiding his bitterness as well as he thought. He let out a short laugh. "No."

She reached over and placed her hand on his forearm. "I'm sorry, Gabe. That's terrible. I really can't blame you for reacting the way you did."

His eyes flicked down to her hand on his arm, but he kept his face impassive, not wanting to spook her. She had been so distant that touching him voluntarily seemed like a real act of trust.

147

"Thanks. I wish I could say I was completely over it. I mean, I forgave my mom, and I have no doubt that things worked out for the best for me, but I still can't understand what he was thinking."

"Do his wife and kids know?"

"They got divorced. Ironically, his wife left him for someone else." He made a face. "At that point, there wasn't any real reason to hide it. His kids know now, which I assume means that his ex does too."

"But he and your mom—"

"Barely speak. My reaction put a damper on that arrangement. She found a new job, a better job, and to my knowledge, they have very little contact."

Kendall took her hand back and a pang of regret shot through him. He found himself hoping that she would return the trust and share something of her own life, but instead she just went back to her sandwich.

And then she asked in a small voice, "Do you know when my grandmother's will was written? Do you think she knew where to find me and that's why she named me as heir? Was it . . . some sort of deathbed change of heart?"

More regret shot through him, this time that he couldn't give her the information she sought. "I'm sorry. I have no idea. Her will came as a complete surprise to everyone."

"It's just that . . . I was in four foster homes

and a group home before I turned ten." She shot him a sad smile. "I was sure that my mom was looking for me, so every time a family wanted to adopt me, I ran away or started causing trouble at school so they'd have to move me."

An undercurrent of pain ran beneath her matter-of-fact tone, and he stayed quiet so she'd keep talking.

"Eventually I figured out that she wasn't coming back. I stopped running away, stayed in the same school, and graduated." She shrugged. "It was pretty okay. The Novaks were good people. It's just that . . . if my grandmother knew I was out there somewhere, knew my full name, I should have been pretty easy to find. So why didn't she?"

Gabe shook his head slowly. "I don't know, Kendall. The date on the will was a couple of years before she died, so I don't think it was a last-minute thing. Maybe she always held out hope you were out there somewhere. I wish I could tell you for sure."

She nodded, her expression shifting to resignation. She opened her bag of chips and popped one after another into her mouth, crunching thoughtfully.

"Do you . . . do you think it would help to have some company to do the inventory?"

She stopped crunching and looked at him, her expression slightly suspicious. She swallowed hard, grimacing at the scrape of chips down her throat, and then said, "Are you volunteering?"

"Yeah, I am."

"But you have work to do. You're the mayor. It's not like you can just take time off to help me."

"Well, I wouldn't be very far away. I've got my laptop and my cell phone if anyone needs anything, and I can still spend a couple of hours in the office in the morning." He also had two models to put together, two possible futures he was trying to compare and contrast for the city council, which meant that he would be spending a lot of late nights on his sofa with his dog. But the glimmer of hope he saw in her eyes made it impossible for him to do otherwise. She needed him, and he couldn't keep himself from stepping up.

"I feel guilty for taking you away from your real duties," she said, but the reluctance in her voice was waning.

"It's fine. I promise. Plus, with two of us, it will take half as long. Though I warn you, I don't know my Chippendale from my Chip and Dale."

The joke elicited a sudden laugh from her. "One is a piece of furniture and the others are cartoon characters. I'm sure you'll catch on quickly." She sobered. "You're sure? I really don't want the entire town mad at me because you're not doing your job."

"Trust me, no one knows what a mayor actually does anyway. A couple of days out of the office isn't going to kill me." He stuck out his hand. "So do we have a deal?"

She hesitated, then placed her hand in his. "Deal."

They shook and Kendall gave him a smile that warmed him to his very core. Once more, he was struck with the feeling of being a complete fraud, this time not because of his work abilities, but because he was pretending to be her friend.

When in reality, he was interested in so much more.

Chapter Thirteen

Kendall struggled to keep her voice even and the topics of conversation light for the next hour, even though the quiver in her stomach made it near impossible. She hadn't meant to share her history with Gabe, but after he'd told her about his father, she'd thought he might be the only non-foster child she'd ever met who could understand what it felt like to be robbed of your own destiny. It wasn't fair that he'd been raised with a father only lurking in the shadows when it had been within "Uncle Bob's" power to step up and be a proper parent. Just like it wasn't fair that Connie Green knew Kendall was out there somewhere and hadn't found her. It seemed like they both understood that kind of unfairness followed you into adulthood, no matter how hard you tried to overcome it.

And the resulting connection she felt with him was altogether unsettling. It wasn't sexual, not exactly, even though she couldn't deny that she found him attractive. It was just the undeniable urge to scoot in next to him and curl into his warmth. To just . . . be close to someone for a change.

But she'd found that was pretty much impossible with men, who took any kind of physical contact to mean she wanted to sleep with them. When she tried to disabuse them of that notion, they either dumped her or tried to force the issue. It was better to settle on this tentative understanding than to risk a short-lived romance. Right now she needed his help. And his friendship.

Other than Sophie, she didn't have any friends.

When it finally grew so cold that her butt was going numb on the metal hood of the truck and her fingers were starting to pale, he gathered up their trash and offered her a hand down. The touch of his fingers sent a little tingle up her arm, but he didn't seem to feel anything of the sort. He just opened the truck door, waited for her to climb in, and then shut it securely behind her. On the way down the mountain, he didn't talk much, so she sat back and watched the headlights cut through the darkness, illuminating the bright silver of the aspen trunks against the dark background of evergreens.

Still, when he stopped in front of the B and B, she half expected him to lean over the console for a kiss. Instead, he sat there with one hand draped loosely over the steering wheel, his blue eyes earnest. "I can go over to the house with you about ten tomorrow. Just tell me if you want to meet there or if I should pick you up somewhere."

She sat there, slightly discomfited by his behavior. "How will I get ahold of you?"

"Oh." He pulled out his cell phone. "What's your number?"

She recited it, and he plugged it into his phone. A moment later, her own phone chirped. "I just texted you. Just let me know in the morning."

"Okay. I will." After an awkward hesitation, she climbed out of the truck. "Thanks again. That was nice."

"It's my pleasure." He smiled at her, his eyes never leaving her face, and she shut the door. When she reached the top of the steps, she looked back, and there he was, still watching her. He gave a little wave, and she realized he was waiting for her to get inside.

Well, that was unexpectedly nice. Or maybe, given her experiences with Gabriel Brandt, it shouldn't be unexpected at all.

It wasn't that late, but the inside of the house was quiet, so she tiptoed up the stairs to her room, which she unlocked with the same key she'd used for the front door. She was just peeling off her coat when her phone rang. For a second, she thought it might be Gabe, checking on her again, but a quick look at the screen showed Sophie's face. Her heart lifted as she answered the video call.

"Soph!"

"Kendall, I'm so sorry. What a crazy day!"

From the background, she could see that Sophie was in their office, dressed in a suit and silk blouse. "The Thomases have turned out to be incredibly demanding, but they're willing to spend a fortune on this remodel, so I can't complain. Guess who's going to be their beck-and-call girl for the next several months?"

Kendall laughed at the reference to one of their favorite movies. "Some clients are like that, but if they're happy, I'd say you're doing the right thing. What else is going on?"

"Well, we have another potential client." Sophie reached off camera for something and then held up an image on her tablet. "Do you recognize this?"

Kendall gasped. "That's not . . ."

"The Woolridge House? It is."

She pressed a hand over her mouth. The Woolridge House was one of the premier examples of Craftsman style in Pasadena, built by an industrialist and privately owned for over a hundred years. Other than the occasional spread in an architectural or historical magazine, the home's interior had rarely been seen. Considering that only a few of the rooms had ever been photographed, Kendall had long suspected that the inside was due for a full remodel or restoration.

"How did they contact you?" she asked when she finally found her voice.

"By phone. I asked them to send over some

photos of the project first so you could see them. I've uploaded them already, and I'll text you the link when we get off the phone." Sophie's expression gleamed with excitement. "Check this out." She began to swipe through the tablet, and Kendall's eyes widened with each successive photo. The first few looked to have been taken straight out of a magazine spread, but the others . . . Well, she'd been right. Varying shades of decades-old remodels had covered the bedrooms and hallways and back living spaces in terrible garish colors, the unique molding painted in some places and water damaged in others. There was no doubt that this was a huge project.

"What did you tell them?"

"I said that our schedule was fully booked, but I knew that you had a special interest in this house, so I would see if there was any way you could fit it in sometime in the next year." Sophie's expression turned uncertain. "That was okay, wasn't it? I didn't want to seem too eager. I figured they'd be suspicious if we dropped everything for them."

"No, no, you did the right thing." Having an air of exclusivity only added to the cachet of their reputation. And Sophie had also been smart enough to buy her time. "Did they say anything about budget?"

"Sky's the limit, it seems. They're after the historical landmark designation."

Kendall's heart leapt with excitement. This was the big project they'd been needing. Something as high-profile as the Woolridge House would land them mentions in every historical and architectural magazine there was, not to mention give them amazing fodder for social media while they were doing the remodel, something she couldn't discount when casting the net for new clients. "Send over the photos. I might need you to do the initial walk-through. Tell them I'm on a special sourcing trip and I happen to have come across some things that will be perfect for that space."

"I take it the process is going well?" Sophie asked, excitement still lingering in her voice.

"Very well." Kendall didn't make the conscious decision to lie, but in the face of Sophie's news, she didn't want to spill how difficult today had been for her. Besides, Gabe was going to help, and she was sure his presence would make a difference in how quickly she could move through the house. He would at least be a welcome distraction. "I didn't get much done today because I had to go buy a heater halfway through, but I think tomorrow will be much better."

"Excellent." Sophie's expression turned mischievous. "I don't suppose there's any good . . . scenery . . . up there?"

Kendall smiled. "It's beautiful. Lots of trees. The sunsets are amazing."

Sophie rolled her eyes. "Not *that* kind of scenery."

"There's some eye candy for sure. The mayor is kind of hot, and so is the town welcome dude. But they're just typical bros." She kept her voice light so Sophie wouldn't guess what she really thought.

Predictably, her friend's expression fell. "Man, if you can't find a good guy in the wilds of Colorado, where can you find one?"

"Don't know, Soph. Maybe they're all gone." She didn't disabuse her of her perception of Jasper Lake, especially when she didn't want her to dig any further about Gabe and Luke. "I did, however, meet a very handsome guy today. He's just a little hairy." She went on to tell her about Gabe's Irish mastiff, knowing her dog-loving friend would get fully distracted from the topic at hand.

It worked. After extracting a promise to get a photo of Fitz tomorrow, Sophie said, "I really need to go and get changed. Sean is picking me up in an hour."

"Have fun, then. Tell Sean I said hi." Sophie's boyfriend was a nice guy, but they'd been dating so long at this point, Kendall was beginning to doubt that he'd ever pop the question. And why should he? They were both so busy that they got together for dinner a night or two a week and Sophie slept at his place when she didn't have an early meeting. It was an arrangement that had to seem perfectly fine to him . . . There wasn't really any motivation to move to the next step.

"Keep me updated. I'll talk to you later." Sophie blew a kiss at the camera and then shut down the video chat, leaving Kendall alone in her quiet rented room.

"Later," she said softly, then tossed the phone down on her bed. Just when she felt the first tendril of loneliness creep in, her phone beeped with an email message. The photos from Sophie.

She pulled out her laptop, connected to the B and B's surprisingly strong Wi-Fi, and began to look through the photos Sophie had uploaded to the cloud. The interiors of the Woolridge House were worse than she'd thought, many of the original features removed during questionable updates. It was her favorite kind of project, one that required meticulous research and layers of detail, not to mention hundreds of thousands of dollars, a percentage of which she would claim as her fee. Maybe they didn't need the money from her houses here after all. If she could land this project, they could potentially get a loan for the purchase of the house, using the commission as a down payment.

Her heart lifted. If she didn't need to sell, then it simplified things for both her and Gabe.

Which was beginning to matter a lot more to her than she'd expected.

Chapter Fourteen

Gabe woke up early the next day with a sense of anticipation. It took him several seconds to remember why—he'd agreed to help Kendall go through her grandmother's house today—and several more to figure out what had woken him up—Fitz whining and nudging his hand from the side of the bed. He pushed himself to a sitting position and scrubbed a fist across his eyes, then stumbled to the bedroom's sliding-glass door. "Okay, Fitz. Here you go. Have at it."

The dog bounded outside to do his business, while Gabe leaned against the cold metal door-frame, letting the bite of morning air chill his skin and bring him to full alertness. A quiver of nerves hovered in his stomach, this time not anticipation but the awareness of all his responsibilities. His to-do list, which had felt so manageable last night, now felt insurmountable. It was a good thing that Fitz's incongruously tiny bladder had woken him before the first glimmer of light had even touched the horizon, because he was going to need all the time he could get.

Once Fitz came trotting back, no more a fan of the cold than Gabe was this early, he locked the sliding door and proceeded to the kitchen to make a big pot of coffee. He dug two leftover slices of pepperoni pizza from the fridge—remnants of his lunch two days ago—plopped it cold on the plate, and lingered in his bare feet by the coffeepot until it finished brewing. His grandfather would be horrified by the idea of cold pizza for breakfast. Gabe had never understood why pancakes or waffles with enough sugar to be dessert were acceptable ways to start a day, but a slice of pizza that encompassed all the major food groups was not.

He grinned at his usual argument, his smile fading when he remembered how annoyed Madeline had gotten over such things. She'd constantly been on him to act more mature, stop being an overgrown frat boy—which was ironic considering she'd always complained to him how distant and focused on their careers her other boyfriends had been. He supposed it was good their relationship had fizzled out, because looking back, it seemed that she wouldn't have been happy no matter how he acted.

"Well, now I'm a town mayor," he said, toasting no one with his pizza. "Doesn't get any more mature than that."

Mayor of a town that desperately needed him to stop reminiscing and get down to work. He brought his food and coffee to the small kitchen table where he'd left his laptop and lifted the lid. He'd made major progress in downloading the town's layout to his drafting software; with the exception of some of the outlying homes, the buildings were more or less present. Now he just had to pull the details into the street view so that they'd look somewhat real on the animation.

The next time he looked up, the sun was glaring through the windows and into his eyes. He glanced at his watch and almost spilled his coffee on his laptop when he jumped out of his chair. Shoot. It was already after eight. He needed to get to the office if he was going to get anything done before he met Kendall.

Twenty minutes later, showered and dressed with his wet hair still dripping onto his collar— something he regretted the minute he stepped out into the cold—he was in his truck and on his way to his office. He raised a hand in greeting at the single car he passed on the way—Mrs. Marshall and her son—but otherwise the town was as deserted as ever.

Would it be so terrible to see some life and excitement around here? his conscience needled him.

No, it wouldn't, but he would far prefer to see the life and excitement that came from a vibrant full-time community rather than the transient flatlanders who arrived along with their expensive Range Rovers and treated the full-time citizens of Jasper Lake like ignorant backwater townies. He might think he was being a little harsh but for the fact that the change was already underway in places like Idaho Springs and Steamboat Springs, and fully realized in Breckenridge and Keystone. Yes, they had vibrant economies and year-round crowds, but they were becoming clones of Vail and Aspen, their former character lost. He was not going to let that happen to Jasper Lake.

He parked in front of his office building, a renewed sense of purpose in his chest, and fumbled his laptop and travel coffee mug while he climbed out of his truck.

"Morning, Gabe."

Gabe twisted to see Bruce McKay, owner of the snowmobile and boat rental, behind him and raised his coffee cup in salute. "Morning, Bruce. You still good to help with the bonfire this weekend?"

"Wouldn't miss it. I've got my propane torch ready."

"Maybe we leave the torch behind this time, eh? We can't afford to burn down the park." Gabe grinned at him, gave another friendly wave, and proceeded into the town hall building.

Linda was already at her desk when he entered, where she no doubt had been since 7 a.m., her earbuds in while she typed once again. She looked up when he entered and gave him a mischievous smile. "Late night?"

He looked at her quizzically.

"Someone saw you with Kendall Green coming

back from the other side of the lake. Decided to show her Make-Out Point, did you?"

Geez. "It's called *Lookout Point,* but yes. I thought she'd like to see the town from above. I'm supposed to be convincing her not to sell her property, remember?"

"Ooh, look who's defensive."

Gabe rolled his eyes. "Of course I'm defensive when you call it Make-Out Point." Though knowing his motives for helping Kendall were neither 100 percent pure nor 100 percent related to the town's well-being, he couldn't protest too much. "I'm going to try to get a few things done and then I'm headed out for the afternoon."

"Kendall?" Linda grinned.

"Yes, Kendall. I offered to help her go through her grandmother's house. She's finding it a little . . . difficult."

Linda sobered. "Can you imagine being in her shoes? Finding out you had family the whole time you were in foster care? That's terrible. She has to feel doubly abandoned."

"I'm sure she does." He paused. "You don't know about any of this, do you? I mean, I knew Connie Green better than a lot of people, but she never let on what happened to her daughter or granddaughter, at least not to me."

Linda shook her head. "I'm sorry. I don't know any more than you. I didn't even hear any gossip about it."

"Which is weird, right? Here, there's gossip about everything. I can't even eat sandwiches with Kendall without you asking me about it."

"Maybe it was too painful for Connie to talk about? If there's no information, there's no gossip. Right?"

"I suppose so." He shook his head. It wasn't relevant to his task, but he still wished that he could offer some explanation to Kendall. Part of the small-town package was everyone knowing everyone else's business, and it was unusual for there to be a huge blank surrounding one of their own. "Anyway, I'll have my cell phone and laptop with me, so feel free to put through any important calls today. Hopefully this won't take more than the rest of the week, and I'll be back to my regular schedule on Monday."

Gabe went to his office and set up his laptop, but he was too distracted to concentrate. It *was* weird that they didn't have any more information on Carrie or Kendall; it was as if they had just dropped off the face of the planet. But the fact that Connie had left her home to Kendall meant she hadn't dismissed her, even if she had merely been holding on to her last shred of hope.

Maybe they would get lucky and uncover something at the house that would give them some hints about what had actually happened . . . and why Kendall was the Jasper Lake daughter the town had forgotten.

Kendall's half-formed plan to get out to the Lakeshore properties early the next day was thwarted by a late night and an exceptionally comfortable bed. When she awoke, sunlight was already streaming in through the crack between the curtains, the chirp of birds alerting her to the dawn of a new day. She threw the covers back, half-panicked, before she realized that she'd never texted Gabe her plans, so she technically wasn't late for anything.

She took her time showering and doing her hair and getting dressed, not willing to admit that she took extra care with her appearance. She'd be lying to herself if she said last night hadn't sparked a glimmer of personal interest in Gabe, but she'd also be lying if she said she had any idea what to do about it. All she knew was that the look he gave her, like he found her enchanting, was something she wouldn't mind seeing again.

Not that it really mattered. She'd be done with this project in three days tops, and she already had the name and number of a moving company that was willing to come all the way to Jasper Lake to pack and ship the furniture she planned on removing from Connie Green's home. There was no future for her here, and it would be best for them all if she managed to remember it.

Still, she fluffed her hair one last time before

pulling her cap on, arranging the waves so they fell neatly over her shoulders, and checked her rear view in the full-length closet mirror to reassure herself that her butt did look as great in these jeans as the saleswoman had promised. She grinned at her own vanity. Before the day was done, she'd be covered in dust and dirt. The job didn't exactly scream sexy.

Downstairs, she declined Mr. Brandt's kind offer of breakfast but gladly accepted a pumpkin scone in a paper bag on her way out. Impulsively, she decided to leave her SUV at the B and B and instead walk the few blocks to town. By the time she stepped foot on the populated part of Main Street, her nose felt numb and her cheeks stung from the cold, but she couldn't deny that she felt invigorated. When she pushed through the door of Main Street Mocha, the warmth of the interior was a delicious contrast to the chill outside.

Delia looked up from the espresso machine at the ding of the front-door bell, and her face transformed into a smile. "Morning, Kendall!"

Wow. The coffee shop owner had remembered her name after one visit. Kendall returned the smile. "Good morning."

"What are you having? Pumpkin pie latte again or do you want to try something new?"

Kendall scrutinized the board. "Mr. Brandt sent me with a pumpkin scone, so I'll try something else. What do you recommend?"

"Cinnamon-vanilla chai," Delia said confidently.

"I'll take that then."

"Great. If you give me your scone, I'll warm it up for you."

Kendall handed it over along with her credit card. Delia studied her curiously while she waited for the card to process. "I overheard your conversation with Burton yesterday."

"Oh yeah?"

"Did you mean it? You're not going to sell to him?"

Kendall didn't remember saying anything of the sort, but the way information flew in this town, her conversation with Gabe could have easily gotten around. "I don't know that I'll have a choice, but it definitely wouldn't be my first one. What's the deal with him anyway?"

Delia grimaced as she returned Kendall's credit card and twisted away to stick the scone in the oven. "Developer. Need I say more?"

"Not all development is bad," Kendall said reflexively. "He's from Denver?"

"Park City, Utah. And I know not all development is bad. It's just that he wants to turn us into a clone of his other resorts to make a quick buck, even if it destroys what makes Jasper Lake unique."

"So what does make it unique?"

Delia smoothly moved to the espresso machine

168

and started steaming the milk for Kendall's chai. "You going to be around this weekend for the Pumpkin Festival?"

"The what?"

"The Pumpkin Festival. Food, music, a big bonfire in the park. We do it every year, and it draws people from towns all around the area, even some people from Denver and Boulder."

Now that she mentioned it, that was probably what had been on the banner Gabe was putting up when she arrived. She just hadn't looked close enough to notice anything beyond the splash of orange. "I don't know," she said finally. "A lot depends on how the next couple of days go."

Delia finished making the chai and handed it over in a doubled-up paper cup. The oven beeped at the same time, and she pulled out Mr. Brandt's scone and returned it to its paper bag. "Well, if you can, stay. You'll see what I mean."

"I'll try." She raised her cup in a salute of thanks and twisted away from the counter.

"Hey, Kendall?"

Kendall twisted back around.

"If you don't have anything to do tomorrow night, we're having a little girls' night out. You think you might like to join us?"

Kendall blinked, startled by the offer. She'd met Delia exactly twice and she was inviting her to hang out with her friends? "Um. Maybe?"

Delia smiled brightly, like she'd agreed.

"Great." She grabbed a business card from the counter and scrawled something on the back. "That's my cell number. Just text me when you know for sure, and I'll give you all the details."

"Okay. Thanks." Kendall tucked the card in her pocket and scurried out of the coffee shop while she contemplated what had just happened.

Delia was probably angling for another opportunity to convince her not to sell to Burton. She shouldn't read too much into things. Then again, she'd seemed to genuinely want Kendall to join her, and she certainly seemed like an interesting person. What would it hurt?

She filed that thought away for later consideration as she rejoined the sidewalk and ambled slowly down the street. Either it was warmer today or she was adjusting to the weather, because between the hot drink in her hand and her cold-weather gear, she was beginning to enjoy the bite of cold on her skin. It had been a shock, truly—a quick check of the weather back home said Pasadena was going to hit ninety-five today—but she could see why so many people retreated to the mountains. A summer resort would certainly be popular for those who were stuck in the sweltering temperatures down below for much of the summer.

She was so lost in thought that she didn't even notice she was walking past the town hall until a familiar voice called her name. She turned to see

Gabe waving to her from across the street, next to his huge truck.

"Hey!" She looked both ways unnecessarily— there were no cars in sight—before crossing over to him. "Good morning."

"When I didn't hear from you, I thought you'd gone over to Lakeshore."

"Sorry, I forgot." Kendall held up her cup. "I got distracted by Delia's chai."

"She blends that herself, you know. She takes special pride in her chai."

"As well she should." Kendall wrapped her hands around the paper cup and took another sip.

"So I was just going to head over there. You want a ride?"

She hesitated. All day with Gabe with no way to leave on her own? Then she realized that was stupid, because he would probably need to leave before she did. "Yeah. Sure. Thanks."

Gabe unlocked the truck with his key fob, and she jumped in the passenger seat before he could open the door for her. He climbed into the driver's seat and started it up with a roar. "Sleep well last night?"

"Like a rock. I know I said it before, but that bed is something else."

"Don't I know it. I keep threatening to steal one for my own house." He cast her a quick look as he backed out of the parking spot and started down the street. "Are you ready for this?"

"Honestly? Not really. But I have a plan. Feel like being my design assistant for the day?"

"What did you have in mind?"

"I'll take photos, but it would be helpful if you could take notes for me. It will save a lot of time."

"What are you going to do with the personal items?" Gabe asked.

Kendall sobered. She'd been trying not to think of that. It was one thing to figure out what to do with furniture, another to dispense with clothes and memorabilia. "I think I'll take out the things I want to ship back, and then anything that's left over can go in an estate sale." She paused. "I was thinking that maybe it could benefit the town. I'm sure you have some charities or an emergency fund that could use the money."

"We do. But, Kendall, that's all rightfully yours. The proceeds—"

"I don't want it," she said quickly. "All those things are from her life here. It's only right that the money go back to the town." And she didn't want to have to see all that evidence of how life had gone on without her, how quickly she'd been forgotten. If she'd had a missing daughter and granddaughter, she would have moved heaven and earth to get them back. Not just given up on them when they disappeared because of some stupid teenage decisions.

"Okay, whatever you want. But maybe let's see

172

what's there before you decide. You may change your mind."

"I won't." Kendall took a deep breath and made her heart hard and her nerves steady. She could do this. The quicker she finished, the quicker she could get back home and start on something that actually did require her attention: the Woolridge House.

When they finally arrived at the Lakeshore homes, Gabe parked at the curb in front of Connie's place, and she hopped out immediately. This time, she knew exactly what key belonged to the front door and stepped into a blast of cold. These old houses were solidly built, but judging from the temperature drop, they were drafty.

"I'll fire up the heater," Gabe said, glimpsing the propane equipment near the front entry. "Where do you want to start?"

"The parlor," she said, heading left. She pulled out her phone and a notebook while Gabe got the heater started, and then handed the writing materials over to him. "Are you ready?"

"You don't waste any time." He flipped open the notebook and uncapped the pen, poised to begin.

She repressed a smile at his earnestness. Most guys would be insulted to be asked to play her assistant, but Gabe was taking her completely seriously. She started with the first item that caught her eye and raised her phone to take several photos of the front, side, and inside. "Numbers 0054 through 0059. Mission oak cabinet." She ran her hands along the interior to assess that everything was solid wood, then pulled out the drawer to inspect for dovetail joining. In the bottom of the drawer was exactly what she was looking for. "Limbert. Between 1902 and 1905."

Gabe scribbled down everything she said, then looked at her quizzically. "How do you know the dates?"

She pointed to the mark burned into the drawer. "You see here how it says *Grand Rapids?* After 1906, it would have also said *Holland.* So we know it has to be somewhere in that five-year period. I have some old Charles Limbert catalogs at home, so if this was an advertised case piece, I might be able to narrow it down even further."

"Is it valuable?"

Kendall smiled. "Quite. And it's well-preserved too."

They proceeded through the rest of the room that way, recording chairs, tables, even lamps, but bypassing an antique grandfather clock that needed so much restoration work it wasn't worth the investment.

"You really know your stuff," Gabe said. "How did you learn all this? Did you go to school?"

"Kind of." Kendall got down on her hands and

174

knees to look beneath another piece, searching for a maker's mark. "I had some design training and I did a certificate program at Sotheby's in London. But the rest has just been lots and lots of firsthand experience. Collecting and studying old catalogs and books. Making some very expensive mistakes."

"Like what?"

"Fall front desk, flame mahogany, unmarked. Probably early nineteenth century."

Gabe stared at her and she gestured to the notepad. He realized that she was talking about the furniture in front of them and quickly scribbled the information down.

"Basically, I got taken in by a good fake, spent way too much, and it was my boss who saved me from putting it in a client's home. He called it a very expensive learning experience. We later used it in another project, where the homeowner didn't care so much about provenance or authenticity, but at a much-reduced cost." Kendall cringed at the memory. She was lucky that Joseph Kramer had been a kind man and hadn't fired her for her mistake, given that she'd made it on the company dime, but he'd also impressed on her the need to thoroughly research every piece before she shelled out any money and especially before she placed it in a client's home. She'd never made the same error again.

Partly because she'd gotten cynical and partly

because she'd expanded her wealth of knowledge to the point she could tell an antique from a fake within the first twenty seconds. And so far, every piece in this house had been real.

"Now the rugs." She took a photo of the Persian rug and then flipped up the back to expose the knotwork. "Wool over cotton, Kashan in cream, red, and gold. 1920 or later, but I'm going to guess 1960s."

"How can you tell?"

"Instinct." Kendall smiled at him. "And wear. The cream fields didn't exist before the 1920s, when Persian weavers started responding to Western demand for more subdued colors. There's a bit of color fading and some wear, typical of a rug that's sixty years old or so. But I might be able to track down the exact pattern to get a better date. Close enough to know it's vintage." She paused. "Connie had good taste."

"Looks like it runs in the family."

Kendall cleared her throat and looked away. The only way she'd make it through this was by hiding behind a veneer of professionalism. She didn't need to be reminded of her personal connection. "Let's go to the library next."

"Kendall, I don't want to push, but this might be an opportunity. To learn a little about your grandmother. To put your past behind you."

She paused in the doorway of the library and inhaled deeply, suppressing her instinct to fire back angry words. His tone was kind and she had no doubt that he meant well, but even considering his experience with his own parents, he couldn't understand. Yes, he had been lied to, but his father had cared enough to be in his life, even under the guise of a family friend. There was no way he could grasp the depth of her anger and hurt.

She leveled her voice, but she didn't turn. "My only family abandoned me, Gabe. A few pieces of furniture will never change that."

Gabe immediately knew he had made a misstep with Kendall, because the easy camaraderie they'd established evaporated. It wasn't that she became rude or even stopped joking with him. She simply erected an invisible barrier between them that he couldn't pinpoint but could feel nonetheless. By even suggesting there might be a way to understand her birth family, he'd unintentionally put himself on their side, not hers. And that couldn't be further from the truth.

Still, as they moved through the remaining rooms downstairs, there was no getting back those early moments of connection or that fragile, fleeting trust they'd established the night before at the lookout.

Why does it matter so much to you? You've known her less than two days. Two days wasn't enough to feel betrayed or like he'd betrayed her.

They were virtual strangers. She had a life in another state, and he was merely a means to an end for her.

And yet he already cared about her. Maybe it was the part of him that rooted for the under-dog—the same part that had led him to take a job with a nonprofit instead of a slightly more lucrative city planner position—that wanted to see things turn out for her. And maybe it was his ridiculous impulse to be a do-gooder that made him want to be part of making that happen.

Or maybe it was just the way she unconsciously pushed a blonde wave away from her face and tucked it behind her ear while she was thinking, looking so appealing that he wanted to reach out and do it for her.

It was definitely not the way her tight jeans hugged every curve and made his mouth dry in unguarded moments.

Probably.

His responsibility here was to the town. Their interests just happened to align at the moment. But if that changed, he knew full well what he'd have to choose. No matter how much he disliked it.

Once the clock started to edge past five and the light outside changed from warm sunset to the bluish hint of falling twilight, Kendall crawled out from under the dining room table and stretched her arms overhead with a crack.

"I don't know about you, but I think I'm done here. All this crawling and contorting has got my back in knots. I don't suppose there's a massage therapist in town?"

"Unfortunately not. And the nearest chiropractor is in Georgetown." He offered a hand to help her up, which after a moment of reluctance, she took. "What do you say we go grab something to eat?"

Her expression shuttered suddenly. "If you don't mind, I think I'll do dinner on my own tonight. I've got some work to do, so I'll probably just pick something up from the sandwich shop and eat in front of my computer."

"Sure. I understand." He was right: he had ruined things between them. She didn't want to spend any more time with him than she had to. "I have plenty of things to catch up on myself."

Now her expression turned unsure. "I'm sorry. I forgot you were playing hooky from your real job to help me. If you don't have time to come over here tomorrow, I totally understand."

"No, it's fine," he said, even though he still had hours in front of the computer ahead, overlaying details onto wireframes for his animation. And that was just one of the townscapes he had to put together. He was definitely going to need to enlist Luke's help to get this done any time this century.

"I don't think it is, but thank you." She paused,

her expression softening. "This would have been much more difficult to do alone."

"It's my pleasure. You ready to go?"

"Sure." She turned off the heater and lugged it into the front entry, then followed him out onto the stoop, where she locked the door.

Knowing full well she was trying to race him to his truck so he couldn't open the door for her, Gabe still got there first and yanked it open. "My lady."

She shot him a knowing grin before climbing in.

The impulse to say something stupid was strong enough that he opted for silence on the way back to town. Only when he stopped in front of the B and B did he finally look at her. "Meet you at the house tomorrow? Say, ten o'clock?"

"Perfect. I'll see you there." She hopped out of the cab and gave him a wave before slamming the door. She didn't look back.

Gabe pulled away from the curb and immediately voice-dialed Luke.

His friend picked up on the first ring. "So. How'd your antiques date go?"

Gabe rolled his eyes. "I managed to tick her off within the first two hours, and now she's gone polite on me. Besides, it wasn't a date."

"Sure it wasn't. You always cut out on work to 'help a stranger.' " Even over the phone, Gabe could hear the air quotes.

He chuckled. "Well, I'm paying for it now, and I could use some help. I don't suppose you'd like to sacrifice your evening to do some really boring graphic design work?"

Luke paused like he was thinking. "What are you offering?"

"Pizza and beer?"

"The good kind?"

"The good kind of pizza or the good kind of beer?"

"Both. My help doesn't come cheap."

"Both then."

"I'll be there in an hour."

Gabe grinned and hung up the phone. He had just enough time to stop by the market that served as both the town pizza parlor and its only convenience store. Fortunately, D'Angelo's had the best pizza in Clear Creek County; the owner was a transplanted New Yorker who used to own a small chain of Brooklyn pizza parlors. A couple of times a year, he imported New York City municipal water to make his dough, not a small feat considering the winter weather conditions on both ends of that supply chain.

Forty-five minutes later, Gabe was walking through his front door, balancing a six-pack of a locally bottled microbrew on top of a large pepperoni and sausage pizza, the steam from the pie making the cardboard box soft and flimsy. As soon as he heard the telltale scrabble of nails against the hardwood floor, he off-loaded the pizza before he ended up beneath it and 120 pounds of dog at the same time.

"Hey, Fitz. How you doing, boy?" Gabe took a couple of minutes to scratch the dog's head and belly, Fitz's tongue lolling out in happiness, and then went to open the kitchen door. The poor canine made a beeline for it, no doubt having eagerly awaited his potty break. Gabe felt momentarily guilty. He usually came home on his lunch hour to walk his dog, but he'd been across the lake the whole day. Now that he thought about it, they hadn't even stopped for lunch. He'd gotten caught up in the juggernaut of Kendall's determination to finish the downstairs today.

When Fitz had done his business, Gabe let him back in, transferred two big scoops of food into his bowl, and gave him one more affectionate pat. He'd just managed to wash his hands and get out paper plates when a knock sounded at his front door. Luke.

"It's open!" he yelled, and a second later came the scrape of the wooden doorframe.

"I would have expected Detroit to give you a little more caution." Luke's deep voice came from the other room, and he rounded the corner, looking like a Norwegian lumberjack in a plaid flannel shirt and work boots. As if the guy did anything more physical during his workday than lift his laptop. Gabe liked to tell him as much.

"Why bother?" Gabe pulled a beer from the cardboard carrier and offered it to Luke, who opened it without comment.

He took a drink and then twisted the bottle around to look at the label. "Nice. Didn't cheap out on me."

"Not tonight. You're doing me a favor. Take the pizza to the dining room?"

Luke complied, and Gabe followed with the plates and a roll of paper towels. They were half-way through their second pieces before Luke finally asked, "So. Kendall Green?"

"What about her?"

"What's the deal?"

"Just trying to convince her not to sell. Thought I could get her to feel some connection to the place, but she's still way too angry at her birth family."

Luke shrugged. "Can't blame her, really. Who abandons their kid like that?"

"Yeah, I know." Gabe took a bite of his pizza, once again regretting letting his mouth get ahead of him. He'd only wanted to help, but the truth was, nothing in his experience prepared him to understand that level of hurt.

After a few moments passed, Luke asked, "Exactly how convincing are you being?"

"Not convincing enough." Too late, he caught the half smile his friend hid behind his pizza. "It's not like that."

183

"Why not? She's gorgeous. In fact, if you're not interested, I thought I might . . ." Luke broke off when Gabe shot him a look. "What? So you *are* interested?"

Yeah, he was interested all right, but . . . "It's complicated."

"Not so complicated. She was flirting with you yesterday. She's interested, you're interested . . ." Luke shrugged. "Seems like a compelling reason to stick around to me."

And that was exactly why he couldn't make a move. Kendall would think he was trying to manipulate her into doing what was best for the town, and she was already suspicious of everyone's motivations here. There was no good way to navigate that minefield.

They ate pizza silently until Luke pushed away the remnants of the enormous pie and pulled his laptop from his satchel. "So. Tell me what we need to do here."

Gabe ran down what he'd accomplished with his current project. "Now the trick is to pull images from the town website and map them to the buildings in the model."

"Oh, that's no problem." Luke connected to Gabe's wireless internet and his fingers flew over the keyboard as he logged in to the back end of the website. A couple of seconds later, he'd downloaded the entire image folder and uploaded it to a handoff site. "What now?"

Gabe had known this was the right play. Luke's back-end access beat having to save every image individually. "I need to come up with a rendering to represent the hotel and resort. All I have is the bare minimum that Burton submitted to the city council."

"Well, didn't you say that he's a Park City developer and all his resorts look the same? Shouldn't be too hard to find images and drawings from his other sites and add them to your rendering. In fact, I bet if we search . . ."

It didn't turn out to be quite as easy as Luke was making it out to be, but after three hours, they had a decent representation of the resort loaded and half the images of the town put in. That wasn't the problem.

The problem was, it actually looked good. Burton was a well-known developer with a talented staff. The resort blended into the natural environment, about as well as a thirty-thousand-foot behemoth could, and he'd thought about ways to maximize both the views and the lake access. The building itself would no doubt be a resounding success. But that wasn't their objection. The objection was the extra traffic and the environmental and economic impact, not to mention the changes to the intangible character of the town. Gabe started rendering four-lane divided highways with their encroachment on the surroundings and then, using his imagination, began working in the strip malls that would inevitably spring up on the side of the newly refurbished highway. He'd seen it before, and good as it might be for the tax base, it was the beginning of the end for the mountain-town character.

Finally Luke yawned and glanced at his watch. "It's almost eleven. I've got some projects to finish, and I have to be up early tomorrow. I'm going to bail."

"Thanks, man. You have no idea how much you helped."

"Yeah, I do." Luke gathered up his laptop and peripherals and shoved them back in his case. "Basketball Saturday?"

When Gabe hesitated, he laughed. "Point taken. You'll be with Kendall. Or at least you hope you will be."

Gabe couldn't even deny it.

Chapter Fifteen

Kendall awoke early, disoriented. Where was she? Why was there something hard and wet poking into her cheek?

Groggily, she lifted her head and the details of her room in the B and B filtered in. One look at herself answered the second question. She was still in her clothes from the night before, and the hard thing was the edge of her laptop, now covered in soggy lettuce from the abandoned sandwich wrapper beside it on the bed.

She groaned, remembering. She'd been up late researching the provenance of the pieces they'd cataloged from Connie Green's house, and somewhere along the line, she must have collapsed in an exhausted stupor. Her eyes felt gritty and her mouth tasted like stale onions. She glanced at her watch. Six a.m. That explained why it was still dark out.

Of course, Gabe wouldn't be over at Lakeshore until later, so there would be no one to know if she caught another couple hours of sleep. But she had way too much work for that. So far she'd managed to avoid going through anything personal in the house beyond a very eclectic CD collection, but as they moved to the upper rooms, she knew that would come to an end. Clothes and other personal belongings, maybe memorabilia. She wasn't sure if she wanted Gabe there for support or if she wanted to be alone in case it turned out to be too much for her.

That brought her back to the memory of last night and how abruptly she had shut Gabe out. Guilt tightened her chest. He had only been trying to help, and she'd practically turned on him.

Except there was no reason to let him in. He was helping her because their interests aligned. However kind and understanding he might be, he had a job to do and so did she. There was no room for personal feelings.

She groaned and levered herself off the bed. First a shower. Then coffee. Then she could worry about the rest.

By the time she was showered and dressed, the sun had just started to peek over the horizon. She packed her laptop and her personal items into her tote, pulled on her jacket, and carefully made her way down the B and B's staircase. She'd told Mr. Brandt that she wouldn't be needing breakfast while she was here—her waistband was already starting to feel a bit tight—but the smell of fresh coffee drew her into the kitchen anyway.

"Good morning," he said when Kendall entered, not at all surprised to see her. "Sleep well?"

Kendall touched her cheek to check if the

outline of her laptop was still pressed into it. "Reasonably well."

"You can't work on an empty stomach. Coffee is not breakfast, no matter what my grandson says. Here." Mr. Brandt stacked sausage and eggs on what looked to be a freshly made English muffin and wrapped it in foil. "You can take it with you to Delia's. She won't mind."

She'd only been here for a few days, and already her routine was that well-known? Or maybe it was just that everyone headed over to Main Street Mocha first thing in the morning.

"Thanks," Kendall said with a smile, tucking the sandwich into an outer pocket of her bag. "I'll enjoy it."

Mr. Brandt waved off her words with his usual brusqueness. "How's the work going over there?"

Kendall hardened herself, but the rush of emotions still surprised her. "Slowly. Gabe has been a big help."

"You know, Gabe was pretty close to Connie."

Kendall frowned. He'd never said anything about that. "Oh yeah? How?"

"She was his Sunday school teacher. Helped straighten out a bit of what had gotten twisted from the situation with his mom." He looked at her significantly. "I expect he's already told you about that."

"Yeah, he did. Connie was a Christian?"

"She was. She was an elder in the church,

taught Sunday school for years. She was a wonderful example to the town."

"It figures. I'm glad she cared about something." Kendall tapped her bag to indicate the sandwich. "Thanks for breakfast."

Only once she was out on the sidewalk did she take a deep breath. It all made sense now. The paragon of Christian virtue had been shamed by her promiscuous daughter and either turned her out or made her feel so bad about getting pregnant that she left on her own. And then once Carrie figured out that she wasn't cut out to be a mother, she'd cut Kendall free. Like an animal who chewed off a limb to get out of a trap.

To both Connie and Carrie, Kendall had been a necessary sacrifice.

She'd like to believe that she was just imagining this, but she'd had too much experience with Christian virtue to think otherwise.

The revelation soured her mood, but she let the fresh air and morning chill wash it away as she walked into town. By the time she made it to Main Street Mocha, the smile of greeting she gave Delia was almost genuine.

"Morning, Kendall," she said. "What are you having?"

"Surprise me. The chai yesterday was amazing."

"How about a Lake Fog then? My tea specialty."

"If it's caffeinated, I'll take it." Kendall paid, then found a table where she could continue the work she'd fallen asleep in the middle of.

She'd barely set up her laptop when a figure blocked the early morning sunshine. She looked up to find Philip Burton standing over her. Dislike instantly spiked through her.

"Kendall Green." Burton pulled up a chair without asking and crossed his legs. He regarded her for a moment. "I was hoping I would have heard from you by now."

"I've been busy. A lot of possessions to sort through at the house."

"Understandable. I heard that the judge closed the probate case finally."

Kendall cocked her head. "You're well-informed. I haven't even heard that."

"I expect you'll be getting a call from Matthew Avery sometime today. He might not even know yet."

The dislike intensified. It was clearly a power play, meant to show her how well-connected he was and how small she was in comparison. It fired every stubborn instinct in her being. "What can I help you with, Mr. Burton?"

"Now that you're the legal owner of the properties, I'm prepared to make you a very nice offer." He took a notepad from his vest pocket and scribbled a number on a sheet. Then he ripped it off and slid it toward her.

$750,000.

She laughed, a genuine laugh. "You've got to be kidding me."

"It's fair. The houses aren't in great condition. They may look nice on the outside, but they need an extensive amount of foundation work due to the proximity to the lake. I don't think you have the money for the repairs."

"Maybe not. But I also know that the land is worth more than that to you. No thank you."

He folded his hands, making a show of patience. "What were you thinking then?"

She opened her mouth to answer what she actually thought it was worth—a million and a quarter—but that wasn't what came out. "Three million."

The pleasant expression slid from his face. "Excuse me?"

"I've done my research too. I know what land would cost you in similar towns, and I know how much it's going to be worth after you build the development. So if you're in such a rush and you really want that land, it's going to cost you three million dollars." Kendall held his gaze, her expression blank, even though her heart was beating so hard she was sure he could see it through the puffy down of her jacket.

"Fine," he said, and for a brief, shocked moment, she thought she'd won. Then he kept talking. "I offered you above market value considering the issues with the homes. But you're not interested in doing business."

"Not if you're going to lowball me, no." She forced a smile, hoping it looked calculating. "I'll consider any reasonable offer, Mr. Burton."

"That was the most reasonable offer you're going to get." He smiled too, and it chilled her. "I hope you don't come to regret your decision."

Kendall sat there stiffly and watched him leave the coffee shop. As soon as he disappeared from the frame of the plate-glass windows, she slumped in her chair. What had she done? She had potentially alienated the only person who was willing to pay a decent price on her properties. It wasn't the $1.7 million she needed for her Pasadena home, but it was almost halfway there. She could do a lot with three-quarters of a million dollars. Her stomach churned with anxiety.

"Here." Delia set a ceramic mug near her hand and then slid into the chair across from her. "That was something to watch. I don't think I've ever seen anyone stand up to him that way. I mean, sure, people yell profanity at him, but that's not the same thing."

Delia's humor cut through her numb sense of horror, and Kendall cracked a smile. "I don't know what got into me. I just . . . I hate that guy. I have no real reason for it either. He's just so . . ."

"Smug? Smarmy? Pleased with himself?"

Delia cocked her head. "I guess that's the same thing as smug, but it bears repeating."

"I feel sick," Kendall muttered, but she reached for the tea and tasted it anyway. It slid down her throat and left a warm trail all the way to her stomach, taking a bit of the nausea away. "This is good though. What's in it?"

Delia grinned. "Trade secret. But mostly tea and coconut milk."

"Well, your trade secret is delicious. Thanks." Kendall took another sip. "You're a business owner in this town. How do you make it all work?"

"That's another trade secret, but it's addictive and possibly illegal." Delia chuckled when Kendall's eyebrows rose. "No, I'm joking. Honestly, a lot of sleepless nights and prayer. I work hard and worry harder sometimes."

The prayer thing snagged in her psyche, but Kendall let it go because she immediately knew this woman wasn't cut from the same cloth as Connie Green. For all she knew, Delia was praying to Buddha. "Wouldn't it be good for you if this became a resort town? A lot of people staying in hotel rooms translates to a lot of money for the coffee shops and restaurants."

"Honestly, it would be. But I moved up here because I needed a respite from my life down below, from all the mindless hustle. The pace of life is what drew me to Jasper Lake, the fact that

194

everyone knows you and has your back. You just don't find that these days."

"No, you really don't." The front door opened with a ding, and Delia cast a look toward the newcomers. Kendall waved her away. "Go. Don't let me keep you."

Delia stood but she glanced back at Kendall. "We're still on for girls' night, right?"

"Wouldn't miss it." Kendall smiled as she left, but the minute she was alone, the sick feeling came back. Telling Burton off had given her momentary satisfaction, but it was short-lived.

What had she done?

Chapter Sixteen

When Gabe arrived at the house, fueled by a mug of Delia's best drip coffee and his grandfather's famous blueberry muffins, Kendall's rental SUV was already parked there. Gabe bounded up to the front door and knocked, but when no one answered, he tried the door. It swung open easily.

"Kendall?"

"Up here!" Her voice drifted down, and slowly he climbed the stairs to find her on her hands and knees beneath a dressing table in one of the guest bedrooms.

He leaned against the doorframe, repressing a smile. "Already hard at work, I see."

She backed out from under the furniture and scribbled something on the notepad he'd been using yesterday. "I've been here since eight. Woke up early and figured there was no point in wasting an early start."

Gabe studied her as she stood and moved on to the dresser beside the table. There was something . . . off . . . about her today. She was always perky, but this was the first time he'd ever seen this kind of frenetic energy from her.

"What's going on?"

Kendall looked at him wide-eyed. "Nothing."

"Liar. What happened?"

She plopped onto the edge of the bed. "Phil Burton found me in the coffee shop this morning."

"And?"

"Made me an offer I had no problem refusing . . . $750,000."

Gabe's eyebrows arched upward. "That's a lot of money."

"I know it is. Which is what he was counting on, me getting blinded by the zeros and forgetting that the property is worth double that—more, considering he needs it for his development."

"So you refused."

"I countered." She grimaced. "Three million dollars."

He just about choked. "Three *million?* What did he say?"

She gave him a crooked smile. "Let's say he was less than pleased with that counteroffer. I have no idea what got into me. It's just that his smug face—"

"—makes you want to punch him in the nose and then take a baseball bat to the headlights of his Lexus?" When Kendall stared at him, he grinned. "Not that I've thought about it or anything."

"Yeah, trust me, I get it."

"So what's the problem? I mean, I imagine he didn't accept your offer, but that's no surprise."

"I don't know. Once I had his attention, I

said I'd accept any reasonable offer, and he said this was as reasonable as he was going to get, or something to that effect. It felt like a . . . warning."

Gabe narrowed his eyes. He already disliked Burton, but now it sounded like he was trying to bully Kendall, and that shifted the dislike into fury. "Did he threaten you?"

"Not in so many words." She shook her head. "You know him. He's so slippery, you come away from a conversation not entirely sure if he really said what you think he said. I know not all developers are like him, but his kind definitely give them a bad name."

"Especially when they make their fortune elsewhere and then come back to pick over the bones of their hometown."

Kendall blinked. "What do you mean?"

"You didn't know? That's part of the reason everyone hates him so much. He grew up here. I mean, he's our parents' generation—" he grimaced at the involuntarily reminder that meant nothing to Kendall—"but he went to the same high school we all did. Left for an Ivy League college, became this big businessman, always claimed he was going to come back and fix what was wrong with this town. Apparently, what's wrong with this town is that it's not Park City." Even saying it aloud made him itch to wipe the self-satisfied smirk off Phil Burton's pampered face. He might have once been a local, but there was be no doubt he thought he was too good for them. When Gabe had challenged him in the city council meeting, Burton had accused him of having a townie chip on his shoulder.

Which might be correct, in some sense, but only when faced with jerks like Phil Burton.

He realized that his internal monologue had run away with him and Kendall was just sitting there mulling the revelation. "Don't worry. There's really nothing he can do to you. As soon as the estate is settled, you're the official owner and you can do what you want with it."

"That's the other thing. He told me it's already been settled and that I should be getting a call from Matthew Avery today. Implied that he knew before my lawyer did."

"So quickly?"

"It was left to me and I'm the only claimant. They were probably happy to get the case completely off their docket."

"What are you going to do now?"

Kendall opened her mouth and then closed it and sighed. "I have absolutely no idea."

For a moment, she looked so disheartened that he realized exactly what she had given up. Three-quarters of a million dollars *was* a lot of money, and it would have made a fine down payment on her house/office in Pasadena. The fact she had turned it down suggested that she was no more anxious to see these homes demolished than he was, but what other choice did she have? Gabe had been so focused on keeping Burton out that he hadn't spent much time considering the alternatives. If he had one flaw—and God knew he wished there was only one—it was that he could jump into things without proper planning, trusting that the right side would win. He called it optimism; Madeline had called it naiveté. Maybe it was. But he had to believe that there was more than one outcome to this situation.

"Right now, we finish doing the inventory of the house," he said finally. "What do we have?"

She handed him the notepad and he saw that she'd already gone through the other bedroom, and with this one almost completed, all that was left was the master. Looked like she had saved it until last.

"Are you ready for this?" he asked quietly.

Kendall shot him a smile, but he didn't have to be a lifelong friend to see the unsteadiness beneath it. "As ready as I'll ever be."

Kendall tried to hide her anxiety with a smile, but from the look on Gabe's face, he wasn't fooled. And why would he be? He had to know how hard this was for her. Guest rooms, living spaces, they were all fairly generic. But the master bedroom was something else, filled with her grandmother's clothes, her personal items, her photographs. She'd left it until last because part of her didn't want to see what she'd find.

Her brave words to Gabe had been a lie, but she had no choice. She scanned the room while she decided where to begin. It was just like the rest of the house: a four-poster bed that didn't strictly fit the Craftsman details of the home, a nice highboy and lowboy pair, some oil paintings that seemed to be more folk than fine art. "Let's start with the bed."

She took a few photos from different angles, but it took supreme force of will to actually approach it. It was a pretty piece, but she knew even before she evaluated it that she would not be taking it with her. "Cherry, quasi-Craftsman, but it's obviously a new piece and not an antique. Doesn't fit any appreciable style, so it doesn't hold any particular value for collectors.

"Lowboy next." She took more pictures, rattled off details, and then pulled open the first drawer and stilled. Shirts filled the drawer, each one folded to precisely the same size and placed in one of three distinct stacks. The musty smell of the drawer said that it hadn't been opened in a long time.

Well, of course it hadn't. Connie had been dead for five years.

Still, Kendall couldn't resist reaching out and touching the top one, a preppy white- and black-striped polo shirt that seemed at odds with the image she'd formed of Connie Green. She'd assumed there would be racks of silk blouses and knife-edge creased trousers, not something so normal as cotton polos. She quickly closed the drawer and opened the next to find lingerie, mostly sensible, but a few trimmed with wisps of lace. She shut that just as quickly. In the bottom drawer, beneath stacks of folded jeans and chinos, she found what she was looking for: a stamp, along with a metal medallion. "Stickley," she said.

Gabe looked impressed. "Even I know that. It's expensive, right?"

"Compared to IKEA, definitely." She threw him a smile. "But this piece isn't antique. It's 1980s, maybe even early 1990s. Good reproduction, though."

"I'm so disillusioned. I never thought Connie would have anything reproduction in her home."

"Don't be too disillusioned. It's still good quality furniture and would have cost a couple thousand dollars new. Hold on to it for another fifty years, and it will be a treasured antique."

"Are you taking it?" he asked.

"Maybe." She wasn't sure about anything at this point. There were some nice pieces, but they all felt so . . . personal. As if they were too linked to their owner and should stay here in the house for as long as it stood. Which might not be that long, all things considered.

That thought made her chest squeeze tight. Maybe she didn't have any personal connection to the house, but working in it for the last few days had given it a familiarity that she found appealing. She could see how this could be a home for someone.

She could see how this should have been a home for her.

"Kendall?"

She blinked and snapped her head around to Gabe. "Yeah. Sorry. Zoned out there for a minute. Let's move on?"

It didn't take long to catalog the rest of the items in the room, and then she had no choice but to move to the closet. She opened the door, stepped into a spacious walk-in, and was overcome with a feeling of inertia, like being thrown into the past. She hadn't misread Connie Green after all; here were the silky button-downs and trousers, the sleek sheath dresses. She'd obviously been a woman of taste and money, as if that had been in question at any point. Running her fingers over her clothes made her feel like she knew her, at least a little bit.

And sparked an anger in her chest that almost blotted out her ability to speak.

There was a small stack of drawers built into one side, and she opened them one by one to find belts, silk scarves, and a tray full of simple, tasteful gold jewelry. It said something about this small town that they knew there was this much of value in the house and yet it had survived for five years, abandoned but intact and untouched. It also served as a reminder that money hadn't been a barrier to Connie's choice to seek out Kendall—or not to.

She shoved the drawer closed, shutting away the glint of all that gold, and looked to the shelves above the hanging rods. There were several white cardboard banker's boxes marked *paperwork* with years on them. As much as she really didn't want to go through old files, there might be important documents relating to the houses. Still, she left them where they were. She wasn't ready for the intimate details of Connie's life.

She retreated from the walk-in and shut the door. "That, of course, wasn't original to the house. She must have put it in sometime in the last few decades. In fact, all the furniture in here is relatively new. Makes me think she did a remodel on the master bedroom."

"You could probably find that out if you really wanted to," Gabe said. "If there was major work done, there would be permits on file. I noticed the kitchen looked newer too."

"Yeah." Kendall sank down on the bed, inexplicably drained of energy. It was only midmorning and yet she felt as if she had run a marathon.

Gabe sat down as well, a few feet away. "Are you okay?"

She rubbed her nose. "I think so. It's just—"

"I know."

"Part of me would have an easier time of it had this place been a dump. If she'd been living in squalor. At least I could believe that she thought I was better off in foster care than here. But this?" She swept a hand around the room, her throat tight. "She had this beautiful life. Even if my mom didn't want me or couldn't take care of me, it's not like Connie couldn't have."

Gabe's hand found hers on top of the bedspread and clasped it tightly. It was warm and strong, and rather than recoiling from the contact, she gripped it back. "I know how hard this must be, Kendall. And I wish I could give you an adequate explanation. But nothing will ever make up for the fact that you were raised away from your family, that you didn't have your mom and grandma. You should have. Does it help knowing that in the end, at least, she was thinking of you?"

"I don't know. Maybe." Kendall took a long, deep breath in and let it out in a whoosh. "Maybe she really didn't know where I was or if I was still alive. Maybe she knew she was dying and so she put me in her will, just in case someone could find me." Deep down, she knew that was wishful thinking, that she was trying to make herself feel better about having been abandoned. But could it be the truth? Could it simply be that

Connie Green had hoped her executor could do what she could not?

"I know you don't want to hear it, but that fits much better with the woman I remember than the idea that she just abandoned you." Gabe squeezed her hand and stood. "I'll give you a minute."

Kendall sat and regarded her grandmother's bedroom, barely registering Gabe's departure. She'd thought that she could just come in here, catalog everything, and ship it off to California. She'd thought she could keep her feelings completely separate, make this whole trip transactional, but now she knew that had always been impossible. Here in this house, in this town, she was being confronted by a past she knew nothing about.

She rose from the bed and went back to the closet, then opened the top drawer that held the jewelry. She ran her fingers over the rows of earrings and necklaces and rings until they touched a simple piece, obviously antique, possibly less valuable than the rest. It certainly showed more wear than the others. The gold band held a cushion-cut aquamarine, and there was an inexplicable familiarity to it, even though there was no way she could possibly remember it. She removed it from its velvet cushion and slid it onto her right ring finger. A perfect fit.

All this time she had been fooling herself. She would never be able to move on until she knew the truth.

Chapter Seventeen

After Kendall parted ways with Gabe, she went back to the B and B, a mission forming in the back of her mind. Gabe had said his grandmother was closer to Connie than his grandfather, but surely Mr. Brandt would know *something*. He hadn't been particularly forthcoming thus far, but she didn't know if that was his regular demeanor or if he was being especially closemouthed to her.

When she arrived at the house, though, the innkeeper was nowhere to be found. Kendall pushed down her disappointment and returned to her room. She had a few more hours to kill until she was supposed to meet Delia and her friends, so she plopped cross-legged on the comfortable bed and opened her laptop. There were still images to download from her phone, furniture to research, and a moving truck to schedule. Regardless of how things panned out with Phil Burton, she was going to have to empty the houses. She might as well do it sooner than later. Though with the amount of furniture she was sending back, she might need to have Sophie rent another storage unit. She doubted that even half of it would fit in the twenty-by-twenty space they maintained for stock, and that didn't count her purchases from Europe that had yet to arrive via sea freight.

But instead of doing any of those things, she found herself flipping through the photos that Sophie had uploaded of the Woolridge House. This was truly an impressive get for a designer, and they'd come to her specifically. Why? There were any number of designers in the Los Angeles area that would be ready and willing to take on the project, many of them with longer careers and better reputations than her. But as she clicked from one photo to another, making note of all the original pieces that were missing, all of the restoration work that needed to be done, she understood. There were designers who could work within the Arts and Crafts style, but she had built her reputation on finding authentic and verifiable furniture and millwork for full restorations. She was less of a designer than she was a historian and plastic surgeon and detective, discovering and fixing what time had ravaged.

If she was really so good at this, she should be able to discover the truth about her past without any problem. Or at the very least, she could discover the truth about her houses. Gabe had said that many of the historical society's records had been damaged in the flood, but he hadn't said all . . . and if she recalled correctly, she had passed their offices somewhere while walking through town. Where was that?

208

Kendall pulled up the town website and searched the listings until she found *Jasper Lake Historical Society*. If she was reading the map right, it was only three blocks north and half a block east, situated in a historic home. She pushed the laptop aside, pulled on her boots and jacket, and grabbed her purse, filled with new determination.

Somehow, when she stepped outside again, it felt like the temperature had dropped a full ten degrees, lending a bite to the cold that stung her skin and seared her lungs, even if the sky was as bright blue and clear as ever. She tugged her gloves out of a pocket and slithered her hands into them. No, it was definitely colder. Must be a front coming in.

By the time she made it to the historical society, she was thoroughly chilled. She walked up the front steps of the old Victorian structure, stamping her feet to get the blood circulating again, and tried the door handle. It opened easily and deposited her into a large, open room, its walls completely lined with bookshelves.

Heated air enveloped her immediately, and she took a moment to luxuriate in the warmth. She peeled off her gloves. "Hello? Is anyone here?"

Footsteps sounded on the wood floor in the back, coming closer until a small elderly man appeared, his back stooped but his eyes bright and sparkling. "Well, hello, dear. What can I do for you?"

Kendall smiled, taking an immediate liking to him. "I'm Kendall Green."

He took his glasses from the chain around his neck and propped them on his nose, blinking. "Why, yes, yes, you are. I'm Patrick O'Neill."

Kendall chuckled. "It's a pleasure to meet you, Mr. O'Neill. I was hoping you might have some information about the houses on Lakeshore. I've inherited them, but I know almost nothing about them."

He tsked and shuffled over to one of the bookshelves. "I'm afraid that I can't help you much there, my dear. Gabriel Brandt was in here looking for the same thing not long ago, and we turned up very little. But I will show you what I showed him." He ran a finger over the leather-bound spines of several thick volumes, pulled out first one and then another, and took them over to an oak desk in front of the window.

Kendall followed him. She paused at the man's shoulder while he flipped the first book open and then followed the columns of spidery writing down with a shaky finger. They appeared to be tax rolls from the late 1800s, which was the first place anyone started when looking for the history of a house this old. Details might be lost, people might pass on, but tax records were forever.

Each line had a date, an address, and a name,

followed by the figure. In this case, the line that Patrick pointed to stated, *1-5 Lakeshore Drive, J. Green.*

She'd been right about all five houses being owned by the same person, at least. And then it sank in. "Green? Who is this J. Green?" The name was common, but surely it wasn't a coincidence.

"That's about as far as Gabe got as well." Patrick leaned against the table and turned to face her. "Constance always said those houses have family significance, so it's entirely plausible that he was an ancestor of yours."

The sharp eyes bored into hers; the man didn't miss much. She glanced back at the book and then at him. "Are there any other tax records for those houses besides J. Green?"

"Yes," he said. "But I'm not sure they're going to help you." He went back to the shelves and, after a moment of thought, took three more volumes down. "I personally knew the owners and the houses had passed through several hands. Unrelated to the Green family. Anything after 1960 is digitized and stored at the county courthouse."

Which potentially meant another trip to Georgetown. Still, she stood by while he found the past records in the book and took photos of them with her phone. She could always track down the families of the early owners and see if they knew anything about the houses. For a moment, she wondered why she was even bothering, but the answer came to her immediately. Gabe.

He had dropped everything to help her, even when she wasn't going along with his plan, even when he had bigger things to accomplish. The least she could do was put her detective skills to work on his behalf.

She was about to thank Mr. O'Neill and leave when something else occurred to her. "I don't suppose you keep copies of the county high school yearbooks, do you?"

Understanding sparked in his eyes. "Ah. No. Unfortunately not. But the high school does. You would just have to call there and make an appointment."

She nodded, trying not to show her disappointment. "Okay. I understand. Thank you for your help."

"It's my pleasure, Kendall. I hope you find what you're looking for."

Kendall smiled, but it was with reluctance that she stepped back out onto the porch of the house. Part of it had to do with how little information she had turned up; the larger part had to do with the cold that hit her, even more bitter for the contrast to the warmth inside. She glanced at her watch. It was still barely two o'clock. She wasn't supposed to meet the girls for dinner until six. She could go back to the B and B and see if Mr. Brandt was back, find out what he really knew.

Or she could walk around town. This was a small town and everyone knew everything about everybody. Surely she could turn up some dirt if she worked hard enough.

She turned her steps toward Main Street, looking at it with a new eye. She had thought it quaint and charming in an abstract sort of way, but every shop and store and restaurant represented a person who lived and worked here, whose livelihood depended on both tourism and local traffic. Were Gabe's plans really in the town's best interest? If they had elected him on a "Save Jasper Lake" platform, that had to mean they agreed with the halt to development and the preservation of their way of life. But sometimes what people wanted wasn't really what they needed. Tourism would bring a much-needed influx of cash.

And then she thought of people like Delia, who had moved from Denver to make a quieter life, probably on a shoestring budget. If the town grew, that meant rents would rise, as would property taxes. Soon, the cost of land and commercial space would outstrip what some of these business owners could afford, especially considering that while income was seasonal, rents were not. She had to believe that they knew what they needed better than some outsider like her or Phil Burton.

The first place she came to was the boat and snowmobile rental, housed in a log cabin–like structure, a few boats on racks, several snow-mobiles chained to trailers. Probably the last place she would voluntarily visit, but that didn't mean she should avoid it now. She pushed through the door with a jingle of harness bells, and a man came from the back, his expression quizzical. "Hi. Can I help you?"

Maybe business wasn't all that good if a potential customer was met with surprise. Or maybe everyone just already knew who she was. "Hi. I, um . . ." Now that she had to explain her presence, she realized that *I just hoped I could pump you for information* wasn't the best opening line.

His expression softened. "You must be Kendall Green. I'm Bruce McKay." He held out a hand, and Kendall shook it, silently blessing him for his kindness.

"I don't really need a boat," she said with a smile. "I'm just trying to get to know the town." She studied him. He was probably in his late forties, which meant he must be about the same age as her mother. "You lived here long?"

"Born and raised right here in Jasper Lake." He paused. "I went to school with your mom."

She blinked at him, feeling suddenly dizzy. "Really?"

Her unsteadiness must have shown on her face because he pulled a stool out from behind the counter and gestured for her to sit. "Yeah. I have to admit, I had the biggest crush on her. I was . . . oh, we must have been about twelve. In fact, I think Carrie might have been my very first crush."

"What was she like?" Kendall couldn't stop the words from coming out, even though she was asking about someone he hadn't seen in almost thirty years.

He smiled gently. "She was fun. Pretty. I think I asked her to marry me."

Kendall chuckled. "I'm assuming she turned you down."

"If I recall, she told me she was flattered, but she knew there were other girls who had a crush on me and she wouldn't want to disappoint them. She was kind that way. Didn't want to flatten my young ego by telling me we were both just kids. We were friends through high school, though. I missed her when she left."

"When she left town?"

"When she left school. You know, got pregnant and started showing."

"Right." It was the same story she'd heard her first night in Jasper Lake. In some weird way, that meant Bruce had known Kendall when she was a fetus. Which probably meant that her mom wasn't the only one he knew. "Did she have a boyfriend?"

He looked at her oddly, like he was surprised she hadn't already figured this out. "Yeah. She was dating Daniel Burton."

Daniel Burton. *Burton.* "As in Phil Burton?"

"Yeah. Dan was Phil's younger brother."

Whoa. If Kendall had not already been sitting down, she would be searching for a chair right now. "So . . . Phil Burton is my . . . uncle?"

Bruce shifted uncomfortably. "No one really knows. There were rumors that Dan wasn't the only boy she was seeing. Was it true? Or was it just people being malicious because of her situation? Only Carrie could answer that. I do know that Dan had a football scholarship waiting for him at CSU, and he wouldn't have let anything jeopardize that."

Kendall took a deep breath in through her nose and let it out in a whoosh. So either her mom had been promiscuous and didn't know who Kendall's father was, or her boyfriend had been selfish and abandoned them to pursue his college football career. "What happened to Dan? Where is he now?"

"Died in a car wreck not long after your mother left. They said he'd been drinking. Sad. Waste of a promising life."

"Does everyone know all this?"

Bruce shrugged, once again uncomfortable. "Hard to tell what people remember. It was a big deal at the time, to hear that someone we went to school with had died. I'm not sure how much the gossip spread beyond the high school."

"But Phil Burton would know that his brother

had dated my mother. That he could potentially be my uncle."

"Oh yeah. He would know that."

A seething anger boiled up inside her and she hopped off the stool. "Thank you, Bruce. You've been more helpful than you know."

"Sure." He paused. "So are you just visiting or are you here to stay?"

"Just visiting," she said. "Thanks again."

He nodded, and she turned. When she had almost reached the door, he called, "Don't miss the bonfire tomorrow. Everyone is going to be there."

Whether he was just trying to be friendly or giving her a hint that she'd have better luck digging up information at the gathering, she didn't know. She just nodded and waved and stepped out into the cold.

And felt her breath vaporize in a way that had nothing to do with the windchill.

Burton knew that he might be her uncle. Maybe he cared as little as his brother, maybe he didn't want her to take advantage of a personal connection, or maybe he was waiting to spring that on her later. But whatever his purpose, it gave her one more good reason to dislike him.

And one more reason to make sure that whatever happened, those properties didn't fall into his hands.

Chapter Eighteen

After Bruce's revelation, Kendall had lost her will to question the rest of the store owners, so she went back to the B and B and took advantage of the en suite bathroom's impressive claw-foot tub. She sank deep into warm, lavender-scented water, courtesy of the bath salts in a glass jar on the shelf, and tried to forget everything she'd just learned. But the thoughts kept coming.

Her mother's boyfriend had let Carrie look like the town slut to shirk his responsibility. His brother pretended that he didn't know who Kendall was so he could take advantage of her.

No matter who they were, no one wanted anything to do with her.

Hot tears slid down her face, and she swiped them away quickly with a wet hand, diluting them with lavender-scented droplets so she could believe it was just a splash of bathwater on her face. She couldn't let this place get to her. She needed to stay strong, finish what she started, get home to her life in California. Her friend and design partner. The Woolridge House. It was all waiting for her.

But sitting there, submerged in the bath, Kendall couldn't even articulate what she needed to accomplish here. On one hand, she'd already cataloged the contents of Connie's house. She could arrange for a truck to arrive and pack things up as early as next week, put the houses on the market for a punishing rate, and let Burton decide whether it was worth it to pay her price. But then it was likely she wouldn't get any money at all, and they'd be back to scrambling to pay their increased monthly rent on the Pasadena house.

It also meant that she would be leaving Gabe to his own devices to save the town.

"So what?" she mumbled, her voice defiant in the silence. "I don't have any responsibility here."

But Gabe had no personal responsibility to her; in fact, he had every reason to see her as the enemy, and yet he was still sacrificing his time and his effort to help her.

And there was that little bloom of warmth in her chest whenever he took her hand that was impossible to deny.

She liked him and she didn't want to see him fail.

"Ugh." She slid down into the bathtub until she was fully submerged and held her breath as long as she could, hoping for some clarity in the echoey expanse of water. When she rose spluttering a minute later, she had made no more sense of her feelings than before; she'd only dissolved her mascara into tracks down her cheeks.

"Fine, fine," she said to no one in particular. She levered herself out of the tub, splashing water onto the antique tiles, and reached for the towel waiting on the warmer. She still had way too much time before she met Delia, but her long, thick hair would take an hour to blow out, so she wrapped herself in the fluffy towel and reached for the hairdryer in a basket beneath the pedestal sink. She took extra care drying it straight and smooth, then turned her attention to her makeup.

Finally, at a quarter to six, she pulled on her jacket and boots and headed out the door, but she was still shocked by how cold the air felt now that the sun had gone down. It was easy to underestimate how much the sunlight contributed to warmth at this altitude until it was gone, and she was shivering before she even made it down the B and B's front steps. She picked up her pace onto Main Street, hoping she would warm up, but the whip of wind around the buildings and through breezeways on each block chilled her to the bone every time she thought she was finally getting warm.

Even so, Kendall could admit how pretty the town looked at night. Old-fashioned streetlamps cast a yellow glow on the buildings, and every time she passed a gap between them, she could see the reflection of the moon on the shimmering lake. She came to the park next, saw the wood piled in the center of a cement-block pit, waiting for tomorrow night's bonfire. Long strings of huge white bulbs swayed between poles and trees and streetlamps, making the sky overhead twinkle like a cloud of dancing fireflies. Finally she glimpsed the Pine View Cantina ahead, warmth and light and voices spilling out through the open door.

She slipped inside, the combined heat of a hundred bodies immediately taking the chill off her. It looked like every single person in town had come tonight, and she was at a loss for how she was going to locate Delia in this madhouse.

And then she heard someone call her name. From a corner booth, Delia waved wildly to get her attention. "Over here, Kendall!"

Kendall made her way slowly through the crush to where Delia sat with four women between twenty and forty, all dressed similarly to her in jeans and vests or puffy jackets.

Delia extracted herself from the table and gave her a hug in greeting. "I'm so glad you made it. Let me introduce you."

The first two were about Kendall's age. Rebecca was a pretty brunette with a flashy manicure and her name on a pendant in gold script. Delia told her that Rebecca owned the gift shop at the end of the street. Next came petite, blonde Eliza—"call me Liz"—who worked as

221

a backcountry backpacking guide when she wasn't pregnant, which she most definitely was now. The other two spanned the opposite ends of the age spectrum: Allison, a twentysomething with pink-tipped hair, was doing her master's degree in social work online while picking up extra shifts here at the cantina as a waitress. And Dawnice, a statuesque beauty who had to be in her early forties, volunteered that she was working on her first novel in Jasper Lake while her husband taught science at the county high school.

There couldn't have been a more disparate group of women, but they all seemed to know each other well, and now they smiled at Kendall warmly. Dawnice scooted over to make room for her next to Delia, and Kendall sat down, feeling equal parts awkward and welcomed. "What's with the crowd?" she asked, looking around. There were people eating dinner, but there seemed to be just as many milling about with drinks in their hands.

"Live music," Delia said. "The Hometown Heroes."

"Now that everyone's here, we can eat." Liz stood and waved to a server, who waved back in a harried fashion. She rubbed her expanded belly and sat back down with a sigh. "I'm starving. I swear this baby sucks every last calorie out of my body."

"Don't be like me," Dawnice said. "I gained forty pounds when I was pregnant with Jaden, and it took me two years to get rid of it. It's nice now, but you regret it later on."

Kendall looked among the women. "Do you all have kids?"

"Just me," Dawnice said, "and of course Liz is about to. The only ones who aren't married are Rebecca and Delia . . . and you, of course. At least I assume you aren't?"

"No, I'm single," Kendall said. A few of the women exchanged glances, and Kendall frowned. She was about to ask what she was missing when the server finally made her way over to their table. Up close, she recognized Julie, who had waited on her and Gabe the first night, but she showed no special sign of recognition. "What can I get you girls?"

Delia ordered something ominously called the Mother Lode to share, and then they ordered cocktails and beers—nonalcoholic for Liz, of course. Kendall looked around the table, struck unusually dumb by the gathering. She'd always prided herself on being personable and comfortable with strangers, but that was usually in a business situation or with men she met in a social setting. This kind of girl gathering was new and entirely unfamiliar. She suddenly had the overwhelming feeling of being an outsider in a place she wasn't sure she wanted to be inside.

Allison leaned across her folded hands and focused with laser precision on Kendall. "So, Kendall, what do you do?"

"I'm an interior designer," she said. "I own a design firm in Southern California."

"Oh, that sounds interesting!" Dawnice exclaimed beside her. "How did you get to do that? It always sounds like a dream job, but I don't know how you get from wishing for it to actually doing it."

Kendall opened her mouth to give her usual short-and-sweet prepared answer, but the curiosity in the women's faces seemed genuine, and she found herself telling them the whole story: how she had needed a job when she moved out at eighteen—she left out the part about aging out of the foster system—and found it as the receptionist at a design school. "I really had nothing else to do but go home to a tragic—and I do mean tragic—shared apartment, so I started auditing classes. Somehow, one of my professors took notice of me and recommended an internship with one of his friends, a well-known interior designer in Santa Barbara. Joseph taught me almost everything I know and gave me the opportunity to work on some projects of my own. When I was ready, I opened my own firm, and the rest is history."

"That's amazing," Delia said. "Sounds like God had it all planned out for you."

"I don't know about God," Kendall said, "but it worked out in the end."

Delia smiled in response, but Kendall caught the looks passed between the ladies and realized her misstep. Oh. She always thought of Colorado as so liberal and progressive; she hadn't realized that she'd stumbled into the middle of a bunch of church people here in Jasper Lake.

But so far they'd been nothing but nice to her, so she swallowed down her discomfort and turned the question back on Allison. "Social work. That's a pretty intense field. How did you choose that?"

"I had my own fairly traumatic experiences with child welfare when I was younger. I grew up really poor—falling-down-cabin poor—and for a while, I got taken away from my mom and put in foster care. But we happened to get lucky and had a really good social worker who was dedicated to reuniting me with my family. I know it doesn't work that way all the time, and now that I'm older, I recognize the challenges that social workers have in an overcrowded system, but I realized the impact a single person can have. I wouldn't be here had she not gotten my mom back on her feet and given her the tools to care for her kids, so I feel like I have a responsibility to do that for someone else."

"Wow." There was really nothing else Kendall could say in the face of that statement. Unlike some of the kids she'd met in foster care, she'd never really blamed the social workers. Even as a young girl, she realized that they had an impossible job with no real options. And most of the ones she'd dealt with were pretty decent people, even when the system got it wrong. If Allison wanted to try to survive in that world, more power to her. There was just a reason why no one in charge of Kendall had ever lasted more than two years.

"Yeah, so now that you've heard all about Saint Allison, go ahead and ask me why I made souvenirs my life's work," Rebecca quipped. The table laughed, obviously some kind of long-running joke, and Allison stuck out her tongue like a teenager.

Kendall grinned. "Why are souvenirs your life's work?"

"Because if I don't sell overpriced, ugly refrigerator magnets, who will?" Rebecca chuckled. "No, really, it used to be my parents' shop, and I took it over when they decided to leave snow behind and move to Arizona. I grew up in that shop. I couldn't stand to see it shut down."

"So what's your feeling about this resort they want to put in?" Kendall asked. "It seems like it would only help you."

But Rebecca didn't get a chance to answer, because all heads swiveled toward the stage, where several musicians were getting into place behind microphone stands and shrugging on guitar straps. She craned her neck to see the rest of the band, but she couldn't see past a large man in a puffy jacket.

Without introduction, the band started into the first song with a scratchy guitar and a sharp rap of drums, filling the tiny space with an explosion of sound. It took Kendall a second to place the song: early 2000s Maroon 5 . . . the only era of the band's music that she happened to like. A laugh spilled out of her mouth when she realized that the band's lead singer was Luke, the painfully good-looking web designer and welcome-wagon guy, and that he was actually really good. She leaned forward to see if she could glimpse the other band members. She didn't recognize the other guitarist or the bassist, but the drummer . . .

Her mouth dropped open. "No."

Dawnice grinned at her. "Oh yes."

Kendall clapped a hand over her mouth, a goofy grin spreading before she could control it. Sure enough, the man behind the drum kit was none other than Gabe Brandt, dressed in jeans and a faded T-shirt and looking like an absolute pro with sticks in his hands. She wanted to ask questions, but she found she couldn't look away from the band—from Gabe. The town mayor was a drummer in a cover band. It was so ridiculous and so perfectly right that she could do nothing but watch in giddy fascination until the end of the song.

When she broke into applause with the rest of the room and looked back to the girls, more than one of them was exchanging a knowing glance with another. "What? Was this a setup?"

"No," Delia said slowly, her voice thoughtful. "Definitely not a setup." But the way she studied Kendall made her once more feel like she was missing some important subtext.

The band started into the second song, which again took her a moment to recognize as Green Day—alt-punk in the Colorado high country? It gave her the chance to be awed at how ridiculously fast the drums were. What did you call that anyway? Drumming? Stick work? She'd never really paid attention to the details, but there was one thing for certain: Gabe could really *play*. She couldn't help but be impressed.

"I don't even know what to do with this," she announced to the table and was rewarded with a round of laughter.

That could have just as easily applied to the platter the size of a trash can lid that a different server placed in the center of their table, heaped high with bar favorites like potato skins, chicken wings, and mozzarella sticks. She took the small plate that Delia passed her and transferred some of the food to it.

The band cycled through some classics before

going to more recent hits, and while Kendall tried to follow the conversation flowing beneath the music, her eyes kept returning to the stage, where Gabe seemed to be having the time of his life. He was friendly and witty on a normal day, but there was an undercurrent of seriousness to him that had made her start to think maybe he was a little . . . dull. There was definitely nothing dull about performer Gabe. She suspected that blond god Luke with the unexpectedly fabulous voice and serious talent on the guitar got most of the attention, but she was far more interested in the endlessly energetic drummer.

Right.

She was interested in Gabe.

For more than just friendship.

Kendall glanced at Delia, who was watching her with a knowing smile. "Seriously, though, this was the whole idea of the girls' night out, wasn't it?"

"Maybe a little." There was still something careful in her tone that made Kendall's stomach flutter inexplicably. "Mostly I thought you wouldn't want to spend your Friday night alone in a B and B, however comfortable it might be."

Kendall flushed, embarrassed that she'd read so much into a friendly invitation, and glanced back at the stage, which didn't help the warmth in her cheeks. She couldn't help but see Gabe in an entirely different light now, and it wasn't because she had a thing for musicians—she was maybe the one woman on the planet who as a rule didn't. It was just that watching him do something he really loved purely for fun reminded her that maybe he wasn't all about business and saving the town. And if he wasn't, maybe she wasn't either.

Maybe *they* weren't.

The band finally went on break, and true to her prediction, it was Luke who was immediately approached by two young women. The other guitarist and the bassist dispersed to what she assumed were wives or girlfriends, but Gabe stood and scanned the crowd for a minute. Surprise registered on his face, and he wove his way toward their table.

"Hey." He addressed the whole table, but his eyes were firmly fixed on Kendall. The women knew it too, because they kept quiet and let Kendall do the talking.

"Hi," she said. "Why didn't you tell me you were playing tonight?"

He ran a hand through his hair and winced. "I don't know. Thought maybe you'd think the cover band was lame. We have fun, though." He glanced at the other women as if just realizing they were present. "Did you guys enjoy the first set?"

Allison responded. "Of course. You guys are always good. Can you play some P!nk on the next set?" She grinned and tugged the ends of her hair.

"I think there might be some on the set list, given prior requests." He grinned at Allison before his eyes traveled back to Kendall. "Can I get you a drink? I'm going to grab a soda before we go back up there."

"Um, sure. But I can get it myself."

Delia slid out of the booth to let her out, and Kendall straightened her sweater self-consciously. She'd spent the last several days with this guy, so why did she suddenly feel awkward? She started to follow Gabe through the crowd to the bar, but when she cast a look back at the table, Dawnice flashed her a thumbs-up. Kendall shook her head with a low laugh.

"So this is where you tell me how impressed you are, right?" Gabe waggled his eyebrows and grinned at her while they waited for the bartender to get to them.

"I would've before you went fishing for compliments. But now I don't think your ego needs any more help."

"Harsh. But probably fair." He glanced back at the table. "Seriously, though, are you having fun? When I ran into Delia, she told me she'd invited you to go out with them, and I thought it was a great idea. They're all nice women and they're smart. Seemed like your type of people."

"Why, Gabe Brandt, was that a compliment?"

231

She fluttered her lashes at him. She hadn't even been drinking that much, but she felt suddenly light and flirtatious.

"I think it might have been." He caught the eye of the bartender, who came over immediately. "A Coke for me and . . ."

". . . sparkling water." She shrugged. "One beer is kind of my limit. And I already stuffed myself with appetizers."

"The Mother Lode," Gabe groaned. "You'll all need a wheelbarrow to leave. It's killer."

It dawned on Kendall that they were making inane small talk like they'd just met, rather than having shared some very personal information about themselves already. But it was like the change in venue—the change in perspective—had landed them in new territory, and she was struggling to find her footing. Should she flirt? Should she bring up business? Should she—?

"Oops. I'm being summoned." Gabe nodded toward the stage, where Luke and the bassist were already taking their places again. He took his Coke from the bartender. "I have to get back up there. I understand if you don't want to stay the whole time. I mean, you're welcome to . . . but don't feel obligated to stay on my account." He seemed to realize that he was babbling, so he took a quick drink of his Coke and cocked his head back toward the stage. "I'm going to go now."

Kendall watched him leave, a smile spreading over her face. The oh-so-smooth and collected mayor seemed to have gotten tongue-tied over her. At least she wasn't the only one thrown by the change of venue. She took her sparkling water and made her way back to the booth.

Delia slid over to make room for her again, but no one said anything, just beamed knowing grins her direction.

"There's really no way I can play this cool, can I?"

"Nope," Rebecca said. "The pheromones are just all over the place tonight."

Kendall felt heat touch her cheeks, but she laughed anyway and gestured for Delia to pass her plate. The coffee shop owner bumped her shoulder in a show of solidarity, and Kendall felt a real glow of warmth in response. She hardly knew these women, but they were clearly rooting for her happiness. And for the first time in a long time, she could imagine what it would be like to have friends.

Chapter Nineteen

Considering how much Gabe struggled to keep his mind on his drumming for the rest of the evening, it was good that they'd started with the most demanding songs. He could sustain a simple rock beat without really thinking about it—a lifesaver given his eyes' temptation to constantly drift to the corner table where Kendall sat with her new group of friends. He could see them chatting beneath the music, or at least the other women were. Every time his eyes landed on Kendall, she was watching him.

Which did pretty much nothing for his concentration.

When he totally zoned out, missed a fill, and fumbled the transition to the chorus on the next song, causing Luke to turn and fix him with a pointed stare, he yanked his head back into the game and finished out the set without another mistake. By the way he was acting, you'd think he was a lovesick high schooler, distracted by his crush in the front row. Which couldn't be further from the truth.

She was in the back booth.

He grinned at the thought and dropped his sticks into his bag, then began to tear down his kit while his fellow band members did the same with their amps, mike stands, and cabling. Luke stopped in front of him while he was disassembling his hi-hat. "I would ask what that was all about, but it's not too hard to figure out."

"Sorry, man. I got distracted." Gabe glanced over to the back table, where the ladies were standing and gathering their coats. He'd given Kendall the option to bail without judgment, but she'd stayed. Was she waiting for him?

"Yeah, I'd say so." Luke nudged Gabe with his elbow and turned to return his guitar to its hard case, shaking his head and muttering about women the whole time. Right. Because he didn't enjoy having women of all ages hanging off him when he played. Not that Luke ever followed through on any of the flirting, for reasons that Gabe could only guess. Guys didn't talk about that kind of thing like girls did. Well, girls other than Kendall. He'd be willing to bet that in the two hours she'd been sitting with Delia and her friends, they'd probably only gotten the barest biographical information out of her.

He was just getting the final piece—the bass drum—zipped up in its canvas cover when a voice came behind him. "Hey."

He whipped his head around to find Kendall standing there, her hands tucked in her coat's pockets. "Hi. You stayed."

"Thought you could walk me home, but I

forgot about your equipment." She nodded to the stack of canvas-encased drums. "All earlier jokes aside, you were really good tonight. Except for that one hiccup."

"You noticed that, huh?"

Kendall grinned. "It's okay. Keeps you humble. Makes you seem like a real person and not a rock god."

Gabe laughed. "I may be many things, but a rock god is not one of them."

"Tell that to your admirers. I didn't think there were so many single women in this town, but it looks like every one of them turned out tonight."

Gabe was about to tell her that had nothing to do with him, but she was already backing away, about to make her exit. He called after her. "It's gotten really cold outside. If you can stick around for a few minutes, I'll drop you at the B and B on my way home."

"Don't go to any trouble. It's only a couple of blocks."

"It's below freezing out there. It's no trouble."

Kendall looked like she was wavering, but her California blood won out and she gave a single nod. "I'll go wait over there, then."

Gabe finished as quickly as he could, then began taking the drums out to his pickup truck, which was fortunately parked just across the street. When he finished with the last one and searched the room, Kendall was engaged in an animated conversation with Luke at the back of the cantina.

Luke waved him over. "Gabe! Kendall was just telling me you hadn't invited her to the bonfire yet."

Kendall turned as well, a glint of mischief in her eyes. "Some mayor you are. I had to hear about it from Bruce."

The bonfire. Right. He'd been so focused on other things, he hadn't even thought about it. They'd started planning for the Pumpkin Festival so long ago, it felt like something that had been over and done with for months rather than still out before him. "You're right. I am shirking my duties. Good thing I have Welcome Wagon Luke to fill in for me."

Luke sent him a murderous glance at the nickname some of the ladies in town had given him, then switched to a smile for Kendall. "And on that note, I will take my leave. Hope to see you two there tomorrow."

Now it was Gabe's turn to shoot a look at Luke for his obvious assumptions, but his friend grinned back in a way that said it had been purposeful. Gabe turned to Kendall instead. "Ready to go?"

"Sure. Thanks."

The cab of Gabe's truck was nearly as cold as the outside air, so as soon as he started it up with a reluctant rumble, he flipped the heater to high. "Looks like there's some snow in the forecast for Sunday morning."

"Really?" Kendall sounded as if she wasn't sure whether to be excited or apprehensive.

"You grew up in Colorado, so it's probably not a big deal to you . . ."

"I haven't been here in a lot of years. If I'm honest, it's maybe the one thing that I miss about my childhood."

Gabe backed out of the parking spot and then turned the truck toward his grandfather's B and B. He knew he shouldn't pry, but he couldn't stop himself. "Was it really that terrible? I'm not judging; I just want to know."

Kendall stayed quiet for a long moment. "It wasn't terrible. Not at the end. I was actually pretty lucky that my last foster parents were great people. But they weren't my blood, you know? And I'm not sure that's something you ever fully get over. It's one thing if your parents die, like in a car accident or something. It's out of their control. They would never have chosen to leave. But in my case, it seems like neither my dad or my mom wanted me, so . . ." She shrugged, her voice trailing off into the silence.

Gabe dared another glance at her, half-expecting to see tears sliding down her face, but she was completely dry-eyed. Matter-of-fact, even. As if that was a conclusion she'd come to long ago and it had become such a part of her that she never questioned it.

"I'm not sure that's true," he said finally. "People make bad decisions when they're desperate or afraid. But I doubt it was because they didn't want you. You know, it was the nineties. She could have had an abortion had that been true."

"Not wanting to kill her baby is different than wanting to raise it," Kendall said flatly, and there was nothing Gabe could say to argue with that. His own father could have pushed for an abortion to keep his affair a secret, but he didn't. Instead he just chose to deny his paternity. Gabe couldn't say that had made him feel any more wanted.

He was about to apologize for prying when Kendall changed the subject. "So. This bonfire festival thing tomorrow . . ."

"Yes?"

She glanced at him, a smile playing over her lips. "Were you going to invite me to go with you or what?"

Gabe chuckled, though part of him was thrown by her lightning-fast change of mood. "Would you like to go with me?"

Now it turned into a full-fledged smile. "I thought you'd never ask."

"I've got some things I need to do first to get ready, but I can come by and pick you up at six . . ."

"No need. I'll meet you there. I'm going to go to the house tomorrow and get a few more things done. In a town this small, you shouldn't be too hard to find."

They'd arrived at the B and B, so Gabe pulled up to the curb and, because it was so late, immediately turned off the engine. Silence fell around them. "I'll see you tomorrow then. Dress warm . . ."

"I will. See you later." She reached for the door handle, and the glint of the streetlight caught the stone in a ring on her right hand, one he was sure he hadn't seen in the days he'd spent with her. But before he could get more than a brief glimpse, she was out of the truck and on her way up the sidewalk.

And not for the first time, he had the feeling that no matter how much time he spent around Kendall, he was never going to know what she was actually thinking.

Kendall slept deeply and awoke the next morning, disoriented once more. It took several seconds for her to realize she wasn't lying in her bed back in Pasadena but in a rented room in the high country of Colorado. She rolled over and checked the digital clock, which showed nine. She frowned at the dim light filtering through the window. Every day this week, she'd been blinded by sunshine before eight. She pushed back the covers and padded to the bay window, where she drew back the curtains. She was greeted by a steel-gray sky and patches of fog clinging to the trees. She was about to back away when she blinked and went for a closer look. Was that *snow?*

A smile spread across her lips. Snow. She might have played it cool last night when Gabe mentioned the forecast, but her inner five-year-old had been practically giddy. Ten years in California had apparently made her appreciate what she no longer had, even if she didn't exactly miss the cold.

For a wild moment, she thought about rustling up a sled or a trash can lid, but her pragmatism just as quickly shut that idea down. It wasn't *snow* snow yet, just a few bare flakes drifting from the sky. And based on experience, she knew that these kinds of clouds rarely produced significant accumulation, certainly not enough to sled on. Besides, she needed to get out to the house and go through those boxes of paperwork. She'd considered bringing them back to the B and B, but most of them were probably related to the house and she'd just have to return them. Besides, she wasn't sure she wanted the past to invade the pleasant cocoon the B and B had become.

She debated getting ready for the bonfire now, but surely she'd be back in time to put on some makeup and curl her hair. Instead, she braided her hair into one long plait down her back, washed her face, and began to layer on clothing that would keep her warm in the frigid house. Fortunately, she'd picked up a pair of thermals before she left, so she slipped on the merino base layers beneath her jeans and the fuzzy ivory sweater from the other day. Over that went her puffy jacket and a scarf, then a pair of warm wool socks and boots. She glanced at herself in the mirror and started laughing. She looked like she was ready to brave the Arctic rather than a few pathetic snowflakes.

She was on her way out the door before she changed her mind and poked her head into the kitchen. Mr. Brandt was there, kneading a huge lump of dough on the floured surface of his marble countertop. He looked up in surprise at Kendall's appearance. "Good morning. Did you want breakfast? I assumed . . ."

Kendall shook her head. "No thank you. I'll pick up coffee in town. I was just wondering if you had a lantern I could borrow. I'm headed over to the house today, and it's pretty dark outside. It'll be hard to sort through paperwork without electricity."

"I'm sure I have something," Mr. Brandt said. "Give me just a minute to finish this knead and I'll go look for you." He gestured across the counter with a floury hand. "You can have a seat if you like."

Kendall perched on the edge of the stool and watched as the innkeeper divided the dough into uniform portions with a bench scraper, then formed them into smooth, grapefruit-size balls. "What kind of bread are you making?"

"Challah. Makes great French toast."

"Mmm. My favorite," Kendall said, her stomach rumbling in response. "You know, your baked goods go pretty fast at Main Street Mocha. If you go in at the end of the day, the case is usually empty."

Mr. Brandt looked pleased at the comment. "How's it going over at the house?"

"Pretty good. Gabe has been a big help in finishing the inventory."

"Has he now?"

Kendall couldn't tell if he was surprised, displeased, or just making conversation, so she moved on. "He has. All that's left is a bunch of paperwork."

"I would imagine you'll find some of the things you need for the houses, the deed and such."

Now that comment was definitely leading. Kendall seized her opportunity. "Gabe said Connie and your wife were close. Did you know her well?"

Mr. Brandt began transferring the dough to separate baking sheets and covered each with a thin cloth. "Not as well as Greta. Connie was a private person. Don't get me wrong; she was outgoing, and she served her community. But as to what was actually going on in her head? It was always hard to tell."

Kendall deflated. It seemed like no one could give her any insight into her grandmother. If Gabe and his grandmother had spent so much time at the Lakeshore house and the family couldn't tell her anything, what were the chances she'd ever uncover the truth?

"Of course, you really couldn't blame her for being private after what happened."

Kendall's attention piqued. "Oh? What do you mean?"

"Her husband. It was a huge scandal. Even now it feels wrong to talk about it."

So this wasn't about her mother after all. It was still information, though. "I'm family. I probably should know."

Mr. Brandt swiveled away and put one baking sheet after another into his oven on separate racks. "Her husband left her."

That didn't sound too scandalous. Sad, yes, but things like that happened all the time.

"For a man."

Okay. That wasn't so common. Kendall was sure her eyebrows had climbed to her hairline. "What happened?"

"He moved out. Moved down to Boulder, if I recall. With the boyfriend." Mr. Brandt shrugged. "You have to remember this was nearly forty years ago. Everyone knew people were gay, but it was somewhat shocking to find that the man she'd had a child with, had lived with for almost a decade, was not who she though he was."

"As it would be for anyone now," Kendall pointed out.

"Well, I suppose that's true, but people are far more accepting now. Or at least they're not as surprised. Anyway, the town rallied around her and Carrie. The men helped Connie with things around the house that Jon used to do for her." Mr. Brandt paused and shook his head. "She and Carrie were so close. Two peas in a pod. They were rarely separated except when Carrie was in school."

This didn't fit the picture she'd formed of her mother's homelife. "Until my mother got pregnant, that is."

"That was shocking, yes, and not what Connie wanted for her daughter, but she stood behind Carrie's decision to keep the baby. To keep you."

"So why did she throw her out?"

"She didn't." Mr. Brandt frowned. "Whatever gave you that idea?"

Kendall searched her memory and found she couldn't come up with any specific incident. "I don't know. Why did she leave, then?"

Mr. Brandt wiped his hands and slid onto the stool beside Kendall. "I have no idea. And more importantly, neither did your grandmother. She was heartbroken. She called the police, but your mother was eighteen, so she didn't count as a runaway. She had just 'moved away.' Connie didn't know if she was alive or dead . . . You know how mothers can worry."

Kendall was tempted to say she didn't know, but it wasn't true. The one time she'd tried to run away from the Novaks' house, they'd found her at a local park with all her things in her backpack. Rather than shouting at her for her ingratitude, her foster mother had dropped to her knees and thrown her arms around Kendall while she sobbed with relief. It was the last time Kendall had ever run away.

"And then one year Connie got a Christmas card with a picture of you." Mr. Brandt thought. "You must have been three. So that would have been, what, 1994?"

"Ninety-five," Kendall whispered. "But she never heard anything else?"

"Not that I know of. Not then at least." Mr. Brandt laid a comforting hand on Kendall's shoulder. "Why don't I go look for that lantern?"

"Thanks," Kendall said, but inside, her mind was spinning. What if her grandmother had kept the card? What if there was some clue to where her mother had gone in the paperwork at the house?

Mr. Brandt came back from the pantry a minute later, holding a chunky plastic lantern with LED

246

bulbs. "I keep this for power outages. It should give you enough light to work by."

Kendall took it from him. "I appreciate it."

"Anytime. Coming to the bonfire tonight?"

"If it doesn't snow, yes."

Mr. Brandt craned his head to peer out the window. "Doesn't look like it's going to amount to much. Just a dusting."

Kendall smiled. Back home, they thought it was fall when the temperatures dipped below the eighties and a few of the trees started to change colors. It wasn't unusual for trick-or-treaters to swelter in their costumes on a one-hundred-degree Halloween. If Jasper Lake considered snowflakes a fall feature, Christmas must not be complete without full snowdrifts.

She drove to town but didn't linger any longer than it took to get her daily drink at Main Street Mocha—this time, the signature Latin Mocha, a dark chocolate coffee concoction with hints of cinnamon and a hefty kick from cayenne and chipotle pepper. She loaded her drink and scone back into her rental SUV and started the drive around the lake, anticipation building in her chest. Maybe the boxes of paperwork would hold the hints to her past that she'd been looking for.

Chapter Twenty

Three hours later, Kendall's optimism was beginning to flag. The banker's boxes had looked so small when she took them down and stacked them in the corner of the master bedroom. They hadn't even looked daunting when she flipped the lid open on the first. But that was before she realized that her grandmother had kept every single receipt for every single thing she'd purchased. It didn't help that Kendall found herself getting sucked into the things she found, especially when they related to the furnishings in the house. There were receipts from antique dealers for some of the older pieces, like the Craftsman cabinet and the Eames lounge chair, which turned out to be an original issue from 1956—the kind of provenance that would increase their value significantly. Others were far less interesting: triple-paned windows in 2005, repairs to the hardwood floors in the upstairs bathroom, a new furnace just ten years ago.

And yet no sign of any personal correspondence.

In fact, everything in the first two boxes save the furniture receipts was so prosaic it made her wonder why Connie Green had kept them in the first place.

She pushed aside the first two boxes on the antique rug and drew the third toward her. Maybe this would be the one. She lifted the box lid off and pulled out a file folder, hoping that she would find anything but receipts: birthday cards, family photos, handwritten letters. Heck, she would take printouts of emails, though she'd seen no evidence that Connie had owned a computer. She flipped the cover open.

Car insurance documents. From 2015.

Kendall sighed and let her chin fall forward onto her chest. Maybe she was expecting too much. She dropped the file folder on top of the box and pressed her fingertips to her eyes, then immediately regretted it. Her skin felt grimy from handling old papers, and there wasn't even any running water to wash her hands with.

Her pulse began to pound behind one eye, a reaction she recognized as stress. She took in a deep breath, held it, and then blew it out through her open mouth with a sigh that ended up sounding more like a foghorn. It was something her childhood therapist had taught her. When she got stressed, afraid, or frustrated, she stopped breathing. Inhaling and exhaling deliberately, even ridiculously, released the tension in her diaphragm and started unknotting the tense muscles in her face, chest, and back.

She was so focused on her loud exhalations that it took her a minute to zero in on the pounding coming from downstairs. She pushed herself to her feet and took the stairs down quickly, her brow furrowed. What in the world?

She yanked the front door open, letting in a whoosh of cold air and snowflakes. Gabe stood there on the front porch, bundled up, stamping his feet. Framed by a wall of white.

"Are you okay? Didn't you see the weather turn?"

Kendall wrenched her gaze away from Gabe to the near-whiteout conditions outside. "No! I've been upstairs with the heater and the lamp." She hadn't even thought to look out the window, too focused on her treasure hunt. She stepped aside to let him in and closed the door behind him. "How did you know I was here?"

"As soon as it was obvious that the storm had changed paths and was going to hit us head-on, I started calling the local businesses to let them know we were rescheduling the Pumpkin Festival for next weekend. Delia asked me if you knew, because you were coming out here. Why didn't you answer your phone?"

Kendall patted down her pockets until she found her cell in the inside pocket. The screen showed five missed calls and as many texts. "I'm sorry. It's on silent."

Gabe raked a hand through his hair, which she initially took as frustration with her but then realized was just a way to get all the snow out.

"Grab your stuff. You can leave your rental here and we'll get it later."

Kendall didn't waste time asking questions, nor did she stop to consider the warmth in her chest. Gabe had been worried about her, and when he couldn't get in touch with her, he'd driven all the way out here in the snow. She gathered her purse, turned off the heater, which she just now realized was only blowing air but not any actual heat—it must have run out of propane in the last few minutes—and grabbed the borrowed lamp. Downstairs, Gabe had his keys in his hand, shifting impatiently from foot to foot.

"Ready?" he asked brightly, but there was an undercurrent of tension in his voice that made her stomach give a little flip.

Kendall pulled her knit cap out of her pocket and tugged it down over her ears. "Ready."

Gabe grabbed her bare hand with his gloved one and helped her down the stairs, which were already covered in at least six inches of snow above a layer of ice. They slipped and slid down the walk to where Gabe's truck was parked, still running. She didn't protest when he helped her around to the passenger side before returning to the driver's side. She couldn't see anything through the layer of accumulated snow on the front windshield. "Are you sure we're going to be okay?"

Gabe turned on the windshield wipers and

double-checked that she was wearing her seat belt. "I've got snow tires, four-wheel drive, and a winch. The road conditions aren't really a problem. The issue is the visibility. But we'll try."

He pulled away from the curb and methodically made his way up the street and back to the highway turnoff. Kendall tried to look unconcerned, but the first time the tires slipped, she lunged for the grab handle and held on for dear life.

"This isn't so bad." Gabe's words were meant to be reassuring, but the tension in his voice said something entirely different. They were going five miles an hour while only seeing about twenty feet in front of them, slipping and sliding on the sheet of ice that had formed early when the snow was still melting on contact with the road. She checked the temperature and saw it had dropped from thirty degrees to only eighteen. He glanced at her. "You okay?"

"Eyes on the road," she gritted out, but it really didn't matter. From what she could tell, there was no road. Only the edge of the lake barely visible to the right of her told her they were going in the right direction. When they finally made it to the highway, her heart was pounding so hard she figured he could hear it over the growl of the diesel engine.

Then a horrible metallic scrape came from the

side of the truck. She whipped her head around, squinting to see outside. "What was that?"

Gabe grimaced and slowed. "Snow marker."

"Like those poles for the plow drivers?"

"Yeah." He peered out the window, thinking. "Okay, I'm calling it. We're going back."

"I thought that's what we were doing. Going back to town."

"Going back to the house."

Relief that they wouldn't have to brave the drive to town warred with anxiety over being snowbound with a virtual stranger. "But there's no heat or water. And my propane ran out right before you got there."

"Don't worry about that. I have supplies in my truck. The storm will blow out by tonight; if visibility improves, we might be able to get back this evening."

Kendall realized he was waiting for her agreement, though he was in charge and really didn't need it. She nodded. "Okay. If you think that's best."

"I do." Carefully, Gabe made a three-point turn until they were facing their tire tracks. The snow was already drifting across them, but they were deep enough that they could follow them all the way back to the house. He parked in front and left the truck running. "Keys? I'll bring the stuff in. You wait here where it's warm."

Kendall handed over the house keys wordlessly

and waited while he retrieved a backpack from the floorboards and a giant duffel bag from the back seat, then trudged up to the front door. The snow had only reached above their ankles when they left; now it was near his calf. That had to be what? Three inches an hour? This wasn't a storm; this was a monster blizzard.

A few minutes later, he reappeared and made his way to the truck. She had the ignition off and the keys out before he got the door open, not wanting to make him stand in the cold any longer than necessary. He helped her off the slippery running board to the equally slippery sidewalk and then up the front steps. "I put everything upstairs for now," he said. "It didn't make any sense to waste a warm room since you've been running the heater the whole day."

They stamped as much snow off their feet as they could before going up the stairs to Connie's bedroom. No, this wasn't awkward at all, stranded in her grandmother's bedroom with a random guy.

Except Gabe wasn't really random anymore.

The room was warm, helped along by the now-working heater. Gabe had hooked up a new propane bottle, but it was turned down low. "Just to keep the chill off. I've got two of these, but we need to conserve, in case we get stuck here overnight. I'm surprised the room didn't lose more heat while we were gone."

"Triple-paned windows," Kendall said. When he looked at her quizzically, she waved at the boxes. "And here I was thinking all those receipts were useless. If our survival ever depends on basic home improvement information, we're all set."

Gabriel chuckled. "I'm glad I had the foresight to stop and tell my grandfather before I came over." He opened the backpack and produced a large thermal carafe and a Tupperware container. "Coffee and fresh banana bread."

"Did you plan on having a picnic here before we went back?"

He threw her an amused glance. "No, I just figured I could distract you from road conditions with snacks."

"Probably true. Though I'm not sure it's really enough to get us through tomorrow. I'm a girl who enjoys three square meals, if you hadn't noticed. Well, two. I don't think anyone else counts coffee as a meal."

Gabe reached into his pack and pulled out two foil packets. "I've got us covered. That is, if you like chicken curry or Swedish meatballs."

"But we don't have any water."

Gabe sent a significant glance at the window, now completely white.

"Oh yeah. Right." She took a packet and flipped it over. "I guess this will be an adventure."

"An adventure with a fully stocked kitchen.

I looked in the pantry and there's still canned goods. I figured we'd be way more comfortable stuck here with real beds and some food."

"Good call." Her eyes widened as she realized something. "What about the bathroom? No water." She looked at the window. "I am *not* going out there."

"That's easy. Toilets will still flush if you have water. Doesn't have to come from the tank. Actually, I'll be right back." Gabe jumped up and disappeared. She heard him rummaging around in the kitchen, and then the back door opened and closed. A little while later, he reappeared in the doorway with two pails, both piled high with snow. He went to the attached master bathroom and set them down. "As soon as they melt, we can use the water for flushing and washing up and stuff."

Kendall stretched her legs out and leaned back against the edge of the bed. So far they'd both plopped on the floor as if not wanting to acknowledge the bed. The parlor would be far less awkward, but he was right. If they wanted to sleep tonight, they would be more comfortable with a bed, and heating more than one room was a waste of fuel.

"So." Gabe nodded toward the box. "What do you say we finish this up?"

Kendall waved a hand. "Be my guest. I've been through two of the three and they don't have anything interesting in them. I was hoping for something that would tell me what happened to my mom."

Gabe lifted the box's lid and took out the folder Kendall had left on top. "Insurance."

"Yeah, I saw that one."

He put it aside and started on the second one, seemingly absorbed in his search. Kendall watched him silently. She'd noticed he didn't shave very often, and the scruffy look suited him. His bright-blue eyes and fine features were almost too beautiful when he was clean-shaven. This way, in his down jacket with a heavy sweatshirt underneath and the boots she'd once thought were ridiculous overkill, he looked like the outdoorsman he actually was.

He felt her gaze on him. "What?"

"I was just thinking that you know a lot more about this survival stuff than I would have expected."

Gabe chuckled. "Just because I know you can flush a toilet by pouring water down it? That's kind of common knowledge, especially if you've ever traveled outside the western world."

"Have you? Traveled, I mean."

He put the papers aside. "Europe after college. Morocco. Thailand. Hong Kong. You?"

"I specialize in European antiques, so . . ."

"Right. Not much need to go anywhere else. Not even for fun though?"

"I've been working since I turned eighteen. I don't have time for fun."

He stopped. "That might be the saddest thing I've ever heard."

"Why? I like my work."

"Yeah, but life isn't all about work."

"It is when it's all you have."

Their eyes met and held, and Gabe's expression turned serious. "Kendall, what are you planning to do here?"

She swallowed and felt something inside her retreat. "About the houses? I really don't know. And don't look at me like that; I'm being honest."

"Come on, you can't tell me you don't see the charm of the place."

"Of course I do! I can see the charm of a lot of places. But that's not enough to throw away everything I've worked for. To you, this is home. To me, this is just the ghost of the past. A ghost that never wanted me to come back."

"Kendall, I know you've got a lot of hurt, but . . ."

His conciliatory tone was more than she could handle. She pushed herself to her feet. "I'm going downstairs to see what there is to eat. You've got a propane stove in that bag, right?"

He nodded and she held out her hand until he reluctantly produced a little case. She left the room, careful not to stomp her way down the stairs. That would be even more childish than

258

leaving the room so she didn't have to continue their conversation. The change in air temperature flowed over her as she descended. The kitchen was frigid, so she zipped up her coat and pulled on her hat and went to rummage through the pantry. Sure enough, there were several cans of soup that weren't even too far past their use-by date. As long as they weren't dented, they should be okay, right? Just to be sure, she left the clam chowder on the shelf and instead picked a beef stew and an Italian minestrone. The acid from the tomatoes should be enough to make sure they were good, or at least that's what she guessed. She'd never really needed to know.

It took a couple of minutes to set up the stove and figure out how to attach the propane bottle, but soon she had the beef stew bubbling in a small saucepan she'd found in the cabinet. Thank goodness she'd left all these things alone when she inventoried the kitchen. For the first time, she felt grateful for the house for reasons other than its value: it was a much better place to shelter in a snowstorm than a truck. Of course, if she didn't have the house, she wouldn't be out here in the first place, so that was a bit of a pointless thought.

The resigned look on Gabe's face was equally pointless to consider, but that wasn't as easy to dismiss. He'd really wanted to talk to her and she'd walked away from him. She didn't want to hear about how she should care about this town that had done nothing for her. But that wasn't really true, was it? Delia had been concerned about her. Gabe had come out all this way for her when she didn't answer the phone. Back home, there was no one who cared enough to look out for her like that. If Kendall didn't come home, Sophie would just assume that she'd met someone or she'd gone to an after-hours party or even taken a quick overnight trip to track down a piece of furniture. She might send a text, but she wouldn't go to any special trouble to find her.

And the worst part was, that wasn't even Sophie's fault. It was Kendall's. There was a time when Sophie had wanted that kind of relationship, thought they'd be BFFs, but Kendall had kept her at arm's length. Friendly, fun, but never deep. Kendall had talked more about herself and her past to Gabe in a week than she had in the seven years she'd known Sophie. Heck, she'd probably said more to the group of girls at the cantina last night than she had to her roommate and coworker.

Again, all her fault.

Because if you didn't let anyone in, you couldn't be hurt by rejection. You couldn't be disappointed. It was easier to be alone by your own choice than to have someone make that choice for you.

But the feeling when someone cared about

you? She hadn't felt that since her foster mother cried at finding her in that little run-down park.

Until now.

Kendall swiped a tear away and poured the now-bubbling soup into a big bowl, then put on the second can to heat.

She'd only known Gabe for less than a week, but he made her feel something she'd never felt with anyone else, whether they'd been around for a day or for a year. Safe. Safe enough to share her innermost feelings. Safe enough to be honest.

So why was she fighting her obvious attraction to him? It was easy to pass off the electricity that shot through her hand when they touched as the cold, easy to say her breathlessness was because of her nerves over the situation and not because she wanted him to touch her again. If there were an Olympic event for denying what was plain in front of her face, she would win a gold medal.

Because she was unmistakably falling for Gabriel Brandt.

And she was screwing it up.

The other soup was finally boiling, so she poured that into another bowl and shut off the stove. She wiped the pot out the best she could with paper towels she'd found in the pantry and used a leftover plastic shopping bag for trash. Of course, the first soup was now cold, but she would take that one and give Gabe the hot one.

She grabbed a couple of spoons from the drawer and picked up the bowls and walked carefully up the stairs.

Too late, she realized she couldn't get the door open while juggling the soup, so she called, "Gabe?"

The door opened immediately. He reached for the bowls, but she skidded by him and set them on the dresser, then spun. "Okay, so here's the thing . . ."

Gabe closed the door, puzzled by the strange opening line. What was she going to say anyway? *Here's the thing: I think I might be falling for you because you're actually nice to me.*

But he was waiting patiently and she still had no idea what to say, so she crossed the space between them, reached up to hold his jaw with one hand, and kissed him.

For one brief, still moment, she thought he was going to pull away. And then his arms went around her, pulling her tight against him. She half expected him to devour her mouth, push her back toward the bed, and at least a tiny part of her thought she wouldn't mind that. But he only kept his hands fixed on her waist, holding their bodies so close that she could feel the warmth pouring off him, his mouth slowly, patiently exploring hers. His restraint was headier than she could have imagined, making her light-headed with need, desperate for more of him. And just when it felt like he might relent and give it to her, he pulled back and stared intently into her eyes. "What was that for?"

"Because I wanted to," she said lamely. She tried again. "Because I realized I really like you." Just as lame, but something lit in his eyes.

"I like you too, Kendall."

She smiled, warmth blooming in her chest.

"But . . ."

A tendril of cold quickly crept in.

"Considering the circumstances . . ."

She pulled away. "Because of the house, you mean."

He looked puzzled. "Well, yeah."

Now Kendall escaped his embrace, disappointment washing over her. "I wasn't trying to persuade you, Gabe. I realize you don't know me that well, but I thought you'd know me better than that."

Now his puzzlement went to full-fledged astonishment, as if she were speaking an alien language. And then his expression cleared. He reached for her and tugged her back into his arms, dipping his head toward her ear. "I mean, because we are completely alone, stranded overnight in a bedroom. Because I can see how easy it would be to lose control with you."

Her surprised gaze met his and the heat in his eyes was undeniable. She caught her breath. "I . . . I thought . . ."

"It would be easier if we were on the same side of the house issue, no doubt, but . . . that doesn't change how I feel about you." He smiled and enunciated each word carefully. "Kendall, I really like you."

Somehow, those five words meant more than a declaration of love could have. She'd had numerous men tell her they loved her, usually while they were trying to get her clothes off. This was different. This was like him saying he saw her and liked what he saw, even with her drama and hang-ups. It was the very opposite of rejection. Who knew that the thing you said to a sixth-grade crush could mean so much as an adult?

They were still pressed against each other, and she couldn't resist sliding a hand up his chest. "I can see the wisdom in what you're saying, but . . . one more kiss wouldn't hurt, would it?"

He grinned. "I really hope not." And then he kissed her again, until she was thoroughly in like and ready to melt into a puddle at his feet.

"Well," she said breathlessly when they parted, "the upside is that both our soups are cold now. Because I really wanted the minestrone."

Gabe chuckled. "I don't understand."

"Never mind." She turned to get their bowls, immediately feeling a chill away from his warmth, but there was a glow in her insides that even the raging storm outside couldn't extinguish.

They seated themselves side by side on the rug again, close enough that their knees touched, and ate their lukewarm soup while they talked. His eyes barely left her face, as if he couldn't bear to lose that little bit of connection. She found herself telling him stories from her past without the melancholy that usually accompanied them: her regret that she'd gotten a design education without actually getting a degree, how she'd met Sophie their last year of school, how she'd kept in touch via social media and pulled her in as soon as she decided to open her own design studio. The way that Gabe watched her in rapt attention and asked questions at the right times made her feel like she'd accomplished something astonishing, like the adversity she'd faced made her that much more incredible rather than tarnished in some way.

And for a few moments, she actually believed it.

Chapter Twenty-One

It quickly became clear that the storm was not going to blow through as quickly as Gabe had hoped . . . and that the small propane heater couldn't keep up with the rapidly dropping temperature. Kendall flicked on the LED lamp as night fell, though it wasn't that dramatic a transition because the snowstorm had blocked out much of the light all day.

"Why do I think this is going to be a long night?" Kendall asked with a sigh. "I'm not even remotely sleepy at the moment."

He wasn't either, but that had a lot more to do with the fact he was still buzzing from her touch, and it was taking supreme force of will to sit next to her like they were just friends, when all he wanted to do was pick up where they'd left off.

Which was exactly why he was maintaining a one-foot buffer between them for the rest of the night. Kendall hadn't seemed nearly as concerned about the prospect of being stuck in a bedroom with him as he would have expected her to be, which made him think maybe she had different views on the subject.

It also brought up a lot of other questions about her beliefs that he didn't particularly want to explore tonight. Especially with the way she'd reacted when she thought he was rejecting her.

"Do we have anything else to sort through?" Gabe asked. The third box had included nothing but medical bills and old insurance policies for a car that appeared to have been sold in 2015.

"There's a bunch of jewelry and accessories in her closet," she said. "I only took a quick glance the other day."

Gabe glanced at the ring on her finger. "Is that where you got the ring?"

Kendall immediately hid her hand. "I just thought—"

"It's yours," Gabriel said gently. "You can do whatever you want with it. I just hadn't seen it before yesterday, so I guessed."

"Right." She took a deep breath as if resetting herself. He was beginning to notice her habit of reacting defensively when she thought he was criticizing her, and he made a mental note to be more careful with his words and tone. She'd done so well at overcoming her rocky start in life, but every moment he spent with her made clear that she was still holding on to some deep wounds.

"Do you think you want to take them with you?" he asked.

"I think so. I'm not sure what they're worth, but it could be a lot just based on the amount of gold in that drawer. Do you want to help me look through it?"

"Sure." He remained seated on the floor while Kendall popped up and retrieved the top drawer from the closet organizer. It slid out easily and she set it between them.

Gabe reached for a jade brooch. "I remember this one."

"Really?"

"Yeah." He searched his memory, but he couldn't come up with more than a vague recollection of it pinned to a white silk blouse. "I don't think she wore it very often, but I saw it on her when she was dressed up one time. Maybe for church."

There it was again, a flicker of an eyelash when he mentioned church. He couldn't let it go. Whether it was a nudge to his spirit from God or simply his own curiosity, he found himself saying, "Should I ask?"

"About what?" She looked genuinely puzzled, so she probably wasn't conscious of her reaction.

"About the church people who hurt you in the past."

Kendall looked him in the face. "How do you know about that?"

He shrugged. "You're uncomfortable with the subject. Most people are indifferent, or they think I'm weird if I bring it up. But you . . . you look like it hurts you."

Kendall studied her hands in her lap and twisted the ring on her finger. For a long moment, he thought she wasn't going to answer. And then she said, "It's because of one of my first foster homes."

He just waited, not pressing.

"I really thought they were going to stick, you know? They seemed great. I liked their church; they were really nice to me, though now I think it was pity. Then I heard them arguing one night. The husband hadn't wanted to take in any foster kids, but the wife said it was their Christian duty, and what would everyone think of them if they sent me away? He said that it wasn't his problem if some druggie got knocked up and couldn't keep her kid, and he wanted to take a vacation as planned." Kendall looked up, her eyes glistening. "I was seven. I really thought they wanted me, and to hear that I was just an inconvenience to their vacation?" Her voice broke. "Well, that was it. Not to mention what they said about my mom. She was *not* an addict. No matter what else I know of her, I know that's true. I would remember." She cleared her throat. "Anyway, that was the first time I ran away. And that was what they needed to justify sending me back."

"Kendall, I'm so sorry." He reached out and touched her knee, but she didn't move or look at him. "That was so unfair and nothing that a seven-year-old should have overheard."

"That's not the point, Gabe. There are good

foster homes and bad foster homes. I should know; I was in both. My point is, I heard nothing but lies. Well-meaning lies, maybe, but lies. And that's all Christianity is. It's there to make you look good and holy, but there's nothing behind it."

The words cut, not because they were directed toward him, but because she'd only had bad experiences so far with his faith. A faith that was supposed to be life-giving and authentic but had cut her down and hurt her. It came down to what his grandmother always said: the only problem with Christianity was the Christians. She'd meant it as a joke, of course, a reference to how they were all sinners, but in this case, he related to its full cutting breadth. He searched for the right thing to say. "I don't blame you for feeling that way given your experiences. Would it surprise you to know I'm a Christian?"

She gave him a look that made him feel ridiculous. "Yeah, I kind of guessed that. Because of . . . you know." She waved a hand that he supposed encompassed the situation and his flat determination that he would not be taking advantage of it. "But I get it. I mean, it's bad enough that you're stuck here with me."

He frowned. "What do you mean?"

"Well, what do you suppose your church is going to say when you don't show up tomorrow because you were out all night with a stranger?"

Gabe grinned. "What, are we sixteen or something?"

She gave him a quizzical look.

"I'm not worried about my reputation, Kendall. It's sound, and even if it wasn't, I wouldn't let what other people might say compromise your safety. What I do in my personal life is between me and God. We know what happened or didn't."

"If you can do whatever you want, then what's the deal with Christians and sex?"

Gabe shook his head, trying not to cringe. As if having to be the lone representative of his faith wasn't scary enough, she wanted him to summarize centuries of sexual mores. "You mean why is everyone hung up on not having it?"

She nodded.

"Well, partly because even if people aren't having it, that doesn't mean they're not still thinking about it."

A laugh slipped from her. "I can't believe you just said that!"

"It's the truth. When I was a teenager, I always thought the adults were just trying to control us and keep us from having any fun. It wasn't until I got older, made some mistakes of my own, that I realized sex adds an intensity to a relationship that maybe it's not ready to bear. And then when the relationship falls apart, you feel like you've invested too much of yourself to let it go. Just please don't tell Luke my explanation because he'll give me a hard time about being all touchy-feely."

Kendall cracked a smile. "I won't. In fact, we never had this conversation. Besides, I don't buy it."

"I was being serious!"

"I know *you* were. But you're one guy. You're a unicorn. You're not the only Christian man I've ever met, and trust me, they don't all hold the same views as you."

"Well, there are a lot of people claiming to be Christians who aren't living it out. And anyone whose Christianity is solely based on who is or isn't sleeping with whom is missing the point. But it doesn't make the whole religion invalid. It just makes some of us really sucky examples of it."

Kendall shook her head, obviously not buying it. "You're not going to convince me, you realize."

"I wasn't trying to convince you. You asked! Trust me, that was the last topic I really intended to discuss tonight."

"Then what do you want to talk about?" Kendall fired back.

Gabe had to think about that one. They'd already delved into deep enough topics, and he was both astonished and touched that she'd revealed as much about herself as she had. It had also given him one big reservation about a relationship that he would have to sort through later. Finally he asked, "What's the dumbest thing you've ever done for a guy?"

"Oooh. You go straight for the throat." She thought. "I almost married one."

"You almost got married? How old were you?"

"Nineteen. I was working the reception job at the design school. He was an artist there. We took a weekend trip to Las Vegas, one thing led to another, and . . ."

"You found yourself looking at a justice of the peace in an Elvis costume?"

Color tinged her cheeks. "That was exactly the case. Fortunately, they decided that we were too drunk to actually know what we were doing and turned us away. Let's just say when I woke up the next morning, I was really relieved that we hadn't gone through with it. Especially since I broke up with him the following month."

"Wow. Close call?"

"The closest. How about you?"

Gabe had to think. "I tried a *Say Anything* moment outside my high school girlfriend's window."

Kendall laughed. "She wasn't a fan?"

"Oh, I'm sure she would have been. I just got the layout of their house wrong, and I was standing in front of her parents' bedroom."

Kendall rocked back with a gale of laughter. "Oh, that's perfect. I can just imagine you all

273

ready for your John Cusack moment and you get yelled at to get off the lawn."

"No, actually, they were really cool about it. Her dad looked annoyed, but I think her mom thought it was cute. She kind of pointed and said, 'She's the other window.' But by that time, the moment was gone and I was so embarrassed I just took my boom box and ran home."

"I can't believe you could even *find* a boom box. I know someone whose ex tried that, but holding an MP3 player over your head just doesn't have the same feel." Kendall wiped her eyes, still chuckling under her breath. "Okay. If you could wake up tomorrow with the knowledge to have a successful career in anything, what would you be?"

"Doctor."

"Oh, come on."

"No, really. They make bank, and I would have my student loans paid off by now."

She squinted at him. "You're really not answering the question in the spirit I meant it."

"Fine then. What would you do?"

"What I do now. I've wanted to be a designer ever since I was twelve and I spent my weekends with my foster mom fixing up the house. It sounds kind of like child labor, but it was actually fun. She let me do my room first, and then we worked on other rooms of the house."

He didn't point out the obvious: she did have

some good memories of foster care, at least one particular placement, but she hadn't realized it because the bad ones overshadowed everything else. "So you're living your dream?"

"Pretty much. I just wish I knew everything I don't know. I don't even know what I don't know . . . you know?"

He grinned at her and she chuckled. "Anyway. I guess we should actually look through these things. I saw some silk scarves in here that might be Hermès."

They both knew they were just killing time. Most of the jewelry was gold, but it was pretty middle of the road. Smallish diamonds, larger semiprecious stones, a few antique pieces that Kendall set aside for appraisal. But she left the rest in the tray and went back for the second one, this time filled with the many rectangles of silk.

Kendall took out the first scarf and shook it out, muttering something about Poochie, whatever that meant. The only Poochie he knew was the cartoon dog from a particularly funny episode of *The Simpsons*. He pulled out a pink-and-green scarf that had a familiar pattern on it—not that he could actually identify it—and then drew in his breath.

"What?" Kendall asked, whipping her head toward him. "Is that a Lilly Pulitzer?"

"No, not the scarf. This." He lifted the wrinkled white packet from the bottom of the drawer, where it had lain hidden by the silk. "I think it might be a letter."

Kendall could swear her heart stopped beating for a full five seconds while she looked at the envelope in Gabe's hand. When it started back up, it was with a thud that nearly knocked the wind out of her. "Can I . . . can I see that?"

He handed over the envelope, his banter silencing, as if he realized exactly what this could mean. Kendall slid her finger under the flap and it freed easily, the adhesive loosened by age. It wasn't *a* letter but *letters,* plural, at least six of them. They were all on regular lined notebook paper, their edges frayed and frazzled from the spiral binding from which they'd been torn. Even from the outside, she could see swirly handwriting in blue pen, pressed so hard that the impressions showed through to the other side.

"I . . . I can't look at them." She lowered the stack of letters into her lap. Instinctively, she knew this was what she had been looking for, but now that the moment had come, she found she didn't want to know. What if everything that Mr. Brandt and Gabe had said was untrue? What if they were angry rants at Connie for kicking her daughter out or, worse yet, something about how Carrie didn't want her kid anymore? She felt faint at the possibilities.

"Do you want me to look first?" Gabe held his

hand out, and after a long moment, she handed them over. As she did, a small, yellowing photograph fell to the floor between them.

Kendall picked it up as gingerly as she would an explosive, her chest too constricted to draw a full breath. The photo was wrinkled and warped, as if it had been exposed to moisture, but the photo was still clear enough to see it was of a woman and a little girl, perhaps three years old, taken in front of a forest backdrop. The girl beamed at the camera, but the woman was instead looking at the child. The expression on her face was laced with such adoration that it hurt to look at.

"What is it?" Gabe asked carefully.

"I think . . ." She dragged her eyes away from the photo, nearly too stunned to form words. "I think it's me. And my mom." She handed the photo to Gabe shakily.

"She looked just like you," he said softly. "No wonder everyone in town recognized you." He studied it for a second before handing it back to Kendall.

Somehow, it had never occurred to her to wonder why there weren't any photos of her or Carrie in the house. Kendall's first impulse was to believe that Connie Green had cut them ruthlessly and definitively out of both her life and her memories. But this photo seemed to suggest otherwise. The wrinkled surface seemed like it had been handled frequently, carried around . . . even wept over?

And the photo itself . . . this was no two-dollar photo booth knockoff. This was a professional studio shot, one that Carrie had paid for and sent to her mother. There was no other way she could have gotten it.

Kendall was gripped with the sudden, desperate need to know what was in the letters. "Open them, Gabe. I have to know."

Gabe carefully unfolded the letter on the top and then another and then another. "They're dated," he explained. "It makes sense to read them in order." He picked up and scanned the first one, then lowered it slowly. "They're from your mother."

Kendall caught her breath, swaying with the kick of her heart. Even after finding the photo, she hadn't dared to hope. "Are they bad?"

Gabe kept reading, and she didn't exhale while she waited for him to answer. A tiny smile surfaced on his face, but it was tinged with sadness. "No, it's not bad. I think you should read it for yourself."

Kendall took the letter with trembling hands. Her mom's handwriting took a minute to decipher, loopy and girlie. She half expected the *i*'s to be dotted with hearts. This was not a woman's handwriting. It was a girl's. The date said that when it was written, Carrie had only been twenty-three. Kendall would have been five. Right before she'd been abandoned. What if this revealed the reason her mom had left her? What if she learned—?

"Kendall." Gabe's gentle tone brought her back to the present. "Just read it. Trust me."

She picked it up again.

Dear Mom,
    I made a huge mistake. I'm so sorry I left the way I did. I was hurt and angry and I thought I was doing the right thing. I thought you were trying to take my daughter away from me. I thought I could do everything on my own.
    I've made a huge mess of things. Kendall is getting so big so fast, and I just can't do this anymore. Not without you.
    Please . . . can we come home?
    Your loving (and very sorry) daughter,
                      Carrie

Kendall swallowed hard, trying to make sense of what she was reading. For the first time in her life, her mother was a real person, with loopy handwriting and the sad perspective of lost youth. Kendall might have had to grow up faster and younger than her mom, but they'd both come to the understanding of how hard and unforgiving the world could be. Whatever the reason

Carrie had left, she'd wanted to come home.

And she'd wanted to bring Kendall with her.

Tears slid down her face and she wiped them away with the back of her hand. "What's the next one?"

The look on Gabe's face as he started reading struck fear into her heart.

"What?"

"I don't know yet, Kendall. Maybe you should let me read through all of them to see how they end first."

"No, I have to know." She'd been looking for this information her whole life, and now that it was right in front of her, she couldn't stop. She put out her hand and Gabe reluctantly passed her the letter.

Mom,
Did you get my last letter? I sent it a week ago and I haven't heard back from you. Kendall and I are in Denver. I'm looking for a job now because we're out of money, but I was kind of hoping I wouldn't need to.

I know I made huge mistakes. I know you may never forgive me. But don't make your granddaughter suffer for my stupidity.

Please let us come home.

Carrie

Kendall blinked. "What? Connie didn't respond?"

Gabe was flipping through pages as fast as he could skim. "No, I think it's okay . . . There's one more like that, here . . ." He passed it over, but from his tone, she didn't even read it, just set it aside. "No, there's a reason. Read this one next."

Mom,
I'm so relieved you're okay and I'm relieved you weren't ignoring my messages. I'm sorry I wasn't there when you called. We had to move motels unexpectedly, but the desk clerk was nice and liked Kendall and saved the letter for me when I went back to see if you'd written. We're at a new place (address below). Don't worry about me, though the money you sent is really appreciated. I have another job interview next week, and I should be able to get a phone set up after that. Let us know when you're home from the hospital. I tried to call, but they wouldn't let me talk to you.

I love you. I've been telling Kendall all about you and she can't wait to meet you.

Love,
Carrie

"Connie was in the hospital?" Kendall remembered the stack of medical files that she hadn't gone through. She'd just assumed that they were from her most recent illness, the one that had eventually gotten the best of her, but it sounded like there had been an earlier one. Not that the knowledge would have helped her without the letters for context. Her heart still beat rapidly. This was like some soap opera or one of those mystery crates that were the rage a few years back. It didn't feel like her life. "What else is there?"

"That's it," Gabe said softly. "That was the last one from Carrie. There's just this." He held up a thicker envelope, one that she had mistaken for a stack of folded letters. It was still sealed, addressed to Carrie at a Littleton motel. A big *Return to Sender* was stamped on the front.

Kendall took it from Gabe slowly, an ominous feeling growing inside. She slid her finger under the flap, the seal still strong after all these years. Here was a full page of slanted, spidery writing that was obviously not Carrie's. Kendall recognized it from the notes in the banker's boxes. Connie's.

Dear Carrie,
My love, I'm so worried about you. I haven't heard anything from you in the

last several weeks. I've called every motel in Denver, Boulder, and Colorado Springs looking for you, but I've gotten nowhere. Even at your old addresses, they say they don't have anyone by that name. Were you listed under an assumed name?

Come home. Your place is here. I know you wanted to get back on your feet first. I know you didn't want to return as a prodigal. Stop worrying about all that. You're so close and I don't know where else to look.

I love you,
Mom

Kendall lowered the paper. "That's it?"

"There's nothing else in there."

"They just . . . lost touch? How could that happen? She was going to come home. She was going to bring me home. . . . How . . . ?" Only when Gabe gathered her against him did Kendall realize she was sobbing. How could this have happened? Carrie had been so close to coming back. Why hadn't she just driven up into the mountains? If she was in Denver, if she had enough money for a motel, surely she had enough money for a car or a rental for the day or even a taxi ride. Knowing what Kendall knew now, it wouldn't have mattered if she'd set foot in this town with nothing but the clothes on her and her daughter's backs . . . someone would have helped them.

So what happened?

All this time Kendall thought she wanted to know the truth, but now the truth was just as incomprehensible as it had always been. Even worse, because now she knew how close she had come to having a real family.

Chapter Twenty-Two

Sleep peeled back from Gabe's consciousness in layers, bringing in the dim light of predawn. He lay there for one moment, reorienting himself, wondering what had awoken him. Then he made a small movement, and the cold, damp air sliced through him like a knife.

His eyes snapped open to see a cloud of breath forming in front of him. He turned his head slightly to where Kendall lay curled up in a ball, mere inches from where he lay beside her on the bed under the heavy comforter and a sleeping bag. He'd held her while she cried for what seemed like hours, until her sobs had stilled and she'd fallen into a deep, troubled sleep, still clinging to him. She hadn't even moved when he'd transferred her to the mattress or when he'd later extracted himself to change the propane bottle in the heater, which had evidently run out sometime in the bitter cold of early morning. It didn't help that he'd had to crack the window to vent carbon monoxide; even that thin stream of cold air had been enough to drop the temperature precipitously. He was suddenly glad that he'd thought to throw the sleeping bag over them.

Carefully he eased himself out from beneath the coverings and thrust his feet into his boots. Kendall didn't stir. Either she was perpetually sleep-deprived—which was entirely possible—or she was just exhausted from the emotional revelations of the night before. Not that Gabe could blame her. After a lifetime of wondering what had happened to her mother, after days of wondering why her grandmother hadn't sought her out, the answers she thought the letters would contain remained just out of her reach.

Gabe took the duffel bag with him as he left the bedroom and descended the stairs to the kitchen, where Kendall had left the propane stove. Had he thought about it, he would have brought up that bottle to use for heat, but they had managed to stay warm anyway. And not in the manner he'd been trying to avoid. Their kisses of the previous evening had been far from his mind while Kendall was sobbing in his arms.

He took the pot Kendall had used for the soup and scrubbed it out with snow, then filled it with more snow to melt for their coffee. A glance overhead showed the clear skies that typified Colorado after a storm, a pale gray in the predawn that would deepen into a blinding blue. From the looks of it, they'd gotten almost two feet from a storm that shouldn't have even netted them an inch. So much for weather predictions. There was a reason why Gabe never removed his cold-weather kit from his truck, even during the summer.

When the snow was finally melted and headed toward boiling, he twisted off the heat and shook in crystals from a canister of instant coffee. No doubt their first stop upon getting back into town would be Delia's, but they'd both need a shot of caffeine in order to brave the cold trip back around the lake. He was just pouring the coffee into two mugs when Kendall appeared in the door of the kitchen, sleep still blanketing her features.

"Do I smell coffee?" she asked hoarsely.

He wordlessly handed her the mug but kept his distance, studying her.

She sipped the coffee and offered him a rueful grin. "Instant."

"Best I could do."

"I wasn't complaining." She stood there, sipping from the mug, until she finally lowered it and looked him full in the face. "Gabe, about last night. I didn't mean to fall apart."

Was she actually apologizing for having feelings? "I would be surprised if you didn't. It's a lot to take."

Embarrassment colored her cheeks and she looked away. "I keep looking around at all of this and thinking, I would have memories of this if . . . but I can't fill in the *if*. What happened? Why did my mom never come home? It sounded like she and my grandmother reconciled. I was found in Denver. Sixty miles from here! So why did no one ever make the connection? What happened to my mom?"

The pain in her voice hadn't eased since last night, but there was something different about it. For one thing, she was calling Connie and Carrie her grandmother and mom. She might not have gotten the answers she wanted—the answers she deserved—but what she had learned had changed everything.

"I don't know, Kendall," he said finally. "We may never know. And even if you could, you might not like what you find out. How important is it to have the whole truth?"

She took a long moment to consider. "I think I need to know everything. It may not be possible, but nothing could be worse than spending my whole life thinking my mother had dumped me because she didn't want me."

And in that moment, Gabe vowed that if it was in his power, he would make sure she found out.

"So what now?" she said finally. "Are the roads clear?"

"I doubt it. The county roads might be plowed, but everything in and out will still be deep. Not that it's a problem in my truck, but we might need to wait to get yours out."

"As long as you don't mind driving me back here until I can get my car, I'm okay with that."

He blinked at her. "I thought you were finished.

Wasn't going through the paperwork your last task?"

"That's true. But there was one space I was overlooking." The corner of her mouth quirked up. "The attic."

Gabe frowned. "This house doesn't have an attic. There's no access in the ceiling and there's definitely no staircase."

"It has an attic. It has a triple window you can see from the exterior." Her eyes sparkled excitedly. "It hit me as soon as I woke up. It got cold, but it wasn't that cold because the house is so well insulated. So I started thinking about what might be over us, between us and the snow on the roof, and then I realized that the roof-line guarantees there's an attic. They probably closed it up to make the house more energy efficient."

Gabe stared at her, impressed. It would never have occurred to him to look beyond the obvious. There were plenty of newer houses that had fake windows to look like attic space when there was really nothing but rafters and mice above. "I wouldn't even know where to look."

"Oh, I do." Kendall seated herself at the kitchen table, mug in hand. "It's in the master bedroom closet." At what must be his shocked expression, she laughed. "It makes sense. It was renovated in the 1980s. The original architecture would never have incorporated a master bath or a walk-in closet. I think the closet is where the stairwell used to be, and the space underneath, which would have been a window nook, got converted into the master bath. If we punch through the ceiling in the walk-in, I think we will find nothing but drywall and insulation, rather than the original lath and plaster."

"Is it possible that you could be wrong?" He imagined going in with a sledgehammer only to break through hundred-year-old wood.

"Anything's possible, but I'm not wrong."

Gabe slowly took the seat across from her. "What are you hoping to find up there? More antiques?"

"No. History. Proof."

"Of what?"

"Of who built this house and why." Her eyes flashed with a glint that seemed just a little bit wild. "I've decided, Gabe. This place is mine. Should have always been part of my life. I'm not letting them tear it down."

His heart leapt, but he quashed his sudden relief with a smothering dose of practicality. "What does that mean? Are you staying?"

Kendall's expression shuttered, and he realized then that he'd been wise to temper his enthusiasm. "Staying? No. I still have a life back in California. But let's just say that there's too much of my history in this house to let it turn into rubble. Especially now that I know Phil Burton is my uncle and he chose to keep that fact from me."

Gabe's mouth dropped open. "Phil Burton is your *uncle?*"

"I take it you didn't know?"

"No! I would have told you. How did you find out?"

"Bruce at the snowmobile place. He went to school with Carrie and my father . . . or at least the guy she was dating at the time. I mean, I could probably do some sort of genetic testing, but I doubt Burton would submit to that."

"He does go to the coffee shop pretty often," Gabe said slowly.

Kendall just laughed. "Steal his DNA? I'm pretty sure that's illegal unless you're the police. And unless he's wanted in a murder or something, that's not going to happen." She sat quietly for a moment. "I don't think it matters that much to me anyway. It wasn't like my father stuck around. My mom was the one who raised me, at least for the first several years. That's more important to me than who might have gotten her pregnant."

Gabe nodded along, though his mind was turning. Kendall might think it didn't matter to her now, but it had only been twelve hours since she had gotten some pieces of her past back. If the other parts turned out to be harder to fill in, she might very well want to connect the dots on the other side of her family. But it wasn't his

291

place to push. She would do what she wanted when she was ready. And given all the trauma involved in her past, she might never be ready.

That only took him back to another glaring question. Yes, she'd kissed him. Yes, there was a definite connection between them. But she wasn't planning on staying. And it was obvious she wasn't a believer. After what had happened with Madeline, he had vowed that he wouldn't date someone who didn't share his beliefs. That meant whatever this was would never make it past that initial stage of attraction.

Except he was already long past that point. He wasn't quite ready to say that he was in love with her, but he was headed that direction. And in those moments after she had kissed him, he'd thought she might feel the same way. If he were smart, he would wish her luck and leave her to her own devices, spare them the pain that would inevitably come if they got any more attached.

But he had a sinking suspicion that if she went straight back to California into her own life, she'd also go back to her comfort zone of an indifferent God, albeit with a slightly improved sense of self from the revelations of Jasper Lake. Away from him, away from her past, away from the truth.

It all came back to the story of who she was and why Carrie had never made it back to Jasper Lake. He had to help her find out the truth, for both their sakes.

Chapter Twenty-Three

In movies, when two people were stranded in an old house together in a snowstorm, either they had sex or they emerged with an unshakable bond. Or they were the victims of a ghost or serial killer, but Kendall wasn't fond of horror movies, so she chose not to count that as an option.

In this case, as if she needed more reminders that her life was not a movie, none of those things had happened. They were still alive, their relationship was still limited to some light making out . . . and most disconcerting, things between them seemed more awkward than ever.

It wasn't that her feelings had changed from last night. Kendall still liked Gabe—more than ever, in fact. Part of her had wondered if the nice guy act was just that—an act—but he seemed genuinely that kind. And if the short religious conversation they'd had was any indication, it stemmed from a sincere faith in God. Maybe she couldn't understand that, but she could respect it. The fact he'd looked so pained when she'd talked about her experiences with her foster parents, his concern that she thought all Christians were hypocrites, seemed to show it came from a deep place. She respected people who stuck to their convictions, especially when it came to relationships.

But the kiss, the feelings, none of that changed the fact she was only here for a short time. Wanting to save the house—just this house, not the others—didn't make any difference in whether or not she would stay. Her livelihood was in California. Her life was in California. But maybe, just maybe, she could do something that would make a difference to Gabe after she left.

What she had not told Gabe, what had occurred to her when she glanced at her phone this morning and saw a text from Sophie about the Woolridge House, was the one thing that could save these homes from destruction.

Designation as a historical landmark.

There was no doubt in her mind that these houses were created by a trained architect with a specific artistic vision. Each of the homes was slightly different, Connie's being more elaborate than the others, but they all displayed a Victorian sensibility for details over a practical architectural style. The whole effect was far more European than American, William Morris versus Frank Lloyd Wright. And yet she was sure these houses weren't from either of those schools.

Which was why she'd texted Sophie to overnight all her Craftsman and Arts and Crafts books and catalogs to Jasper Lake. Kendall couldn't remember whether that was a backpack full or a truckload, but from the string of shocked emojis, followed by ten of the poop symbol, she suspected it was closer to the latter.

"Kendall? Did I lose you?"

Gabe was studying her face, and she realized she had completely zoned out. She gave an embarrassed little laugh. "Sorry. I'm still sleepy. And I was thinking about the house. I don't suppose you know anyone who could help us cut a hole in the ceiling, do you?"

"I could probably find someone."

Kendall narrowed her eyes at Gabe. "We need someone who can cut a neat square in the drywall and then patch it back up. Not someone who's going to bust it up with a sledgehammer."

Gabe laughed. "Then that leaves out Luke. Seriously, though, I know some contractors in town who could help us."

"For how much?"

"For the chance to stick it to Phil Burton? Free."

Kendall smiled. The small-town thing was starting to pay off. "Good. And tell them to bring a ladder. If I'm right, we're going to need a way to get up there and look around."

"Exactly when are you thinking about per-forming this little bit of surgery?"

She blinked. "Today."

"Church is about to let out and then every-one heads to lunch. Earliest I'll be able to get someone out here is tomorrow."

Kendall didn't truly believe that every single person in town went to church, but she didn't argue. Probably any friend of Gabe's who would help for free was the churchgoing type. Besides, she was feeling cold and grimy, and the only thing she really wanted to do right now was take a long, hot bath and brush her teeth . . . twice. She'd never thought of herself as particularly high-maintenance, but she'd never been without running water or heat for twenty-four hours either.

Finally, when both their mugs were empty, Gabe pushed back from the table. "Ready to go? I'll take the pots and dishes and wash them at home. Don't want to risk critters."

"I am more than ready to go," Kendall said. "I'll just go get my stuff." She handed over her mug and then took the stairs two at a time to the bedroom, where the mussed bed and the spilled contents of her handbag were the only evidence of their sleepover. She dumped the items into her bag, straightened the bedspread, and then rolled up the sleeping bag and stuffed it back in its sack. She lingered for a long moment over the stack of letters on the nightstand, scanning the old photo as if it still had more secrets to impart, then tucked everything carefully away into one of the pockets of her bag. All the while ignoring the one nagging fact that she couldn't reconcile. Gabe had smiled, but he hadn't reached for her. Hadn't kissed her. Hadn't given any indication that anything out of the ordinary had happened between them, besides her epic meltdown.

There was no doubt that he'd been into that kiss last night, but he'd been awfully determined not to let it go any further. What if his reaction hadn't had anything to do with the propriety of the situation? What if he actually wasn't interested, and given all the emotional upheaval of this week, he hadn't wanted to hurt her feelings?

She blinked away the pang of disappointment, refusing to acknowledge it ran deeper. She'd been here for less than a week. There was nothing here that she couldn't turn her back on when she went. But for Gabe, this was home. Saving the town was his greatest goal. And if she knew what was best for both of them, she would focus on that instead of whatever kind of feelings his presence seemed to summon in her.

Kendall grabbed her purse, the sleeping bag, and one of the banker's boxes, and descended the stairs to the first floor, where she dropped her load before returning for the other two boxes. The rumble of Gabe's truck outside told her he'd gone to warm it up. He still had her house keys, so she laced up her boots and waited for him to reappear at the front door.

When the door opened, he stayed on the stoop, blowing into his cupped hands. "Ready?"

"Ready. Can you help me with these boxes while I lock up?"

"Of course." He fished the keys out of his pocket and traded them for the file boxes while she locked the dead bolt behind them. Cold air seared her lungs, but she took a deep breath anyway, relishing the fresh, pine-scented air. She carefully picked her way down the front steps onto the walkway and turned a half circle, taking in her surroundings. It looked like a painting or a movie, the shapes of the houses and bushes indistinct under mounds of snow, the lake beyond an inky dark blue against the blanket of white that crept to the water's edge. Even for someone who regularly saw the Pacific Ocean, it was the most breathtaking view she'd witnessed in years.

Gabe slowly moved to her side. "It's pretty, isn't it? The highway won't be so nice once it's plowed and the ice melt is laid down, but this side of the lake always stays pristine."

"Do you come over here often?"

"To fish and kayak, sometimes. There's a footpath that goes between here and town. It's a couple of miles through dense forest, but if you don't mind packing your gear in, it's a beautiful walk." He flashed her a quick smile. "I wouldn't recommend it in the snow, though."

"I'll have to try that sometime," Kendall said, only remembering once the words left her mouth that she wouldn't be here when the snow melted. For a brief moment, she daydreamed about sitting in the library next to a roaring wood fire while white flakes sifted down outside the window like the view from inside a snow globe.

But that was impossible. Besides, she was getting swept away in a romantic daydream of what a snowy winter would be like. Based on the numbness that was creeping into her toes, even inside her insulated boots, she figured she would be over the whole thing in a month, tops.

"So what do you think? Get back to town?"

Kendall flushed at once more being caught in her daydreaming. "I think that's a great idea. You're sure we're safe to drive?"

"Absolutely." He led the way through the knee-deep snow to the side of his truck, where he opened the passenger door for her before trudging around to the other side.

Kendall gripped the overhead handle for dear life when they took off, but she managed not to gasp when the truck fishtailed through its U-turn.

"Okay?" he said, glancing at her.

"Fine. Don't mind me. I never really had to drive until I moved to California, and we panic at the first sign of raindrops."

Gabe chuckled. "If it makes you feel better, there are still some people in town who grumble every time there's snow in the forecast. I can't completely blame them. It does make daily chores a little more difficult, especially the commute. They'd never survive someplace like Minnesota."

"*I'd* never survive someplace like Minnesota." She stared out the window as they slowly rejoined the highway, a spray of snow kicking off the truck's massive tires. "Do you know how to trace a genealogy?"

"Uh, that's a change in subject. Not really, unless you call logging in to one of those online databases tracing a genealogy. Where did that come from?"

Kendall shifted on her seat to face him. "I was thinking about the people who originally moved to this area to seek their fortunes and how hard the winters would have been. So then I started thinking that the builder of the houses was probably a newcomer. There is a mention of a J. Green in the tax rolls from the end of the nineteenth century."

"So you thought that maybe you could trace your family line back to this J. Green and discover who the architect might have been. It's a good idea, but wouldn't it be easier just to google 'J. Green architect'?"

She shot him a reproving look. "I've already done that. Nothing came up. There doesn't seem to be a record of any such person, at least not in any of the books or databases I searched. I even searched the county library's online catalogs thinking they might have some local history books, and nothing."

"Hence the attic."

"Hence the attic. We better pray that the Big Guy in the sky is smiling down on us when we cut a hole in that ceiling. Because if there's nothing in the attic about my grandmother's house, we're out of options."

Now that she'd invested herself in saving these houses and their connection to her history, she felt sick at that possibility, even though it was the most likely outcome. After all, it stood to reason that the attic had been emptied before it was closed off. What if she never knew what had happened to her mother or who had built the house? Was she destined to remain ignorant of the town's connections to her past?

"Hey." Gabe glanced her way and reached for her hand, wrapping his cool, strong fingers around hers. "Don't give up. We've still got options. Including some we haven't thought of yet."

Kendall's gaze drifted down to their linked hands, and her heart gave a little kick. Surely he couldn't do that and feel nothing, not remember how well they'd fit together, how natural their kiss had been, completely devoid of the usual first-kiss awkwardness. That had to mean something, didn't it?

He didn't immediately pull his hand away, but then he put on his blinker to make the turn off the highway to the Jasper Lake access road and needed two hands to navigate the truck

301

through the huge snowbank left by the county's snowplow. Kendall took advantage of the truck's jostling to thrust her hand back into her pocket and grip the grab handle tighter. She didn't want to know if he would reach for her again when he could steer with one hand.

Before she'd kissed him last night, her conclusions had seemed so simple. But now she realized that she couldn't have complicated things more effectively had she tried.

Chapter Twenty-Four

As soon as Gabe pulled up to the curb of the B and B, Kendall reached for the door. "Thanks again," she said. "You really saved me last night. Let me know about the contractor friend?" And then before he could respond, she wrenched the door open and jumped out of the truck into a pile of fluffy white snow.

Gabe lifted a hand in farewell, a frown creasing his face. Kendall forced a smile and waved back, even though inside she was cursing herself. He must think she was demented, practically throwing herself out of the truck before it even came to a complete stop. But she couldn't stand waiting to see what his farewell would be. A kiss on the lips? A kiss on the cheek? A friendly punch in the shoulder as if they were buddies?

No, that one wasn't his style, at least.

So instead, she grinned at him like an idiot and trudged up the sidewalk to the front stoop of Mr. Brandt's B and B. She struggled with the key in the cold lock, but the minute the door opened, footsteps rang out from the back hallway, and the innkeeper appeared beside her.

"Ah, Kendall! No worse for the wear, I see." The man gave her an awkward pat on her shoulder.

Kendall chuckled at the uncomfortable show of affection. "Did Gabe tell you he was with me?"

"He did, but that's not the same as seeing it with my own eyes. Is he here?"

"Oh, um, no. He had to run into the office and check on things, I think. With the canceled bonfire and everything." Kendall was fully making it up, and she hoped that Mr. Brandt didn't question her too closely.

"Come get warm then. Can I make you some coffee?"

"Thank you, that's very kind, but I think I just want to take a hot bath if you don't mind. Even with my little propane heater, it wasn't that warm in the house."

"Understandable. If you need anything, just let me know."

"Thanks. I will." Kendall smiled at Gabe's grandfather and then turned and made for the stairs.

She threw her bag down on the bed as soon as she entered the room and made her way to the attached bathroom, kicking off shoes and stripping off clothing as she went. The tile was cold underfoot, as was the edge of the tub when she perched on it to run the water, but just the prospect of a long, hot soak made some of the tension seep out of her body.

But once she was ensconced in the hot water, complete with lavender-scented bubbles, she couldn't wait to get back out. She needed to talk to somebody about the situation with Gabe. She almost reached for her cell phone, placed just out of reach on top of her sweater by the tub, but she and Sophie didn't really have that kind of relationship. They'd never discussed anyone they were seeing, unless it was to complain about the guys' bad habits once they'd broken up with them. Besides, Kendall wasn't usually the type to agonize over a man. She met a guy, went out with him, and decided to either keep dating him or let him down easy. Or in the case of the really obnoxious ones, immediately ghosted him. But talk about feelings, go around and around about the nuance of a conversation or a look? Not since middle school.

Fantastic. Gabe had reduced her to a middle schooler.

Still, Kendall couldn't shake her restlessness, so she stayed in the tub just long enough to defrost her fingers and toes and then wrapped herself in a fluffy bath blanket while she thoroughly dried her hair. Not out of vanity, but out of survival instinct, considering it would freeze solid the minute she ventured outside. When it was finally dry and braided under a warm wool hat, Kendall layered up like she was braving the Arctic, pulled on her damp snow boots, and headed back out into the cold.

A block away from the B and B, she began

to regret her choice, but it wasn't like she had any other options. Her car was at the Lakeshore house, Uber didn't exist up here, and she certainly wasn't going to call Gabe to drive her to the coffee shop so she could talk about him with Delia.

No, she shouldn't think of it that way. She was gathering intel from someone who knew him. It was only sensible. Delia might be a friend of his, but she was also a woman, and in these situations, sisterhood always trumped friendship.

By the time she reached Main Street Mocha, Kendall was a teeth-chattering icicle. Her cheeks burned from the cold, her nose was completely numb, and she'd ceased to feel her feet about a block ago. Maybe she wasn't as adapted to the cold as she thought. Even two blocks in subfreezing temperature made her feel like she might die of hypothermia.

Thankfully, the coffee shop was open, but it was packed with people warming up over mugs of coffee and tea, some of them dressed like they'd come from church. Maybe Gabe's claim was right—maybe this was a town of churchgoing folks, though that made her feel more out of place than she already had. A quick skim of the counter revealed a teenage girl working the espresso machine. So much for her hope of seeing Delia.

And then the woman bustled in from the back, carrying a large box, and started to transfer stacks of paper cups to the cabinets under the counter. Kendall skirted the line and moved to the side of the counter. "Hey, Delia."

Delia twisted and then broke into a smile. "Kendall! You made it! I thought you might have decided to crawl back under the covers, not that I would have blamed you."

"I was actually hoping to talk to you," Kendall said, then quickly amended, "Just a chat. Nothing important."

Yeah. Gabe was turning her into a total idiot.

But Delia smiled. "Sure. I just came by to check on things. Mary couldn't find the extra cups, and she was worried about running out with the after-church crowd. What can I make you?"

"I hate to jump the line . . ."

Delia leaned forward and winked. "Advantages of being a friend of the owner."

Kendall's guilt wouldn't let her choose anything complicated, so she said, "A peppermint tea would be great actually."

"Coming right up." Delia went to the hot water dispenser at the bar and came back a minute later with a paper cup. "Come on. We'll grab that little table in the corner."

Kendall studied Delia as she wove her way through her coffee shop. Despite her youthful, alternative appearance, there was something settled, even wise, about her. Those were two things Kendall wasn't sure she'd ever be. Or maybe it was just that Main Street Mocha was Delia's home, her business, her happy place.

"I am so glad you're okay," Delia said when they were seated in the corner, away from listening ears. "When Gabe came in looking for you, I was afraid you might be stranded somewhere."

"I would have been, if not for you. Thanks for sending him out to the house after me. It would have been a long, cold night if he hadn't shown up when he did."

Delia nodded, saying nothing, just looking at Kendall in that focused way of hers.

Kendall sipped her tea and tried to figure out how to broach the subject.

Finally Delia sighed and cocked her head. "Okay, Kendall, spill. What happened?"

Heat rose to Kendall's cheeks for maybe the ninetieth time today. What had happened to the self-assured woman who didn't need anyone's validation? "How do you know something happened?"

"Because you just told me it did." Delia sobered. "Are you okay? Did you . . . do something you regret? Did Gabe do something you regret?"

Kendall's eyes widened when she realized what Delia was implying, though she was warmed by her sudden sharp tone. She was ready to jump behind Kendall if she needed the support. "No, nothing like that. I mean, we spent the night together, but we didn't sleep together."

Delia exhaled. "Okay, good. I didn't think that was Gabe's style, but sometimes you don't know people as well as you think you do."

"But I did kiss him."

"Oh." Her mouth rounded in surprise. "And? He wasn't bad, was he? You're not trying to figure out how to let him down easy?"

Kendall laughed at the scandalized look on Delia's face. Clearly this had been a topic of conversation at one point among the women, though it only took one look at Gabe to understand why. She lowered her voice. "No, it wasn't bad. It was . . . good. Really good. Like, put on the brakes before this goes too far sort of good."

"So where's the hang-up?"

Kendall bit her lip, not sure how to explain the situation. "This morning, he was distant, like he regretted everything. I know he's really religious, but it's not like there's anything in the Bible against kissing, is there?"

Delia's brow furrowed. "No, thank goodness. But what do you mean, *really religious?* That's not exactly how I would describe him."

"I just mean his faith is obviously important to him. How many guys would purposely not take advantage of the situation? No one around, things heat up a little . . ."

"Well, yeah, that's Gabe. His faith does mean a

309

lot to him, and I'm glad to hear that it applies to all areas of his life. Frankly, that's kind of hard to find." Delia studied her thoughtfully. "Kendall, are you a believer?"

Kendall shrank back from the question and cupped her hands around her tea. "I mean, I believe God exists. But I don't go to church or anything."

"So you wouldn't call yourself a Christian?"

Kendall choked on her mouthful of peppermint tea. "No. Definitely not."

Delia rubbed the side of her nose. "Yeah. I think this is a conversation you need to have with him and not with me."

"Why? Did I do something wrong?"

Delia reached for Kendall's hand and gripped it hard. "No, you didn't do anything wrong."

"Then why won't you tell me what you're thinking?"

Delia looked like she didn't want to answer, but finally she sighed. "Okay, you cannot be mad at me if I got this wrong, because you really need to talk to Gabe. But if I had to guess, I'd say that he's putting on the brakes either because you're leaving soon or because you're not a Christian."

"You're kidding me, right?" Kendall blinked at the other woman. "So it doesn't matter how much we like each other or how compatible we are—he's not interested because I'm not a church person?"

Delia smiled gently, but there was a tinge of sadness in her eyes. "It's not a church or no-church thing, Kendall. Christians generally only date people who believe the same thing because it would be like . . . trying to operate the same machine while using two different manuals. You'll inevitably have conflicts because you're approaching life in completely different ways."

"And that's really important to him?"

"I can't speak for him. But I do remember him saying he and his last girlfriend broke up because they wanted and believed different things. So yes. I imagine that could be a factor."

"Wow." Kendall wasn't sure what else to say. She felt blindsided by the revelation, and she couldn't decide if she felt better or worse. So maybe he really did like her, really was attracted to her, but he'd realized after their conversation that there couldn't be a future between them.

"I'm sorry, Kendall. I really do think you two should talk, however awkward it might be."

"No, it's fine. I thought that maybe I'd done something wrong. But now I know it's because I *am* something wrong." Kendall pushed back her chair. "Thanks for the information. I appreciate it."

"Kendall—"

She waved Delia down. "I'm okay. Thanks for the tea." She turned on her heel and marched as quickly as she could out of the coffee shop, determined to make it outside before hot tears spilled from her eyes onto her cheeks.

That's what she got for not leaving it alone, for pushing boundaries that had no business being pushed. Because now it wasn't nervousness or fear that she felt; it was hopelessness. She might not be entirely sure what she wanted from Gabe, but he'd made it more than clear he wanted nothing from her.

Chapter Twenty-Five

After dropping Kendall off at the B and B, Gabe went straight home and was nearly knocked off his feet by an overly excited Irish mastiff. He'd had Luke come over and feed and play with the beast, but it wasn't the same as having his master home. Gabe chuckled from his position on the floor and scratched the dog until Fitz was nothing more than a squirming pile of happiness.

"Ready to eat?" he asked. The dog's ears perked up, and Fitz followed him into the kitchen, where the bowl was conspicuously empty . . . as it always was. Gabe scooped out the food and filled the bowl, but inwardly, his mind had gone back to Kendall. He wasn't sure what to think about how they'd left things. They'd never really managed to talk about what came after their two passionate kisses, because they'd gone into a religious discussion and then found the letters from Kendall's mom. This morning, things had been more than awkward . . . even before she'd practically leapt from his truck so she didn't have to deal with his goodbye.

That had to be his fault. He shouldn't have taken her hand on the way back. It had been a moment of weakness, a sudden need to reestablish a connection with her, even though he had no business doing so.

Her coolness should make things easier for him. If she wanted to put the brakes on, it saved him from the hard, messy conversation of why they shouldn't take their relationship any further. Even if that was the last thing his heart actually wanted.

He blew out his breath and swore softly. There wasn't any point in trying to deny it, trying to call it something else to preserve his self-respect. He was falling in love with Kendall Green.

"Well, you've really managed to step in it this time." The very thing he said he would never do again, he went and did again.

But it wasn't fair to compare Kendall to Madeline. They were nothing alike. For one thing, the only detail he and Madeline had in common was their choice of profession. He and Kendall, on the other hand, shared a sense of humor, a sense of history, and from the way Kendall had been singing along at his gig, the same taste in music. Never underestimate the importance of radio station harmony in a relationship. And yet Kendall was so wounded by her past experiences, he wasn't sure she would even consider the possibility that she needed God in her life. So far she'd been taught that the only person she could depend on was herself.

And now, by pulling away, he was just reinforcing that belief.

He groaned. What did he do now? The one thing he couldn't do was disappear after he'd said he would help her uncover everything she could about her past. The first step to doing that was finding someone who could cut a hole in the ceiling tomorrow morning. He pulled up his contacts list on his phone and scrolled through the names and numbers. There. Mike Millan. He was a retired contractor who did handyman work in the area, small jobs that other contractors couldn't get to because of their workloads. He also lived right in town. He dialed the number and was pleased when Mike picked up on the first ring.

"Hey, Mike, it's Gabe. I have a favor to ask of you." He explained the situation and what they wanted done.

"You had me at 'searching for hidden treasure,' but ticking off Phil Burton is a bonus. I'll be there at nine."

"Perfect. Thanks. I owe you one." Gabe clicked off, satisfied that at least that was lined up. But even if they were to uncover something that would help them find out the history of the home and the identity of its architect, it didn't tell Kendall anything else about what had happened to her mom and why she had never been brought back to Jasper Lake. For that, they needed something else entirely.

Could he . . . ? Would Kendall blame him for invading her life or thank him for it?

No, that wasn't the way he should approach this idea. Kendall needed to know, once and for all, the truth of her own provenance. She might not thank him for it, might even be angry, but that didn't mean it wasn't the right thing to do. Gabe found his laptop in the other room and searched the web for several minutes, then picked up the phone. In mere minutes, the plan was set in motion.

For better or for worse.

Kendall didn't make contact with him for the rest of the day, leaving Gabe checking his phone compulsively like an idiot. Finally he texted her that their contractor would meet them the next morning at nine, so he would pick her up at the B and B. He expected some sort of reply or comment about how she was excited to see what was in the house, but all he got back from her was a thumbs-up symbol.

She had completely detached.

"For the best," he told himself out loud. Fitz cocked his furry head as if he didn't believe him. That was okay. He didn't believe himself either.

When Gabe couldn't stand his restlessness any longer, he pulled on his coat, hat, and boots, shoved his laptop in a backpack, and ventured out in his truck. Even he wasn't crazy enough to trudge through a foot of snow to get coffee. Apparently everyone else had the same idea, because the street in front of Main Street Mocha was crowded with cars in both directions and the plate-glass windows were fogged from the heat of so many patrons.

Gabe kicked the snow off his boots before he entered the coffee shop. Delia's part-time employee, a high school girl named Mary, was working the register and the espresso machine like she was born to it, which was practically the truth—she'd been working here since it was legal for her to have a job at fourteen. Whoever said that teenagers weren't capable and reliable had never met the girls who worked in Delia's business.

He ordered an Americano, extra hot, then wandered over to a corner table, where he plopped down in a chair and pulled out his laptop again. He might have downplayed the situation when he was assuring Kendall of his help, but in reality, he still had massive amounts of work to accomplish. The first model was almost finished—the one that showed what Jasper Lake would become with Burton's interference—and he was beginning to think that he'd done too good a job. It looked modern and appealing, like Breckenridge or Vail. But he hadn't yet added in the traffic or subtracted the businesses that would undoubtedly be pushed out by bigger corporate-owned entities once Jasper Lake became a legitimate money-making proposition.

And he had yet to put together the model of his own vision, something that would build on what the town had already established rather than take away from it.

He'd been counting on Kendall's help to catch that particular vision.

A cup was plunked down in front of him, sloshing coffee onto the table, dangerously close to his laptop. He looked up and saw Delia standing in front of him, still dressed for church, her hands on her hips. "Well. You've done it this time."

"Nice to see you too, Delia," he said placidly, even though her words and her expression sent dread into his gut. "What's going on?"

She pulled out the chair opposite him and sat, drumming her fingers restlessly on the tabletop. "Kendall came to see me."

Uh-oh. He had no idea why that would be a bad thing, but from the look on Delia's face, it was.

"Why did you start something that you know you can't commit to?"

Gabe winced and rubbed his hand through his hair, stalling. "She told you about that."

"That you kissed her and then froze her out? Yes."

"Hey now, that's not entirely true. She kissed me first."

She cocked her head. "Yeah, and you were not at all a willing participant."

She did have a point, but it wasn't as if he'd slept with her and taken off. A kiss was . . . a kiss. An exploration. Sometimes it went somewhere and sometimes it didn't. But he knew he was justifying himself.

Delia's expression softened. "I thought you said you weren't going to get involved with someone who wasn't a Christian."

"Exactly why I put the brakes on things."

"Yeah, you should have put the brakes on first."

He frowned. "I know we're friends, Delia, but where's this coming from? Other than pushing me to date more, you generally don't have strong opinions about my love life."

"I do when it hurts someone else I consider my friend. Kendall came to me for advice, and I had to tell her."

"You had to tell her that . . . ?"

"That you didn't date women without the same beliefs as you."

"Delia!" Gabe gaped at her, a burst of anger filling him. "That wasn't your place!"

"Well, she was there thinking she did something to offend you. What was I supposed to tell her? She's a friend, Gabe. I wasn't going to lie to her."

"But still . . ." He had no idea how Kendall would have taken that information, but he suspected it wasn't well. "I need to talk to her."

"I told her that she needed to discuss this with you as well, but I'd be surprised if she brings it up." For the first time, Delia looked remorseful. "She kind of shut down. I thought it might make her feel better that it didn't have anything to do with her. After all, you guys have known each other for all of a week. It's not like it's anything serious."

"Right," Gabe said, but inwardly he knew that wasn't true. Maybe they'd only met a week ago, but there was . . . *something* . . . between them that transcended the usual one-week relationship stage. Something that told him they'd connected on a real, deep level.

What was he supposed to do with that?

Delia drifted away, leaving Gabe to sit there and think about what he'd done. He'd been pretty much on autopilot when it came to Kendall, ignoring the feelings that he knew were brewing. He'd let his own blindness keep him from consulting God on what he should do about the relationship, had inadvertently hurt someone he cared about.

He pulled out his phone and texted Kendall. Do you have time to talk?

She took so long to answer that he thought she was either asleep or ignoring him. And then finally she replied, I'm catching up on some work at the B&B. We'll chat tomorrow when you pick me up.

That was the last thing he wanted to do: have a serious conversation while in the cab of his truck, on their way to do a little demolition. But Kendall's response was a clear brush-off, an indication that he'd legitimately hurt her. He would have to do this on her terms.

And it was probably good that he had some time to think. Because he needed to know what he wanted and be prepared to stick to it, no matter what it might do to their burgeoning friendship.

He just had a feeling that when they were finished, there wouldn't be a friendship to speak of at all.

Chapter Twenty-Six

Kendall ignored the ache in her chest every time she thought of Gabe and instead focused on her computer screen. She had no right to be upset, no right to expect things that Gabe hadn't promised her. It was good, actually, that she'd had things put into perspective for her. In a single week, she'd forgotten the whole reason she'd come to Jasper Lake—to sell her property here and buy the house that had been the closest thing to home for the last several years. Going through the photos of the Woolridge House, making notes on her pocket notepad, was a good way to realign her focus.

But she had to admit that Gabe wasn't the only thing dragging her mind back to Jasper Lake. She'd resisted any feeling of connection to this mountain town, the missing pieces of her past leaving painful jagged holes inside her. But finding her mother's letters had changed all that. Yes, there were still gaps in the narrative; it didn't change the fact that things had gone wrong in ways she couldn't even begin to comprehend. But it showed her that the one thing she'd always feared was untrue.

She'd been loved.

Her mother had been trying to bring her back home to her family, trying to give her a better life. No matter what had interrupted that goal, she could hold on to the knowledge that she hadn't been dismissed as damaged or a deadweight or unworthy of love.

No matter what Gabe might think of her.

Kendall sighed and put aside her notepad. There was no way she was going to focus on the California house, and to be honest, there was very little she could do. For reasons she didn't fully understand, she hadn't been able to get herself to contact the owners of the home and tell them she would take the job. Something told her she'd never be able to move on with her life without some closure in Jasper Lake.

There was no point in putting it off. She had to know.

She brought up the genealogy site and opened an account, then entered her credit card number for the monthly trial that would give her access to all the original records they had on file. She then found herself staring at a clean white screen with a search box.

She sat there, her fingers hovering over the keys. Then she typed *Kendall Green* followed by her birthday. At the last minute, she entered her place of birth as Colorado, though she had no idea which town she was born in.

An animated symbol indicated it was searching,

and Kendall held her breath. Only to receive the message *No results found.*

Hmm. That was disappointing, but not completely unexpected. She typed in her mother's name, *Caroline Green.*

Nothing.

She thought for a second and then typed *Constance Green* and *Jasper Lake* in the keyword box.

Nothing there either.

Clearly she needed a birth date. She turned to open the file box containing her grandmother's medical records . . . and realized she'd been in such a hurry to escape, she'd left them in the back of Gabe's truck. She winced, weighing the need to get the information against the awkwardness of texting him after she'd blown him off.

The desire for information won out. She texted, I forgot my boxes in your truck. I don't suppose you're someplace you can reach them?

A minute later, he replied, Sure. What do you need? Do you want me to bring them over?

No, that was the last thing she needed. She was on a roll and he was only a distraction, especially if he wanted to talk about what had happened. No, I just need my grandmother's birth date. It should be on the medical records.

Several minutes passed, and Kendall couldn't help wondering where he was. At home? Eating lunch? Obviously she'd sent him out in the cold and snow to check the boxes.

And then he came back with 04-01-1951. Need anything else while I'm looking?

Don't think so. Thanks.

She put the phone aside and carefully typed the birth date into the search box. This time when the little animation was done spinning, it brought up three records. One had been filed in St. Louis, Missouri, the second in Charleston, South Carolina. But the third? Longmont, Colorado.

Kendall's heart pounded as she clicked on the arrow that led to the record. She'd expected it to lead her to a birth certificate, but instead it led her to the deed of an old house in Denver, owned by Jonathan and Constance Green.

She wanted to slap her hand to her forehead. She was looking up Connie's married name. But now that she remembered her grandfather's name, maybe she could find a marriage certificate.

It took several permutations of her search before she came up with a plausible record: a marriage license between Jonathan William Green and Constance Amelia Jankowsky.

Kendall gave a sharp laugh. She was part Polish? That was something she'd never expected.

She typed in Connie's maiden name, almost giddy with anticipation of what she'd find.

No records found.

She sighed and slumped back against the pillows on her bed. That was anticlimactic. Here she'd been sure she was about to uncover something important about her past, something that might even help her with the house, and she'd hit a dead end.

She stared at the ceiling for a long moment, tracing the smooth slope of plaster into the cove molding, letting the sense of failure wash over her. And then she sat bolt upright.

She was an idiot. The original owner—or at least an early owner—hadn't been a Jankowsky. He had been a Green. Related to her grandfather, not her grandmother.

Kendall rolled her eyes at her own sluggish thinking and typed in her grandfather's name and birth date. This brought up a short list of records—marriage certificate, the deed to the Denver house, even a military enlistment record. Apparently Jonathan Green had been a Navy man. Well, that would explain why he had repressed his true identity for so long. Gay men in the military were barely tolerated today; back then, they would have been prohibited from serving at all.

And then she came across something that she should have expected but hadn't: a death certificate dated November 5, 1993.

An unexpected wash of disappointment flooded her. It wasn't as if she had given her grandfather much thought until now; she'd been much too focused on her relationship to Connie and Carrie. But now she realized that in the back of her mind, she'd hoped he might still be alive out there somewhere, one of the last links to her family. And as much of a long shot as it might have been, one of the last links to the provenance of the house.

She shut the lid of the laptop in frustration. It was slightly more than she'd known before—she was a Jankowsky on her grandmother's side— but it didn't give any more insight into the house and how it had made its way back around into the hands of a family member. If indeed J. Green and Jonathan Green were even related. It was a common enough name; she could be reading into things far too deeply.

No, if they were going to find out anything helpful about the Green family line and how these houses fit into the history of Jasper Lake, they'd have to do it through the house itself. She just hoped that when they cut into the ceiling of the master bedroom closet tomorrow, she was left with more than drywall dust to show for it.

Chapter Twenty-Seven

Kendall was waiting for Gabe on the front walk of the B and B when he pulled up to the curb the next morning—shivering, but more than ready to see what secrets the house might be hiding. At least it had gone from the teens to just below freezing this morning—already the snow was starting to melt around the edges, though she couldn't quite conceive of how, given the cold, silvery sunshine. She hiked her bag onto her shoulder and picked her way carefully down the slippery walkway to the door of the truck, climbing in before he could get out and open the door for her. They weren't dating, so there was no reason to act like they were.

"Morning," she said brightly when she settled into her seat and fastened her seat belt. "Are you ready for this?"

Gabe blinked at her a couple of times, then seemed to pull himself together. "I just hope that we're not making a big mess for no reason."

"Think of it as treasure hunting. You don't always come across something valuable, but the possibility is the exciting part." She might be overdoing the perkiness a bit this morning, but it was the only way she was going to get through this day with him. Complete denial. The sooner she pretended that he didn't mean anything to her, the sooner she would start to actually believe it.

They pulled away from the curb, and Gabe made his way slowly down the now-plowed road. "Kendall, I think we probably should talk."

"No need," she said briskly. "Delia already told me."

"Yeah, I wish she hadn't done that. It was something I should have told you myself."

Kendall waved a hand. If only she could wave off the sudden pang to her heart as easily. "It's okay. She did me a favor. I didn't realize that you were so strict about who you dated. Had I known, I would never have kissed you."

Gabe came to a stop at the intersection that led to the highway and put a hand on her arm. "Kendall, this is my fault, not yours. I'm really sorry. I never meant to hurt you."

"It's okay." Kendall shrugged. "We've just been hanging out. It's been an emotional trip, given everything I've discovered. It's only natural that I would get a little carried away. But I am going home soon, so anything that we might have thought was . . . forming . . . between us would have to end anyway."

Her pronouncement seemed to shut Gabe up. He nodded and pulled out onto the highway, making the rest of the short drive around the lake in silence. Kendall watched the scenery out her window like she'd done the first time she made the trip with him, but the landscape was so different under a heavy load of snow that it looked almost like a different place. The shapes were now soft and indistinct, hard edges blanketed by white that sparkled in the sunshine like a layer of diamond dust. She'd forgotten how much she loved the light on freshly fallen snow. Even as a child, it had filled her with such a sense of possibility, like it would melt off to reveal a totally different world than the one that had come before. As if everything would be reborn.

But now that she was an adult, she knew that for what it was—a child's fanciful imagining. It had taken years for the realities of life to adequately sink in.

When he finally pulled up behind Kendall's SUV, the house looked exactly as they'd left it, complete with their footsteps marring the otherwise-perfect sheet of white. She hopped out of the truck directly into a snowbank. The snow melted on contact with her warm jeans and soaked through to the skin, crept into the top of her boots. Great. She'd be wet all morning now. And there was no chance of heat inside to dry her out.

Gabe was just climbing out of the truck when an old, battered Ford pulled up behind him, a ladder strapped to the top, tools sitting in orange five-gallon buckets from a home improvement store in the bed. An older man with a gray ponytail and a battered army-green jacket climbed out of the truck gingerly, like he wasn't quite sure yet if his legs were going to hold. But he trudged through the snow to shake Gabe's hand and then turned to Kendall across the bed of Gabe's truck. "You must be Kendall Green. I'm Mike Millan. I hear we're going to be doing some surgery on the master bedroom ceiling."

The word *surgery* calmed whatever fears she might have had, so she nodded. "Hoping to find some clue to the house's architect or builder up there."

"Let's get started then." Mike went back to his truck and pulled out one of the buckets, then gestured to Gabe. "You could grab that ladder for this old man if you wanted to make yourself useful."

Kendall grinned at Gabe, who just chuckled, and led the way up the walkway to the door. She unlocked it and kicked some of the snow off her boots before she walked in, but Mike continued straight inside. She would have to track down some towels or something before the snow melted into the hardwood floors and marred the pristine finish.

"Let's go see what we have. If Gabe ever gets here with the ladder." Mike winked at her, and

Kendall realized he'd given him the task just to be contrary.

"Follow me." Kendall led the way up the stairs and down the short hall to the master bedroom, then gestured to the closet. "From my understanding of typical Craftsman floor plans, I think this area used to be a staircase."

Mike walked inside and started rapping on the walls with his knuckles. "Could be. This doesn't sound like lath and plaster, but with a house this old, it could be anything. It's hard to tell until you open up the wall."

"We're not going to do that, though," Kendall said in alarm.

"No, I don't think it's necessary."

Gabe finally appeared in a rattle of metal, out of breath and lugging the ladder under one arm. "Okay, where do you want this?"

"Set it up in here," Mike said, moving out of the way. "I'll start with a jab saw and see what's underneath the drywall before we fire up the generator."

Right. A generator. Because it was hard to use power tools when there wasn't actually any power to the house. Kendall was glad he'd thought about that little detail or the whole trip would have been a waste of time.

When Gabe had finished setting up the ladder, Mike found what looked like a pointy, serrated bread knife in his bucket and climbed up the first couple of ladder rungs. She held her breath when he plunged the saw into the ceiling and began sawing. "Not lath and plaster," he said. "Probably not the original ceiling." The saw stopped abruptly. "That's a joist."

"So what does that mean?" Kendall asked, her heart beating fast.

He didn't answer, just kept cutting until there was a three-foot square scribed out in the ceiling. And then he shoved his hand in the gap and pulled. The section came away in two pieces, taking with it bright-pink insulation and a shower of dust. Mike pulled out a flashlight and pointed it up into the space left over.

"We've got an attic," he said. "Don't even need the saw, I think. Give me that screwdriver, will you, sweetheart?"

Kendall allowed herself a covert eye roll at the endearment but found the battery-operated screwdriver and handed it up to him. He removed several long screws from something. "Hammer?"

Kendall held her breath again as he hammered a piece of two-by-four out of the ceiling and yanked it out. Then he climbed up another step, stuck his head inside, and looked around. When he climbed back down, he said to Kendall, "You were right. It's an attic space. You want to take a look?"

A giddy sense of excitement built in her chest as she squeezed by Mike and carefully climbed the ladder into the void. Cold air—even colder than the rest of the house—hit her as soon as her head breached the space. She held out a hand and Gabe passed the flashlight to her. She flicked it on and shone the beam around her.

It was an attic all right, dark, drafty . . .

And completely empty.

Disappointment slammed into her, sucking both the air and the hope out of her chest. "Well. That was a waste of time and mess." She climbed back down.

"What were you hoping to find exactly?"

"I don't know," Kendall said. "Paperwork? Old furniture? A big portrait of the owner with a flashing sign that says, 'I built this house'?" Her voice cracked on the last word, spoiling the flippant effect. Gabe shot her a sympathetic look. "So far I've hit only dead ends when it comes to the architect of the house."

"You're looking for blueprints and the like?"

Kendall nodded. "I need something that shows who the architect was. It's the only way for me to determine the exact age and historical significance of the place."

Mike moved past her again and picked up the piece of wood he'd taken out of the ceiling. "Did you look in the newel post?"

Kendall blinked. "The newel post? Like for the railing?"

"Yeah, sometimes architects of these old houses

would leave the blueprints in the newel post. Or behind the fireplace mantel." He scratched his beard. "You know, one time I found something under a floorboard when I was replacing the original floors. But I doubt you would want to do that."

Kendall exchanged a look with Gabe that made her think they were thinking the same thing. They'd just cut open a ceiling when they should have started with a newel post or fireplace. And then her heart sank. If there were plans in this house, they could be anywhere. She wandered back out in the bedroom and sank down onto the edge of the bed, deflated. They could tear this house apart and come up with absolutely nothing.

The sound of the power screwdriver whined from the closet as Mike replaced the support beam in the center of the space he'd cut out. Gabe came to sit beside her. "Admitting defeat already?"

"What's the point? I'm not going to destroy my grandmother's house looking for something that probably doesn't exist."

"That's what you heard? Because I heard something about checking a newel post and a fireplace mantel. Well, technically two, because this house has two fireplaces."

Gabe's tone brought a spark of hope back into her gloom. "Mike, do you think we could get the cap off the newel post without damaging too much?"

"We can try," he shot back.

Gabe grinned. "See? We can try. Not exactly a resounding yes, but at this point, I'd say we take it."

Now that there was a plan B, she could barely sit still while Mike sent Gabe down to get the other bucket, which had drywall tape and joint compound and all the tools he needed to repair the ceiling. By the time he was done, all it needed was to dry and then get another coat of paint, and no one would ever know they'd cut a hole in the closet.

Mike climbed off the ladder and wiped his dusty hands on his jeans. "So. We cracking up a newel post or what?"

"Easy there, Mike. Kendall just turned white as a sheet. We want to do it as carefully as possible."

"Well, yeah. But the varnish is old, so I just want you to be realistic."

In the end, though, it wasn't that complicated. Mike ran the tip of a box cutter around the seam between the post and the cap. Then he removed a rubber mallet and gently tapped the cap off. He peeked in.

"What's in there?" Kendall asked, almost afraid to look.

Mike stepped aside. "Look for yourself."

Her heart fell as she approached the post.

Somehow, it had never occurred to her that it wasn't a solid piece of wood, but rather four pieces seamed together with a void in the middle. She took the flashlight with dread and shone it into the space inside, expecting it to illuminate bare wood.

Instead, it revealed a sheaf of rolled paper.

Chapter Twenty-Eight

Kendall's heart thumped against her rib cage as she reached into the newel post and withdrew the roll. There could be no doubt about what the papers were—the dark-blue color gave them away—but the pages were wrinkled from exposure to moisture, and the rubber band that held them together crumbled the instant she touched it. She held her breath while she slowly unrolled the stack.

It was the exterior elevation of the house, marked above the image in elaborate, old-fashioned script, with the words *No. 3 Lakeshore Drive.*

Kendall glanced at Gabe, her eyes wide. "These are them." She looked around, so stunned that she could barely form a complete thought. He guided her to an occasional table beneath the window in the front parlor and helped her unroll the papers flat while Mike hovered curiously in the periphery.

"Does it say anything about the architect?" Gabe asked quietly over her shoulder.

Kendall scanned the entire page for the second time. All it showed was the exterior, only slightly different from how it stood now. She shook her head. "I don't see it."

Gabe carefully lifted the fragile paper and rolled it up again, then put it aside so they could view the second print in the stack. This one declared *No. 3 Lakeshore Drive, Ground Floor,* and showed the floor plan with all the pertinent dimensions.

"Still no signature," Kendall murmured. "But at least we know one thing: the architect was British. Or at least European."

Gabe frowned at her, puzzled.

"Americans call the bottom floor the first. Always have to my knowledge. Only Europeans use the term 'ground floor.'"

"I guess there's an easy way to find out." Gabe lifted the second sheet to reveal the third. Sure enough, it was the upper floor of the house, marked *No. 3 Lakeshore Drive, 1st Floor.* "Looks like you're right."

Kendall's excitement started to build once more. Maybe that's why she hadn't been able to turn up any records on a J. Green. If he had recently emigrated to America when he designed the houses, there might not be any records, especially if he didn't come through Ellis Island, which was one of the few institutions to digitize and categorize their old paper records. She looked more closely at the plans and felt a sharp spike of satisfaction that she'd been right: the old staircase had indeed been placed between the master bedroom and the upstairs bathroom.

She hadn't lost her touch when it came to architecture.

"No full signature yet?" Gabe inquired by her ear again. She jumped, startled, her skin prickling at his sudden nearness.

"Not yet." What architect didn't sign his plans? Kendall's stomach twisted. Was it possible that after all this, they might still be no closer to knowing his identity than they were before?

And then she turned over to the last page and inhaled. It was an extensive drawing of the decorative woodwork in the house, showing cross sections and profiles of each piece of molding, even the columbines she had admired on her viewing, with notes on what kind of wood and varnish should be used for each. And at the very bottom were the words *No. 3 Lakeshore Drive, Clear Creek County, Colorado—Jasper Green, Architect, London, England, 1899.*

A chill rippled over her skin. She slowly turned to Gabe. "Jasper Green. As in . . . Jasper Lake?"

His expression shifted as the implications sank in. "I always thought it was named for the rock that's found around here."

"Kind of an ironic name, don't you think? Green jasper?" Kendall chuckled, but most of her mind was still focused on the possibilities. Now that she knew the architect was English, she had a place to start. Her expertise was mostly centered on the American Arts and Crafts movement, which might be why she'd never heard of him. But given the use of the William Morris wallpaper and the decorative elements that had struck her as far more European than American, it made sense. Why had she not thought to research Morris's students in Britain?

"This could be big," Gabe murmured, drawing her thoughts back to the present. "You realize what this means? If Jasper Green really lent his name to Jasper Lake, he could be the founder of the town. These could be the first structures built in the entire place." He grabbed Kendall's hands and squeezed. "You might have just saved everything." And then he pulled back. "How do we find that out, though?"

"First things first. Let's try to see if Jasper Green was a known architect. That alone makes the houses worth saving." She pulled up her cell phone and found the tracking notice that Sophie had sent when she FedExed the books, then searched for the package number. "It says the research books I had sent from home have been delivered."

Gabe jumped up as if he'd been sitting on hot coals. "Mike, can you close up the post again? We need to get back to town."

Mike had been watching the whole proceeding with vague amusement. "All I want to know is if this is going to ruin Burton's plans."

Gabe and Kendall exchanged a glance and simultaneously declared, "Oh yeah."

Mike grinned. "That's all I needed to know. Let me clean up here and we'll lock up."

Kendall shifted from foot to foot impatiently while Mike tapped the cap back onto the post and gathered his tools. Gabe carefully rerolled the plans and handed them over to her for safekeeping, but she could do little but clutch them and marvel over the discovery. If Jasper Green was anyone important or if he was involved in the founding of the town, they had the tools they needed to win over the city council and stop the zoning change. They'd found their smoking gun.

And Kendall might have found a little-known bit of her past. She stared at the prints for a moment in wonder. Was that where she'd gotten her love of architecture and design? Did it literally run through her blood?

"Ready to go?" Mike asked, poking his head in through the front door. Kendall jolted back to the present and impulsively hugged the handyman. "What was that for?"

"Thanks for helping us. If you hadn't mentioned the post, we would never have thought to look there. How did you know about it?"

Mike shrugged. "My wife likes to watch those English mysteries on PBS. Always something hidden in a post or a fireplace, isn't there?"

Kendall looked at Gabe and they both started to laugh. "Then thank your wife for watching all those mysteries."

They locked up the house and made their way to the trucks parked at the curb. The whole time Kendall crossed her fingers mentally and sent up prayers to whoever would listen that the books waiting back at the B and B would illuminate something about their architect. They paused between the bumpers of Gabe's truck and Kendall's SUV.

"That was some stroke of luck," Gabe said. "Now we just need to see if we can track down how Jasper Green came to Colorado from England. It kills me that all those old records were lost. Surely there was some information about him in there."

"Maybe not. After all, if he founded the town, he might have predated the town records. And who knows? Back then people would settle in a place, the town would grow up around it, and they'd name it after the founder posthumously. He might not have even survived to see his namesake."

"Yeah, but what about the J. Green in the tax rolls?"

Kendall paused. He had a point. "There's no way of knowing whether or not that was Jasper. Could have been a child or a widow."

"I guess you're right. It feels like every time

we get a little bit of information, it just shows us how much we still don't know."

Kendall flashed a rueful smile. "Don't I know it."

Gabe reached for her hand. "We're going to find out about your mother, Kendall. Somehow. I promise you that."

For a long moment, she wanted to believe him, wanted to keep her hand in the warmth of his grasp, but then she remembered that no matter what she might feel for him, the relationship was doomed. She drew it away slowly and kept her voice light. "Don't promise things that you can't deliver, Gabe."

Gabe looked at her sharply, and only then did she realize that her words could have been taken two ways. She hugged her arms around herself.

Well, he shouldn't promise that either. But they didn't have time to dwell on a relationship that was dead before it even started.

Just as the silence began to get awkward, Gabe nodded toward her SUV. "You have a snow brush for all that?"

"A what?"

Gabe chuckled. "Hold on." He went to the truck's back seat and returned with a long plastic tool, sporting a soft brush on one end and an ice scraper on the other. She reached for it, but he ignored her and began to brush the accumulated snow from all the windows. Kendall flushed.

Even after all the weirdness between them, he still treated her with kindness.

Perhaps that's what made her pause halfway to the driver's side door. "You're still coming back to the B and B with me, aren't you?"

He seemed surprised. "If that's okay."

She gave a single nod. "I could use the help. Follow me back?"

"I'll see you there."

Kendall faltered for a moment, then unlocked the door and climbed into the frigid interior of her rental vehicle. She almost regretted picking up the SUV, not because she wanted an excuse to spend time with Gabe, but because the silence inside gave her far too much time to think. Far too much time to dwell on the possibilities. She was glad when they finally arrived in front of the B and B, Gabe parking behind her at the curb, and they quick-walked up the slippery path to the front door.

As soon as they stepped through the front door, Gabe lifted his voice and called, "Opa?"

A moment later, Mr. Brandt appeared, wearing an apron and wiping his hands on a kitchen towel. "There you are. Kendall, you got a delivery. The box is on the floor right there behind you."

They turned to see a large cardboard box, battered and water stained, but intact. Gabe asked, "Opa, can we use the dining room? We've got a bunch of books to lay out."

He shrugged. "Don't see why not. Doesn't get used for anything else anymore." He cocked his head curiously. "What have you got there?"

"We found the architect of the Lakeshore houses," Kendall said before Gabe could answer. "We need to see if there's anything about him in my reference books."

His eyebrows rose. "You shipped them all from California?"

"Oh, this isn't even close to all. This is just a small section of my collection. My entire library is filled with reference books and catalogs." The words filled her with a sudden pang of home-sickness for her Pasadena house. She'd only been gone a week, but it felt like she'd completely separated from her old life, as if it were a half-remembered dream. How could her detour here feel more real than the life she'd so painstakingly made back home?

She looked at Gabe and her chest clenched. It was his fault. From the moment she had laid eyes on him, she'd been pulled in like there was some invisible band that connected them. Even when she was trying to deny everything—her attraction, her hope for what she would find here—she had been slowly falling for him. His kindness. The soft way he touched her when he wanted to comfort her but didn't know how. The passionate way he'd kissed her and the restraint he'd shown afterward. It all added up to someone she could love.

And he didn't want her.

Tears pricked her eyes. "You know what?" she said suddenly. "Why don't you leave them to me?"

Mr. Brandt looked between the two of them, obviously deciding there was more than met the eye going on, and excused himself. But Gabe wasn't quite so intuitive. "It will go faster with both of us."

Kendall stared at the floor. "I can't do this, Gabe. I can't pretend this with you."

"What do you mean?"

She laughed harshly, but she still didn't look him in the eye. "I can't pretend not to be falling in love with you. And I don't believe that you don't feel something for me. It's just your stupid, rigid beliefs that are in the way, and I can't look at you without being angry and hurt and absolutely baffled that an intelligent person like you would be bound by some outdated standard."

"Kendall . . ."

She brushed past him and picked up the box, struggling under its weight. She was going to hurt herself, but right now she was too angry to let him think she couldn't handle it. "I'll call you if I find something. Otherwise . . . I don't think we have anything to say to one another." She started up the stairs, teetering precariously, but he didn't come after her. She didn't know if that made her feel better or worse.

When she got up to the landing, he said her name again. She turned, hoping that maybe what she'd said had sunk in, that maybe he was going to change his mind. But he was only watching her with a sad look on his face. "I'm sorry, Kendall. I know you probably hate me right now. Outdated standards or not, it's what I believe. And I can't change that for you or anyone."

Kendall gave him a sharp nod. She pushed through into her room and bumped the door shut with her hip, then lowered the box to the floor with a thud. Where she landed beside it and cried like her heart would break.

Except it hadn't. Wouldn't. Couldn't. You couldn't break something that had already been destroyed long ago.

Gabe knew he should go back to work, but acting like nothing had happened after the confrontation with Kendall was impossible. Instead, he found himself walking to Main Street Mocha, inviting the biting cold as punishment for his own stupidity.

This whole thing happened because he was trying not to hurt Kendall, knew that if they continued down this road, it could never work out. His mistake wasn't sticking to his beliefs; it was forgetting about them in the first place. He'd let his own attraction to her get out of hand, let her think that there was a future for them. It might not have been logical, but matters of the heart never were.

And now he'd done damage to someone he truly cared about.

His misery must have shown on his face, because when he stepped up to the counter to order, Delia took one look at him and made a face. "Uh-oh. That doesn't look good."

"Thanks," he said. "Can I just get a small Americano?"

"You can if you tell me what's going on with you."

Gabe glanced around. There were a handful of people in the coffee shop in the afternoon, but he wouldn't call it crowded. Still, he didn't feel like spilling his guts standing at a cash register. "Caffeine first."

"Okay. I can respect that." She waved him off when he pulled out his wallet. "You can wait to pay until I decide if I feel sorry for you or not. If I do, no charge. If I don't, double."

That made Gabe smile. Delia never failed to cheer him up, even when he was feeling completely wrecked. "Deal. Make it a large, then. I have a feeling I'm going to come out on the right side of this one."

Delia gave him an amused look and then pointed sternly to the table in the corner. "Plant it there. I'll bring you your coffee in a minute. Have your wallet ready."

Gabe chuckled, though inwardly he wasn't feeling much like laughing. He took the seat by the window that she indicated and drummed his fingers on the table while he waited for his drink. A few minutes later, Delia set a stoneware cup and saucer in front of him and plopped herself into the chair opposite.

"I'm in love with Kendall," he said.

Delia didn't react.

"But for obvious reasons, that can't work out."

She said nothing.

"The thing is, I didn't mean for it to happen. There's just . . . something about her. I can't help it. She's smart and funny and . . ."

"Wounded?" Delia suggested.

Gabe blinked. "Well, kind of. But that's not why I fell for her."

Delia folded her hands on the table. "Gabe, I say this out of love. But you're confused here."

He sat back in his chair, feeling vaguely offended, though he wasn't sure why. "Of course I'm confused."

"She's been here for a week. You're not in love. You've found someone you admire and you're attracted to. There's a difference. What you're in love with is the chance to fix her."

"No! That's not it at all."

Delia reached across the table and placed her hand over his. "Gabe, you're a fixer. You always have been. It's why you came back to Jasper

Lake and ran for mayor. You saw a problem and you thought you could do something about it."

"And that's a bad thing?"

"No, that's a very good thing. It's one of the things that makes you a great friend and potentially a great mayor. Jury is still out on that second one, but I have high hopes for you." She winked at him. "But since Kendall Green came into town, I'm not sure you've seen her as a person. First you saw her as the solution to the town's problems. And then you saw her as someone you could help, someone you could fix." She looked at him closely. "Tell me that's not true."

He wanted to protest, but he thought of how he'd promised that *they'd* uncover what happened to her mother, of the steps he'd already taken to accomplish it. "Okay, maybe you're right on that count. But I still don't think it's a bad thing."

"It's not a bad thing! Not at all. But it's not love. If it turns into a relationship, it's codependency." She held up her hands. "I'm no psychologist. But I have spent enough time in a therapist's chair to know relationships that start because two people *need* each other are doomed. You've got your stuff. She's got her stuff. Maybe you should be focusing on how to work out that stuff rather than how to be together. And after that? Who knows?"

What Delia said made a lot of sense, but he couldn't accept it completely. Not when his free

351

Americano was on the line. "She's leaving this week. I may never see her again."

"Then it wasn't meant to be." Her smile turned gentler. "Tell me, Gabe, who's in charge here, you or God?"

The obvious answer was God, but when he opened his mouth to respond, he couldn't in good conscience pretend that he was letting Him lead. "Okay, fine, you've made your point." It didn't mean he had to like it. Why would Kendall have come into his life other than to have a relationship?

He felt so stupid even thinking that, when the answer was clear. Of course there were other reasons. Saving his town. Helping Kendall find the truth of her past, heal from the trauma of her abandonment. When he said as much, Delia fixed him with a pointed stare. "You're stepping into your savior complex again, my friend. You ever hear the phrase 'Physician, heal thyself'?"

"Yeah, yeah." In his heart, he knew there was something to Delia's words, but he couldn't deal with that right now. Or maybe wouldn't. "I've got other news you might be interested in, but first I have to know if I'm paying for my own coffee."

Delia smiled. "It's on the house. You're just pathetic enough to qualify."

"Gee, thanks."

"So what's the news?"

"We found the plans for the Lakeshore houses,

or at least one of them. A British architect named Jasper Green."

Delia's eyebrows flew up. "Interesting. Do you think the town was named after him?"

"It's entirely possible. That's the next order of business, to try to dig up some information on who he was and where he came from. But this is the very break we've been waiting for. Either way, I think we can make a case for the historical significance of the houses and stop the rezoning."

"That's great news, Gabe. I'm so happy." The front door dinged as another customer entered, and Delia rose from the table. "Keep me posted, okay?"

"Will do."

He sat there and sipped his Americano, mulling over what Delia had said before he could be tempted to shift away from the uncomfortable topic. Was he really confusing love with his desire to help?

He couldn't deny the possibility. After all, wasn't his talent envisioning how things could be, rather than how things were? It's why he'd chosen his career, why he'd run for mayor, why he wanted to save the houses. He had grand visions of the future, what he could accomplish with a little work and time. And if he were honest, mostly what he *felt* right now was run-of-the-mill attraction. It seemed crass to call it lust, but he didn't know Kendall well enough to know if he loved her. He just knew that there was a connection he wanted to explore, a possible future in which they could be happy together.

And he simply didn't want to give up that vision of the future.

He downed the rest of his coffee and pushed away from the table. There were multiple versions of the future, and he didn't want to see the one where Main Street Mocha was replaced by corporate chains and potentially important pieces of Colorado architecture were destroyed in favor of a summer resort.

It was time to get to work.

Chapter Twenty-Nine

The materials that Sophie had sent her might not be a truckload, but they were definitely more than a backpack full. Kendall ripped off the packing tape and opened the box, taking out the heavy books two by two. Some of them were academic tomes on the history of the Arts and Crafts movement. Some were books on Craftsman furniture, Morris wallpaper designs, and the architectural variations of the style. And then there were a handful of catalogs from Christie's and Sotheby's auctions from the last several decades. How Sophie had managed to determine which ones were relevant, Kendall had no idea. Unless she'd actually gone through each and every one . . . which, knowing her former assistant turned designer, was entirely possible.

Kendall started with the architecture books, plopping on her bed and dragging one heavy volume after another onto her lap. Even just skimming the contents, hours passed before she got through them all without even a single mention of Jasper Green.

She blew a stray tendril from her face in frustration. She'd been banking on there being some information on him somewhere. She'd even take a photo of woodwork that was similar as a direction to start hunting down information. Architectural styles didn't develop in a vacuum, after all.

For one mad second, she was tempted to call Gabe and ask him to come over and help her sort through the mess. But he'd made it pretty clear what he thought about her. Maybe he didn't bear her any ill will, but he certainly wasn't interested in her beyond her relationship to the houses and what their sale could mean for the town. She dumped the last heavy book off her lap and dragged the next one onto it.

She was about to call it impossible when she lifted a slim book—little more than a pamphlet, really—that she'd picked up at a conference in England long ago. It was poorly printed and bound, clearly the efforts of an antiques professional who had no publishing knowledge, but she remembered thinking that the information in it was solid. It was about the Art Workers' Guild, a society formed in Britain to bring together practitioners of both the fine arts and the applied arts on equal footing—a little-known outgrowth of William Morris's ideals, if not his specific tastes. Kendall found herself sucked into the history, half-forgetting what she was supposed to be looking for as she read about the early masters of the guild and their philosophies. And then, halfway through the pamphlet, she came across this passage:

In the spirit of the guild's philosophy that there should be no dividing line between art and architecture, many of its earliest members were both accomplished architects and fine artists. One member that clearly expressed the tension of the era was Jasper Green, a sculptor, decorative artist, and architect who defected from the Royal Academy because of their increasing hostility toward the applied arts.

Kendall's heart rose into her throat, losing its rhythm for what felt like an eternity. She quickly skimmed the rest of the short book, this time having her eyes attuned only for the name, but Jasper Green never surfaced again.

But he existed. He was an architect, sculptor, and applied artist—the old term for what they now called industrial design. She knew he was once a member of the Royal Academy and the Art Workers' Guild, which meant she'd been right about him being British. Of course, it still told her nothing about how he'd ended up in America, building houses with Carpenter Gothic exteriors and Craftsman interiors, but at least it was a start.

It was a confirmation.

Kendall jumped off the bed and lunged for her phone. At this moment, she no longer cared about her vow not to contact Gabe, not when she

357

had a solution to their problems. She dialed his number and didn't even wait for him to say hello. "I've got it, Gabe! Jasper Green was a member of the Art Workers' Guild in London in the 1880s. That makes these houses significant both for the architecture and the age. We can apply to have them placed on the National Register of Historic Places."

The line stayed quiet, and for a second, she thought he'd hung up on her. Then he replied, his voice careful, "And how long will that take?"

"It varies from state to state, but usually about ninety days. Why?"

He cleared his throat. "We don't have ninety days, Kendall. They're scheduled to be condemned in thirty."

Twenty minutes later, Kendall and Gabe claimed a quiet corner table in Main Street Mocha, the decision to meet on neutral ground almost automatic. Ever since Gabe's pronouncement, Kendall's brain had been spinning. How could the houses be condemned, and why hadn't she been notified as the owner?

No, that was far more coherent than what she was mostly thinking: *Why? Why? How? Why?*

Delia looked between them curiously when she set down their drinks, but she didn't interrupt. Kendall ignored the peppermint mocha and pitched her voice low, below the buzz of the coffeehouse. "So what do you mean my houses are being condemned?"

Gabe pulled out a folded piece of paper, which looked like it had been crumpled and then smoothed out again. "Burton delivered it to my office as a 'courtesy,' which really means that he wanted to gloat about it. Apparently he found out that we have the original plans for the houses and that there have been changes made to them. There aren't any permits on file for the changes. That, combined with the foundation issues . . . you'll have a notice tacked on the door by the end of tomorrow, if it's not there already."

Kendall sat back, stunned. "I don't understand. How did he find out so quickly? We only just found the plans today."

"My guess? Mike ran into him and bragged about finding the plans. I'm sure he didn't think it could hurt us, but he underestimated what Burton was willing to do to get the property."

"Burton has been threatening something like this from the beginning, I just didn't understand the hints." Kendall kneaded her temples, forcing herself to think rationally despite the surge of adrenaline flowing through her body. There had to be a way out of this. "I thought home-owners could make changes themselves without permits?"

"Well, we have no evidence it was done by the homeowner. Actually, it's very unlikely that it was. And if the work was unpermitted and done by someone other than Connie or Jonathan Green, then it can't be grandfathered in. Basically, Burton is claiming that the houses are unsafe because of unpermitted work and deferred maintenance, and we're being given thirty days to demonstrate that we can bring them up to code or they'll be condemned as a public safety hazard."

Kendall stared at Gabe, horrified. "How can he possibly do that? They haven't even looked at the houses to know what's been done or if they're actually dangerous."

His tone soured. "Best guess? Burton has someone inside the county government."

Her mouth dropped open. Of all things she thought she would face up here—bureaucracy, the slow pace of small counties, resistance to change—corruption was not one of them. "So you think—" she lowered her voice when it came out much too loud and the neighboring patrons turned toward her—"he paid someone off?"

"I don't think it was anything that blatant. I think it was more like a well-placed word to someone that his project will bring in a lot of money in permits and property taxes to the county and he has a legitimately legal way to make that happen." Gabe slumped back in his seat, looking defeated. "He's not wrong. That's the way the county code is written. Though I'd be surprised if it's ever been used to demolish homes to pave the way for a commercial project."

"Yeah, it makes eminent domain look like it's on the up-and-up," Kendall said bitterly. "But wait. You said we have thirty days to demonstrate that we can bring them up to code. Not that we actually have to do the work in thirty days. Right?"

Gabe nodded. "That's correct. We need to respond to the notice, file all the requisite permits, etc."

"So we do that, then. Easy."

"Not so easy, Kendall. These things take money. Not to mention if you manage to save them, you still have to return them to their original plans in order to get them listed on the registry."

Now it was Kendall's turn to slump back in her seat. "I don't have that kind of money."

"Yeah. Neither do I."

"What I don't understand is how he could condemn the houses and get them demolished, but I still own the land."

"Which is now worth significantly less without the improvements on it. He doesn't have to pay you what the houses are worth, just the lots. Given the price of property up here, that's much less. *And* it doesn't do you any good to hold on to empty, barren land."

Even through a sudden surge of blinding rage, she had to admit that Burton was smart. He'd worked through every angle. He'd warned her. And since she had made it clear she wasn't going to cave to his initial offer, he was starting to apply pressure.

Completely unethical, but entirely legal.

Gabe was staring into space now. She peered into his face. "Gabe, are you okay?"

He focused on her, but the wry twist to his mouth said that whatever he was thinking about wasn't pleasant. "I might know someone who could help us."

Kendall blinked at him. "You do? Why have you waited so long to contact him, then?"

"Because I said I'd never speak to him again, and I've kept that promise. But now I may have no choice." Gabe rubbed his hands over his face wearily. "I have to call my father."

Chapter Thirty

Gabe didn't tell anyone else what he was planning. Not his grandfather and certainly not his mom. His grandfather would no doubt be cautiously optimistic. Opa had always told him that he was only hurting himself by ignoring a relationship with his father. His mom? He couldn't even imagine what she might say. After he'd found out about his true parentage and been shipped off to Jasper Lake, they'd never discussed it in depth again.

And that didn't even begin to address what his father might do.

No, not his father. The man who was biologically responsible for his existence. Robert Miller.

Despite the fact that Gabe had barely been in the office since Kendall arrived, he called Linda to inform her that he would be out of town on business for a day or two. Then he arranged for Luke to come feed and walk Fitz while he was gone. It was only a little over an hour from Jasper Lake to his father's office in Denver, but he had no idea if Robert would be in or willing to see him. It could take more than a day. He packed an overnight bag, shoved his laptop into a backpack, and hopped into his truck as the sun crested the horizon of the nearest peak.

As soon as he hit the boundaries of the town, Gabe exhaled. He felt like he hadn't taken a full breath in months, and that was compounded by how twisted up in knots he'd been since the confrontation with Kendall. He still couldn't think about the hurt, stricken look on her face when he'd told her there could be no future for them because of the differences in their spiritual beliefs. Every time, he wondered how he could have done things differently. How he could have spared her.

How he could have spared himself.

Because now, knowing that they were nearing the end of their time working together, that she intended to return to California in less than a week, the idea of her absence made it hard to breathe. In just a short period of time, she'd worked herself into his daily life in a way that he'd never thought possible. He couldn't effectively explain it. They had a few things in common, yes, but there was no denying the connection that he'd felt since the very first time he'd laid eyes on her, and it wasn't merely attraction. It was like . . .

. . . he'd found his missing piece.

It just seemed that God hadn't gotten the memo.

Gabe squeezed the steering wheel, knowing that thought wasn't fair. If there was anyone who'd misread the situation, it was him. He couldn't reject the possibility that she'd been brought into his life for a reason other than his happiness. He'd helped her uncover some details about her mother and grandmother; he'd at least managed to talk to her about his faith, before his faith became the thing that drove a wedge between them. Maybe that had to be enough.

No matter how the idea made his heart ache.

"Your plan hasn't changed, Gabe," he told himself sternly as he rejoined the highway that would take him to I-70 and then down the mountain into Denver. It had always been to save the town. That's why he had been brought to Jasper Lake, and that's what he was going to do. Even if it meant breaking a promise that he'd made to himself and his mother so many years ago.

By the time the road flattened from the steep downhill through Genesee into the gentle slopes of Jefferson County, he had a game plan. He wasn't going to approach Robert as his son. He was going to approach him as a civil servant making an appeal to a businessman, one that could be very profitable for him. After all, if there was one thing he knew about his birth father, it was that he looked out for his own interests. Gabe was suddenly glad that he'd decided to don a button-down shirt and his sport coat, even if the waterproof boots weren't quite the business image he wanted to portray. But this was Colorado, after all. People took meetings in

Wranglers and cowboy boots, went to four-star restaurants in fleece pullovers. He doubted that his father's office was any different.

It had been so long since he'd been to the building, Gabe had to rely on his phone's GPS to take him to the downtown block where Miller Property Group was located. It was a multi-story brick Victorian building, two floors of which were taken up by the various divisions of Robert's company: real estate, development, investment, and architecture. It was a testament to Colorado's rapid growth that what had started off as a residential architectural firm had grown into something spanning all areas of property development.

The difference between Burton and Robert Miller was ethics. Robert's firm specialized in restoration and preservation, converting buildings to new uses while still retaining their architectural and historical details. Ironic, considering it was his lack of personal ethics that brought Gabe into this world in the first place.

Gabe parked in the underground parking garage and took a moment to straighten himself before he yanked the door of his truck open. He took a deep breath. Now or never.

He had to check the directory in the old-fashioned Victorian lobby to see which floor his father was on and stepped onto the equally old-fashioned–looking elevator. He was relieved to see that the inside was all new stainless steel and chrome, despite the original brass doors that opened to admit him. He punched the 3 button and held his breath as the doors slid closed and the elevator glided soundlessly to the third floor.

The doors opened again and deposited him in an ornate hallway that opened into a large reception space. He walked directly to the mahogany desk and forced a smile for the young woman who sat there. "Gabriel Brandt here to see Robert Miller."

Her eyes widened slightly—obviously she knew who he was—but she managed a friendly smile and gestured to the waiting area to the right. "I'll see if he's available. Please make yourself comfortable. There's coffee and tea while you wait, if you'd like."

"Thank you." Gabe returned the smile even though he was shaking inside at what he was about to do. He hadn't spoken to Robert in . . . what? Over ten years? And only then because he'd accidentally run into him at a Denver Christmas party. Apparently they had professional connections in common. Rather than taking a seat, he helped himself to a cup of coffee from the machine. The first sip hit his nervous stomach and turned it sour.

"Gabe! What a surprise!"

Gabe spun at the male voice and put down the Styrofoam cup quickly on the edge of the table.

He blinked. His mental image hadn't taken into account the passage of time: in the last decade, the lines around Robert's eyes had gotten more pronounced, his dark hair tinged with silver, the athletic build a little softer. And despite all that, no one could look at the two of them and not know that they were father and son.

He found his voice and was pleased that it came out strong and steady. "I'm sorry to just drop in on you like this. Do you have a minute?"

"For you? Always." He stepped aside and gestured for Gabe to precede him down the hall into the back of the office. Gabe was relieved he didn't try to embrace him or touch him in any way. In fact, he was treating him like a friendly business associate. Which, in this case, was exactly what he was.

"First door on the right," Robert said in a low voice, and Gabe turned in to a surprisingly small office that was decorated only with a mission-style desk, a matching credenza, and two conference chairs. Paperwork spilled from piles on the desk, and the walls were hung with dry-erase boards covered with various property addresses rather than the fine art he'd expected. Instead of taking a seat in the imposing leather chair behind the desk, Robert turned one of the guest chairs so he could face Gabe.

"What can I help you with today, Son?" The word seemed to be almost automatic, as directed toward a younger man, not to his own actual son, but it still grated on Gabe's nerves.

"I have a business proposition for you."

Robert studied him for a long moment, then gave a nod. "I'm listening."

Gabe hesitated, but Robert seemed to be serious, so he started at the beginning. How he'd been elected mayor of Jasper Lake to preserve the town's character, how Burton's development threatened that, and how the nasty behind-the-scenes dealing was threatening to demolish Kendall's houses. When Gabe finished, Robert just sat there, his head tipped toward the ceiling, thinking.

"That is a tricky situation." Robert finally focused on his face. "I don't see how I'd be able to help directly. The fact is, we're exclusively focusing on Denver at the moment, and my firm is integrally involved in lobbying for zoning changes to prevent some of the irresponsible development that's happening in the less affluent neighborhoods."

Gabe's hopes plummeted. He could understand where his father was coming from, but he wouldn't make an exception, even for him? He didn't know why he'd come here. He'd burned these bridges long ago, and it was only stupid hope that made him think some remnant of paternal responsibility would induce Robert to help. Worst of all, Gabe really couldn't blame him.

But Robert wasn't finished. He grabbed a note-pad from his desk and scribbled several names and numbers on a sheet of paper, then tore it off and handed it to Gabe. "The first number is an attorney I work with, Pam Martinez. First thing you do is call her and ask her to file an injunction on the condemnation proceedings pending a historical places designation. She's well familiar with the county court systems, and most of the judges won't bother ruling against her because she has a reputation for tying them up with motions until they give in." A small smile surfaced on Robert's face—either he liked this woman or he admired her pit bull approach. Maybe both. "The second, Winnie Johnson, is a friend I know involved in Colorado historical preservation projects. She's also part of the board that reviews grant applications for historical preservation. The deadline was a couple of weeks ago, but I happen to know that they haven't awarded this year's grants yet. They may be willing to fudge the deadline if you tell her what you've told me. That could at least buy you some time to get the houses up to code and lift the con-demnation proceedings.

"In the meantime, you and this Kendall you mentioned need to put in your application for the National Register. As in yesterday. Pam is going to need that as part of her filing. And then, based on those things, you push—and push hard—to get the city council to change the zoning. Immediately. Bring a motion and make them vote on it. Show the dirty tricks this guy is willing to employ to destroy the most unique characteristics of your city. Ask them how much their autonomy is worth to them." Robert's eyes sparkled. "If there's one thing I know about Coloradans, especially in the high country, it's that they prize their way of life and their independence. Show them that they're letting an outsider determine their future." He held Gabe's gaze. "This isn't a matter of facts, Gabe; it's a matter of emotion. Of personality. Like it or not, you chose to be the leader of this town. So lead. I have no doubt that you're capable of swinging this your way."

Gabe skimmed the paper in his hand, but he really didn't see it. This was not what he'd expected when he'd shown up here today. He'd been hoping that Robert would swoop in with his checkbook and save the day. Maybe feel a little bit of guilt about how he and his mom had struggled when he was a child.

Instead, he was acting like . . . a father.

A father giving him advice, shoring up his confidence. Except unlike a real father, he hadn't been there. These were all just empty platitudes. A way to get him out of his office quickly so he could get back to his real work. "How do you know I can lead?" Gabe shot back. "You know nearly nothing about me."

The corner of Robert's mouth tipped up, but it was almost a grimace, not a smile. "That was by your choice, Son, not mine. And I venture to say I know a lot more about you than you think." He tilted his head toward the credenza behind them.

For the first time, Gabe noticed the photos sitting there. Several of them were of Robert's daughters, as he might have expected. But there was one of him with his mom at his high school graduation, beaming off to the side in a way that made it obvious they'd been smiling for someone else's camera. Another photo of him shaking the hand of the president of his university as he accepted his graduate school diploma, obviously taken from a distance and cropped.

"I stayed away out of respect for your wishes," Robert said quietly, his voice a little hoarse. "But that doesn't mean I didn't care. Or that I'm not proud of you." Now the grimace turned into something more like a smile. "I've followed from afar. I hope that doesn't upset you."

"I don't know how I feel about that." In some ways, it felt intrusive, almost creepy, that Robert had been present at his graduations and he didn't know it. Of course, it wasn't like he was following Gabe around town with a telephoto lens or something, but the idea that he'd been there and Gabe hadn't known . . .

Robert gave a single nod. "Call Pam and Winnie. Today, even. They'll take your calls and they can help guide you through the process. Save your town, Gabe." He pushed himself to his feet. "And when you decide how you feel about the rest, even if you just want to talk, vent, tell me what a terrible absentee father I was—" a wry twist of a smile surfaced again—"you know where to find me."

Gabe stood as well. He hesitated before gripping Robert's outstretched hand. "Thank you for seeing me. Thank you for the advice."

"Good luck. I trust you know your way out? I'm overdue for a meeting."

Gabe nodded slowly and turned toward the door, aware of Robert following him out. But he didn't turn back to see if he was looking, to see if he turned down the intersecting corridor toward some unseen conference room. He didn't want to see whether he looked proud or disturbed or sad.

Robert Miller didn't get to have that kind of effect on Gabe. Not now. Not yet. Maybe not ever.

Gabe smiled at the receptionist on the way out and made his way to the elevator, simultaneously unsettled and excited. He had a plan of attack now. A way to save both the houses and the town. It didn't help Kendall with her house back in California, but it did prevent her from losing all the value in her property.

If only it could stop him from losing her completely.

Chapter Thirty-One

The entire time that Gabe was in Denver, Kendall felt like holding her breath. He'd finally told her what his father did and how he might be able to help them, but despite what he wasn't saying, she knew it was a long shot. What man would receive his son with open arms when he'd been reviled for over a decade? Kendall certainly didn't expect anything. Which meant that she would be responsible for making these next steps work on her own.

Somehow, Kendall had thought that this was going to be a simple process—just download the appropriate forms, fill them out, and email them in. She should have known better, especially considering that it was a governmental process. It took her nearly all morning to parse the National Park Service's website and download all the requisite forms for the national registry, which then sent her to the state's historical society, History Colorado, for information on the state registry. It seemed that they gave grants up to $200,000 for the preservation of historically significant properties.

It was then that she made two unpleasant realizations. First, she had missed the fall deadline by mere days. And second, just because they got the properties listed—*if* they got the properties listed—it didn't mean that they would be automatically protected. Private owners were within their rights to demolish, renovate, change, or rebuild the properties as they saw fit, with no interference from state or local governments. Which meant the county could still choose to condemn the houses if they deemed them dangerous.

In short, the magic bullet might turn out to be no more effective than a Nerf dart.

Kendall sighed and dropped her head into her hands. She was beginning to think that she really might not come out of this process with anything. Somewhere along the lines, she'd stopped worrying about buying the house in Pasadena and started agonizing over the idea of losing the last tenuous link to her past. Now that she knew, however late it might be, that she'd actually had a family who loved her, Connie Green's house meant something to her. The town meant something to her.

Gabe meant something to her.

But that last part wasn't to be. He'd made that clear. And it had no bearing on what she had to do here. For the first time in her life, for reasons she couldn't understand, she was tempted to pray.

But that was stupid. She wasn't even convinced that God would acknowledge her existence. He certainly had never made Himself known to her in those years when she'd needed Him. So why would He bother to rouse from His slumber for something as insignificant as saving a home she didn't even know she had a few weeks ago?

And yet . . . she found herself thinking the words in her head, if not to God, to the universe. *Please. Please don't let me lose this house. After everything I've lost, I think that would be unbearable.*

The words had barely surfaced in her mind before her phone rang and jerked her out of her thoughts. She snatched it up and saw Gabe's name on the screen. After a moment of hesitation, she punched the Accept button and raised it to her ear with a tentative "Hello?"

"Kendall. I'm glad you picked up. I just left my dad's office."

Her hopes rose. "Will he help you? Is he interested in investing?"

"Not exactly," Gabe said, and those hopes crashed to the ground, as fragile and brittle as antique china. "But he did have another idea." Gabe filled her in on what his father had suggested about contacting the state historical society and applying for a grant.

"I already found that," Kendall said, trying to keep the disappointment from her voice. "We missed the deadline."

"Yes, but before we didn't have the recommendation of a member of the organization and the personal contact information of one of the decision makers. Not that she can sway them to our side, but he was pretty sure they'd accept the late application given the unique situation and the urgency."

Kendall's heart lifted. "Really?"

"Really. But there's more. He gave me the name of an attorney. I already called her and she'll see me this afternoon while I'm in Denver. She's willing to file for an injunction on the condemnation proceedings in county court, and she's pretty sure she'll be successful."

For reasons that she couldn't fully explain, tears sprang to Kendall's eyes. "Really?" she repeated, her voice choked.

Gabe's voice softened. "Really, Kendall. We're not going to let Burton succeed. We're going to fight this, and we're going to win."

Emotion swelled in her chest and she found she couldn't answer for several seconds. "Thank you, Gabe. I mean, I know this is for the town too, but . . ."

"I know how much it means to you, Kendall. I know it wasn't what you were looking for when you came here, but I don't blame you for wanting to hold on to that connection to your past."

Kendall swallowed hard and nodded before realizing he couldn't see that gesture. Hope joined the ache in her center, fragile but new.

"Thanks, Gabe. I'm going to get started on the registry application now."

"Good plan. I'll call you when I'm done with the lawyer." He paused. "God willing, we'll have this all locked down by the time you have to leave."

"Great. Let me know what happens." She clicked off the line, but his words stuck with her: *God willing.* Maybe it was just a saying, but now she wondered. The timing of his call felt altogether too convenient given her tentative prayer moments before.

But that was silly.

Wasn't it?

Kendall pushed her laptop off her lap onto the bed and thrust her feet into the boots standing on the rug at the bedside. She needed to work on the registry application, yes, but the checklist had clearly said that she needed photographs documenting the homes and their historic elements. Given the fact that there was no electricity there, she needed to snap some photos while it was still light outside. She might as well give it a shot now. They didn't have much time to waste.

Kendall pulled on her jacket over her fuzzy sweater and yanked her knit cap down over her ears, bracing herself for the cold. Fortunately, the roads were hard-packed and reasonably stable between the mounds of snow on the shoulders, so she drove far more confidently than she had the day after the storm.

And yet when she pulled up to her house, there was a big black SUV sitting in front. Slowly Kendall climbed out of her rental, her brow furrowed. Tracks in the snow around the outside of the house showed someone had been there recently . . . or was still there.

"Hello?" she called, hating the fact that her voice sounded so tentative. For the first time, she realized exactly how isolated she was out here, on a side of the lake that had no structures except for the occasional hunting shack. The town itself was so friendly and benign that it had never occurred to her to worry about the isolation. But now . . .

Don't be stupid. It was probably the city inspector tacking up the notice on the door. Now that she had crossed the street to the sidewalk, she saw the piece of paper that had indeed been pasted to her front door.

And then a crunching of snow from the back of the house alerted her to the owner of the footprints. She braced herself as a tall figure rounded the side of the house, resolving into an all-too-familiar sight: Phil Burton.

The fear she'd felt moments ago dissolved into pure, unadulterated fury. She planted her hands on her hips and stared him down as he approached, an amused smile on his face.

"Good morning, Kendall. Didn't expect to see you out here. Come to say goodbye to the place?"

Very rarely had she considered a person evil, and she'd mostly thought of Burton as an opportunist. Maybe she had an uneasy relationship with development, but she'd never really hated him. Until this moment.

He was trying to upset her, wanted her to know that he'd won. Basically he was gloating. Kendall didn't take the bait. Instead she said evenly, "You're trespassing. This is my property, not yours."

"Come now, Kendall. We both know it won't be your property for long."

She didn't want to tip her hand, so she just clenched her jaw. "All you've managed to do is get condemnation proceedings started. They might tear the houses down, but given that you're behind it, what makes you think that I would ever sell the land to you?" She turned and surveyed the lake. "I mean, since you're thinking about developing around it, I was thinking I might hold on to it as an investment. I figure in about ten years, this lot will be worth . . . what? A million or two at least? If I'm patient, I'll get what I want out of it."

For a second, Burton's expression flickered into uncertainty. She'd at least planted a seed of doubt. But it steeled again and he smiled. "If that's what you want to do, I have no objection.

Hold on to the land. I'll build around it and take advantage of the unobstructed views of the lake through your property. Because really, who's going to want to build a multimillion-dollar house that backs to a resort?"

He had her there, and he knew it. But this had been about misdirection—she didn't want him to think for a second that they were going to fight him in court or that they were going for a History Colorado grant. Let him bask in his own glory while he could. The thought of his shock made her smile inwardly. If he wasn't so determined to make this personal, she probably wouldn't be so determined to enjoy his inevitable defeat.

But that brought up another question. Why exactly *was* this so personal to him? She could understand trying to secure the lot for a development, but there was plenty of land on this side of the lake. In fact, her houses didn't even have the best views. The section just a half mile down had a protected cove that would be perfect for launching paddleboards and rowboats come summer. So why was he so determined to have *this* spot for his resort?

Secure in his victory in their little skirmish, he brushed past her, striding out into the snowy street.

Kendall called to him, "What do you get out of this exactly?"

He paused. "What do you mean?"

"There are better places to build a resort, and given the amount of money you were willing to throw at this piece of land, I know that finances aren't the main issue. So why are you so determined to knock down these houses?"

Burton went still, and she knew she'd scored a direct hit. For a long moment, she didn't think he was going to answer her. But then he strode back toward her, his expression ugly. "You really want to know why?"

Kendall backed up a step, but she squared her shoulders. "Yes. I want to know."

"That witch ruined my family. She killed my brother."

Kendall blinked at him, in shock. "I thought your brother was killed in a car accident. And he left my mother, not the other way around."

"I see you're not surprised by the family connection." He gave a harsh laugh. "I'm not talking about your mother, though she was another piece of work. I'm talking about your grandmother."

Kendall swallowed hard. "I don't understand."

"Of course you don't. Because if there was one thing Connie Green was good at, it was hiding the truth. She hid the truth about her husband for a decade though she had to know he batted for the other team. No, my brother was in love with your mother. For reasons I still can't understand, he was willing to give up everything for that little tramp. He just wanted to finish college first. Be able to provide for her and his brat." He smiled slightly, as if only now realizing that he was talking about Kendall. "He had a football scholarship waiting for him. But no, Connie Green pushed and pushed. Demanded that his baby not be born out of wedlock, because God forbid that anyone think the daughter she raised was less than perfect."

Kendall stared at him, shell-shocked. This was not the story she'd heard, not even the story she'd imagined. "He was going to marry her?"

"He left school for her. Abandoned his responsibilities to his family, got the only job that would hire a stupid nineteen-year-old college dropout, the gas and oil fields in southern Colorado. It was on his way back to work after visiting her that he got into the car wreck that killed him."

The revelation took Kendall's knees out from under her, and she looked around for somewhere to sit, but there was nowhere. Not unless she wanted to plummet to the bottom of a snowbank. "I thought he was drunk driving."

"That's what the coroner said, but he was wrong. Did you know that blood alcohol level can rise after death and cause a false positive? Look it up. He didn't drink, never did. He had a reputation for being a partier, but that was only because he was on the football team." Burton's expression shifted far away, and she realized he had momentarily forgotten about her. "He was the good one out of the two of us. He was going to be a doctor. The football player who wanted to be a doctor. My parents were counting on him taking care of them in their old age." Burton laughed harshly. "Guess who that fell to after he died?"

Kendall could barely breathe at all the revelations. She hadn't been abandoned by her mother, and her mother hadn't been abandoned by her boyfriend. Somehow, Connie Green had a small part in the whole situation because of her rigidity.

One bad decision that had snowballed and destroyed an entire family.

No, two. Because now as she looked at Phil Burton, she didn't see evil. She saw bitterness and sorrow and a deep thread of unforgiveness that was eating him alive. He held her family responsible for everything that had happened to his, even though it was nearly thirty years ago and his brother had been an equal participant in the act that had brought her into the world.

And even more unsettling, she saw a small bit of that in herself.

"You have to let it go," she said softly.

It was clearly the last thing he'd expected her to say. She continued, "I've spent my whole life hating my mother for abandoning me, my father for being absent, and now, my grandmother for not coming to find me even though she knew I was alive. I intended on selling these houses as quickly as possible, because like you, I wanted to erase all memory of the family I should have had."

She took a deep breath and fixed her gaze on him. "But you know what I've realized? It doesn't matter. It doesn't change anything. I wasn't hurting them with my hate. I was only hurting myself." She gave him a sad smile. "You can raze these houses to the ground, but long after they're gone, your hate will still be here, eating you alive."

They locked eyes, and Kendall held her breath, waiting for his response. For a second, she thought she'd gotten through to him. Then he sneered, "Enjoy your last thirty days with the houses and with your forgiveness. I'll take my retribution."

He spun on his heel, marched across the street, and climbed into his vehicle, slamming the door so hard the window rattled. But he shot one last searching look at her as he pulled a U-turn in the street and headed back toward the highway.

Kendall managed to remain standing until his taillights disappeared, and then her knees gave out. She stumbled up the walkway and collapsed on the icy front steps of Connie Green's house. And for reasons she couldn't exactly understand, the tears she'd been holding back overflowed their gates and spilled down her face.

No, she did understand.

Her mother had wanted her. Her father had apparently loved her mother enough to give up his future plans for her. And her grandmother had made so many mistakes, but she had tried to rectify them. It had just been too late. Chance, bad luck, whatever you wanted to call it, had intervened and set Kendall on a path that no child should have to walk.

She didn't know how long she sat on the front steps of the house, weeping for the life she should have had, weeping for the life she'd actually lived, feeling the sorrow that she would never know the people who had unintentionally set her down this path. She held every single one of them responsible for their choices.

Then she forgave them.

And when she finally pushed herself to her feet—her face tear-streaked, her insides hollowed out, and her butt numb from the cold concrete— she felt like a different person.

A person ready to face whatever life had for her.

Chapter Thirty-Two

Gabe turned off the highway onto the road to Jasper Lake after dark that night, his head spinning but his heart hopeful for the first time in months. The meeting with the attorney had taken a good part of the afternoon. He was glad he'd brought snapshots of the blueprints to the lawyer, because once she'd seen those, she was 100 percent in agreement with his father.

"There's no judge in the county who is going to let the condemnation proceedings go forward," she'd said definitively. "Not with the preservation efforts happening in the high country. No one wants to be responsible for destroying part of Colorado's history, least of all if it could someday become a tourist attraction." The motion would be filed in the county court by the end of the week, and she thought they'd have a ruling on it within a few days. The compressed nature of the process meant an extraordinary amount of work on the attorney's part, but she hadn't seemed to mind. Gabe suspected that was because of the personal referral. When he'd looked her up, he'd seen she'd done an extensive amount of work with his father's company.

As Gabe's truck slowly rolled through town,

he contemplated going straight home but found himself automatically navigating to the bed-and-breakfast instead. He let himself in the front door with his key and started up the stairs before he thought better of it and texted Kendall. Can you come down to the parlor? I have news.

A minute later, he heard footsteps upstairs and the opening and closing of a door drifted to him. Moments later, Kendall appeared at the top of the stairs. "Gabe! I didn't expect you back tonight. Did you get everything wrapped up?"

"Let's go in the parlor and talk," he suggested, gesturing toward the comfortable sitting room. Her face creased into a quizzical expression, but she followed his lead and settled in one of the overstuffed chairs by the fireplace.

"I talked to the lawyer this afternoon, and she's going to file for a temporary injunction at the end of the week. It should be wrapped up by the end of next week, if not sooner. Of course, the temporary injunction will have to turn into a permanent one, but if we get the grant, we should be able to pull the permits and get the condemnation order lifted anyway. This is basically just a stopgap measure until we can figure out what to do. That means a lot of work on our part, getting plans ready for the permits, but I think if we work hard over the next week or two, we should be ready—"

"Gabe," Kendall interrupted. "I'm leaving."

His words stumbled to a stop. "Leaving? Now?"

She didn't quite meet his eyes. "We've done what we set out to do. If you're so confident this is going to go in our favor, there's nothing that I can't do remotely from California. I've been gone too long already." She hesitated. "I accepted a new project in Pasadena that starts next week."

Gabe felt stricken. She was leaving? Well, of course she was. There was no reason for her to stay. He'd known she would go back to California at some point, but he hadn't really internalized what that was going to mean. What it was going to be like to work on this without her. What it was going to mean to his daily life for her not to be in it.

"Kendall, if this is because of us—"

"It's not," she said definitively. "I'm not running away. I'm not trying to punish either of us. I just realized it's much too difficult to do . . . this . . . with the two of us, if there's not going to be the two of us." She swallowed hard. "So I've decided to put the houses into a trust. And I'm making you a coexecutor."

He stared at her. "What? I thought . . . Didn't you need . . . ?"

Kendall shook her head. "Here's the thing, Gabe. I ran into Burton today, and he told me the reason he's going after these properties so hard. It's punishment because he holds the Greens responsible for his brother's death. And I realized that there are a lot of people, me included, who have put too much importance on a house. On any house." She gave him a wan smile. "Including my house in Pasadena. I would hate to lose it, but I'm not going to rush into anything before I've thought it through. I'm certainly not going to be pressured to sell something that's been in my family for generations without giving it some serious thought."

She took another deep breath and continued. "But I am going to have difficulty making some of the decisions and getting the permits together, so I'm giving you the decision-making authority. Assuming you'll accept it. I know it's a lot to ask."

Gabe sat there, so shocked by her revelation that he didn't know what to say. And that's when he noticed the subtle difference about her: a peace that until this moment she'd never displayed. The tiny lines on her forehead were relaxed, the corners of her mouth tipped up so slightly that he realized he'd never noticed her faint frown. She seemed . . . settled. What had happened today to create such a change?

But she was waiting for an answer to her offer. "Of course I'll accept it. Thank you, Kendall. It's generous of you to hand over control of your own property for the good of the town."

Kendall lifted a shoulder in a tiny shrug. "Not

really. It's in everyone's best interest. You know this town better than I do, and I trust you."

It was those three words that hit him harder than anything else she said. The pain bloomed in his chest. "Kendall—"

She rose from her chair. "Don't make this harder than it has to be, Gabe. I know we're not meant to be. But maybe we were brought together for a reason." She gave him a sad smile. "I'll be done with the historic register application by the end of the week, and I'll file it before I leave. I'll send you a copy. And I checked with Matthew Avery. He's going to call you to get your signature on the trust paperwork."

"Kendall, thank you." Gabe rose as well, not sure what he was going to say. But there wasn't anything else to say. This was the end of something that had barely gotten started, a blip in their lives, two weeks that Kendall would forget as soon as she got back to California and dove into her new project.

Somehow Gabe didn't think he would be able to forget her as easily.

And then she surprised him. She walked to him and slipped her arms around his middle, drawing herself in for a long hug, her head resting on his chest. When she pulled away, she reached up on tiptoes and brushed a light kiss across his lips. "No. Thank you. I don't think I could have handled this all without you."

And then before he could think of how to reply, she was gone upstairs, her door closed, not with a thud of finality, but a soft, barely perceptible click.

Kendall closed the door quietly behind her and leaned her forehead against the solid wood panel, unable to move any farther from Gabe than she already had. All this time, she'd been so good at protecting her heart from the pain of goodbye. She'd never looked back when she had to leave a foster home, never let herself think about what she was losing, what she might be walking into. She'd built the hard shell around her heart so securely that nothing could penetrate it. Not love and not loss.

And yet now she felt the cracks as if they were physical, a pain in her body, a tearing. She took a long, shuddering breath as tears slipped from her eyes. All these years, she'd been afraid of heart-break. Afraid that it would be the sharp knife of betrayal and loss. Only to find out it felt much more like the thawing of frozen limbs after a long day in the cold. Painful, prickly . . . and yet with a sense of rightness, a sense of balance being restored.

She wiped the tears from her eyes and moved to the bed, letting herself feel the sorrow, marveling that it didn't crush her. She was going to miss Gabe. She wished things could have turned out differently, but she couldn't pretend to be someone—something—she wasn't just for him. And maybe that was the biggest indication that she'd actually learned something here.

The question was, who was she?

She'd always seen herself as a foster child, unwanted by her own mother. But she hadn't been unwanted. The title didn't fit.

She'd seen herself as someone who could rely only on herself, even when she had people around her willing to help. But now she was willingly handing over control of her property to someone she barely knew because she trusted him.

What other titles had she assumed that would turn out to be false?

Someone who couldn't love? The twist in her stomach when she thought about Gabe seemed to prove that one wrong.

Someone who was unloved? Both her father and mother had made huge sacrifices for her, even if they hadn't worked out in the end.

Someone who had been forgotten by God?

It was only then that a memory surfaced, cloudy with age, so ephemeral that she couldn't be sure it was actually a memory and not something she'd conjured. Sitting on a woman's lap, flipping through a picture book. No, a picture Bible. Singing a song.

"Jesus Loves Me."

Could that have been her mother?

It couldn't be. But it had to be. She knew for sure that it wasn't any of her first foster homes. There had been little to no physical contact with those foster parents; certainly none of them would have hauled her onto their lap. She remembered going to Sunday school a few times with the one foster family, the one she'd overheard condemning her mother.

By the time she'd gotten to the Novaks', where she'd lived until she was eighteen, she was far too old to sit on anyone's lap and she certainly would have remembered it.

No, it had to be her mother.

She turned the image over and over in her head as she got ready for bed, as she washed the makeup from her face and pulled on her pajamas. And the more she did, the more she was convinced it was a memory. Because there was a sense of happiness, of comfort, associated with it, something she'd rarely felt about any other part of her childhood.

Except for maybe the warmth she felt in that park when Nancy Novak had pulled her in and wept relieved tears that she'd been found.

She held those two memories close as she crawled into bed, let them fill her up as she drifted off to sleep, feeling a little less alone than she could remember in a long time.

Chapter Thirty-Three

Even working around the clock, it took Kendall nearly the entire week to finish the historical register application. Part of it was the wild-goose chase of paperwork that the various web pages and applications and links sent her on, checking and double-checking everything that was required for a successful application. She reviewed the samples History Colorado provided. She retook photos when the first set didn't adequately show the details of the architecture and edited them to show the houses in the best, most preserved light. She actually had to drive to Georgetown before she could find someone who was confident in handling the brittle blueprints so she could scan and attach them. She had the same print shop scan the passages in the pamphlet that mentioned Jasper Green.

She also did more research and was able to find a few other mentions of the architect online—one in a slideshow from an art school in Chicago and another in a catalog on eBay, which she overpaid for and then overpaid again to have FedExed to her overnight. She managed to find his name in the Royal Academy roster and a couple of photos of sculptures housed in obscure English museums. And yet, she was still only partially confident that she'd established the importance of the architect and his relationship to Colorado. It was a call to the Art Workers' Guild in England that yielded the final piece, a photograph of his name on the fresco that lined the inside of the guild hall, right next to the most important decorative artists and architects of the age. If she couldn't establish his importance, at least she could establish his proximity to the most influential people of the Arts and Crafts movement. Surely the rarity of his work should help emphasize that it was crucial not to destroy what little was left.

It was Friday afternoon when she finally clicked Send on the email, the application sent via blind copy to Gabe. Her bags were packed, her flight scheduled out of Denver the next day. She closed her laptop and took a deep breath. She'd head over to the attorney's office to sign the trust into existence, and he'd assured her he would wait until she was gone to have Gabe come in.

Because, of all the things she was preparing to leave behind, he was the most difficult. Knowing he was just across town in his office was torture. She'd avoided Main Street Mocha in case she saw him, instead opting for French press coffee in the bed-and-breakfast kitchen. She caught sight of him out the window one day, walking Fitz by the house, and dropped the curtain when he glanced up to her room. Probably just a coincidence, not an indication he was looking for her. She had to believe that was the case. It was too difficult to leave him behind otherwise.

She half thought he would show up to see her off when she checked out of the B and B the next morning, but it was only his grandfather who met her when she hauled her duffel bag down the stairs.

"What do I owe you?" she asked.

He waved a hand and wouldn't meet her eye. "Pshaw. It was a pleasure having you. Especially after all you've done for Gabe and the town."

It seemed like overstating something she'd done mostly for her own benefit. She reached into her purse and counted out a handful of hundred-dollar bills, what she estimated the room would be worth back home, and Mr. Brandt's eyes widened. "That's far too much."

Kendall removed one hundred from the stack to placate him and then pushed the money into the man's hand. "Please. It's my pleasure. I appreciate the place to stay. And the coffee and breakfast." She gave the innkeeper a rueful smile, knowing that he understood the true reason she hadn't been venturing out lately for her morning cup of joe. She would have to stop by Main Street Mocha and say goodbye to Delia before she left. It was a shame that she wouldn't be sticking around permanently. She had a feeling the owner could turn out to be as much of a friend as she'd been an impromptu mentor.

Unexpectedly, Mr. Brandt gave Kendall a hug, and she had to escape before tears pricked her eyes again. Surely she could get out of this town without crying. Or without seeing Gabe. She had to.

When she walked out to her rental vehicle parked at the curb, however, there was a thick package sitting on her windshield. She shoved her duffel in the back of the SUV before carefully removing the package and bringing it into the driver's seat with her. It appeared to be a hardboard file folder, at least an inch thick, wrapped in heavy clear plastic. She frowned and unwrapped it.

A note was paper-clipped to the front of it, written in blocky, masculine writing that she somehow knew was Gabe's even before she saw the signature. *Kendall, I'm sorry if I overstepped, but there are some things you need to know before you leave.*

Fear struck her heart without her really knowing why. She flipped it open and found a cover letter from Alvarez Private Investigation.

Dear Gabriel,
Please find enclosed the information requested regarding Kendall Green and her mother, Caroline Green. I feel con-

fident that had this occurred today, with integrated computer systems, Ms. Green would have been reunited with her grandmother shortly after she was found. Unfortunately, in the 1990s, local law enforcement and social services used independent systems. This is both a failure of technology and of manpower to reunite a child with her family. I hope the enclosed police reports can give Ms. Green some closure on her situation.

Kendall's heart pounded so hard she felt dizzy. The words blurred on the page. Had Gabe actually hired a private investigator to look into her past? It took several minutes of breathing in and out, staring through the windshield, before she could find the courage to look past the cover letter.

And what she found there was unbelievable. She had to read through it multiple times to understand what the reports were saying, to piece together the significance of what had happened.

On April 21, 1997, a woman matching Caroline Green's description, identified only as Jane Doe, had been struck and killed in a crosswalk on a street in Golden, Colorado. She hadn't been carrying a purse or identification, though police speculated that a witness to the hit-and-run had stolen her possessions since she was dressed nicely and likely would have had a handbag. After scouring missing persons reports and running her fingerprints, no matches were found. No one ever came forward, and she was cremated in accordance with the city laws for unclaimed bodies.

Far south in Littleton, Colorado, on that same day, a five-year-old child identified as Kendall Green was left at a drop-in day care and unclaimed at closing time. The employees hadn't noticed anything suspicious about the woman who dropped her off and only became concerned when she hadn't returned for hours after she'd said she would. The child had been well cared for and was left with a backpack with her name inked on the inside. Police suspected she had been abandoned by a parent or perhaps even kidnapped and then dropped off. When no matching missing person report was turned up nationwide for a five-year-old girl of her description and no one came forward to claim the child, she was handed off to child protection services, where she entered the foster care system. A new birth certificate and Social Security number were issued, and without an exact date of birth, no one made the connection to a Kendall Green born in Clear Creek County.

Kendall sat there in frozen disbelief, unable to process what she was reading. Her mother hadn't abandoned her after all. She'd never come home because she couldn't. She'd been killed—doing what, Kendall couldn't possibly guess. Maybe meeting with a lawyer. Maybe looking for a job. Maybe just shopping for a used car or any other possibility. And because of bad luck and a failure of governmental communication, no one had ever connected a hit-and-run with an abandoned child a single county away.

Kendall expected tears to come, but she couldn't even cry through her shock. Deep down, some part of her had hoped that her mother was still alive. That she would be able to ask her what happened. That her mother could say something to explain everything she'd been through, to somehow take away the hurt.

That hope was over.

The words on the page blurred, and she shoved them away. She wasn't denying the pain that would come. There was time for that later. There were still pages in the file.

She flipped past the police reports and found a transcript of an interview with Bill and Nancy Novak, her foster parents. She scanned the basic questions that established who they were and then found these words:

JA: How did Kendall Green come to live with you?

NN: We were on the list to foster to adopt. We couldn't have children, and we were determined that we would adopt a child who needed a family. When the agency came to us with a girl who had already been in four homes and been returned to social services because she kept running away, we wanted to refuse the placement.

JA: Why didn't you, then?

NN: God. It's the only explanation. I was on the phone, ready to tell them we wouldn't take the placement because she had refused to be adopted by her previous families, and instead I asked when she would be here. [laughs] I got off the phone and looked at Bill and asked, "What just happened?" He shrugged and said the situation had been taken out of our hands.

JA: And how did Kendall settle into the placement?

BN: It was rough. She was defiant and distant by turns. And then one night she ran away. We didn't know where she was for six hours. My wife was in a panic. All we could think about were all the things that could happen to a little girl out there and how badly we'd failed her. We drove all around the city and eventually found her in the park next to her old elementary school. We were so relieved. Nancy just held on to her and cried for what felt like an hour.

NN: When I went to tuck her in that night, she was sitting on the edge of her bed with her bags packed, fully dressed. She thought she was going back. I unpacked her clothes and gave her pajamas and told her she needed to go to bed if she didn't want to be late for school the next morning. [NN wipes away tears] She might not have softened much, but she never tried to run away after that.

Kendall paused, the pressure in her chest almost unbearable. She'd remembered that moment when Nancy had clutched her and cried, but until now she hadn't remembered her misery all the way home. How she'd sat up for hours while her foster parents talked about what to do with her, thinking it was only a matter of time until she was sent back again. She'd finally gone one step too far, screwed up the only good thing she might ever have in her life. The memory of that sick feeling hit her so hard she had to swallow her nausea down several times before she continued.

JA: You mentioned earlier that you wanted to adopt. Did you change your mind after that?

NN: No! We still wanted to adopt. But Kendall made it very clear that she believed her mother would be coming back for her someday. She refused.

BN: It was hard for us. We wanted her to be part of our family, but we decided ultimately it was more important to do what she needed than what we wanted. She needed a stable home and we could provide that for her. It was the least we could do after what she'd been through.

Kendall blinked at the words. What were they talking about? She didn't remember having said that. She had only a vague recollection of her teen years, feeling like an outsider because she was a foster kid, because they'd never taken the step of giving her their last name.

Was it possible she'd blocked that out? Was it possible she'd had it wrong the whole time?

Had she been letting an erroneous assumption affect her whole life without realizing it?

She glanced at the SUV's clock. She still had five hours until her flight. She looked back at the page, where the address for Bill and Nancy Novak was written.

She had no choice. She had to know the truth. The whole truth.

Chapter Thirty-Four

Kendall sat outside the 1960s ranch-style house on a quiet street in Littleton, studying the front like she was on a surveillance detail. She'd put the address of her last foster home into her phone's GPS, thinking she probably wouldn't recognize it after a decade, but the minute she drove onto the street, she locked onto the home like she was following a beacon. Memories flooded back, ones she could fully understand repressing: the nights crying in her new room, wanting to go back to the last foster home because it was familiar even if it was unhappy. Being the new girl at school yet again and trying to hide her foster kid status for as long as possible. The day that everyone found out anyway and the whispers began about why her parents had abandoned her.

But that wasn't all. There were also memories that shouldn't need forgetting: riding a bike up and down the street on Christmas Day, her foster father Bill running beside to steady it until she got the hang of it. Sitting out on the front porch drinking hot chocolate with Nancy after a hard day at school. Backing down the driveway in the Novaks' station wagon on her sixteenth birthday, right after she'd gotten her driver's license.

And the day she'd packed up one suitcase full of stuff, the clothes and shoes that she'd bought herself with money from a part-time job, and walked away from this place without a second look.

Kendall swallowed hard, tears pricking her eyes. She should probably have called ahead. There was no guarantee they'd even want to see her, and her flight back to Burbank left in three hours. She didn't really have time to be making this unplanned stop.

And yet she knew this was something she should have done long ago, that she would never be able to move on with her life until she dealt with her past. Now that she had some of the answers, maybe Bill and Nancy Novak could fill her in on the rest.

There were two cars parked in the driveway, the old station wagon and a newer SUV, so she knew they were probably home when she left her rental vehicle and crossed the street to the house. She braced herself for an uncertain reception. With the way she'd left without another word, not even a card or a phone call to say how she was doing, they might not even want to scc hcr. They might have spent the last decade thinking about how ungrateful she'd been for their help when she'd had nowhere else to go.

They wouldn't be totally wrong.

Kendall took one more deep breath and then

shook off her hesitation and rapped sharply on the door. For good measure, she pressed the doorbell too.

From deep inside the house, a dog barked twice and then a woman's voice shushed it. Kendall's heart rose into her throat. Bill and Nancy had never had a dog; if it hadn't been for the familiar station wagon with the same small dent in the bumper from where she'd accidentally backed into a trash can, she might think they'd moved.

And then the door swung open, revealing Nancy Novak, holding on to the collar of a panting, smiling golden retriever. She looked older than Kendall remembered, of course, a touch more silver woven into her blonde hair, but she looked as trim and healthy as ever. She straightened with a smile for whoever she thought was at the door, and then it slowly slipped off her face. "Kendall?"

Her name on her foster mom's lips struck a pang into her heart. For a second, she'd wondered if she would even recognize her. "Hi, Nancy. I didn't mean to drop by without notice, but I was in Colorado . . ."

Nancy's eyes welled with tears, shimmering in a film. She turned away and yelled, "Bill! Come here! You won't believe who's here!" Kendall was still standing there, but Nancy seemed momentarily unable to figure out what to do.

"Can I come in?" Kendall asked tentatively.

Nancy shook herself. "Come in, come in. I was just surprised. I didn't expect . . . I never thought . . ." She snapped her mouth shut and stood aside for Kendall to enter. The instant she let go of the dog's collar, he started dancing around Kendall's legs, sniffing her and nudging her hand.

"You probably smell Fitz on my boots still," Kendall murmured, kneeling down to scratch the dog. She was aware she was really just delaying the inevitable, but it was much easier to face the friendly dog than the unknown expression of her foster mom.

Bill came around the corner from the back of the house and froze. "Kendall?"

Kendall straightened. "Hi, Bill. I'm sorry to drop in on you two so unexpectedly. I was in town and . . ." She broke off, aware she was bungling this reunion, but right now she wasn't even sure if it was welcome or not. "Could we sit down and talk for a minute?"

Bill recovered faster than his wife and smiled. "Of course, Kendall. You know you're always welcome here. You just surprised us. Although not as much as getting a visit from a private investigator." He held his hand out toward the adjacent living room, and Kendall took tentative steps toward one of the chairs placed near the front window.

"Yeah, sorry about that. I didn't hire him. A . . .

friend of mine . . . took it on himself to get some answers for me. I had no idea he was even doing it."

Bill and Nancy took seats on the leather sofa opposite her, Nancy automatically reaching for Bill's hand. The gesture instantly made Kendall nervous. She recognized it from nearly a decade with this couple; Nancy always reached for him when she was uncertain about what came next. They were as unsettled as she was.

"It's no problem, Kendall," Bill said. "We weren't sure if we should even talk to him. But his questions weren't that intrusive . . . or at least it didn't seem like it was anything that could hurt you or make you susceptible to identity theft or something like that."

That was Bill, the practical one. Nancy was still staring at Kendall like she was a ghost, almost shaking.

"I don't even know why I'm here," Kendall said finally. "I just got the report this morning and . . ." She tried to order her thoughts. How could she have lived with Bill and Nancy for eight years and feel like they were strangers now? Maybe because she'd been away for longer than she'd known them. She'd lived two-thirds of her life without them.

"My mother didn't abandon me. She was killed. Actually, both my parents were, at different times."

Nancy's hand flew to her mouth, tears coming to her eyes again. Kendall had forgotten how tenderhearted she was. "I'm so sorry, Kendall. That must have been difficult to learn."

"It was. Kind of. And to be honest, it was kind of a relief." Kendall swallowed hard, feeling guilty even thinking the words, let alone saying them aloud. "I didn't realize how much I hoped my mom was still out there, that I would find her someday and she could give me an explanation."

"That's absolutely understandable," Nancy said. "It's why . . ." She broke off and glanced at Bill, who gave her a nearly imperceptible shake of his head.

"No, what were you going to say? 'It's why' what?" Kendall looked between the two of them. "Please. Tell me."

Bill cleared his throat. "It's why we never pushed to adopt you after the first time you refused."

Kendall blinked. "You asked to adopt me?" She'd read it in the investigator's report, but she also hadn't completely believed it. She would remember something like that, wouldn't she?

"About a year after you came to live with us," Nancy said. "You seemed like you were settling in. Making friends. You seemed happy here."

Kendall hadn't really remembered being happy there, but now that she said the words, there were flashes, recollections of stretches where things were peaceful. She had settled in. But it felt less about being happy than having finally accepted her fate.

Aloud she said, "I think I must have been. What did I say when you asked me?"

Nancy chewed her lip. "You said that your mom was still out there somewhere, and you were going to find her someday. You said that we'd never be your family." Tears glistened on her foster mom's lower lashes, and she swiped them away quickly. "We didn't blame you, of course. But after that, you pulled away. Stayed in your room. Wouldn't see your friends. We thought . . . well, we thought it was better to let it go than to push you. To unsettle you."

Kendall flushed hot and cold. The only things she remembered from that time were emotions she couldn't deal with, ones she now recognized as guilt. Guilt that she liked living with Bill and Nancy. Guilt that some days she didn't even think of her mom. And extra guilt when she realized she couldn't remember her mother's face, if she'd ever really committed it to memory.

"I'm sorry," Kendall said softly. "I never meant to hurt you."

"No," Bill said resolutely. "We don't blame you. We understood what we were signing up for. Even if it was . . . difficult at times."

Restlessness overtook Kendall and she pushed

412

up from her seat. Wandered around the living room for a second, looking at all the things that had changed, all the things that had stayed the same. Remembering all the details she'd hidden away: family dinners at the scarred oak dining table every night, Nancy picking her up from school every day, Bill helping her with math homework at the coffee table in this room. The Christmas tree that would go up in the corner the Sunday after Thanksgiving, and the yearly trip to pick a new ornament to hang on the tree. The birthday banner with her name that went up over the fireplace every year.

Kendall made two realizations. One, she had no idea what her actual birthday was.

And two, this whole time she'd been thinking she was an orphan, she'd actually had a family.

All the years she'd spent thinking she was alone, she'd had people caring for her and holding her up.

She'd just been so mired in her own loss and pain that she hadn't been able to see it.

She turned to Bill and Nancy, forcing down the lump in her throat. "Thank you for everything you did for me. I'm so sorry I didn't . . . that I couldn't . . ."

Nancy let out a strangled noise and leapt from the sofa, crossing to Kendall's spot near the fireplace and enfolding her in her arms. "Kendall, sweetheart, we've missed you so much. But it wasn't our place . . . We didn't want to force you to do anything you didn't want to."

Bill stood and moved to their side, his warm hand settling on Kendall's shoulder. "The important thing is that you came home. We were hoping you might someday."

It was that word, *home,* that finally broke her. The tears that had been hiding behind her eyes welled up and spilled down her cheeks, poured out of her in indelicate sobs to wet Nancy's sweater. Bill encircled both of them, his arms around their shoulders while they cried. She had no idea how long this went on, but when she finally pulled away, she figured she was completely red and swollen. But Nancy and Bill were smiling at her.

It was Nancy who spoke first. "We were just about to have lunch. Do you want to join us?"

And despite the fact that she was going to miss her flight, Kendall nodded. "I'd love that."

It was surreal being back in this house, sitting at the familiar oak table. Nancy bustled around the kitchen, putting together roast beef sandwiches.

"Can I help?" Kendall asked more than once, but Nancy waved her back to the table, where Bill was busy asking questions about her life for the last ten years.

She'd already told them how she'd gotten a free but completely undocumented interior design education in California while she was working as a receptionist and moved on to her business. "I'm about to start a project in Pasadena on Monday, restoring an old Craftsman in the historic district."

"So what are you doing in Colorado, then?" Bill asked, puzzled. "I assumed the private investigator was because you lived somewhere far away."

"That's kind of a long story."

Bill and Nancy exchanged a glance; then Nancy smiled. "We've got plenty of time."

That led to the story of how she'd inherited the homes in Jasper Lake and how she'd found the letters between her mother and grandmother. Nancy gasped. "You were so close and no one had any idea?"

Kendall shook her head. "No. Something to do with unconnected computer systems. I'm told it would probably never happen today."

Nancy set the platter down in the center of the table, sandwich halves stacked neatly alongside freshly washed grapes and dill pickle spears, her usual casual offerings for company. They were treating her like a guest; Kendall wasn't sure whether to be honored or hurt. After ten years, she guessed they were feeling as awkward as she was.

Bill took Nancy's hand and then held out his other hand for Kendall. "Shall we say grace?"

Kendall blinked. She tentatively joined hands with both Bill and Nancy and they bowed their heads. She followed suit, though she still studied them through her eyelashes.

"Dear Lord," Bill prayed, "we thank You for bringing Kendall back to us today. We thank You for Your grace and protection over her for the last ten years and for granting her many successes. We pray that You'll help her find exactly what she's looking for. Amen. Oh, and bless this food."

Kendall and Nancy laughed at the last-minute addition and pulled their hands away, but the last words lingered with her. *Help her find exactly what she's looking for.* What *was* she looking for?

Nancy gestured for her to help herself, and she took a sandwich half and some grapes automatically. She never had liked pickles. "So when did all this happen?"

"When did what happen?" Bill asked.

"The prayer thing. I don't remember you being particularly religious when I was growing up." She winced at how accusatory the words sounded as they left her mouth, but Nancy and Bill didn't seem to notice.

"Well," Bill said slowly, "I was raised Episcopalian, but I wouldn't say I was ever really a believer."

"And I would have called myself an agnostic." Nancy laughed a bit self-consciously. "Though I think it was less a matter of not knowing if God existed and more wondering why, if He existed, things didn't go my way more often."

Kendall winced, hearing her own thoughts come out of Nancy's mouth.

"But after . . . I guess we needed some comfort. Bill asked me to go to church with him—bullied me, really—and we realized that the thing we were looking for all these years was something we already had."

"What was that?" Kendall asked.

"Family."

She couldn't hear that word without feeling a pang, but now she was curious. "What do you mean?"

Bill reached for Nancy's hand and squeezed, but his eyes remained fixed on Kendall. "Did you ever wonder why we fostered, why we wanted to adopt?"

Not really. It was a testament to her childish self-involvement that it had never occurred to her to wonder.

"We tried to have a baby for years," Nancy said softly. "But after six miscarriages, it seemed like it was never meant to be. So we decided to foster. We were really looking for an infant, to be honest. But then we got a call and they needed an emergency placement for a ten-year-old girl, and we . . . well, we couldn't say no."

Kendall knew this part from their interview

with the PI, but she wanted to hear it from their own mouths. "Why?"

Bill chuckled. "Well, now it seems pretty obvious that it was God working behind the scenes. We thought we wanted a baby, and we got a preteen. We thought we wanted to adopt, and we ended up fostering."

Guilt struck Kendall. She put down her sandwich. "I'm sorry. If you hadn't taken me, you might have gotten your baby."

"That's what we're trying to tell you," Nancy said. "We're not sorry at all. You were just what we needed. You made us realize that it really wasn't about us, what we wanted." She got teary again. "You made us parents."

Kendall's own eyes swam in response, and she rubbed her nose to make the stinging sensation go away. She'd already done more crying on this trip than she'd done in the last ten years, and she was afraid her mascara was probably now ringed around her eyes like a raccoon's.

"But part of being parents is letting go. And after you left, we realized that we'd devoted ourselves completely to you—which is not a bad thing, by the way—and the hole that was left made us start to question things. We saw the emptiness of our life."

"And that's when you found church," Kendall guessed.

"That's when we found Jesus," Bill corrected.

"In something that was absolutely not a coincidence, the first service we came to talked about how God has predetermined us for adoption as sons and daughters through Jesus. I remember hearing that verse when I was growing up and it not making any sense to me." He looked a little embarrassed. "I always thought the status of adopted son was less than. But now it made sense to me, for the first time in my life."

"Kendall, we couldn't have loved you more if we gave birth to you," Nancy said softly. "But the choice to be adopted or not was yours and yours alone. We weren't going to force it on you. We could only love you the best we could."

"And we realized that's exactly what God had done for us. He was just waiting for us to take Him up on the offer." Bill smiled. "The rest is history."

Kendall shifted uncomfortably in her seat, though she didn't know if it was because of the talk of God or the talk of her rejected adoption. As memories filtered in of nights sitting at this table, of how well they'd treated her, of how much they had actually loved her, she couldn't push back the guilt swelling in her chest. They'd accepted her as a member of their family, and she'd scorned it. She'd been too busy thinking about all she'd lost to ever realize what she was gaining in return. There was no real need to have felt alone for the last decade.

She barely noticed when tears began falling again. "What happens when you realize that too late?" she whispered.

Bill and Nancy reached for her hands at the same time, but it was Nancy who spoke. "It's never too late, Kendall. You're our daughter, legal or not. You've always been part of our family if you want to be. We were just waiting for you to come home."

It was too much. It was all too much. The knowledge of her birth family, Gabe, the understanding of what she'd thrown away with her foster family. She pulled her hands away and jumped to her feet so quickly that she knocked the chair backward onto the kitchen's tile floor. "I'm sorry. I can't do this."

She fled the kitchen and found herself standing on the front porch of the house that had been home for much of her childhood. But found she couldn't walk down those stairs. Couldn't walk away again. Her feet were rooted to the spot as surely as if they'd been poured in the cement of the steps. She swallowed and rubbed her raw eyes and instead settled onto the porch swing. It had a new flowered cushion, but it still creaked in the same way when she sat on it, the chain squealing with every push.

After a few minutes of swinging, the front door opened. Bill stepped out and closed the door quietly behind him. "Can I join you?"

Kendall scooted over to make room, but she didn't look at him. He sat beside her but didn't say anything, just started the swing swaying again.

Finally Kendall couldn't stand the silence anymore. "I'm sorry."

"For what?"

"For how I treated you and Nancy. I should have said yes."

Bill stopped swinging abruptly. "It's not your fault, Kendall. Maybe we shouldn't have told you. We never meant for you to carry our burdens."

She glanced at him. "I don't even remember you asking to adopt me."

"You were hurting. You'd had a lot of change in your life. We understood."

"That makes one of us," Kendall said. "I've spent my entire adult life feeling like I had no one to count on. Like I was just one bad decision short of being on the street, with no safety net."

Bill nodded and resumed swinging. "You know, it's not too late."

"I'd say it's about a decade too late."

"Not necessarily. There's something called adult adoption."

Now it was Kendall's turn to still the sway of the swing. "You're serious about this."

"Of course we are." Bill looked at her. "It's a little different because you're a fully independent adult, but it would still make it legal."

Kendall's heart swelled in her chest and she felt like it might stop. She had just discovered her Green roots. She'd just learned that had things turned out differently, she would have been a Burton. And now Bill was asking her to consider becoming a Novak? She had no idea how to answer that question. And yet the fact he'd asked . . .

She reached for his hand and squeezed it. "You have no idea what that means to me. But it's a big decision. I feel like my last name is the only thing I have left, the only connection I have to my mother's family."

Disappointment laced his voice. "I understand. And we thought you might feel that way. That's why Nancy didn't come out with me."

Because she couldn't stand another disappointment. The unspoken words hung between them.

"But there are other kinds of family, aren't there?" Kendall asked softly. "Just because it's not legal doesn't mean . . . Well, I mean, I've always wanted someplace to spend Christmas."

A slow smile spread over Bill's face. "We still have your stocking, you know."

"Are you sure that's okay with you guys? I know it's not really what you'd hoped your family would look like . . ."

He smiled and squeezed her hand. "We loved you, Kendall. We never stopped. We'll take you however we can get you."

The tinge of self-deprecation made her laugh and her heart lifted. Even Bill had to know that what he offered was too much for now, maybe ever. But to know that she wasn't alone . . . to choose a family based on love and gratitude for what they'd done for her . . . that had to mean more than anything a judge could pronounce.

And yet reality called. She glanced at her watch. "I'm not sure I can still make my flight, but I should probably try."

Bill looked disappointed but he nodded. "Let us wrap up your lunch. You can eat it at the gate."

"Thanks." She rose and smoothed her hands down her jeans-clad legs. "But I'll be back. And I can call you guys, right?"

Bill put one arm around her shoulders and squeezed. "Of course you can."

Kendall lingered on the porch, and when Bill came back, Nancy was with him, bearing a care package for the plane—her uneaten sandwich, some chips and grapes (no pickles), and a couple of homemade chocolate chip cookies. She gave her foster parents one last hug goodbye and promised them she'd be in touch, feeling both wrung out and lighter than she had in years.

She waved one more time after she climbed into her rental and put it in gear. That was absolutely what she had needed to do, and if she wasn't mistaken, they'd needed it just as much. Even though she would soon be twelve hundred miles away, knowing that they were there waiting for her, that she'd see them at Christmas, filled a spot in her soul that she hadn't realized needed filling.

But she'd also realized that this house was not her home now, any more than it would have been had they been her birth parents. Children were supposed to move on and have their own lives. And however abruptly it had happened, regardless of the ties unnecessarily severed, they'd unknowingly given her that gift of wings.

It was time to fly home.

Chapter Thirty-Five

It turned out that Kendall needn't have hurried. Storms elsewhere in the country had delayed her plane's arrival in Denver, and by the time she finally walked through the door of her Pasadena house, it was well past dark.

Very dark. The front porch light, always on a timer, had been left on, but the interior of the house was pitch-black. Kendall flipped on the entryway light. "Sophie? Are you home?"

It was a silly question. It was Saturday night. Of course Sophie wasn't home. Either she was with her boyfriend or she was out with friends, just as Kendall would have been, had she stayed home. And yet somehow, her life before Jasper Lake, only two weeks in the past, felt completely foreign. As if her "glamorous" California existence had been a dream, and the time in the Colorado mountains had been her waking up to reality.

Don't be overdramatic, she chided herself. She headed down the hall to her room first, unlocked her door, and dropped her bag inside. Only then did she notice the note taped to her door, surprisingly analog for Sophie: *Spending the weekend at Sean's house. Will be back Sunday night. XOXO, Soph*

Well, that explained it. As much as she wanted to see Sophie, she couldn't much complain about having Sunday to herself. Kendall wasn't sure she could adequately answer all the questions Sophie would likely have. She wasn't even sure if she could answer them for herself right now. It was probably good to give herself a little space and silence to sort through everything she'd found out in the past several days.

It also gave her some uninterrupted time to sort through the inevitable mess that had been left in their office. Sophie was many things, but neat was not one of them.

But she didn't yet have the energy to deal with that, not without a hot drink. She went into the kitchen, flipping switches as she went until the house was blazing with light. It was completely neat, no dishes in the sink, the dishwasher unloaded and empty, the countertops wiped off. That probably meant that Sophie had been working outside the house for the entire time Kendall was gone. She flipped on the electric kettle, which stood in its place of honor next to the coffeepot, and plopped a tea bag in her mug, wishing for a second for Delia's amazing coconut milk Lake Fog. But good old-fashioned English tea would have to do.

Minutes later, she walked back to the office with her steaming mug and kicked her boots off at the entrance of the office space. She braced herself and clicked on the light.

She blinked. For a second, she was tempted to turn the light off and on again to see if the results would be the same. Rather than the mountains of paperwork and books that she'd anticipated, the office was pristine.

Kendall wandered over to her desk, which was usually overflowing with mail and paperwork. Not this time. Her in-box had a number of new items in it, but instead of being tossed haphazardly into the bin, still in their envelopes, they'd been removed, flattened, and tagged with sticky notes where necessary. Two staggered columns of paperwork sat on her desk as well. The left side appeared to be items that Sophie had responded to, bills she'd paid, and other urgent items, all documented with sticky note explanations. The other, shorter column were things that Kendall needed to address when she returned, all annotated with their due dates.

Kendall just stared for a moment, then moved to Sophie's desk. It was even cleaner than hers, the usual detritus of inspiration photos and fabric samples transferred to the pinboards behind her desk.

Who had kidnapped Sophie and replaced her with a pod person while she was gone? Who was this organized dynamo?

Out of curiosity, she clicked Sophie's mouse

to bring up the computer monitor, and it opened without a password. It was just the two of them, so they'd never felt the need to protect their computers. The screen opened to a drafting program showing a floor plan: the mid-mod that Sophie had taken on last month. Kendall realized that she'd never checked on how the project was going or asked if Sophie needed any help. She clicked the 3D button that would show her the animation of what the finished project was going to look like.

And drew in a breath.

It was completely different from what Kendall would have done, but that was part of the wonder of it. Having spent so much of her career specializing in restoration, she would have been tempted to create a faithful representation of the house's 1960s identity. But Sophie had almost gone the opposite direction. Mid-century pieces mixed with sleek contemporary furniture and stately antiques. A clean-lined mid-mod sofa sat over a muted Persian rug before a white enamel Danish coffee table, Saarinen-style. And in a choice that seemed shocking but worked amazingly well, the entire room was papered in a muted yet dramatic wallpaper.

It was lovely.

Kendall plopped into Sophie's chair, suddenly struck with a mix of shock and guilt. She'd completely underestimated her assistant. Not her assistant anymore, her design partner. She'd thought she was mentoring Sophie, but really, she'd been holding her back.

Only then did Kendall see the blinking light on the office phone that indicated a message on their main business line. She punched Speaker and then the message light. It dialed into the voice mail and then began to play.

"Hello, this message is for Sophie Daniels. My name is Roberta Lyons. I'm a friend of the Thomases; you're currently redoing their home in Long Beach? I would love to talk to you about a remodel project in my own home here in Glendale. It's a mid-mod as well, though certainly not as important as theirs, but I love the direction . . ."

Kendall punched a button to save the message as unread and then clicked off the phone. It looked like Sophie was making a name for herself. She waited for the expected feeling of jealousy, of hurt, but curiously, she felt nothing but a vague sense of pride. It was time Sophie got recognition for her work. She had obviously not only kept the place running while Kendall was gone, but she'd brought in three new jobs for the firm. Maybe they didn't need the sale of the Jasper Lake homes to keep their spot here in Pasadena after all. The new clients would go a long way toward solvency.

But once the thought of Jasper Lake was in her

head, it was hard to dismiss. After spending time in Connie Green's house and then the Novaks', the big, beautiful house that surrounded her now, which had once felt so familiar, felt like . . . just a house. A house that had sheltered her, provided her a home base and a living, given her something to call her own, but an ordinary structure all the same.

She pushed herself off Sophie's chair, feeling unaccountably restless, and headed down the hallway to her bedroom. Surely what she was feeling now was just a knee-jerk reaction to all the change, all the revelations she'd experienced. It was like the culture shock she experienced every time she traveled to Europe and again when she returned to the United States. A recognition of all the things she took for granted and a realization that there were things in both places she'd missed.

Occasionally there were people she'd miss too.

Kendall sighed and unzipped her duffel bag, then pulled out the papers she'd slipped into the zippered lining. The packet from the PI, the letters between Connie and Carrie. She traded her jeans and sweater for a pair of joggers and a tank top and climbed beneath the fluffy comforter on her bed, draping it over her crossed legs. And then she started sorting out the paperwork in front of her.

After a few minutes, she realized she was

forming a timeline, looking for something. Looking for what, she didn't know. The revelations surrounding her abandonment softened her bad memories but didn't eliminate them. They didn't erase decades of feeling unloved, unwanted, unmoored. The desire to have a family of her own, who actually belonged to her, instead of being assigned to her. The fact that, unbeknownst to herself, she'd been striving and working and searching for who she actually was, always trying to prove that she was more than just an orphan shuttled between foster homes with all her worldly possessions in a black plastic trash bag.

But when she looked at it objectively, laid out in front of her in paperwork and photos, her life didn't appear as unmoored or random as it had felt at the time, even the recent developments. If she had learned all this even a few years back, would she have been prepared to accept it? Or would she, with her always closed-off heart, have dismissed anything having to do with the people she thought had hurt her?

Without truly realizing what she was doing, she picked up her cell phone and dialed.

Gabe picked up on the second ring, his voice surprised. No, shocked. "Kendall! I didn't expect to hear from you. Is everything all right?"

She fell back against her pillow, tears pricking her eyes. Until now, she hadn't realized how much she was going to miss him, how much she wanted to hear his voice. Regardless of what had happened between them that single night, he'd become a friend, someone she truly cared about, whose opinion mattered to her. And she realized that she didn't know how to answer his question. "I don't know."

A long pause from the other end of the line. "Do you want to talk about it?"

She pulled the comforter up to her shoulders and rolled over as she pressed the phone to her ear, almost completely buried beneath her covers. "Do you believe everything happens for a reason?"

"Like, do I believe everything that happens is meant to be?" Gabe asked.

"Yeah, I guess."

He took a moment to answer. "Not really. I mean, I believe in a grand plan. But I also think we make our own role in it through our choices. I've made bad decisions that took me way off course. I've done things that I knew were wrong, or at least that I knew weren't good for me, and I've had to deal with the consequences."

"But you do believe there's a grand plan. You think there's a God up there pulling the strings."

His voice softened. "You know I do, though I wouldn't say pulling the strings. I'd say gently guiding and nudging. Where's this coming from, Kendall?"

She swallowed hard. "I visited my foster parents today."

"You did? How did that go?"

She realized that she hadn't thanked him for hiring the PI yet, but that would have to wait. She wasn't ready to derail their current conversation, not when she was still desperately seeking an answer to a question she couldn't yet fully form. "It was good, actually. And bad. I realized that my memories of my childhood weren't completely accurate."

"Oh? In a bad way or a good way?"

"I just saw everything through the lens of my own trauma. When I went back, I remembered all the good things they did for me. The normalcy I had for eight years."

"They were good foster parents after all, then."

"They were good parents, period." She swallowed down the lump in her throat. "I didn't realize how much I'd hurt them by rejecting their love."

"You were a kid, Kendall. A kid who went through something incredibly traumatic, followed by all that uncertainty and shuffling around in the system."

"But I did eventually land somewhere good. And it's thanks to them that I was able to grow up and become a productive adult, even if I didn't realize it at the time."

"And now you're feeling guilty for that?"

Kendall licked her lips, almost afraid to voice the thoughts bouncing around her head. "It's just that . . . if I was so wrong about them, what else was I wrong about?"

Gabe's voice turned cautious. "Like what?"

"Like . . ." She almost couldn't voice the words. "Like about God."

She heard Gabe exhale and it struck jitters in her stomach, not unlike what she'd felt before she made the decision to kiss him. What was he thinking? Would he make fun of her? Did he think this was just a way to get him to talk to her again? A way for them to be together?

That thought hadn't occurred to her until now, and she pushed it away. Even she knew this question was way more important than a guy.

Finally Gabe said, "I can only tell you my experience, Kendall. You know I was angry at my parents because of what happened, and I was angry at God, too. I wanted nothing to do with Him, especially considering my mom was supposed to be a Christian, then had an affair with a married man and lied about it for a decade. I let the problems with her relationship with God affect my relationship with Him."

"So how did you get past it?" Kendall asked. "What was the tipping point?" She couldn't believe these words were coming out of her mouth, but she really wanted to know.

"I don't know. It wasn't one big thing. I guess

it was just seeing how my grandparents believed. And believe it or not, *your* grandmother. I can only think that she learned her lesson after what happened with your mom, because she was all about grace and God forgiving our mistakes and the weakness of our faith. And I just kind of realized . . . that God had been waiting for me to come around. Patiently. Not forcing anything."

"Huh." Kendall found she couldn't say anything more eloquent, her mind spinning too fast.

"Kendall, talk to me. You can tell me anything, you know. We can still be friends, regardless of what else we might have been."

Those words gave her a heart cramp. What else they might have been. No, she couldn't go there right now. And Gabe was maybe the only person who could understand how she was feeling, what she was wrestling with.

"I guess . . . I've always blamed God for what happened to me. Like, He was sleeping on the job and He let me down. And I don't think I'll ever understand how He could let both my parents be killed in car accidents just a couple of years apart. You've probably got a better chance of being hit by lightning than that happening."

Gabe made a sound that could have been agreement or just acknowledgment, but she took it as support.

"But when I look back . . . a lot of positive things happened that were equally implausible. I

435

got taken in by a really good couple who tried their best to mitigate all my trauma, even if I didn't realize it at the time. And then 'chance' took me to the design school, where I found my new career. And then by more chance, I found my mentor. And opened my own place. Found a partner . . . who, by the way, has done a better job running the business while I was gone than I've ever done . . . And then just when I was maybe ready to hear it, I uncovered all this. I met you." She chewed her lip. "What if that wasn't all by coincidence?"

"I don't believe in coincidence or chance, Kendall. I only believe in consequences of our actions and God's providence. And thank God that a lot of the time His providence overrides our stupid decisions."

His wry tone made her laugh, unexpectedly. "That would be comforting if it's true."

"It is true, Kendall. I know it. I've experienced it. And you forgot one more bit of supposed chance. It's not just your life wrapped up in this timeline. I found out about your house reverting to the county right as I took office a couple of months ago. Which only happened because I lost my job . . . which, quite frankly, felt like the worst thing that could happen to me at the time. Had that not unraveled an entire chain of events, would you even be asking these questions?"

Her heart was pounding a little too hard now. "I guess not. I just . . . What do I do now?"

"Only you can answer that. Tell me one thing, Kendall. What do you know in your heart to be true? Not what you've been told or how you've protected yourself, but do you still believe everything in your life has happened by coincidence?"

A single tear breached her lower lashes and slid down her face. "I guess not."

"What do you want to do about it?"

She knew, but she couldn't say it. "It's too late, Gabe. I wouldn't even know how to begin."

"It's never too late. God loves you, Kendall. He always has. He never stopped."

The words, so close to what Bill had uttered mere hours before, stopped her in her tracks. "What did you just say?"

"God takes us as we are. Broken and confused and unfaithful and insecure. All we have to do is accept Him. Recognize that the emptiness we're all trying to fill can only be taken up by Him. It's why He sent His Son to be sacrificed. To build that bridge between us, across the chasm that our sin caused between us and God. It's just our choice whether or not to walk over it."

Kendall was crying for real now, and she didn't even know why. She wanted so much to believe that what he said was true. That there had been, if not a purpose, at least a plan at work in her life.

Someone guiding her steps. That she wasn't as alone as she'd always believed.

But then, hadn't that been what she'd thought about Bill and Nancy? That when she walked away, they were done with her, when in reality they were just waiting for her to come home? To accept the gift of being in their family?

Gabe made coming to God seem just as easy.

"What do I do?" she whispered.

"Believe," Gabe said, his voice equally quiet. "It's a choice, Kendall. To believe or not."

And for the first time in her life, it felt like an easy choice.

"I choose to believe."

Gabe exhaled as if he'd been holding his breath. "Then welcome to the family, Kendall."

It was those words more than anything that broke her. She could do nothing but cry into the phone for long minutes, so long that she had to look at the screen to see if the call was still connected. She couldn't find the words to express how she felt as everything she'd held in—loneliness and grief and fear—poured out of her. Somewhere in the back of her mind, she knew Gabe must think she was crazy.

But he was still there.

When her tears were finally spent, it was his quiet voice on the line that brought her back. He talked to her about what her decision meant. Encouraged her to find a church with a pastor who could help guide her down the right path. To get her own Bible and read it. How many times had she wished for an instruction manual only to find out that one existed?

She thought it would take a while to be able to call herself a Christian, with all the emotions and bad memories loading that word. It was going to have to be enough to say she'd found God and she was getting to know Jesus. That was honest, at least.

It was early morning by the time she hung up the phone with Gabe, her heart aching and raw for reasons she couldn't even explain. She'd thought when someone made a decision like this, it was all light from heaven and choirs singing and inexplicable joy. Not this raw, painful feeling that the things she'd always held close—her beliefs and her prejudice—were being ripped away and replaced with something new.

But maybe that's what healing was like. She suddenly remembered the time she was thirteen and she'd dislocated her knee. It was so painful she didn't want anyone to touch it, least of all the doctor. The process of putting it back in place was agonizing, but it was followed by relief. And then an ache as the swelling subsided and the joint got stronger again.

As hard and emotional as the experience felt, as she closed her eyes and drifted to sleep, there was relief.

Chapter Thirty-Six

Gabe hung up the phone and sank back into the couch cushions, at once wrung out and completely wired. When Kendall had called, he'd certainly had no idea that she was wrestling with the ideas of God and salvation. The whole time he had been talking, he'd had a running litany of prayer in the background that went something like: *Please God, don't let me lead her astray. Don't let me screw her up. Give me the right words.*

And God had answered apparently, because by the time they'd hung up, Kendall was a new person.

Fitz nudged his hand, an indication the dog didn't appreciate that he'd stopped petting him, as he'd done for hours while talking to Kendall, an unconscious action. He chuckled and scratched the dog's ears. "You attention fiend. Now you're going to expect hours of doggy massage every night, aren't you?"

The shifting of bushy eyebrows could have meant either "That's not an option?" or confusion that he was even questioning the wisdom of the action.

After all the crying Kendall had done, she was

likely sound asleep now. But Gabe had an idea that was not in the cards for him. He could think of only one thing.

The only barrier against them being together was gone.

And yet at the very thought of pursuing her romantically, he slammed into a big mental brick wall.

No.

God rarely was so clear with him, but there could be no questioning that answer.

Was that what this was all about? Was their friendship, their barely begun romance, merely a vehicle to bring Kendall to Christ? Was Gabe just a stop on whatever path God had intended for Kendall all the time? When she'd called, he'd been half-hoping she'd gotten home and realized that California wasn't where she wanted to be, that she wanted to come back to Jasper Lake.

But now he couldn't deny the possibility that none of it had been for his benefit, only for hers.

No, that wasn't true. They'd needed to work together. The attorney had filed for the injunction and felt confident it would be granted on Monday or Tuesday. His dad had called to say that he'd heard from his friend at History Colorado who confirmed that the grant application had been received and would be considered, even though it was late. Turned out she was a history buff and actually had a deep appreciation of the Arts and Crafts movement in England. Another thing that couldn't possibly be a coincidence.

Had Kendall not come, he wouldn't be raising a motion to the city council to change the zoning on Monday. And he certainly wouldn't be on speaking terms with his father again, something that felt a little bit like an ill-fitting suit. They'd grown out of the family friend relationship they'd had when he was a boy, and now they were going to have to figure out what a new father-son relationship looked like. If he were completely honest, it was something he'd always secretly wanted but never wanted to admit.

But now he wasn't sure if it was enough.

Because talking to Kendall made him realize that in two short weeks, she'd become one of the most important people in his life. It seemed impossible. They'd worked together and kissed twice. But he couldn't help but admire her bravery, particularly because she didn't recognize it as such. In two weeks, she'd had her world turned upside down. She'd had to reevaluate everything she thought she knew about her past and her family. She'd reconnected with foster parents and realized the error of her memories. And she hadn't been afraid to abandon her long-held belief when faced with the evidence that, indeed, life was not haphazard. That she had been guided all these years by a loving and patient God.

How could he not love her? Whether or not they ever had the chance to fall in love, he wanted the best for her, even if it was at his own expense.

For that reason, he was going to heed the warning in his spirit that said to do nothing. To not let on the depth of his feelings. Because what he wanted right now seemed not to be important, not if it interfered with another new relationship she would be working on.

"You know, Fitz," he said with a sigh. "Be glad you're a dog. Because sometimes being a human sucks."

Fitz just wiggled forward so he could get more of his body on the couch.

"Yeah, thanks, buddy. I've got you as long as I keep the kibble and the scratches coming."

Gabe might fully believe God had a plan. He might be willing to be obedient to it.

But that didn't mean he had to like it.

Sophie was supposed to be at her boyfriend's house, so Kendall nearly jumped out of her skin when the front door slammed late the next morning. She leapt out of her office chair and poked her head out of the office, a hand held over her pounding heart. "Soph? Is that you?"

Sophie stopped short. "Oh, sorry, Kendall.

I just came home to grab something. I didn't expect you to be here."

Kendall blinked at her. Breezy, confident Sophie just stood there guiltily. "I texted you that I'd be home yesterday. Didn't you get the text?"

"Yeah, I did. I just . . ." Sophie shifted from foot to foot, looking around the room.

Kendall narrowed her eyes. "Soph, what's going on? Level with me."

Sophie gestured for them to take a seat in two of the chairs at the round table they used for design consultations. "I really didn't want to do it this way."

Kendall blinked. "Do what this way?"

Sophie grimaced. "I got a job offer."

"What?"

"And I took it." Sophie rushed on, "I'm so sorry, Kendall. I really value everything I've learned from you, and it's been great working with you, but the past couple of weeks have proved to me that I'm capable of more than what I'm doing here. The Thomas project is going really well, and someone else wants to hire me . . . My clientele is taking off." She reached for Kendall's hand. "Can you ever forgive me?"

Kendall sat there, frozen in shock. And then she started to laugh.

Sophie suddenly looked terrified.

"How long have we been friends, Soph?"

Sophie looked like it was a trick question. Only

then did Kendall realize that what she'd seen as a friendship maybe didn't mean the same thing to Sophie, who had a life outside of the design group. Kendall had been a mentor, a roommate, but had they ever really connected with each other on a deep personal level?

"How long have we worked together?" she rephrased. "Four years, right?"

Sophie nodded.

"In all that time, I was afraid to let go of any of this business because it was all I had. I had to make it work, because as you know, I have nothing to fall back on. But leaving and coming back to all this . . . I realize I've been under-utilizing you. You are capable of so much more than I gave you credit for. You're an excellent designer in your own right, and you're also apparently a good businessperson." She took a deep breath. "In fact, I was about to ask if you wanted to become a full partner."

Sophie looked at her, her eyes wide. "I . . . I don't know what to say."

"Say yes. Or no. It's your choice."

Sophie hesitated. "Here's the thing, Kendall. I've watched everything you've had to do to get this business up and running. I see the money going out. I see how close we are to being in the red every month. And I just don't think I have it in me to take on that kind of responsibility."

"I understand," Kendall said, though the hope

she'd felt moments before deflated. "You're sure you won't stay? As a designer, of course, not as my assistant."

She cringed a little. "Kendall, the offer is with Joseph Kramer."

"Wow." Kendall sat back in her seat. Joseph Kramer? "Wow."

"I hope you don't feel like it's a betrayal because he gave you your shot. Because it was partly the fact I worked with you that made him want me. He had nothing but great things to say about you and your work. But we both know that I'm a different designer than you are. And . . ." Sophie shrugged. "I can make a lot more money there. I know that shouldn't be the deciding factor, but it is. Southern California is expensive. It's the difference between having my own place someday and continuing to live where I work. And I know you love it, but sometimes I just have to get away. That's why I spend so much time at Sean's place."

Hearing it put that way, Kendall realized how backward she'd had everything. For Sophie, this was a job, not her home; she'd never been as dedicated to keeping this house as Kendall had. Now Kendall wasn't even sure why she was so attached to it.

"I'm actually kind of glad to hear you say that," Kendall said. "Because I'm letting this place go."

Sophie gasped. "You're kidding me. Is it

because you couldn't sell the properties in Colorado?"

"Partly." She didn't tell her that it was because she'd chosen to keep them, for reasons she was only beginning to understand. "But also because I was holding on to it for the wrong reasons. I thought it was my home, and I thought home meant everything, and now I realize there are things that are more important."

"So . . . what are you going to do?"

"Well, we didn't sign the lease, so I suppose I'm looking for a new place to live," Kendall said. "I'm committed through Christmas, but I'm going back to Colorado for the holidays, so I guess we need to be out of here by then. Is that going to be a problem?"

Sophie shook her head. "I'll just put my furniture into storage until I find an apartment. I'll stay with Sean until then."

"Good. I think." Kendall sat back, her hands in her lap. What else was there to say?

"Kendall, are you okay? You seem . . . different."

Kendall took a deep breath, but she couldn't keep the smile off her face, even if it was tinged with irony. "You have no idea."

"The trip to Colorado was a good thing, then?"

"It was exactly what I needed," Kendall said. "I feel like a different person." She would wait to tell Sophie that she'd found God. . . .

Right now, with all the changes Kendall had announced, Sophie might think she'd joined a cult and was pledging all her money to it or something. Besides, Kendall wasn't sure how to put the experience into words. Didn't know what it really meant to her yet. Other than it felt like after carrying the weight of the world for years, she'd finally shifted it to the rightful shoulders.

"I have to tell you I'm really relieved by your reaction. I thought you might feel betrayed."

Kendall took the words in and nodded slowly. "A month ago, I would have. Because this was all I had. I was hanging all my hopes on the success of this business. But now . . ." She shook her head. "It's important, but it's not the only thing."

Sophie was still staring at her like she'd grown another head. "So I guess we'll discuss the plans for my transition on Monday?"

Kendall nodded. "You should take the new client with you. I know they called here, but they asked for you. And quite frankly, mid-century modern isn't my thing. I think I'll stick with the historical restorations."

Sophie was trying not to look giddy, but she was failing. She stood and unexpectedly threw her arms around Kendall's neck. "Thank you, Kendall. For everything."

"You're welcome, Sophie. You're ready. Everyone saw it except for me, and for that I'm sorry."

Kendall disentangled her. "Now go. I know this was just a quick stop-in."

Kendall watched her assistant—former assistant, soon to be former employee—leave the room and then sank back into her chair. She'd made the decision to give up this house on the spur of the moment, but it had been percolating in her mind ever since she'd decided to keep the property in Colorado. She had enough of a reputation to continue working out of a smaller house, without a showroom. All the furniture would shift to the warehouse she was already paying for, and she could get out from under this crushing lease.

It felt like the right move.

And then she wondered if maybe she should pray about it. It was a new idea, running her thoughts by God. She didn't even know how He would answer. With an audible word? With a sign? With a feeling that she was doing the right thing?

Will You show me my next moves? I don't want to make a mistake.

Maybe not eloquent as prayers went, but Gabe made it seem like it was that easy.

Now she just had to wait for an answer.

Chapter Thirty-Seven

The motion passed, seven votes to two. As soon as Burton heard the decision, he stormed out of the room and slammed the chamber door behind him.

Gabe wasn't sure which was more satisfying—the fact that the city council had taken his leadership on the rezoning issue or the fact that Burton was furious over it.

Actually, he suspected it was the cocky expression on the developer's face that had swung a couple of votes in Gabe's direction; his unofficial poll had made him think it was going to fall five to four in his favor. But those swing votes were tricky—they could have gone either way.

The temporary injunction had helped, though, coming through early this afternoon just as the attorney had predicted. It only granted them a stay of execution—even though the zoning had been changed, the condemnation proceeding was on file and they were going to have to deal with it one way or another. They had to bring the homes up to code, and then they would be safe. Permanently.

Gabe desperately wanted to call Kendall and let her know, but every time he tried to dial her number, he was met with a suffocating wall of *No.* God was not messing around. When he felt no such check at typing her email address, he sent her a quick message: *The injunction was granted and the city council voted to change the zoning to historical residential. We're safe for now.*

He shoved his phone back into his pocket, refusing to mark the minutes until she replied.

Because if she didn't . . . that would feel like more of an ending than even God's clear direction.

"I don't understand," Kendall said. "We were all set to start today."

Louise Marquette, the owner of the Woolridge House, regarded her sympathetically. "I'm so sorry, Kendall. When we didn't get a reply from you confirming, we assumed that you were just too busy. And although you were definitely our first choice, we thought perhaps we would be better off going with someone who would be more committed to the project."

Kendall stared at Louise in shock. This couldn't be happening. She'd counted on the deposit for the Woolridge job to take her through Christmas, to help pay for the move and the first month's rent on whatever house she ended up leasing. She wanted to argue, but their minds were made up, and anything more would be unprofessional. She stood and held out her hand. "Well, I'm very sorry it didn't work out. It's a beautiful home, and I hope you're thrilled with the way it turns out."

"We hope so too. Thank you, Kendall. I'm sorry again."

Kendall walked out the front door of the home, climbed in her car, and immediately started to search her phone for the email she'd sent confirming that she would indeed start the job today.

And found it. In her drafts folder.

She blinked at the phone in disbelief. Had she really done that? She'd forgotten to press Send? With everything that had been going on at the time, she supposed it was possible, but it wasn't like her.

She pushed her hands through her hair and forced down the panic. " 'All things work together for good to those who love God,' " she repeated to herself, a verse she'd learned when she'd tentatively walked into a neighborhood church last night. "You have some way of reinforcing lessons."

She could only hope that God had a sense of humor. Because this faith thing was already new enough without making Him mad.

Then again, it wasn't like He didn't know what she was thinking anyway.

"Okay. What next?" She directed the words to the car's ceiling and, not surprisingly, got no distinct response back. Hopefully some kind of answer would come before she ran out of money and a place to live.

She leaned her head back against her car's headrest and concentrated on taking deep breaths to calm her fluttering heart. This was fine. It wasn't like she didn't have any prospects. She'd had a few inquiries for projects after the holidays, and there was a quick kitchen refresh between Thanksgiving and Christmas—one Sophie had just emailed her—that looked promising. Just because the big one had fallen through didn't mean she was in trouble. She just needed to figure out a way to keep things afloat while she was moving into a less expensive place and Sophie was transitioning out.

Her phone dinged, her email notification. Her heart rose into her throat when she saw the sender: Gabriel Brandt. She opened the message and read it: *The injunction was granted and the city council voted to change the zoning to historical residential. We're safe for now.*

She frowned and reread it. That was it? Not that she wasn't thrilled to hear that they'd prevailed over Burton and his revenge plans, but she and Gabe had spent five hours on the phone on Saturday night. That was all he had to say to her? No asking her if she was okay. No wondering if she'd found a church like he recommended or if she'd actually bought a Bible.

Nothing saying that he missed her or wished

she was there to help with what came next in Jasper Lake.

Kendall shook her head angrily to clear those thoughts. She wasn't mad at him; she was mad at herself. Hadn't part of her thought that maybe, now that they shared the same faith, however new and tenuous hers was, there might be hope for them? That he might reconsider his decision not to pursue a relationship with her?

But that wasn't really the point, was it? That wasn't why she'd decided to follow Jesus. She'd made that choice because it was no longer possible to ignore how God had already worked in her life, using the disasters for good, or at least better than it might have been.

She needed this relationship for herself, not just as a stepping-stone into a romance with Gabe.

She tapped out a reply, as brief and careful as his message had been: *I'm so glad to hear that. Keep me posted. And let me know if you need my help with anything.*

She dropped her phone into the cup holder and twisted her key in the ignition, ignoring the ache in her chest that didn't seem to want to fade now that it had taken up residence. But she had plenty to keep her distracted. Plenty to keep her from dwelling on the irony: she was finally letting go of her fear of relationships, but it came too late for her to have the one she really wanted.

• • •

Gabe had his work cut out for him, keeping his mind off Kendall. She was first on his mind when he woke up in the morning and last on it when he went to bed. But his guidance had been clear, and as much as Gabe wanted to believe her brief reply changed the rules, he knew he was just trying to think up reasons to hear her voice again.

It wasn't as though he didn't have plenty to do. Now that the injunction had been issued and the zoning had been changed, it fell to him to start thinking about what they were going to do in place of the resort. The situation that he had been hired to remedy hadn't changed: the town was still in danger, but this time the danger was the likelihood of it fading away slowly, dying season by season. Just because he was opposed to the development that Burton had wanted to bring to Jasper Lake didn't mean he didn't recognize the need for it to grow and thrive.

The answer came from a most unexpected place, carried by the most unexpected person. Gabe looked up at a knock at his office door when Linda was out to lunch, expecting to see one of the Jasper Lake citizens hoping to catch a minute of his time.

Instead, it was his father.

Gabe rose from his chair immediately, shocked into silence. He finally found his voice and stuck out his hand. "I didn't expect to see you here. Do you want to have a seat?"

Robert shook his hand tentatively and then pulled out one of the armchairs in front of Gabe's desk. "This is impressive, Son. It's a nice little town."

Gabe seated himself awkwardly behind his desk again, feeling as if he were meeting a stranger whose motivations he didn't quite understand. It wasn't so far from the truth. "First time you've been here?"

"First time in years. Back before the flood, it was quite the tourist destination. I'm not sure any of the towns up here have recovered."

"They really haven't," Gabe said, glad to be on familiar footing. "But we're working on some ideas." He studied his father, who looked as uncomfortable as he felt. "What brings you up here? You know you could have just called if you needed to speak with me."

"I know. But I wanted to talk to you in person." Robert leaned forward a little in his chair. "I have a proposal for you."

"Oh?"

"A business proposal actually. Given how the grant application turned out—"

"Wait. What? You've got news on the grant application?"

Robert looked confused. "You haven't heard. When I got a call from Winnie, I assumed you'd already been notified. She was open to considering your application, but the rest of the committee didn't feel it was fair to allow you to submit past the fall due date. They've pushed it to the spring. You've got a good chance of winning the grant from what I hear, but the earliest anyone will decide on it is May or June. And from what I understand—"

"—that's going to be far too late. You're right. The injunction is only temporary. And even getting a historic places designation isn't going to be enough in the long term." Gabe sat back in his chair, the wind knocked out of him. He'd been relying on the grant to make the updates on the houses. Had all their work been for nothing?

But then he realized that Robert had led with a business proposal, so surely he hadn't driven up here to deliver bad news in person, especially bad news that he thought Gabe had already received. "What's the proposal? Since clearly we are going to need other ideas."

"Right." Robert pulled out a hardback portfolio from his bag and slid it across the desk to Gabe. "This belongs to a young architect who has been working for me for the past couple of years, Astrid Elison."

Gabe flipped it open. The images inside were pretty standard for a college architecture graduate: renderings and diagrams of her designs interspersed with black-and-white photos that helped convey the feeling of the structures. But they were arranged in a way that told a story, as much a picture book or a graphic design example as an architectural portfolio. In Gabe's work at the nonprofit, he'd seen more than a few of these, and he couldn't help but be impressed.

But he still didn't know what it had to do with him. He said as much.

"Astrid's focus is on sustainable architecture and multiuse spaces, but she's particularly interested in how that intersects with historical preservation and city planning. Which is part of the reason she approached me for a job." Robert smiled. "Hounded me is a more apt description, actually. She is a finalist for an architecture grant based on her portfolio, but she needs a subject for the final round of the grant competition. I mentioned something about Jasper Lake."

Gabe's eyebrows flew up. "She wants to come here and do what?"

"Well, that's what you'll need to work out with her, if you're interested in going forward."

"Why isn't she here talking to me herself?"

"I would be partially underwriting the project since she would continue to be my employee. And if we can come to an agreement on something that would be beneficial for the town, Astrid, and my firm, I'm willing to make a substantial investment." Robert smiled faintly. "And . . . I didn't really want to share the second

458

conversation I've had with you in decades with a twenty-two-year-old."

Gabe couldn't help but return the smile, though his mind was whirring. "What if she doesn't get the grant?"

"If it makes financial sense, I'll still invest. But we're months away from that determination. These things take time to set into motion."

Gabe leaned back in his seat. There was still something missing in the idea; Astrid surely wasn't the only one interested in sustainable architecture and preservation in this day and age. They needed a hook, a new idea, if she had the slightest chance of winning the grant. And then it came to him, so obvious that he felt like an idiot for not thinking of it sooner. "How does she feel about technology?"

Robert's brows knit together. "What do you mean?"

"What if her proposal was to demonstrate a remote-working community? It fits into the sustainable model because it's a fully walkable/bikeable town. Requires no commuting, which consumes no fossil fuels and creates no pollution. Coworking spaces. Multiuse buildings. 'Work virtually in the most beautiful town in Colorado.'"

Robert's expression turned thoughtful. "This isn't something you just came up with."

"No. Kendall did. We were spitballing a couple

of weeks ago, and she floated it as an idea to attract the younger set to the town. Low cost of living for start-ups. Work-life balance. As she said, millennials are into that, and if we're going to survive, my generation is the one who will have to decide to come back to small-town living. And it's also the generation that patronizes yoga studios and mountain bike shops and organic markets."

"Which brings more retail to town . . ."

"Which then makes us more of a fully functioning, self-sufficient community, not as dependent on other towns for our goods and services," Gabe finished.

Robert sat with the idea for a long moment, then smiled. "I like it. Let me propose it to Astrid and see what she says. And if she's interested, I'll put her in touch with you."

"I have one request though."

"What's that?"

"I want Kendall Green on the design team."

Another smile played at the edges of his father's face. "And would this be for personal or practical reasons?"

"A little of both, to be honest. Her specialty is historic preservation and blending architectural styles. Trust me, we want someone like her helping us."

"Are you asking me to give her a job?"

It wasn't what Gabe had been thinking, but

now that Robert said it, it sounded like an ideal solution. He hadn't been sure she would come back if he asked her, and the salary he could offer her as a Jasper Lake employee couldn't compare to what she was making as a designer. But if she was instead working for Robert and only tangentially with him . . . He waited for the familiar smack in the head that had met him every time he tried to contact Kendall, but it was conspicuously absent. Apparently God was okay with this course of action. Or at least Gabe hoped He was, now that he'd already put it out there.

"That's exactly what I'm asking."

Robert held Gabe's gaze for a long moment. "When we get things underway . . . if and when I make the decision to invest and we move forward . . . I'll contact her. But, Gabe . . . understand this. It's not a quick fix. It will take a year to break ground. Maybe ten before we see the full expression of the idea, and maybe even longer before we see if it's successful. Are you willing to be in this for the long haul? You may not be mayor by that point, but Jasper Lake is going to need someone to see it through to the end. Are you sure you're that person?"

Even six months ago, he wasn't sure how he would have answered that question. Jasper Lake, the mayoral race, had been something to do because he'd lost his way, wasn't sure where God was leading him next. It seemed his season in Jasper Lake was not to last a year or two but a decade. With or without Kendall.

Slowly Gabe nodded. "If we can make this happen, I'm in it to the end."

Robert stood and offered his hand. "Then I'll talk to Astrid and have her get in touch. From what I know about her, she'll take your idea as a unique challenge . . . and I think it gives her a good chance of winning the grant as well."

Gabe stood too and shook his dad's hand. "Thanks for coming in person." He watched his dad pick up his bag and turn on his heel. Before Robert reached the door, Gabe called, "You know, it's almost lunch. I don't suppose you want to grab a bite to eat? The cantina down the street has fantastic barbecue."

Robert turned, surprised. Then he nodded. "I never turn down barbecue."

Gabe closed down his computer and grabbed his jacket from the back of the chair and his keys from the drawer. Then he grinned and tossed the keys back. "Never mind. It's walkable."

Chapter Thirty-Eight

Kendall thought it would be difficult to leave the Pasadena house, but as she made one last trip through the empty interior, she realized once more what she'd always known: it was just a house.

And yet it had been more than that. A place of shelter. An escape. A waypoint when she needed it, wasn't sure of her next moves.

The one thing it had never been was a home.

Satisfied that she hadn't forgotten anything and that it was in the same condition as when she'd moved in, she stepped out onto the stoop and locked the front door for the last time. All her personal items and furniture had been moved into the firm's storage facility, pending the signing of her new lease when she returned from her Christmas vacation in Colorado. She'd finally decided on a place—a much smaller but just as charming foursquare in nearby Glendale—but the owner was dragging her feet on sending over the lease paperwork. Kendall had left her a message telling her to email the paperwork when she had it and she would overnight it back. She wasn't taking any chances on losing her new start.

And yet nothing about that new start was as

nerve-racking and gut-fluttering as this trip back to Denver. Bill and Nancy had been texting her almost nonstop for the past week, confirming her arrival at the airport, telling her that they had her room ready, double-checking that she hadn't developed any food allergies since she moved out. It was both funny and heartening that they seemed as nervous about this reunion as she felt.

She hadn't yet decided if she was going to spend some of the next two weeks in Jasper Lake. She hadn't heard anything from Gabe in weeks, and the last email had just been to check in and let her know that her houses were okay, the injunction still stood, and he was waiting for grant decisions before they could do anything more about the permits on her houses.

Nothing personal. Nothing to make her think she was on his mind as much as he continued to be on hers. For all she knew, he was dating someone in town. More than likely, actually. There weren't that many young singles in Jasper Lake, and it seemed to her that they would pair up quickly.

Still, the idea of him with Rebecca, for example, made her stomach clench.

"Easy there. You're going to have to get used to that idea. You can't avoid Jasper Lake forever." She'd been paralyzed when it came to the idea of selling the houses, but she couldn't deny that they weren't doing her or anyone else any good sitting there vacant. It was a miracle that they had stayed as well-preserved as they were. Houses were like people: lack of activity made them deteriorate.

She mulled over the thought the entire way to the airport and while she was sitting at the gate waiting for her flight. By the time she walked down the Jetway to board the 737, she had decided that she was going to bite the bullet and get in touch with Gabe. He was the executor of the trust, after all, and they needed to decide what they were going to do with the houses. Even if seeing him would stir up all sorts of feelings she had no business experiencing. Even if he told her that he was in a relationship with someone else.

As soon as she was on board, she pulled out her phone and sent a text message: Headed to Colorado for two weeks to spend Christmas with Bill and Nancy. We should probably meet and discuss what we're going to do with the houses.

And then she put her phone on airplane mode so she didn't have to deal with the reply until she landed.

She spent the two-and-a-half-hour flight flipping through magazines she'd picked up at the airport's newsstand, things that required nearly no attention on her part, considering that she was instead hyper-focused on what awaited her in Denver. As soon as the plane touched down on the runway—after the same bumpy descent that had met her last time—her stomach started jumping nervously. When the Fasten Seat Belt sign went off, she turned off airplane mode.

Immediately messages started ringing through.

She held her breath, expecting one of them to be Gabe, but his name never came up on the list. Instead, they were alternating messages from Bill and Nancy.

On our way to the airport.

We're here. Just let us know when you land.

Have you landed yet?

A smile came to Kendall's face and she tapped out a reply to both of them: Just landed. No checked bags. Should be out in 20-25.

It was a new experience, having someone anxiously awaiting her arrival. And she couldn't deny that it warmed her from the inside out. So this was what it was like to have a family. And even though she was sure she was putting too much pressure on this trip to Colorado, she couldn't help but be glad she'd taken the leap.

She had only been out of the airport doors on the arrival concourse for three minutes when the new burgundy SUV pulled up at the curb. Kendall blinked as Nancy and Bill leapt out of the front seats. Nancy made it to her first, enfolding her in a tight hug that seemed to say she'd been afraid Kendall wouldn't come. Bill took her suitcase and shoved it into the back of the vehicle, then came around for a much more restrained hug. "Ready to go?" he asked.

Nancy made for the rear door, but Kendall shook her head. "No, no. Kids sit in the back, right?" She grinned at them and slid in, settling her backpack next to her.

They climbed back in and pulled out into the airport return. Bill shot her looks in the rearview mirror, but Nancy turned fully around. "How was your flight? How was closing up the house in California? Was it hard?"

Kendall smiled. "The flight was fine. And leaving the house wasn't as hard as I thought. I'm waiting for an email from my new landlord, in fact. I found an adorable house in Glendale that has room for an office and client meeting space, so I think I'll be fine. It's much more affordable, so that's a relief."

"Well, I hope you don't mind that we made plans while you're here," Bill said.

"Oh, of course not. I didn't expect you to hang out with me the whole time," Kendall said, even though she'd been hoping that very thing.

"No, silly," Nancy said. "We mean we made plans for . . . or rather, with . . . you. We were able to get tickets to this year's Christmas home tour. We went last year and it was lovely, all these beautiful homes in Belcaro and Bonnie Brae. This year's tour is all historic remodels and restorations in University Park. We thought it might be right up your alley."

"Oh! That sounds wonderful. Sophie and I

did the Holiday Look In Home Tour last year in Pasadena to benefit the symphony."

"You know, given your interest in historic architecture, you might find a lot to your liking here in Denver. There's not a lot of Spanish and mission style here, but there's plenty of mid-century and Craftsman. And if I'm not mistaken, those are your main interests."

"Sophie is the mid-mod designer, and she's no longer with me. But yes, I love my Craftsmans." Especially the ones up in Jasper Lake, but she didn't voice those thoughts. "I'm not sure I could ever leave California, though. I'm established there, well-known, and unfortunately that doesn't really transfer across state lines. I'd have to start completely from scratch, and I've spent too long building my business to give it up now."

"You sound like you've given it some thought," Bill observed blandly.

She had . . . and she'd given it a fair amount of prayer, too . . . but that didn't mean she would ever really do it. It didn't make sense for her to pick up her life and move, unless there was a compelling reason to do so. She glanced reflexively at her phone. Gabe still hadn't replied.

But her future landlord had. She got momentarily distracted from Nancy's explanation of why Denver was a wonderful place to live—forgetting that Kendall had spent most of her childhood there—and opened the message on her phone.

It was short, and the contents made her heart sink.

Dear Kendall,
I'm so sorry to do this to you at the last minute, but my tenants have decided to renew their lease for another two years. As they've already been with me for five and they're currently occupying the house, I feel it's only fair to give them the lease.
I hope that I haven't put you in a bad position. Thank you for your understanding.

"Kendall, is something wrong?" Bill was looking at her with concern in the rearview mirror.

Kendall pressed the trash icon on the message. "No. Nothing's wrong. Just a work email, sorry."

"I certainly hope you'll be able to relax a little while you're here," Nancy said tentatively. "From what you've told us, you work so hard."

"Oh, I'm sure I'll be able to relax. I just needed to take care of a few last-minute things." She dropped her phone into her backpack. "In fact, I'm done here. I'm all yours."

"In that case," Nancy said, "we thought we'd stop for lunch on the way home."

Kendall smiled and said, "Lunch sounds great." And she meant it.

Her enthusiasm lasted about four days.

It wasn't that Bill and Nancy weren't nice or loving or any of the things that parents should be. In fact, they were *all* of the things parents should be, including concerned, nosy, and insistent.

Kendall had made the mistake during the tour of homes—which was lovely and inspiring, in fact—of saying that she'd lost her place to stay in California, which then instigated a full-court press on Nancy's part for Kendall to stay in Denver. Bill, on the other hand, was concerned about her financial solvency and whether or not she could survive if she had to start from scratch. Nancy was quick to offer up their place as a short-term solution. Kendall was quick to politely decline.

And yet, even while their invasiveness disturbed her, it also gave her a warm, fuzzy feeling. Whenever Sophie would complain about how her parents butted into her business and tried to give her advice, Kendall had been secretly jealous that she had people concerned enough to bother. Now that she was in the same situation, she understood how irritation and gratitude could coexist.

She also understood that she would not be living with them for longer than a vacation.

It might have been this state of mind that made

her snatch up her phone without hesitation when Gabe's name flashed on the screen. "Gabe! I was wondering if you'd gotten my message."

"Hey, Kendall." His voice, deep and familiar, poured over her like warm honey, sending a sensation through her body that was almost like an inward sigh. "I didn't want to intrude on your vacation with Bill and Nancy."

Kendall glanced around the living room, and though all signs pointed to them still being in the front yard adding lights to the Christmas land-scaping, she stepped into the backyard instead. "Oh, trust me, I'm glad for the intrusion."

His tone turned concerned. "Not going so well?"

Kendall laughed. "It's going exactly as I imagine a typical visit home to the parents would go."

"Ah. Yes. I understand. Well, in that case, I don't suppose you would like a distraction? Tomorrow is our Christmas tree lighting and bon-fire up here in Jasper Lake. I seem to remember us missing the other bonfire because of weather."

Kendall flushed at the recollection. They'd been warming up all right, but it wasn't stretching hands toward a bonfire. She hesitated before she answered. This was what she'd been waiting for, but was it really what she should do? What purpose could seeing Gabe in a social environment have if she was just going to get her heart broken?

"I don't know," she said slowly. "I flew out here, so I don't have a car."

"I'll come down and get you. You're not that far. Besides, I'd like to meet the foster parents."

"No!" Kendall blurted, imagining what they would do once they got a look at Gabe. If they found out she was entertaining romantic thoughts toward the mayor of Jasper Lake, she would never hear the end of it. "I'll borrow a car. I'm sure they wouldn't mind. We need to discuss what we're going to do with the houses anyway."

"Yes," he said. "We do."

"So I'll drive up there tomorrow afternoon then? That will give us enough time to discuss business matters before the bonfire."

His voice turned warm again. "I can't wait. I'll see you then."

"I'm looking forward to it. See you tomorrow." Kendall clicked off the line and stood there for a moment, her stomach fluttering.

Stop reading into this. It doesn't mean anything. Why would he suddenly contact you after two months if it wasn't because you texted him saying you needed to talk?

"Looking forward to what?"

Kendall spun to see Nancy standing behind her, wearing work gloves and holding a huge spool of Christmas lights. She had a knowing look on her face.

"Oh, it was just Gabe, the guy I'm working with up in Jasper Lake on the houses."

"Just the guy who hired a private investigator to find out your past for you?"

Kendall flushed again despite herself. "Gabe is the mayor of the town. It was—" She couldn't think of any legitimate official reason for him to have done it for her, and from the look on Nancy's face, she knew it. "I was going to head up there tomorrow. I might stay overnight or not. Would it be possible to borrow a car? I can always rent one if need be . . ."

Nancy waved her hand. "No, take the SUV."

"Oh, I didn't intend to take your new car—"

"It has four-wheel drive and winter tires. I'd feel better if you drove that, especially going into the high country in December. There's no snow in the forecast, but you never know. Weather changes on a dime."

"Yes, it does," Kendall agreed faintly, knowing just how true that statement was and feeling slightly disappointed that she wouldn't have the opportunity to be stranded up there again.

Stop it! If you have any chance of making it through this intact, you have to keep things strictly professional. Friendly, but not romantic. Because you won't survive another rejection.

"Thanks," she said finally. "I'll be back for Christmas Eve, obviously."

Nancy studied her for a long moment and then

walked over to place a gloved hand on Kendall's shoulder. "You know how much we've enjoyed having you here this week, don't you?"

Kendall smiled. "Yes. And I've enjoyed being here."

"We want you to always feel welcome here. We consider this your home. But, Kendall . . . if you find that you want to do something different . . . say, stay up in Jasper Lake for Christmas . . . we absolutely understand."

"Why would I want to stay in Jasper Lake?"

Nancy shot her a knowing smile. "You forget that I raised you through your teenage years. And you've never been very good at hiding it when you've got an interest in some boy." She chuckled. "Well, in this case, a man. Can you really tell me that this Gabe is just a friend or a business partner to you?"

Kendall chewed on her lip in response.

"That's what I thought." Nancy pressed her into a brief hug. "Don't worry about us. All we've ever wanted is for you to be happy. And if it turns out that spending Christmas in Jasper Lake with Gabe makes you happy . . . well, who are we to interfere? Besides, your Christmas presents will keep."

Kendall forced a smile, but the words had sent a new round of jitters into her stomach. She intended to say thank you, but instead she said, "And what if I'm misreading this whole situation? What if he really does just want to talk business like I told him?"

"Well, in that case, he's an idiot and you're better off without him." Nancy winked at her. "Now why don't you come out and help us with the last string of lights? I'm afraid if you don't tell Bill enough is enough, he's going to go buy some more."

Kendall followed her foster mother through the house into the front yard, where Bill had indeed turned a tasteful Christmas display into something similar to the Griswolds' house, viewable from space. She surveyed it for a long moment, then slid an arm around both Bill's and Nancy's waists to pull them close. "Thank you, both of you. It's perfect."

Chapter Thirty-Nine

Everything was ready for the tree-lighting ceremony and bonfire tonight, but Gabe still circled the square and walked up and down Main Street, making one last check. They traditionally held the tree lighting and bonfire the Saturday before Christmas, but the town had been slowly transforming into a holiday wonderland since the beginning of December. Garlands decorated the eaves on all the shops and buildings, and wreaths hung on nearly every door. Swags of fake greenery decorated the old-fashioned streetlights, and each street corner was punctuated with a covered fire bowl that put out heat for the shoppers and visitors that flocked to Jasper Lake during the holiday season. He paused in front of the one just down the street from the town municipal building and held his hands over the heat emanating from the wood fire. Even with his gloves, the daytime temperatures were chilly, as evidenced by the cloud of condensation that formed in front of his face every time he exhaled.

The sound of an engine turned his attention to an SUV coming up the street, and for a moment, his heart skipped a beat. Until Gabe realized that it belonged not to Kendall but to his father. Robert pulled up in front of the building and stepped out a moment later, bundled in a down jacket and boots. Gabe wandered in that direction and waited on the curb for his dad, who immediately pulled him into a tight embrace.

"Is she here yet?" he asked by way of greeting.

"Not yet."

Robert bumped his shoulder. "Don't worry. I'm sure she'll respond favorably to your proposal." When Gabe arched his eyebrows in response, he grinned. "*Our* proposal. The business one. Of course."

"Yeah, thanks." Gabe shoved his hands into his pockets to keep himself from fidgeting. He had been as restless as a racehorse at the starting gate since he got Kendall's text message, but it hadn't been the right time to respond until yesterday. He'd always tried to be sensitive to God's leading, but he'd never experienced such definitive communication until Kendall came along. Given her fledgling faith and how he'd left things with her, he wasn't about to jump the gun.

And yet his feelings for Kendall hadn't faded a bit. In fact, he'd gotten a fair amount of clarity in the last couple of months. They didn't know each other well. They might not work out at all. But despite the flirtation of a few of the single women in town, which had become more pronounced since Kendall left, he had absolutely no interest in anyone else. He had no interest in *having* interest in anyone else.

Which he could only take to mean that he had to give this thing with Kendall a shot.

Of course, she still lived and worked in another state. And he couldn't deny that no matter how gently he'd tried to do it, he'd hurt her when he said he wouldn't pursue a relationship if she wasn't a Christian.

Maybe God just wanted them to settle this once and for all.

"You look as nervous as a man on his wedding day," Robert observed, and Gabe shot him a glare. He chuckled. "Sorry. Which are you more worried about? That Kendall will turn down the job offer or that she'll turn down *your* offer?"

"Both," Gabe said honestly. "Though I think she'll be too intrigued by the job to turn it down. Or at least I'm hoping that's the case." He and Astrid had worked closely together for the past couple of months to come up with a workable preliminary town plan to submit to the grant committee. They wouldn't know the results for months yet, but Robert had been impressed enough by their vision to pledge several million dollars to the cause.

"Seen Burton around much?" Robert asked with a wicked glint in his eye.

"Oddly enough, not so much." Gabe grinned. "He's still sore over the loss of all that property."

Turned out that Kendall had been right. Without the acres of lakefront property she owned, Burton's land hadn't been as valuable as he thought—not to mention that he didn't actually own some of it. Much of it had been contingent on him getting the entire waterfront. He'd been bluffing mightily to get her to give up without a fight. Gabe felt a surge of pride that she'd seen through his bluster. Now he just couldn't wait to show her what they had in mind.

"Astrid isn't coming?" Gabe asked, checking his watch. Kendall had texted saying she was on her way over an hour ago. She should be arriving any minute.

Robert didn't miss the gesture, but at least he didn't comment on it. "No, she flew home to Minnesota to be with her family for Christmas. She said she had confidence in your ability to present the plan, since you did more than half the work."

"Hardly. I just—" The words trailed off when he caught a glimpse of an unfamiliar red Honda driving down the street toward them and held his breath. It could be anyone—they had a lot of visitors during the tree-lighting weekend. But then he caught a glimpse of a familiar face surrounded by waves of blonde hair, and his heart jolted into double time.

"Showtime," Robert murmured under his breath. "Why don't I go wait inside?"

479

"No, stay." He reached out and stilled his father while Kendall parked and climbed out of the car.

How had he forgotten she was so beautiful? She had dressed more warmly than last time—she'd apparently prepared for the below-freezing temperatures—and the hit of cold air instantly put a tinge of pink in her pale cheeks. Her expression reflected his own uncertainty as she shut the door and shouldered her handbag.

"Hi, Kendall," Gabe said warmly, waiting for her on the sidewalk. He debated for a second and then went for it and enfolded her in a hug. After a brief hesitation, she wrapped her arms around his midsection and hugged him back tightly. It felt right. It felt like she should have never left. He inhaled the scent of her perfume, jasmine and vanilla, and then released her reluctantly.

Kendall's eyes were wide and confused, and she seemed unable to figure out what to do next. Gabe stood aside. "I'd like you to meet Robert Miller, my father."

"It's a pleasure to meet you, Kendall." Robert went for the hug as well, and Gabe could have kissed him for making his own greeting a little less awkward by comparison.

Kendall disentangled herself and laughed breathlessly. "Well, that was a welcome. Nice to meet you, Robert."

"We're a family of huggers," Robert said with a shrug, and Gabe wondered if that was actually true. His mom was, but now he realized how little he actually knew about his dad, even after working with him for the last couple of months.

"It's cold out here. Why don't we go inside?" Gabe gestured toward the front door of the town hall and held it open for them. Once inside, he scooted ahead to divert them to a conference room rather than his office.

"Why are we going in here?" Kendall asked.

"More room," Gabe said. "We have something to show you."

He hung back while Robert and Kendall entered, gratified by her sharp intake of breath. On the conference room's fabric-paneled walls, they'd clipped the renderings that he and Astrid had finished of the new developments in town.

"What is all this?" she asked, moving from one to another.

"This is our submission for the National Society of Sustainable Planning and Architecture," Gabe explained. "A mouthful, I know. The buildings were designed by Astrid Elison, one of my dad's architects. The city plan was done by yours truly."

A smile was forming on Kendall's face. "Bike paths? Coworking spaces? And what's this? Green Village?"

Gabe moved up beside her. "I admit this was my idea. This right here is your plot of houses." He indicated with his finger. "The rest are a mix of condominiums, apartment buildings, and single-family homes. All designed in Jasper Green's signature style using sustainable materials and built around community green space." He grinned. "Your last name lends itself to all sorts of useful puns."

Kendall laughed, but wonder still laced her expression. "It's incredible. I never expected . . . And what's this?" She moved to the last board, which showed several pieces of marketing material.

"This is an advertising campaign that a local agency worked up for us. Do you recognize the slogan?"

" 'Work virtually in the most beautiful town in Colorado,' " she breathed. "That was my idea."

"And it was a brilliant one. We want to maintain the community feel, but we recognize that we need young singles, couples, and families if we're going to continue to exist and grow. We've already got a couple of companies that use virtual workers who are considering sponsoring our efforts here." He nudged her with his arm. "This is all you, Kendall."

She turned in a circle, taking in all the plans at once. "This is amazing, Gabe. I love it. You and Astrid and, I assume, you, Robert, have done a wonderful job here."

"We're just missing one component," Robert said, stepping closer. "It didn't seem right to go forward with this project, especially Green Village, without the remaining Green descendant working on it. I've looked over your work, Kendall. You have an impeccable eye for preservation, but you also have a deep understanding of how modern spaces need to function. We could use a designer with your eye to join us."

Kendall's mouth dropped open. Gabe could see this was the last thing she'd expected. "You're offering me a job?" She looked between the two of them.

"I am," Robert said. "You'd be a full employee of Miller Property Group. Compensation package to be negotiated, of course. I imagine we'd want you to be full-time in Jasper Lake, however."

"For how long?"

"Well, we're expecting the first phase of the project to take about five years. It may be ten before we're completely finished."

"Five to ten years?" she asked faintly.

"Think about it," Robert said. "We can talk about the details later. I know this is a lot to take in." He gave her a nod and a smile before discreetly slipping from the room.

Kendall did one more wide-eyed spin. "This is amazing." She smiled. "And it preserves my homes."

Gabe lifted a shoulder. "It doesn't get you your $1.7 million, I'm afraid to say."

Kendall gave him a sheepish smile. "I let the Pasadena house go."

"What?"

"I let the house go. Sophie went to another company, and I realized there was just no reason to hold on to it." She shrugged. "I thought owning something would make the difference, but no matter how much I wanted it to be, it wasn't home."

"It seems like a lot has happened since we last talked. Want to take a walk around town and tell me about it?"

Kendall smiled at him. "I'd love to."

Chapter Forty

The air was frigid, but Kendall felt flushed enough with the afternoon's revelations and Gabe's nearness that she didn't even feel it. All she noticed was the warmth of his body soaking into her arm through his coat as they walked together down the street.

"Your poor hands," he commented, looking down at her fingers, which were turning bright red in the cold. She'd forgotten her gloves in the car. He tugged his glove off and interlaced her fingers with his, then pushed both of their hands into his pocket. "Better?"

"Better," she said breathlessly. She might have been able to tell herself that she could do without him, that she could get through this day without any feelings, but the mere touch of bare skin showed that lie for exactly what it was.

"Tell me everything that happened," he said after a few moments.

"Everything? I hardly think you want to know everything."

"But I do." His gaze held an intensity that was likely to give her a heart attack if she didn't settle down her unruly nerves.

She took a moment to focus on the Christmas

decorations that had turned the street from a charming mountain town into a veritable Christmas village. "I've done a lot of thinking," she said finally. "After I . . . became a Christian, I had to look differently at everything I thought I knew about my life. I had been searching for stability and meaning everywhere I wouldn't find it. In work. In my house. Even in my anger and bitterness. I had lived with it for so long, told myself that I could only rely on myself, that I couldn't let anybody in. I thought Sophie was a friend, but I never really let her be a friend. Bill and Nancy wanted to be my parents, but I wouldn't let them."

Gabe just walked alongside her, listening quietly, his presence a stabilizing force for the frantic zing of her emotions.

"Even worse, I let all my bad experiences color the way I looked at God. But no matter how much I denied Him, He was still there. He was still working behind the scenes. I don't know if I realized how much. Maybe I'll never realize how much."

Like the fact she'd lost her house in Glendale four days ago, she had no clients lined up, and today she'd been offered a job. Here in Jasper Lake.

Was this really an example of God working, or was this a test that she was supposed to pass? A temptation she was supposed to overcome?

"That sounds like a full couple of months," Gabe observed quietly.

"How about you? What have you been doing?"

"Missing you."

Kendall halted on the sidewalk. "But . . . you never even called or texted. I thought . . . I just assumed . . ."

Gabe smiled helplessly. "I picked up the phone every day. And every day, God told me, 'Not now.' "

"As in, a voice from heaven?"

"More like a vise around the chest or a kick to the head. For whatever reason, He didn't want me contacting you, and I think I understand why."

"That makes one of us," Kendall mumbled, though she understood what he was saying. She had been working out deeper issues, and that would have been impossible to do if she was distracted by Gabe. "I thought you didn't care. I thought you'd forgotten about me."

Gabe abruptly turned toward her, pulling their hands out of his pocket and reaching for her other one. "Kendall, I didn't stop thinking about you for a single day. It killed me to stay silent. Of course I tried to convince myself I would be fine without you, but I didn't really believe it."

Her heart was beating so hard that she could barely breathe. "What are you saying, Gabe?"

Gently he pulled her to him, one hand going to her waist, the other rising to brush a strand of hair away from her cheek. "I'm asking you to stay here. With me. I don't know if this is real, true love, Kendall. Maybe it's too soon to know that. But I'm asking you to give us a chance to find out."

Then he was lowering his lips to hers, brushing them in a kiss that felt both familiar and new, questioning and assured. When she wrapped her arms around his neck and returned the kiss in a wash of emotion that swept her away, she completely forgot they were standing on a public sidewalk. There was only the two of them and this moment, laced with hope and passion and uncertainty. Without guarantees.

But she had a guarantee. That if she took a leap, if she risked her heart, there was Someone there to catch her. Whatever decision she made, she didn't have to make it from fear because she wasn't alone.

When they parted, she looked up into Gabe's face. Her heart pounded and her stomach danced nervously. She was taking a chance on him, leaving everything behind. And yet hadn't her way been paved to this very moment?

She stretched up on her tiptoes and kissed him again, a gesture that was supposed to be affectionate and short but turned into something entirely different. She broke away laughing.

"Was that a yes? You'll stay?" Gabe asked, his eyes sparkling.

"That was a yes."

Gabe took her hand again, beaming, his expression reflecting the giddy feeling inside her. Only then did she notice the trickle of people walking toward the square where they were getting ready to flip the switch that would illuminate the giant spruce growing in the center of the park. As they joined the crowd, she saw a couple of amused glances thrown in their direction, making her wonder how many people had seen them kissing with abandon in the middle of Main Street.

The crowd started counting down, and Kendall stretched to whisper in Gabe's ear, "Isn't this supposed to be your thing?"

"I passed off the honor to Luke. I wanted to be standing here with you when they lit it."

"Five . . . four . . . three . . . two . . . one . . ."

The switch was thrown and the tree illuminated in a wash of sparkling white lights of all different sizes, looking so much like a column of swirling fireflies. Gabe bent down to kiss her again, making her completely lose her train of thought and sense of place, until applause and hoots of approval rang out around the square. She looked up, wondering what they'd missed, until she realized that they were aimed their direction.

Heat rose to her face and she buried it in Gabe's jacket, but he only chuckled and nudged her so she could look back around at the smiling faces.

"Welcome home, Kendall Green."

A Note from the Author

I don't know about you, but no matter how long a good story is, I'm never ready for it to end! That went double for *Provenance*: Gabe and Kendall are some of my favorite characters ever, and I wasn't ready to let them go.

So for those of you who feel the same way, I've got good news: I've written an exclusive epilogue to keep the happily ever after going a little while longer! Find it at my website:

carlalaureano.com/provenance-epilogue

Thanks for accompanying me on this ride. You have a lot of books from which to choose for your pleasure reading time, and I'm so honored that you've chosen mine!

Acknowledgments

One of the greatest unexpected blessings of the publishing industry is how many amazing people you get to meet. Books don't happen in a vacuum, and I've been fortunate to work with some of the best on this book.

My most heartfelt thanks go to Jan Stob, Sarah Rische, Elizabeth Jackson, Andrea Garcia, Amanda Woods, Andrea Martin, Mark Lane, Eva Winters, and Steve Laube. You are the ones who made this book happen and I'm so grateful!

Hugs to the special people in my life who help me maintain perspective and love me on the frustrating days as well as the good ones: my husband, Rey; my sons, Nathan and Preston; Mom and Dad; my faithful friends Lori Twichell, Amber Lynn Perry, and Courtney Walsh. I'm blessed to have you all in my life.

Discussion Questions

1. Most of us have daydreamed about a surprise inheritance or windfall that changes everything. If the Jasper Lake houses came to you, what would you do with them?
2. Kendall has a special knack for tracking down the provenance—the origin and history—of the pieces she uses to decorate her clients' homes. What do you think inspired that curiosity? How do those skills serve her in new ways when faced with her Jasper Lake inheritance?
3. Gabe feels a deep connection to Jasper Lake—a place he credits with saving his life. How does that connection steer his decisions? Is there a place that holds similar roots for you?
4. For much of Kendall's life, she's had a bad impression of Christianity, going back to her foster-home experience. How does that history initially color her impression of her grandmother Constance? Of Gabe? Gabe remembers his grandmother joking that "the only problem with Christianity was the Christians." Have you felt truth in that?
5. Gabe is accused of being "a fixer." How

does he play that role in Jasper Lake? In his relationship with Kendall? Do you relate to his impulse to jump in and fix things? Where does that serve him and others well? In what ways might it be harmful?

6. Kendall realizes she has put labels on herself that aren't true, like *abandoned* and *unwanted.* It makes her wonder, "What other titles had she assumed that would turn out to be false?" If Kendall had always known the truth about her mother and grandmother, how do you imagine it would've changed her life? Have you found yourself carrying titles that aren't true? How have you worked to discard them?

7. Kendall comes to see that her memories of her past are incomplete, with the bad crowding out much of the good. How does filling in the gaps change her perspective? Have you ever been forced to look at your past through a new lens? How did it change things for you?

8. Gabe tells Kendall, "I don't believe in coincidence or chance. . . . I only believe in consequences of our actions and God's providence. And thank God that a lot of the time His providence overrides our stupid decisions." Do you agree with his perspective? Can you think of a time in your own life when God's providence has softened

the consequences of your actions or brought good out of a bad decision?

9. Kendall initially believes she won't be able to move on without knowing the full truth about her family. But at the end of the story, many of her questions remain unanswered. How does she find peace with the things she might never know? How important is it to have the whole truth?

10. Kendall has spent much of her life searching for a place to call home. What does *home* mean to you?

About the Author

Carla Laureano is the RITA Award–winning author of contemporary inspirational romance and Celtic fantasy. A graduate of Pepperdine University, she worked as a sales and marketing executive for nearly a decade before leaving corporate life behind to write fiction full-time. She currently lives in Denver with her husband and two sons, where she writes during the day and cooks things at night.

Center Point Large Print
600 Brooks Road / PO Box 1
Thorndike, ME 04986-0001 USA

(207) 568-3717

US & Canada:
1 800 929-9108
www.centerpointlargeprint.com